CRISIS

The Fifth Kelly Turnbull Novel

CRISIS

By

Kurt Schlichter

Kindle Paperback ISBN: 978-1-7341993-2-1

Crisis - Kurt Schlichter - Paperback - Complete - 111920 – v79a

For Irina

ACKNOWLEDGMENTS

None of these books would be possible without the help and support of a bunch of people.

First, of course, is my hot wife, Irina Moises. She has been there every step of the way, reading and critiquing the manuscripts and always demanding one more read to purge them of the hated scourge of typos.

Lots of other folks contributed (sometimes unknowingly) and I can't list them all, but I'll try to name a few in no particular order: Cam Edwards, Drew Matich, Robert O'Brien, Matthew Betley, Larry O'Connor, Glenn Reynolds, Chris Stigall, Seb Gorka, Tom Sauer, Hugh Hewitt, Tim Young, Jim Geraghty, WarrenPeas64, Big Pete, fellow Nevada vet Pat O'Brien, and many more.

I want to give a special shoutout to Adam Kissel for his tireless work on the manuscript. I also want to thank Bill Wilson of Wilson Combat for his amazing support and help. Kelly Turnbull uses a Wilson Combat CQB, which better gun guys than I have deemed the greatest production version of that venerable classic ever made. I carried a regular M1911A1 for years in the Army as my service weapon, but since I have had the chance to shoot a Wilson it is not too much to say that I had never really shot a 1911A before. Thanks for everything, Bill!

Let me also offer my thanks to my Twitter pals for their support and their "patroning," to quote that half-wit AOC (who shows up in the book). Thanks!

My cover artist J.R. Hawthorne, *aka* Salty Hollywood, has continued his legacy of excellence with this cover.

Like Montgomery Burns did in the acknowledgement to his memoir *Will There Ever be A Rainbow?,* I want to thank you, the reader. It's hard for me to fully express my gratitude to those of you who have disregarded the lies of the venomous sissies and who have embraced the Kelly Turnbull novels.

And, finally, I always thank Andrew Breitbart, because he saw the power of culture to fight the power of the Establishment. Andrew, I hope you are reading and digging these books up there!

KAS, November 2020

PREFACE

This is the fifth novel in the Kelly Turnbull series.

With *Crisis*, I am finally getting around to telling the story of how the United States split in two, after the last one, *Collapse*, told the story of how it might come back together.

I wrote this one during and after the pandemic and the George Floyd riots. I was often tempted to stop writing and just transcribe what was happening. It takes place when the "Split" happens (think of it as around late-2022). Of course, the fact that this is being finished right after the 2020 election complicates things plot-wise, but I'm going to try to finesse that. With the election disputed at the time of this writing, I had to make a call, and I'm basically going with Biden winning because that smooths out the plot. In the four years since I started writing, events have often overcome my speculation (like Trump did!), so if something seems not to quite match the prior books, chill – I'll be revisiting them and tweaking them. You have to suspend a lot of disbelief with these novels – sadly, not enough in light of the rising tide of liberal insanity.

Just go with it.

As I write in the prefaces to all these books, this is not some sort of eager fantasy. No matter what the loser Never Trump sissies and professional liars of the left say, this story is not what I want to happen. This is what I fear *might* happen if we let people like them win. Like its four companion volumes, *Crisis* is a warning, but one that I hope you find entertaining. Do what needs to be done to ensure it never comes true.

And I will set the Egyptians against the Egyptians: and they shall fight every one against his brother, and every one against his neighbor; city against city, and kingdom against kingdom.

Isiah 19:2

BOOK ONE

1.

Kelly Turnbull took the news of his death with remarkable calm.

Clay Deeds broke the news to him personally, which surprised him. Deeds had left Baghdad several months before, called back to the United States for some cryptic reason. He had not told Turnbull the reason, being a master of mushroom growing – that is, keeping his operatives in the dark and feeding them manure. But Turnbull, who disliked politics as much as he disliked mustard, terrorists, and other people in general, figured the reason had to do with the deteriorating state of things back in CONUS.

His instincts were sound.

Earlier that evening, Turnbull had been out with his team visiting bad people and escorting them off this mortal coil. From across the room Deeds caught a pungent whiff of sweat and gunpowder wafting off of the Army captain, who wore a camo uniform stripped of all names, rank, and insignia. The spymaster was sitting back on Turnbull's ancient couch in the dingy office at the top of the fortified police commando headquarters building that doubled as Turnbull's bedroom. There was a manilla envelope on the cushion next to him. Outside the locked door, his security team waited to ferry him to another location to notify another operative of his own passing.

"Now that you're dead, you can come back to the continental United States," Deeds said, not using "CONUS," the military slang for the homeland.

"Why would I do that?" Turnbull asked. He was sitting at his wooden dinner table, his M4 broken down in front of him, and he was a bit irritated to have been disturbed during his post-mission weapon cleaning ritual. "You can keep CONUS. I have everything I need right here."

"You mean that here, you have a green light to do what you do," Deeds countered.

Turnbull shrugged. He ran with a crew of seasoned Iraqi special forces. They picked their own targets, and they dealt with their targets in their way without interference. Deeds had kept his promise when he pulled the young captain out of the traditional Special Forces organization and set him up as one of his off-the-books, go-to guys. But now, Turnbull's team was kind of running out of targets, having shot its way out of a job. Still, Turnbull figured he could play this out to the end, and that this gig would last at least a little while longer.

"I need you back home, Kelly. I can't promise you a green light, but I can promise you a yellow one."

"Is everyone still wearing masks back there? That's so dumb."

"Only the ones trying to make a statement."

"Nah, thanks for the offer, but I'll stay here."

"Except you can't, having been sadly killed in action and all."

"Yeah, about that, Clay. Why am I dead?"

Deeds leaned back on the threadbare cushion. Turnbull was one of a number of Deeds' operatives to whom the enigmatic spy had broken the news of their demise in a tragic helicopter accident that had conveniently taken place over the water, resulting in their corpses not being recovered despite an exhaustive search.

"No one looks for dead guys, Kelly. That's why you'll all be dead."

"'All'? So, you're putting together a team," Turnbull said, annoyed. "Clay, you know how I feel about working with others."

"You manage to work with a team here."

"Only one of them speaks English and he's afraid to talk to me except out in the field. Our relationship is perfect."

Deeds leaned forward. "Kelly, I need you. I need your skill set. It's getting serious."

"It's all politics. And I don't do politics. I do terrorists."

"I think it was some Bolshevik who observed that you might not care about politics, but politics care about you."

"I hate Russians too," Turnbull said. He picked up a cleaning rag and threw it back down again. "I don't like this. It's one thing to pull ops out here against foreigners. Screw them. It's another thing when it's back home."

"You haven't been home in a few years, Kelly. It's different than it was when you left. People are at each other's throats. Whole cities are under radical militia control. The federal government is paralyzed. The military brass is completely unable to deal with what is coming."

"Incompetent generals and admirals? I'm shocked. Shocked."

"I'm serious, Kelly. It's bad, worse than anyone ever imagined."

"Yeah, I know," Turnbull said bitterly. "The last time I called my idiot brother, he told me I needed to 'check my privilege.' My privilege? When I called him, I was lying in a crappy Iraqi hospital ward because Ali Nasrami had shot out a chunk of my kidney."

"In Nasrami's defense, at the time you were in his house with a rifle trying to kill him."

"First of all, you sent me. And second, I succeeded. But that's not the point. There's nothing back in CONUS for me, Clay. I belong out here, hunting down *jihadis* and Iranian Revolutionary Guards and all the other assorted lowlifes that make the Mideast the special wonderland of love that it is. That's my thing."

Deeds sat back on the couch for a moment, weighing whether to tell Turnbull that when the officers went to make the death notification, his brother – Turnbull's closest living relative – had taken the news very well indeed. In fact, his composure was such that his first question was whether he was the beneficiary of any kind of life insurance benefit from the government. As it happened, he was not – Turnbull had listed his beneficiary as the National Rifle Association. Deeds decided to avoid that tangent and to continue his pitch.

"Well, the first mission I need you for tracks with both your priorities and mine. The Venn diagram of *jihadi* assholes and leftist assholes overlaps because of a Hezbollah banker who goes by the name 'Saladin.' Yeah, Saladin – he's pretentious all right. Anyway, he's in New York City right now trying to leverage the left's ties to street gangs and the bureaucracy to help him import a huge amount of Middle East heroin. They both get untraceable funding that way."

"And you want me to what, go to the Big Apple and kill everyone involved?" asked Turnbull sourly. "I mean, it's a jungle under de Blasio, but people might take notice if I whack a dozen targets."

"No," Deeds replied with a tinge of horror. "We are not going to kill any Americans. And I don't even want you to off Saladin. We just need you to disrupt their cooperation."

"See, you're already cramping my style."

"This needs doing, and you, being dead, are the perfect, untraceable means to do it."

Turnbull looked at his superior quizzically. "Why don't you just, you know, call the feds and they can arrest him, which I understand is traditionally how one deals with drug dealers in the US of A."

"What feds should I trust, Kelly?" Deeds asked. Turnbull assessed that his handler was not being sarcastic. That it was a serious question took him a bit aback.

"I don't know. The FBI? The DEA? Some other bunch of guys in suits with badges and guns and three letters?"

Deeds shook his head and smiled a bitter little smile. During these kinds of discussions, he always gave off the vibe of the cunning, ruthless Roman senator the rest of the senators always turned to when they needed to plan the conspiracy against a bizarre emperor who had gone too far and married his horse.

"How do you know they don't know about it? How do you know the folks on the top floor have not been told to look the other way, Kelly? You assume that they would not want it to happen. Can you assume that?"

Turnbull considered this for a moment. "I'd like to be able to assume that. Seems like stopping this kind of thing is their reason for existing. Are you saying the whole bureaucracy might be corrupt?"

"I'm saying I can't trust anyone in the bureaucracy to take America's side instead of his own faction's side. Their interests and America's interests no longer necessarily correspond. I do not say that lightly. I've worked in our government for a long time. But the old rules and norms are gone. Think about what the last decade has shown us, Kelly. We have seen the media reject objectivity. We have seen our elite excuse, if not outright embrace, political violence. We know the FBI tried to pull off a coup to frame President Trump for collusion with the Russians. We know prominent politicians and tech companies and key institutions were all willingly bought by China. And I know a lot of things that have happened that you have not read about in the newspapers."

"There are still actual newspapers?"

"For all intents and purposes, no. Figure of speech. But my point is that allowing its radical allies a nearly bottomless supply of untraceable cash is potentially advantageous to a liberal elite playing footsie with violent left-wing extremists. Revolutions don't pay for themselves, and while a bunch of tech titans and left-wing donors have given millions to fund Antifa, BLM, the

People's Militias, and the rest of the radical left, if you are one of these rich check-writers, there's a risk that if someone goes too far and someone in law enforcement actually does his job and traces the money back to you. The untraceable money this could generate could create massive havoc."

"I'm still not really buying it, Clay. If what you're saying is true, America is way down the road to a very bad place."

"You're usually a stone-cold cynic, Kelly, but here you're adorably naive. You think there are still norms and rules, but there aren't. That's the crisis," Deeds said. He continued: "The midterm elections probably won't be settled for months. We can't even hold an election without getting at one another's throats. Maybe something will set us back on the right path, but probably not. It's all about power, who will dominate the culture and the government. You need to take off your rose-colored glasses and see clearly that our country is in grave danger."

"And you want me and some other dead guys to come back to America and help you fix things?"

"I need a team in place to do the things to protect America and its stability that we can't rely on the squabbling politicians and bureaucrats to do anymore."

"A team of dead guys?"

"It's called Task Force Zulu," said Deeds.

"Should be 'Task Force Zombie,'" Turnbull replied. "Special ops of the living dead."

"We can bring you all back to life when it all calms down again. Until then, there are things we need to do to keep the country safe because the people who should be doing them are too busy competing for power. And the people doing those things will need to be ghosts."

"'Zombie' works better with 'Zulu' than 'ghost,'" Turnbull said. "You know, the 'Z' and all."

"Stop trying to make 'Zombies' happen, Kelly. It's not going to happen."

"Yes, it is," Turnbull insisted.

"You need to pack," Deeds said.

"I'm not sensing that I'm being asked to volunteer. I'm guessing that I'm being voluntold for this mission."

"Good guess," Deeds said. "You leave tonight."

"Do you put me in a coffin for transport or what?"

"There's a thought, but you're flying less comfortably," Deeds said, handing over the manilla envelope that had been sitting beside him on the couch. "Your papers, itinerary, and your mission brief. Burn whatever you don't need before you leave."

"I know how tradecraft works," Turnbull said grouchily.

Deeds ignored the irascible captain and went on. "Now, once you hit New York, you are on your own. There's no support in place to give you even if we could. We have to have total deniability. You'll need to get your own gear, including weapons, and figure out how you are going to do the op. He's in town for 96 hours, so you don't have a lot of time. We have one date/time when we know he'll be somewhere in particular."

"You can't even put a piece in a dead drop for me?"

"Nope. This is wet work. You are on your own and we'll disavow if you are caught or killed."

"You mean killed *again*. You know they'll just run my DNA and prints and ID me."

Deeds shook his head. "We have allies in the bureaucracy too. They run your DNA or prints and it will come up blank. Just don't get taken alive."

"Do or die?" asked Turnbull.

"Something like that," Deeds said.

They both knew it was exactly like that.

The Army likes to distill things into mnemonic lists for its leaders. One of those that they teach you very early, even before you become a lieutenant, are the troop leading procedures. It's a list of about ten things you do, starting from getting a mission to completing it.

Turnbull remembered two from near the top of the to-do list: "Make a tentative plan" and "Begin necessary movement." He did both.

The movement came first. His employer had flights set up all the way to New York. He had a new passport and various credit cards, documents, and pocket litter that all identified him as Andrew Matich, a "media rep" who lived in a hipster enclave in the Echo Park part of Los Angeles, an area he knew well enough so that he could answer basic questions about it if asked. There was also $3,453 in well-circulated dollars and a similar amount in euros, enough to buy what he needed but not enough to trigger a freak-out at customs if they searched him and found the cash.

Turnbull did not bother with a shower. Instead, he changed into his one set of civilian-ish clothes, a pair of 5.11 tactical trousers and a polo shirt. Being June, it was still hot at 9:00 p.m. His Iraqi lieutenant drove him to the Baghdad International Airport, and he got in line at the Austrian Air counter to check in to Kennedy, with a three-hour layover in Vienna. He took no checked bags. There was not much in Baghdad that he wanted to take with him back to America.

Turnbull left his Iraqi-issue M4 back at the police commando base, but he would never have traveled across the recently pacified city completely unarmed. Nor would he spend a moment outside the secure area without a piece. Before he went through the security checkpoint, he slipped into the filthy men's room and buried his Kimber .45 and his spare mags in a trash can under a pile of rough paper towels. All he took on the plane was his stinking self and a copy of the only English language book he could find at the police commando base, a sci-fi paperback called *The Paradigm Shifters of Sirius* that had a cover showing an androgynous human kissing an alien that was likewise androgynous. The book was in pristine condition.

He sat in a window seat near the back of the plane, a Boeing 767-300ER with the red and white color scheme endemic to the airline. An Arab man sat down in the aisle seat, surveyed his reeking seatmate with the rumpled clothes and, despite this, politely said, "Hello." Turnbull feigned ignorance of the language – English – and stared out the window. After a while, he took out the paperback and found out within a few pages that the indigenous aliens were the good guys and the Earth colonists were the bad guys, except for one human who rejected rigid gender identities. Xe was the hero and allied xirself with the aliens to fight the humans. Turnbull got about 15 pages in but finally put the book in the magazine pouch for the next lucky passenger after reaching a point where the book mentioned a "dense matter object" and had a long footnote about how calling a black hole a "black hole" is racist and the book would have no part of it.

He shut his eyes and began making his tentative plan.

Vienna had an old, cramped airport that probably looked like something from about ten years into the future way back in 1967. But aesthetics aside, it was jam-packed with shops and stores, which is exactly what Turnbull needed. He purchased, with cash, a shaving kit and a black backpack to use as a carry-on bag. He then bought some civilian clothes, including a pair of soft European jeans. He also bought a couple shirts, some socks and underwear, a casual dark windbreaker, and a nice German-made leather jacket.

These he took into one of the airport layover guest rooms, where for about 50 euros he could rent a small room with a bed and a shower for an hour. He shaved, then cleaned up, changing out of his filthy duds and into his new clothes. The tacticool clothes he had flown in went into the trash. He looked in the mirror, wearing the leather jacket. He was forgettable – the very look he was striving for.

Turnbull sat down on the small Germanic bed, which had no sheets and just one large down comforter. He slept for the balance of the hour then caught his flight.

The United 777 landed at JFK at mid-morning. There must have been 350 people on the plane, about half of whom insisted on wearing masks. Turnbull did too, not because it made it harder for viruses but because it made it harder to identify him.

He did not get off the plane until he counted about 120 folks, and then he slipped into the conga line. It took a while to get to the door and people battled to take their carry-ons out of the bins. He feigned patience even as he mentally cursed them.

Eventually, he got to the door and stepped out without making eye contact with the stewardess who thanked him for flying United. On the wall of the jetway, which was filthy, there were a dozen posters informing new arrivals of the various demographic groups whose lives mattered, and a sign further letting visitors know that "HATE IS NOT WELCOME HERE." That poster's graphic was a cartoon transexual Statue of Liberty kissing a sexy immigrant wearing a sombrero.

The other passengers went left at the sign pointing to the baggage claim; Turnbull broke right and went straight through customs. The lines were short, but Turnbull stood in the longest one. The busier the agent was, the less likely she would be to spend time on him. She took his passport and declaration form, confirmed he had no bags without following up on why, then welcomed Andrew Matich back home to the United States.

He headed toward the ground transportation area. A cab was unloading a woman and her kids, but Turnbull slid in before she could shut the door. The cabbie was an Armenian, which Turnbull noted from his placard, and he vigorously shook his head.

"Sir, no, I cannot pick up here. You must go to the taxi stand."

Turnbull silently handed him $100. The cabbie shrugged and hit the gas. A quick glance backward confirmed that no one seemed to be following them. He relaxed on the ride into Manhattan. He had been to the island before, spending a couple weeks there as part of a special ops urban tradecraft course – basically, learning how to operate surreptitiously in a big city.

The cabbie dropped him in Midtown in the center of a block packed with wholesale shops and pizza places. Turnbull threw him the $70 fare then added another $30 and off the driver went.

New York, he noted immediately as the smell of fresh urine warmed by the hot sun wafted into his nostrils, had changed, and for the worse. Bums and drugged-out losers huddled in doorways. Most of the people walking briskly along the sidewalk, eyes down, not making eye contact. Many of the people wore masks in fear of COVID-22 or whatever earlier COVIDs might still be lingering in the air.

There were fewer cars than he remembered, and whole streets seemed to be blocked off to accommodate unused bike lanes. The city seemed emptier and quieter than he remembered it, even if it was dirtier and more menacing. On 6th Avenue at West 44th Street, someone had painted, on the blacktop in giant yellow block letters that went from curb to curb, "ASIAN TRANS AND NONBINARY LIVES MATTER." It had not been laid out and centered very well, since the concluding letters "ES MATTER" crossed through the intersection and went on down the next block to end somewhere beyond West 45th Street.

He got moving. Several blocks along, Turnbull saw a sign for a Best Western. The clerk was a young woman listening to her iPhone, and his sudden approach surprised her. She put the device down, but it tore the earphone out of her ear and Turnbull heard "...here's, the King of Conservatism, Teddy King!" She gathered it up and turned the podcast off, then stared in horror at him.

"Are you okay?" Turnbull said.

"I'm, I'm sorry," she stammered.

"For what?" Turnbull said, himself running through his mind what social errors he might have forgotten while he was gone, and failing.

"Just – that was accidental."

"I'm kind of confused."

"That show. I don't want you to think I was listening to it on purpose."

"Well, how else would you listen to it?" asked Turnbull, genuinely baffled.

"You're not offended?" she asked, looking around. "You're not going to complain to the manager?"

"Not at the moment. I'm no Karen. It's a free country."

"Is it?" she asked. "If anyone asks, I just say I'm listening to a D-Yazzy jam."

"I don't know what that is," Turnbull said, handing over his ID. "I need to check in."

She took the license. "It's good to meet one of us. Especially here. If my boss found out, I'd be out of here and there're no jobs."

"One of us?"

"A conservative," she whispered, and then she smiled. "We gotta stick together. I'm totally giving you an early morning check-in. And upgrading you."

"Andrew Matich" paid cash for two nights. In his room, he showered again and emptied the backpack except for the leather jacket. He slept for a while, then got ready. He wore jeans and a polo and a windbreaker when he went back outside with the backpack.

The clerk gave him a low-key thumbs up sign as he walked through the lobby. He returned it, unaware that the media had declared the thumbs-up gesture racist after conservatives adopted it from Donald Trump's famous photo taken while he walked to Marine One heading to Walter Reed Hospital after being infected with COVID-19 a few years before. As a result of the uproar, all episodes of *Happy Days* had been removed from cable circulation and Netflix due to The Fonz's promotion of white supremacy. Moreover, Henry Winkler was canceled after he went on Twitter and called the imbroglio "crazy," the charge being that he was "minimizing the threat to the safety of oppressed peoples posed by his promotion of racist hate."

A couple blocks from the hotel, he bought blue, black, and gray masks from a vendor for $20. He slipped on the blue one. A good bunch of the people out wore masks, so he'd fit right in.

Turnbull walked farther along the sidewalk until he came to a street full of small shops. The electronics storefronts were piled with boomboxes and flickering monitors. He had to go inside to find what he wanted, prepaid cell phones. Favorite tools of deadbeats and drug dealers as well as tourists, these were essentially disposable cell phones with a few hours of time included in the price. Turnbull bought one for $70 cash. There was also a rack of knockoff Swiss Army knives by the register. Turnbull checked the edge on one and, satisfied, paid another $20 for it. Later, he got a small pack of Windex wipes at a Duane Reade.

Now Turnbull needed a gun.

There are several ways to get a gun in a strange place. You can be issued one. Deeds had told him that that option was out. You could go and buy one legally, but this was New York and the Second Amendment didn't apply here. You can buy one illegally, but that invites a host of problems, like the expense, the fact the weapon is likely to be of sub-par quality, and the risk inherent with dealing with the kind of people who deal in illegal guns.

Or you can take one. The best place to get a good, high-quality weapon is from someone who carries one professionally. Here, that meant a cop.

Turnbull walked about ten blocks toward downtown, veering into ever more empty, ever more rundown areas. On the way, he removed the windbreaker, figuring that the people in the electronics places would primarily remember it if asked. Other than a surly crew of six young men dressed in Yankees uniforms, their faces white with greasepaint, there were few people around. Those who were out mostly seemed in a hurry and were not much interested in one more random guy out on the street. He walked and watched, passing gyros vendors, passersby yapping into cell phones, and the ever-present vagrants.

But there were no beat cops. He kept walking. Did the NYPD even do foot patrols anymore? He had seen a few cop cars go by, most with obvious riot damage. But there should be some fuzz somewhere. It was not like in the sketchier areas of town, where the People's Militia had, at least informally, displaced the police.

At 2:00 p.m., he spied two cops on foot across the street, shooting the shit outside a café. They must have talked for 20 minutes before they split up. The younger – and smaller – one was coming his way.

There was an alley a half block down from them, and Turnbull went ahead and slipped into it. At the far end was a fairly busy street. Halfway down it was a row of garbage cans; Turnbull put the backpack in a relatively clean space behind them. There were no windows overlooking the alley, and no clear line-of-sight views from any of the surrounding buildings.

The cop would pass right by the alley's mouth. Perfect.

When the cop saw the well-dressed guy lying there moaning, he muttered, "Shit" and trotted over to kneel beside the injured man.

"Hey fella..." he said and touched Turnbull's shoulder.

Turnbull spun and drove his fingers into the cop's windpipe. The cop gagged, grabbing his throat and leaving his temple exposed. Turnbull smashed it hard with his knuckles. The cop went over and his eyes rolled back. Turnbull rolled onto his feet and kicked him hard in the nose, smashing it. The cop gasped.

Turnbull liked cops as a general matter, but he needed what he needed. In his condition, there was no way the officer was going to resist or remember anything except that there was some guy lying on his face in an alley before everything went black.

Using his brand-new knife, Turnbull slit through the loops holding the cop's gun belt, then sliced through the belt itself. He took it off as one piece and then pushed the officer over facedown with his right foot. Turnbull also checked his ankles. Bingo. There was a Walther PPK backup gun in a holster with a second mag strapped over the cop's left foot. Turnbull took that all in one piece.

He stuffed the ankle holster and the whole belt, holster attached, into the backpack after removing and donning his leather jacket. The jacket on, he walked briskly out the far side of the alley and turned onto the sidewalk. The cop was still lying prone at the other end.

"Sorry," he muttered.

There was a subway station three blocks up. Turnbull didn't make eye contact with anyone as he went down inside it, got on a train and exited five stops later. Coming up onto the street, he hailed a cab and returned to his hotel serenaded by tunes from what sounded like a Top 40 station in Mogadishu.

It was a good score. The guy had a well-maintained Glock 19 nine-millimeter service weapon. Turnbull now had three 15 round magazines of hollow point ammo. Not a .45, but he wasn't one to look a gift gun in the barrel. The PPK was a nice bonus.

He also had a can of pepper spray, which might come in handy. There were handcuffs and a key, another always useful item. Part of his tradecraft training was to always have a key concealed on himself, and he was taught a number of ways to keep it handy if he ever anticipated getting cuffed involuntarily. They ranged from somewhat to highly unpleasant, but none was worse than not having a cuff key when he needed it.

Finally, there was a black 21" ASP expandable baton. As his old team sergeant observed when seeing one demonstrated for them at Bragg, "That could put a hurtin' on somebody."

The PPK was well kept and, unlike the Glock, had no NYPD serial number stamp. There were only two mags of seven 7.62mm rounds each. It was small, but readily concealable.

Today was working out nicely.

Turnbull dressed for the rendezvous in his leather jacket and jeans, with the Glock in his waistband at his back and the PPK in his jeans pocket. He carried all his mags and the burner smartphone. He was unshaven, and he wore a Mets cap he bought from a sidewalk vendor the day before. His pack was over his shoulder, and when he walked out of the hotel room, he had wiped down every surface that might bear his fingerprints – just in case.

Before the elevator opened into the lobby, he had slipped on a gray mask and two blue latex gloves. Now he was just another New Yorker who was paranoid about viruses.

Turnbull got to the public library at about 8:30 a.m. and scouted it out. It was surrounded by buildings that overshadowed it from every angle. Lots of windows, he noted. There was a statue out front of Maxine Waters on a horse for some reason, and another of Karl Marx; Turnbull vaguely remembered that the pedestals had previously been occupied by lions. Apparently, the big cats were racist and had to go.

The adjacent Bryant Park was one big kill zone. Fifth Avenue out front was busy even though the sidewalks had fewer pedestrians than he remembered from previous visits. It might have been the protest going on in the park. It appeared to be a perpetual one, since there was actually a semi-permanent stage set up in front of, and blocking access to, the ornate Josephine Shaw Lowell Memorial Fountain. Above the stage there was a very long banner announcing that "Black-Trans-Asian-First Peoples-Nonbinary-Otherkin-Latinx-Fatx-Allies Lives Matter." BTAFPNOLFA Lives Matter was one of the major radical organizations in the city, one that Mayor de Blasio particularly celebrated.

On stage stood a very angry woman, screaming about the racism inherent in the American Constitution and the "secret amendments" she insisted foreshadowed the mandatory return of slavery if the "racist, sexist, colonialist power structure, including the police and the prison-industrial complex" was not immediately abolished. She had some attentive listeners in the park, several of whom were chiding others who applauded as "aggressive" and "creating unsafeness with their hand striking."

The proper way to show approval, they asserted, was to up-twinkles, waving one's fingers in the air. This, in turn, was met by a demand that the critics "decolonialize their class privilege" and stop "otherizing our allyship" regarding the applause versus up-twinkles debate.

The passersby were mostly immune both to the BTAFPNOLFA Lives Matter speaker's speeches and to the argument over how to demonstrate support for it. For his part, Turnbull was hoping they would start punching each other and silently put his money on the pro-applause contingent. The up-twinkles faction seemed pretty soft.

This great debate died away and Turnbull moved on, a bit disappointed that it didn't get physical. At the library, there were plenty of people just sitting on the steps under the statuary, some drinking their coffees, some reading, some deep into their texting, and others just sort of staring. A few vendors with food carts lined the curbs. There was plenty of sound too – lots of honks, brake screeches, and the occasional lawyer yelling into his Android. Of course, the BTAFPNOLFA Lives Matter speaker could always be heard droning on in the background.

Turnbull was on alert, because as public as it was, it was also dangerous out there. An unexpected aggressor could take you high from a window or drop you from the sidewalk and just keep walking and you would never see it coming. It was a great choice for a meeting place if you did not trust those you were meeting with, not so great for unknown threats. And Turnbull resolved to use that to his advantage.

He left the park and walked back around the library and a few blocks down 5th, then stepped into a Starbucks, switching into full anonymity mode, not making eye contact, making no sudden movements. The barista fetching his latte seemed a bit puzzled at being paid with cash instead of with a card or an iPhone. He had to get his manager to help him make the $1.38 in change from the $20.

Turnbull took his cup and a banana and sat down, facing the door. He had clear fields of fire across the breadth of the storefront and could escape and evade by leaping over the counter and through the back if it came to that. His tentative plan established, he sipped his drink and nibbled his fruit. He was in no hurry.

At 10 a.m. exactly, Turnbull was standing on 5th in front of the library between the Maxine and Marx sculptures. A few meters to his right was a vendor's cart offering breakfast burritos – that would do for short term cover if all hell broke loose. There were a couple escape options, but he was going to be exposed for at least 15 seconds whether he bolted across traffic toward the high rises or back around through the trees in Bryant Park.

A dark-haired man in a blue suit stood out from the crowd. It wasn't that he was big, though he was certainly big. It was that he walked with a purpose, with the confidence of a guy who knew he could deal with whatever came along. He had focus, and Turnbull saw it 50 meters away.

Turnbull's kill plan was simple – he'd draw and fire twice, center mass torso, as he brought the Glock up and finish with a forehead shot, since the guy most definitely had a vest, and then he would move fast toward the park. He casually wriggled the fingers on his right hand to loosen them up.

At 20 meters, the man put a phone up to his mouth, said something, then put it back into his coat pocket. Turnbull scanned the periphery for any compadres who might be lurking.

The big man waited by the curb, and Turnbull waited while watching him. It was about two minutes until the car Turnbull expected arrived, a black Mercedes AMG that glided up to the curb. The big man got the door, and a short but exquisitely suited man stepped out onto the sidewalk. He matched the photos of Saladin, though the gentleman hardly looked like the scourge of the crusaders. Maybe the scourge of maître d's and escort service madams.

Deeds had had only one piece of information to share with him, that Saladin would be at the library entrance for a meeting in nearby Bryant Park at this time on this day with his contacts. It seemed at first blush to make no sense, to do business in a place that was so public. Yet that flaw was also a feature – the kind of people the Hezbollah money manager was dealing with could very well cross him, and vice versa. Doing things in a big crowd kept everyone cool. And, Turnbull figured, with the protesters in the park, there was zero chance either the NYPD or the feds would have the area under surveillance. A judge in Hawaii had found that the Constitution barred law enforcement from watching such assemblies – not expressly, but impliedly, via the various penumbras and emanations of the actual text therein. Oddly, this constitutional prohibition only applied to groups like BTAFPNOLFA Lives Matter and Antifa – some conservative groups had tried to invoke the same rule when federal law enforcement began harassing them, only to be told the Constitution was different when it came to the right.

The Mercedes disgorged two more guys who were obviously security. They flanked Saladin, and when three younger folks – two men who looked like they were in the drug game and a 20ish blond woman, who looked like a junior at Wellesley who wanted to tick off her dad – approached him, the guards blocked their path until Saladin motioned them forward. They started walking together around the library and up West 40th Street. Turnbull followed at a short distance as they walked to the rear of the park, and then went in among the crowd. Turnbull followed, running scenarios through his head. He had no real plan beside his default one, which was shoot everyone. And that was the one plan he was not supposed to execute.

They walked through the trees and by the various cafes and outside tables toward the torn-up, brown grass that had been co-opted into a demonstration area. There were few normal folks around. The park belonged to the radicals now. This explained the trash, a mix of Starbucks cups, water bottles, and the occasional needle – as well as even less savory cast-offs that showed that romance was still alive even among the left.

A new speaker was on stage, a very thin one of indeterminate gender apologizing for having "skinny privilege" and segueing into how America not providing a basic income was killing "our Earth Mother Gaia." A few people were listening attentively, most of them appearing to be high, while the rest of the crowd talked among themselves. Saladin and the three were having an animated conversation, while his trio of security men stood off a few feet and not-so-gently pushed members of the crowd back when they wandered too close. Turnbull had still not cracked the code on what he was going to do when the big guy pushed a pimply protester to the ground for coming too near to their principal.

The pushed person screamed like a teen girl seeing BTS in concert. The Hezbollah guards all fixed on him, astonished at the caterwauling the kid was issuing from his piehole for merely having been shoved down onto his ass. Now Saladin was raising his voice at his security men, chiding them in Arabic about the disruption, while the two dealers were watching it all unfold. The Wellesley girl joined in by screeching about how the guard was a transphobe. This confused Saladin, who began to argue with her.

The nearest guard had his back toward Turnbull, a huge mistake, but the tableau was just too fascinating to look away from. Turnbull saw his opportunity, weighed the options, and channeled Patton's admonition to his commanders.

Audacity, audacity, audacity.

He flicked his left wrist. The ASP snapped out and locked at 21 inches, and Turnbull swung it up and across the nearest security man's left temple. It connected solidly, so solidly that the sound of the "whack" drew Saladin's attention away from the various howling millennials that surrounded them.

As his guard's legs buckled and he collapsed like a puppet whose strings had been snipped, Saladin stared in horror. His two other guards pivoted, their hands diving inside their suit coats. But Turnbull had his Glock 19 out in his right hand and fired two rounds dead center mass into the chest of the big guard, then two more into the second. They both dropped as the crowd scattered.

He was pretty sure they would both be wearing vests, and that the hollow points would not penetrate. Pretty sure.

Saladin stood frozen, with the Wellesley girl screaming to his left and the two dealers gone. The shot security guards gasped for air, groaning from their broken ribs.

Turnbull lined Saladin up center mass from habit, then dropped his barrel and put a round into each kneecap. Then he turned, the Glock hanging in his hand at his thigh, and started moving through the crowd as Saladin rolled and howled on the ugly lawn.

A rich Lebanese businessman with Hezbollah connections kneecapped in the midst of a large Black-Trans-Asian-First Peoples-Nonbinary-Otherkin-Latinx-Fatx-Allies Lives Matter demonstration was going to invite embarrassing scrutiny. Hopefully, it would scare the *jihadis* and/or their prospective partners off the deal. But if it didn't, at least it guaranteed Saladin would not be joining next year's cast of *Dancin' with the Stars: Beirut.*

People were running everywhere through the park – the surrounding office buildings had created a terrific echo chamber that amplified the sound of the gunshots. The thin activist on stage was yelling about how this was a police attack on innocent protesters. Turnbull moved away as fast as he could without sprinting. No sirens yet, but it was only about 30 seconds since he dropped his target. And the nice thing about an anarchist demonstration is that its security, if any, is not particularly well organized.

But the problem with such groups is that a lot of dumb people, often on drugs, try to get in on the action. Turnbull spotted the pair right away and pegged them not as cadre, not as live-action role players like the screaming girl with Saladin, but as street punks who latched onto the movement because it provided them a green light to run rampant.

Now, they were running rampant at Turnbull, one shirtless, stocky, and skin-headed with incomprehensible tatts across his chest, the other long-haired and carrying a skateboard, which he presumably intended to use to brain Turnbull. This intent was confirmed when the long-haired one took a swing with it, targeting Turnbull's noggin. Turnbull dropped and it sailed over his head, exposing the elbow of the assailant. Exploiting that opening, Turnbull brought the ASP hard against the bone of the exposed joint, pulverizing it. The skateboard went flying as the attacker's left hand went to his shattered limb. This exposed long-hair's face, and Turnbull smashed in his nose. A gusher of scarlet erupted.

As long-hair was collapsing into the dirt, the skin-headed one was charging, thinking that Turnbull was preoccupied while beating his comrade senseless. But Turnbull was not too busy to bring up the Glock and level it at the man's face.

"Think about it," Turnbull hissed.

"F---," began the attacker just as his head exploded.

Turnbull eyed his gun, thinking that perhaps it had gone off. But it hadn't. Turnbull bolted just as another round cracked through the air and planted itself in the dirt a few feet from where the dead man was lying face down. Turnbull dodged behind a London Plane tree, and another round smashed into the bark, kicking up splinters. He glanced out from his hiding place, scanning the face of the nearby office buildings.

The sniper was using a silenced weapon; Turnbull himself might be the only one who knew the sniper existed. Well, the only one who knew the sniper existed and who was still alive.

There was movement in a fifth-floor window, and then another shot, also slamming into the tree. Turnbull fired off the rest of the mag at the window, aiming a bit high, hoping to suppress the shooter. The last round went off and his gun's slide locked back, and that was Turnbull's cue to bolt.

He sprinted by an ugly statue of a squatting Gertrude Stein. Someone had used gray spray paint to scrawl "TOO WHITE" across its dark bronze surface. As Turnbull darted past, another shot dinged off her forehead.

He was running full-bore now, but so were all the other folks in the park, and he drove into a crowd heading toward West 42nd Street. He did not hear any more shots cracking by, but there was no way whoever it was – probably a fourth Hezbollah security man – was not up in some window still waiting for a clear shot. That's why he was so happy to get under the intermittent concealment of the trees, even if their leaves were largely gone.

There were bums and vagrants lining 42nd, and Turnbull slowed down as he passed the heaping shopping carts and dirty tents of the homeless – though it was now a misdemeanor to call the unhoused that. He tossed his Mets cap into one open flap and slowed to a walk as he approached a bank of Port-A-Potties set up by the city in a futile effort to keep people from dropping their used soup kitchen dinners on the sidewalk. Of eight outhouses, only two were showing green on the door handle. He pulled one open and a sad man with a belt around his bicep and a spike in his arm stared back. Turnbull shut the door and went to the second, possibly unoccupied, one. This one actually was empty, and he went inside and locked the door.

It was as dank and as horrid as one might expect. The graffiti invited him to every act of perversion imaginable, and also suggested that one perform unnatural acts upon policemen. It occurred to him that it was at least two minutes since he had kicked off the chaos and he still did not hear any siren.

Though he had on the latex gloves, he had to be certain there was no biologic evidence that could link him to the weapons. He took out the Windex wipes and carefully wiped down the ASP. Satisfied it was clean of prints, he dropped it into the cess tank beneath the seat. He repeated this for the Glock and its magazines. They all went to the bottom, and it was highly unlikely anyone would be looking for anything there. They might be found when the vileness was pumped out, but that was fine. If it all worked out, he'd be long gone by then.

He realized that he was glad that he was wearing a mask.

Next, he gave the bare skin of his right arm past the glove a good scrubbing with the Windex wipe. That might or might not get the gunshot residue off him so that if he was tested, he might not come back as having fired a weapon recently. It was worth doing, just in case.

Lastly, he took the PPK out and made sure there was a round in its chamber, then replaced it in his jeans pocket. He used a wipe to flip the latch and pushed the door open with his foot.

More people running, and a now there was finally a siren in the distance.

He stepped out and took off his leather jacket. He rolled it up and tossed it into the entrance of another of the ragged tents lining the street. The subway station was ahead. Most folks were running past the entrance, but some were descending into it. The subways had an unsavory reputation again, like they had had a half-century before, but Turnbull figured it was his best way out of the area.

At the head of the stairs, a face caught his eye. One of the two dealers he had seen with Saladin was looking at him quizzically from a dozen yards away. Turnbull broke eye contact fast, but it was too late. The man sprinted after him, reaching under his loose shirt for something that would likely go "Bang."

Turnbull launched himself down the stairs into the subway station. A sign hanging above the turnstiles read "FARE AVOIDANCE IS A VIABLE REPARATIONS STRATEGY FOR OPPRPESSED PEOPLES" and Turnbull, feeling mighty oppressed with the armed drug dealer following behind him, leapt over the turnstile. Next to him, a very heavy woman struggled to get herself over the one in her lane.

He sprinted on through the dark corridors, nearly slipping on a puddle of orange vomit and hopping over several junkies passed out perpendicular to the passageway. There were many posters, most of them soliciting membership in the People's Militia or taking a stand that racism is bad. There was one with Mayor de Blasio and the words "FIGHTING FOR SOCIAL JUSTICE" across the top; someone had taken a Sharpie and drawn in a speech bubble where de Blasio admitted that "I have no dick."

Turnbull noted that every single camera in the place was trashed – every single one. At least this would not all be memorialized on video. He kept his mask on regardless.

He made hard for the nearest track platform, not caring about the direction the train was running – uptown, downtown, he just needed to get to some other part of town. There was a noise from behind, a shot, and the round sped past his ear.

He came to the platform and broke right at a full clip, but he immediately pulled up to a stop past the lip of the entrance and spun 180 degrees. The dealer came out of the entrance, clutching his Smith & Wesson MP9 Shield pistol, and Turnbull tackled him at speed. The gun flew out of the dealer's grasp and clattered across the floor as the other riders scattered. The pair went down on the filthy concrete floor, sprawling in a blizzard of punches and kicks. The guy was not formally trained in combatives, but he was strong, and he connected hard with Turnbull's side. Turnbull returned the favor to the man's nose, crushing it with a brutal right jab.

Turnbull scrambled to his feet, his back to the tracks as the dealer leapt up and charged. There was a flash – the dealer had a blade in his right hand. Turnbull pivoted and dodged his charging opponent, slamming his left foot into the man's shin as he passed. The dealer's momentum carried him on while he staggered, unable to stop as he flew off the platform into the darkness of the tracks.

The train could not brake in time, and it made an awful crunching noise.

Turnbull pivoted back to the entrance, and there was a young transit cop, eyes and mouth wide, trying to take in what he had just stumbled into.

His hand was on his service Glock as Turnbull's PPK loomed in his face. The cop froze.

"Don't die for that drug dealing asshole," Turnbull said, breathing heavily through his face mask. The Walther did not waver, locked between the patrolman's eyes.

"I didn't see shit. I can't even see your face," said the cop. "And good riddance to him. You think I care about that scumbag?"

"I'm leaving," Turnbull said.

"Can I shake your hand first?"

"Gimme the Glock."

"You take my piece and I'm screwed."

"I'm borrowing it. There's a trash can at the entrance. I'll dump it in there. You wait two minutes and come get it. That's my deal."

"Okay."

"And you forget me." Turnbull noted that the platform was clear. No one wanted to be a witness – everyone had fled.

"Like I said, the only thing I want to do to you is give you a medal," said the cop. He handed over the weapon and Turnbull bolted.

Good to his word, after a quick wipe with a Windex sheet just to be safe, he dropped the weapon into the overflowing garbage can at the entrance to the station, making sure it was underneath an empty bag from Chick-4-Just-Us, the woke Chick-fil-A offshoot that operated in the liberal jurisdictions that had banned the original brand. He then left the subway station and blended in with the crowd as he got far away from the scene.

He was near Columbus Circle when he took out the burner cell. From memory, he dialed a number.

"Who is calling?" asked a voice on the other end.

"Andrew Matich."

There was a pause. A long one. The voice returned. "Newark Airport Holiday Inn. 1600 hours. Understood?"

"Roger." Turnbull hung up, broke the phone on a stone bench and tossed the pieces, then hailed a cab. "Newark Airport Holiday Inn," he said as he pulled shut the door. The cabbie grunted, and they pulled into traffic.

There was a monitor playing local news on the back of the seat. The anchor reported that there had been a shootout between suspected drug dealers at Bryant Park, according to the NYPD. The anchor seemed to put more faith in the story provided by the BTAFPNOLFA Lives Matter organizers, who claimed that a dozen Proud Boys had attacked the peaceful demonstration as part of their racist violence agenda. The organizer, labeled "BTAFPNOLFA Lives Matter Spokesbeing Enola Gaines," promised "concrete retaliatory actions tonight." The anchor stated that the NYPD was preparing for escalated and fiery peaceful protests, the term "riot" having been banned by the station's style rules.

The anchor also briefly mentioned that a young honor student had been killed in a tragic subway accident at the Bryant Park station that afternoon while returning home from church. She then moved on to a discussion of Mayor de Blasio's controversial initiative to solve climate change by banning cheeseburgers. "We can no longer have it our way!" it showed him telling a group of pale, weak vegan weather fanatics.

Turnbull shut his eyes and tried to sleep as the cabbie drove him to his pick-up rendezvous, thinking that he had done okay for a dead guy.

2.

"Death to fascist racists and transphobes!" something that was very angry yelled at Kelly Turnbull as the operator walked by. That was one of its nicer comments. Most of its catcalls involved insinuations of transgressive sexual proclivities that, in other circumstances, the malignant creature would have strongly advocated.

The something was pink-haired with a blue streak parting the 'do in the middle, and it was sort of oblong-shaped, suited-up in a vinyl jacket that probably cost his or her or whatever's daddy a pretty penny. The something was standing north of Turnbull across Constitution Avenue from the Mall, protected by a police barricade with about a thousand of its friends. Many were wearing masks, but less because of the peril of viruses than to make a statement. Mask-wearing meant acceptance of the official expert position that the country was in a state of perpetual pathogen siege and that this justified the government exercising vast emergency powers. The fact that almost no one was still sick that November was irrelevant; to deny the need to wear masks forever was to deny science itself. And science denial was bad, unless the science was inconvenient, in which case science denial became a moral imperative.

They pressed together, official science having determined that leftist protesting in close quarters with lots of howling conferred immunity to disease, while congregating in churches or to demand liberty promoted it.

All of them behind the barrier, whether masked or unmasked, were shouting similar obscenities in similarly high-pitched voices. A thin line of nervous District of Columbia cops, a few of them specially allowed to be armed for the occasion in the wake of the "de-policing" of the city following the riots of 2020, separated them from the huge and highly illegal gathering of normal people around and before the Lincoln Memorial.

None of the normal people wore masks. Most did wear jackets to protect themselves from the fall chill they expected once the sun went down.

Turnbull was among them wearing jeans and a newish leather jacket, his compact B&T APC9 9mm submachine gun and SIG Sauer M18 pistol underneath with a half-dozen interchangeable mags. He surveyed the something that was screaming at him from across the street, and it was flustered by his cold stare and his lack of reaction to its taunts. But he was reacting on the inside. Turnbull calculated that he could, if necessary, pretty easily put a hollow point into its forehead across the 35-meter distance. The apathetic cops would likely not even be an issue – the relatively few urban police officers (now officially called "Community Resource Guides") remaining after the "policing reforms" were loath to put themselves at risk for a populace that hated them, or for a government that would happily throw them to the wolves if someone's phone camera caught them in the ugly act of policing thugs.

No one ever got fired, indicted, or imprisoned for not intervening. The people of DC, and most big cities, were on their own, as the stratospheric crime stats illustrated to anyone who cared. The politicians certainly did not.

Having completed his contingency plan to eliminate the threat – to the extent the big mouthed strange-o constituted a real threat – Turnbull commenced to ignore it and, after he scanned the rest of the motley – and surprisingly small and relatively restrained – band of leftist counter-protesters for potential danger, he moved on.

For his trouble, he got called a "cis-gender queerbait" with an unnatural attraction to his mother, which struck Turnbull as conceptually confused on every level.

But he had no time to waste on the ravings of spoiled college students performing live-action revolutionary role-playing for the media. Somewhere in the crowd of normal folks were some bad people who were packing more than just big mouths. He was sure of it.

Turnbull was there for them. And Turnbull was no browbeaten big city cop.

A trio of Metro squad cars came up Constitution, the bullhorn on the lead vehicle blaring.

"This is an illegal demonstration! You are ordered to disperse! You are making racisms and sexisms and risking infection by the European virus and...." The reader paused, seemingly unsure of the next allegation in the litany. "You are also racist. I repeat, this is an illegal demonstration and you are ordered to clear the area by order of the Main Facilitator of the Community Resource Guides of the District formerly known as Columbia!"

Now it was the turn of the people on Turnbull's side of the street to start jeering even as the something and its friends cheered on their new pals, the DC cops. It was the stubbornly normal-looking people gathering on the Mall who were in violation of the law, not the freakshow leftist counter-demonstrators. The crypto-Marxists were on the same side of the street as the White House, and on the same side politically as its current occupant – in fact, he occupied it all the time, rarely going out in public. One could get banned from social media for referring to it, as many had, as the "perma-lid."

But the normal folks were not going anywhere. In fact, there were more and more of them pouring into the Mall even though the police had tried to block off the bridges from Virginia and had even shut down the subway system. All of this was to prevent the rally, because in the eyes of the establishment, it was the wrong kind of rally.

Most of the attendees looked like they had just come from church, or at least a mega-church – there were a lot of polo shirts and some cargo shorts, as it was an uncommonly warm fall afternoon. Some carried signs. Some brought kids in strollers. None wore masks, though the threat of the now-renamed "European virus" – the term "Chinese coronavirus" had been decreed to be racist as all get out – was one of several reasons the authorities gave for banning this gathering.

Yet the protesters were cheerful – there was no ominous vibe despite the circling police presence.

These people were there to take their country back, a country they were watching being stolen from them.

It was not merely the disputed mid-term elections a couple weeks before, where the fraud in favor of leftist Democrats was open and extensive, that outraged them. The four-justice leftist bloc controlling the Supreme Court after Justice Kavanaugh's tragic keg accident had been quite busy in recent weeks. Where there is no majority, a four-justice vote upholds the lower court's ruling, and the Ninth Circuit had been busy. It had discovered, lurking within the Constitution, a new right to be "free of hate speech." To the surprise of no one, "hate speech" seemed to correspond exactly to whatever the current Democrat administration did not want said out loud. There was also a new right to citizenship for illegal aliens – if you get here, you had a right to vote Democrat. The Donkey Party was registering millions of them to be ready to vote as instructed in the next election, though considering its aggressive fraud, enrolling new voters was almost superfluous.

And there was a new right to "be free of the terror of gun violence." *Carpenter v. New York* overruled *Heller* and *McDonald.* In a flash, American citizens had gone from having the right to keep and bear arms to having a right to not have other American citizens keep and bear arms. And protesting this was, according to the mayor of the city formerly known as Washington, "hate speech."

Dissent went from being patriotic to being treason right at the very same moment that the left had taken power.

Chief Justice Roberts had supplied the fourth liberal vote validating the Ninth Circuit's opinions in all of these cases, initially earning cautious praise in a *Washington Post* editorial, though that tepid applause was withdrawn in a subsequent *mea culpa* disclaimer that ran on the front page after the newsroom's Intersectionality Committee that reviewed all the paper's contents complained. "We apologize for the pain and hurt we caused by praising someone many accurately see as a symbol of patriarchy and racism, even if after many long years of complicity in oppression he seems to have begun to make amends through his rulings," the abject apology read.

Clay Deeds had been standing near Turnbull at an airport when CNN's Jake Tapper gleefully read this live and wondered aloud for his audience of frequent flyers and shut-ins if the Chief Justice's guilt over his privilege and complicity had driven him to become a reliable liberal vote, prompting Deeds to mutter something like, "No, I've seen the photos." Turnbull, steadfastly disinterested in politics, had ignored him and gone about his business.

In fact, Turnbull had always made an effort to ignore politics, even as politics became impossible to ignore. The impeachments, the arrests, the Department of Justice prosecutions of a dozen Republican senators on charges that Democrat senators skated on, and then the midterm election that was still embroiled in a continued post-election vote count fight – he had heard of these things as they happened, but he was focused on his missions. America still had foreign enemies, and those became Kelly Turnbull's enemies. The schemes and conspiracies of the politicians back home repelled him, so he simply chose not to pay attention. And then one day last summer he was pulled out of the Middle East by his boss Clay Deeds, and suddenly he was walking around whatever they were going to change the name of

Washington, DC, into in the middle of November with an automatic weapon under his coat.

Turnbull knew what an unstable society felt like – he had experienced them all over the world. And it disturbed him that he was getting the same feeling here in America.

There was a discreet mic on his collar and he wore a low-vis earpiece. It now came alive.

"This is Hufflepuff-One, you got anything?" It was Ted Hiroshi, his fellow Zombie, somewhere in the crowd to the west near the Vietnam Veterans Memorial.

"Nope," Turnbull, aka "Hufflepuff-Two," replied quietly, refusing to use the *Harry Potter*-inspired call signs his friend had selected, no doubt to annoy him. A little kid holding his mom's hand stared, wondering why the scary man was talking to himself. Turnbull ignored him.

"Does Ravenclaw-One have anything?" asked Hiroshi. Turnbull winced. Wasn't *Harry Potter* the one with hobbits?

"Negative," came back Joe Schiller. "I got nothing." He and his own team were on the far side of the growing crowd. There were four teams from Task Force Zulu on the ground, mingling, eight operators in all.

Turnbull moved on down the sidewalk. For an illegal gathering, it sure seemed festive. Moms, dads, kids – many were wearing star-spangled clothes, patriotic t-shirts, and sometimes hats reflecting their military service or their desire to make America great again once again.

In America, these were now the criminals, the bad guys.

That made no sense to Turnbull, who felt right at home with these folks and who was totally alienated from the jeering mutants on the other side of the avenue. How it came to this, where these patriotic citizens were the problem, was beyond him. But he had decided that such questions were beyond his pay grade.

His job was to keep these people safe.

And he had been doing that for years, in Afghanistan, Iraq, Syria, and elsewhere, first in the sketchy world of traditional Special Forces and then through the looking glass after being recruited by Clay Deeds for off-the-books jobs that it was better the powers that be just didn't know about. He had done that all over the world, violently and well, but this was different.

This time he was doing it at home, in the United States. And the enemy was American, at least nominally. But his green light was gone. There were rules. In fact, it had been almost half a year since he had killed anyone, which smashed his previous post-enlistment record by several months.

But his oath specified all enemies, both foreign and domestic.

The domestic enemy that day was Merrick Crane III. He should have been on Wall Street like his father and his father's father, making tens of millions a year doing whatever Wall Street people did. Instead, Crane was a guy who played footsie with Antifa until he decided that Antifa just didn't have the will to do what was really necessary to achieve the revolution. That's when he had helped start the People's Militia movement in the cities. Rumor had it that he now found even that organization to be insufficiently committed.

Word from the informant inside Crane's organization was that something was going down at today's "Rally for Liberty's Reawakening." Of course, that morning they had fished the body of the informant out of the Potomac next to a delightful waterside restaurant called Sequoia, ruining its legendary weekend brunch buffet. The corpse's fingers had been snipped off with a garden clipper, and its tongue was melted out from the Drano that someone had poured down the snitch's throat.

Turnbull kept moving, watching and ready.

Merrick Crane III could smell them as he walked through the crowd. Maybe not actually smell them, but the value of mere objective reality paled in comparison to the fierce urgency of the narrative. These creatures were disgusting, with their racism and sexism and homophobia and their stupid Jesus and their brutal embrace of guns and, worst of all, their selfish refusal to comply. They stank of their Americanism, their childlike and malevolent love of this blighted country, born in genocide, forged in slavery, and built on a tyranny over the working class.

That the people he hated so much were largely working class themselves never occurred to him. He was no expert on the working class – he prepped at Phillips Academy-Andover, graduated with a sociology degree and masters from Harvard, and interned on Capitol Hill with Chuck Schumer (who owed his father many favors) before the unpleasantness with the photos and the crotchless vinyl costume led to the Democrats reluctantly cutting the Senate leader adrift. If only he had not been with a buxom, traditionally attractive blonde, the ex-senator could have gotten through the scandal and perhaps even enhanced his position within the party.

Crane had never earned a paycheck in his life. But he did not eschew money or what it bought. In his file, Turnbull had found a note that his target still underwent a daily five-step facial cleansing and moisturizing regimen even while underground.

To Crane, the working class was wonderful in theory but in practice, he found its members dull, stupid, and in dire need of the guidance of those with the ideological credentials to rule.

People like him.

To make that happen, history needed a shove, and not merely a gentle nudge. Starting in 2021, Antifa had gotten even more into arson and property bombings, but it never went all the way. It never went the next step. Crane intended to do so. His time on the Hill had taught him well that real change would not come in through bourgeois conceits like elections and debate.

It would come in on a tide of blood.

He had worked on the Bernie Sanders campaign before the elderly communist's embarrassing penchant for secret Bahamian bank accounts became public knowledge. Socialism was weak sauce, and democratic socialism weaker still. He had flirted with Antifa, earning his stripes within the hierarchy of the allegedly hierarchy-free organization during the 2020 riots and actually rising in the ranks of a movement that was not supposed to have ranks until much of its East Coast activities were under his personal dominion. But then they pushed him out, claiming he was going too far after some unpleasantness involving informants and chainsaws.

Crane rejected the concept of going too far.

So, he left Antifa, bringing along those individuals who he had identified as ready to take the next step with him. After all, you weren't serious if you weren't ready to shed some serious red.

This had initially led to the People's Militia movement, an Antifa without the ridiculous anarchist fixation that understood that organized power – combining cadres, disaffected scions of the middle and upper classes, and people the oppressors called "criminals" – required building a force that would replace the defunded and abolished police forces of the oppressors. But while necessary, even the People's Militias – which were springing up in many left-wing enclaves – were unprepared to go as far as was necessary. So even as he coordinated People's Militia activities, he built his own personal force that would be free to act without artificial restraints and restrictions. While Antifa and the People's Militias embraced shedding blood in theory, Merrick Crane III reveled in it in practice.

His first big score was hitting a National Guard armory and liberating fifty M4 carbines, mags, and crates of ammunition. He might have likened it to the raid on Harper's Ferry had he ever bothered to study American history – history was just a litany of racist outrages, so why bother? – and learned who John Brown was.

Looking across the road, he saw the White House back in the distance behind the leftist counter-protesters. These Neanderthals all around him called the occupant "the most leftist president in history," and perhaps that was true. But the redistribution, the suppression of dissent, the Green New Deal that was destroying the fossil fuel industry and impoverishing vast swathes of Middle America – these were mere half-measures. His true agenda would make them shiver.

And he had allies, powerful allies, ones who saw the value of someone who would push the envelope while they sat back in their comfy sinecures. They would let him do the back-breaking and dangerous work of forcing open the Overton Window, and then swoop in once he had done so with his unspeakable tactics to reap the rewards.

Or so they thought. The complicit mainstream fools who thought they were playing him did not realize that they would be the first against the wall when he achieved his goals.

His watch told him there were ten minutes to go. He looked along Constitution Avenue at the throngs walking by the t-shirt vendors and food carts, and he smiled.

Turnbull had gone south into the crowd on the Mall itself. The rally organizers had set up a stage on the top steps of the Lincoln Memorial. This was highly illegal, of course, but it had happened so fast that the depleted and defunded DC cops could not organize a response before the tens of thousands of patriots had gathered. The algorithms created by the leftists who ran Facebook, Twitter, and the rest of social media had been unable to fully suppress the word of the rally – the patriots were constantly figuring out new ways to avoid being blocked and locked no matter how hard the Silicon Valley types tried to suppress them. But it was a never-ending cat and mouse game – patriots sought to spread the word and leftist twenty-somethings in Cupertino sought to identify and squelch those unapproved messages. Of course, to the extent that the mainstream media would mention the rally, it would be to highlight its myriad thoughtcrimes.

Behind the platform, the patriotic protesters were scrubbing off the spray-painted, often obscene, graffiti that had accumulated on the columns, the walls, and on Abe's statue itself.

A couple leftists had gotten close to there and were screaming incoherently that this act of community and political hygiene was "literally murdering us" and that they were "literally shaking." A couple of guys in tank tops who looked like they lived in a gym picked them up and carried them shrieking out to Constitution Avenue, where they literally threw the vocal leftists onto their asses on the asphalt.

The cops, realizing that no matter what they did they would be crucified, just watched. This set the penned-up left-wing protesters across the street to screaming even more about the tyrannical police state that they seemed unaware that their own allies ran in DC. The officers were just glad that, for whatever reason, the mob was behaving itself today. Perhaps the short notice for the counter-rally had kept enough of them from gathering to create a critical mass of riotous idiots.

From below the podium, at the base of the white marble stairs, Turnbull scanned the crowd. Finding nothing threatening, he moved north back toward the street. The speakers' voices were already echoing across the masses from the big amps that had been snuck in. Turnbull was not paying any real attention to the speakers, but what he caught resonated. It was a lot of stuff about the Constitution and God and freedom, and as apolitical as he considered himself, he was for all of those things.

"We were created by the Lord with those rights, and we'll be damned if we let them be taken from us!" the current speaker shouted with the hint of a North Carolina drawl behind his words. Turnbull recognized the man, an actor, from a recent movie titled *Love's Savage Fury* that he had watched between missions back at Bagram. He was a fan of Nick Searcy, but the star's nude scene had been a bit jarring, especially since it was with an equally buck-naked Kate Upton. It had left the audience of Green Berets in the camp with very mixed feelings.

The MC, radio host Larry O'Connor, took over to introduce the next speaker, Senator Lindsey Graham, who proceeded to talk about how his continuing investigation into the Russiagate scandal was going to lead to accountability for the conspirators very, very soon. The crowd booed him.

Turnbull ignored the speeches. He had a job to do.

Turnbull returned to the sidewalk next to Constitution Avenue, which was lined with vendors of all kinds hawking shirts, hats, tacos, Cokes, whatever. The angry leftists were still there across the street, making a fuss, and chanting about how if there was no justice there would be no peace, but the attendees were generally ignoring them. The DC cops were looking positively dejected, unable to do much of anything except keep the two groups apart. They certainly did not have the numbers to stamp out the traditionalists' protest, as much as their bosses would have liked them to. Such were the wages of defunding.

Plus, there was always the possibility that these gun rights protesters were actually exercising their now-nonexistent rights, and few of the Washington flatfoots felt like personally rolling the dice to enforce the administration's gun confiscation fetish.

Graham got offstage quickly, and the crowd erupted so loudly as O'Connor announced the next speaker that Turnbull paused and took notice.

"And I am proud to present a legend, a true hero, a martyr to the cause of freedom, Lieutenant General Karl Martin Scott!"

On the stage, the general, his familiar face lean and worn but focused and fixed, raised both hands to greet the crowd. Turnbull had little use for either the news or flag officers, but even he knew that Scott was not supposed to be making public statements as a condition of his pre-trial release.

"I fought for this country," he said, his amped voice rolling over the now silent crowd. "And I told the truth when those in power wanted to hide it. They can throw me in prison. They can even shoot me. But they cannot ever silence me!"

That was it. He was still up there talking, but the crowd was going crazy for their new hero, the guy who had defied the president and was as universally loathed in the blue states as he was adored in the red.

In Iraq, his no-quarter war against ISIS had earned him the nickname "Killdozer 6." Back home, his nickname was "Second Amendment Scott."

He spoke a little more, but it was hard for Turnbull to make out exactly what he said except for the "God bless you" that came at the end. He walked off to a sustained roar. Turnbull looked at the cops, but they weren't reacting. Real problems would start if the authorities decided to take him back into custody here and now – that could be a disaster. But none of the authorities made a move, and the rally continued.

Nearby, an ABC News reporter was looking into his camera explaining to the network's dwindling audience how the rally was "a tsunami of racist hate spewed by racists."

Turnbull kept moving along the sidewalk, looking for anything out of place, and looking for Merrick Crane III in particular. But finding him here was unlikely. Terrorist bigwigs rarely got their own paws dirty. They generally left the actual bloodletting to their minions.

Except, at that moment, Crane was about 200 meters north of him, and coming his way.

"Hey," said a woman's voice from behind Turnbull, one with a lightly suppressed Southern lilt. "You in the leather jacket."

Turnbull pivoted, assuming he'd draw the SIG and go for a Mozambique drill on his interlocutor – two in the chest, one in the hat rack – if it came to that. But his kill plan wasn't necessary, at least not at that moment.

The woman calling to him was a pretty blonde in her early 30s, clearly a reporter since a cameraman was standing next to her, munching on a green apple and looking bored. He was dressed like a hobo, as field cameramen generally are, but she was extremely put together. She looked like she was about to walk into her suburban Georgia Baptist church for the first time after getting divorced, with a slightly too-tight red dress that hovered above her knees, loads of make-up, and every hair locked into its assigned place. The mic she held said "Trump News Network" in gold letters.

"Sir, would you like to tell my audience why you are here?"

"No," Turnbull said. He observed the cameraman was not shooting yet, which was good. Having his face plastered all over basic cable would be a bad thing.

"You know who I am, right?" she asked.

"No."

"Avery Barnes, Trump News Network?" She nodded, expectantly.

"You say that like I should know and/or care. Adios."

"Hey," she said. "Come on. You at least look a little sketchy. Everyone else around here looks like they're on the way to Sunday school or is hoping to walk some old lady across the road. Help a lady out."

"Bye, TV girl," Turnbull said.

"I'm so bored with people talking to me about the Founders and natural rights. Something tells me that you'll totally say something that will go viral. Come on. Let me make you a star."

"Yeah, no," Turnbull said, pivoting.

"What the...?" Avery said, looking toward the speaker, her attention completely gone in that fraction of a second. There was a commotion up on the stage.

"I think Kanye West just grabbed the microphone away from Dana Loesch," Avery said to no one in particular.

"Speaking as the representative of Jesus, I say these Democrats are Pilate reborn!" began the rapper, his voice booming over the Mall as he tugged at the microphone from beside the podium.

"Get this, Lou!" Avery shouted, forgetting about her interview subject. Now the cameraman dropped his fruit and scrambled to catch the moment, and with the reporter distracted Turnbull moved away. He got about twenty feet before all hell broke loose.

Merrick Crane III stepped over to a youngish man with a scruffy beard who had been handing out hot dogs to hungry protesters from his metallic wheeled cart at $9 a pop.

"Ready?" Crane asked. The man swallowed and nodded. He was on edge. That was why Crane was here himself. With him present, they would damn well come through. It was part of his leadership strategy, ensuring that his troops were more afraid of him than the enemy.

"Good," Crane said. "For the revolution."

"The revolution," the man repeated, like a scuzzy parishioner calling back the Church of Marxism's version of "Amen."

Down the street, the rest of the half-dozen *faux* vendors were watching the exchange, taking their own cues.

The minion opened up the top door of his cart and reached deep inside past the hot dogs and soggy buns to pull up and out an M4 with a 30-round mag locked in the well.

Crane stepped backwards onto the sidewalk, where several passersby had noticed what was happening and stood stunned, watching the people who just a minute before had been hawking their wares producing loaded assault rifles. Crane kept his own 9mm Walther Q4 TAC automatic under his jacket – Merrick Crane III was not going to carry some battered Beretta M9 liberated from a West Virginia Army National Guard maintenance unit's armory.

Turnbull was moving along the sidewalk as West and Loesch were playing microphone tug o' war on stage, and then a young woman at a stand displaying a variety of hats bearing statements like "Make America Great Again Again" reached under her table into a cardboard box and came back up with a loaded M4.

The liberty protest attendees knew exactly what it was – a benefit of being gun-fluent – and after a second to get their bearings, they scrambled. Being generally law-abiding, even where the law was an ass – as it was in gun-hating DC – none of the civilians was carrying concealed. If this had happened in, say, Texas, it would have been a very different story.

But Turnbull *was* armed, and he reached back for the compact Brügger & Thomet APC9K submachine gun hanging under his coat. The woman was faster, up on her feet with the M4, looking at the rally for a moment as she brought her weapon to her shoulder. Then she turned 180 degrees to face the line of DC cops and the leftist protesters.

So did the rest of the shooters, a total of six of them.

Turnbull processed this unexpected turn of events even as he brought his submachine gun up, the carrying strap long enough for him to maneuver with it still attached. He had expected the shooter to open fire on the normals gathered for the rally, but his target – like her comrades – paid the patriotic attendees no mind. Somewhere up the street, the first of the shooters opened fire on the leftists, then all of them joined in before Turnbull could take aim.

They were spraying across Constitution Avenue into the mass of counter-protesters, and mowing down any police officers in the line of fire.

The woman was ripping off her second three round burst as Turnbull set the red dot sight on her center mass and squeezed. His 9mm rounds came out of the compact weapon in a burst of six, all of which slammed into her, stitching up her body from her gut to her mouth. She dropped her M4 and fell backwards, collapsing the stand and being partially buried under an avalanche of novelty ballcaps.

People were running everywhere, and Turnbull knew they were truly scared because no one was slowing down to film the chaos with their cellphone. The road itself was empty except for dark shapes, the bodies of police officers murdered where they stood. Across the road was chaos as burst after burst of 5.56mm rounds slammed into the leftist crowd. Scores of the counter-protesters fell. It was pandemonium over there.

Turnbull searched for targets among the vendors. Some were obviously innocent, but not all. There was more shooting up the road, and he sprinted ahead.

Behind him, Avery Barnes was on her knees, and turned to her cameraman.

"Are you getting this, Lou?"

He nodded, the adrenaline overcoming his common sense.

"Come on!" she yelled and ran forward, with Lou tagging along.

There was a guy with an M4 at a taco stand wearing a t-shirt with a picture of Dan Crenshaw riding a giant eagle while casting lightning bolts from his one good eye. The shooter was firing away across the street with his gun resting on the top of his cart for support.

"Hey!" Turnbull yelled as he approached, his APC 9K ready.

This got the shooter's attention and he turned, bringing the rifle around. Turnbull emptied what remained of his 20-round mag into the man, who sprawled back with the eagle and the SEAL shredded upon his chest.

There were too many civilians around for an automatic weapon, Turnbull decided. He let the submachine gun hang by its strap and drew his SIG pistol. The bad guy at the next stand was in the process of being tackled by two burly protesters, who were trying to wrest his M4 away. The muzzle was going every which way – if someone pulled the trigger, civilians were bound to get hit.

"Step off, I'm a federal special agent!" Turnbull yelled, and the two men let go. The shooter stood there, weapon in hand, puzzled.

Turnbull shot him in the face, then stepped over and put another slug through his forehead. Turnbull figured if there was ever a green light, firing an automatic weapon into a crowd was it.

The two civilians stared at him, shocked.

"I'm a very special agent," Turnbull said to the incredulous civilians. "You didn't see anything."

"See what?" one of the men responded.

"Screw that piece of shit," said the other, and then he spit on the twitching corpse.

Turnbull moved ahead, leading with the handgun. He became aware of the cacophony on his radio as the other Task Force Zulu members closed in.

"Tango down, moving to engage the next one!" It was Ted Hiroshi.

"I did three, looking to run up the score," Turnbull said. He was aware of sirens in the distance. People were running everywhere. In the street, an armed DC cop was bravely engaging a target with his pistol, then there was a burst and he fell backward in the street. Turnbull could not see his target ahead – too many people – but there were more shots.

"Tango two down," Hiroshi announced.

"I'm coming your way," Turnbull said into his mic as he ran, the SIG in a two-hand grip searching for targets, and then he froze.

Merrick Crane III, clear as day, on the sidewalk, 25 meters ahead, an automatic in his left hand. Their eyes locked.

Turnbull aimed. The gun sight was dead on the bastard's smug, moisturized mug.

Civilians darted between them, in all directions, running and shouting. He had no clear shot. Turnbull could see a smile on Crane's face, and the terrorist gestured with the handgun as if to ask, "Should I kill some of these fine folks?"

To his right, there was more shooting as the scuzzy man from the hot dog stand ran down the gutter on Constitution Avenue with his M4, firing off random bursts.

"Shit," Turnbull hissed, pivoting. The running scuzz caught sight of Turnbull too late to react. He took two rounds mid-sternum and dropped backwards on the asphalt.

Turnbull pivoted back. Crane was gone. Long gone.

He walked over to the ventilated terrorist, whose white t-shirt was marred by two thorax holes surrounded by rapidly expanding circles of crimson. He was not moving and didn't seem to be breathing, but why take a chance? Turnbull casually shot the man in the forehead, and the brass shell casing clinked as it bounced down Constitution Avenue.

"Tango four dead," Turnbull said into the mic. "I saw Crane, but he's in the wind."

"Roger! We're on the way!" Schiller said. There was plenty of chaos, but no more gunfire.

"Negative, negative, I think it's done." Turnbull said. "Clear the area. Clear it. The civvies will be moving in. Get out of here."

Turnbull relaxed a bit and turned back the way he came.

Avery Barnes was there, in his face, wide-eyed and excited. Her cameraman was with her.

"I knew you were something," she said, out of breath. "I didn't know what, but I knew it by looking at you."

Turnbull pointed his SIG at the cameraman, who dropped his rig and stepped back, hands up.

"We filmed everything," Barnes said.

"Yeah?" Turnbull said, then he shot the camera on the ground twice. It began smoking.

"Holy shit, man!" shouted the cameraman.

"Forget me," Turnbull directed, and not nicely.

"You think the video's in the camera?" Barnes said, giddy. "It uploads automatically. I got you on tape killing three terrorists."

"Four," Turnbull said.

"Look, we can cut around the footage of you. That never has to come out."

"Why would you do that?"

"You have to give me your story. Off the record, but everything. Unless you want to be a star."

Turnbull contemplated shooting her, though in fairness he always contemplated how he would kill everyone he met. He decided against. Terrorists were one thing, but someone might miss Miss Avery Barnes.

"Give me a story," she said. "Find me." The sirens were getting louder.

"And how do I do that?"

"Oh, I have a feeling whoever you work for can find whoever it wants whenever it wants to."

There were a swarm of red and blue flashing lights coming up the road. Turnbull tucked his pistol into his holster and walked off without another word.

"Nothing was uploaded yet. The memory card is wasted," Lou said as he surveyed the wreckage, but Avery Barnes was already on her cell talking to Trump News headquarters back on 6th Avenue in New York.

"We're right in the middle, Mike. Right in the middle of it! They shot up our camera! Yeah, Lou's fine, I guess. Look, I want to go live off my iPhone video right freaking now!"

3.

Turnbull was the last Task Force Zulu member to arrive back at the safehouse, a brick townhouse in Alexandria with white trim and two signs out front, one reading HATE HAS NO HOME HERE and the other NO SOLICITORS – THIS MEANS YOU. The anti-hate sign had a little rainbow on it and a circle of multi-ethnic cartoon kids hugging.

Ted Hiroshi let him in the front door and locked it behind him securely. The pleasant wood door's exterior hid the metal plating on the inside.

"He's waiting," Hiroshi said. He had a Glock on his hip. A tricked-out M4 lay against the wall within easy reach.

"Everyone here?"

"Now they are."

"I got delayed," Turnbull growled, and indeed he had. The police had tried to seal off the Mall after the massacre, but 150,000 patriots determined to get home were not about to be corralled. They pushed through the hastily erected barricades and streamed out of the city. Turnbull faded into the mass and had to go the long way.

It was a somber migration – the entire crowd was aware that something terrible had happened. He heard rumors as he walked – everyone was walking – of a hundred, two hundred people dead. That sounded high, but there were a lot of bodies littering the capital city. He resolved that if Crane was ever in range again, he would unload, and if civilians were in the way, well, he'd try his best to miss them.

The cops were out in numbers, many armed with long weapons and very much on edge – not a shock since a bunch of their own had just been gunned down. Turnbull was briefly concerned that conflict might escalate with the crowd. After all, the media – well, the majority of it – was reporting that it was the patriots who had opened fire on the peaceful counter-protesters.

The narrative was already being baked into the mainstream media's message during the three hours it took Turnbull to get back to Task Force Zulu's temporary sanctuary. It asserted that those conservative monsters on the Mall were not just literal Nazis but murderers as well.

Ted motioned for Turnbull to follow him upstairs.

Clay Deeds was talking to Joe Schiller. Casey Warner was sitting on a couch at the top of the steps on the second floor cleaning his HK P30 pistol. Other operatives were prepping their gear as well. Brad Essex was loading 7.62mm rounds into his SCAR's magazine. Cole Suthern was cleaning his M4. Wes Albert was repacking his med kit. Turnbull had worked with most of them overseas; together, he assessed Task Force Zulu as quite a dangerous clique.

The TV monitor was on – it was CNN with the volume low but audible. The chyron read "RIGHT WING BLOODBATH IN DC."

"Is this an airport lounge?" Turnbull asked as he got to the top of the stairs.

"Gotta watch the liberal media as part of our 'know your enemy' program," Casey replied.

"That's enough of that crap," Deeds said, his face etched with obvious distress. "We are non-political. That's not what we are here for." Schiller stood there, his face blank, clearly not buying it.

Casey nodded sullenly, but he was absolutely political. He had about 100,000 followers of his Twitter account @FullAutoGalt. A hardcore fan of Ayn Rand, he liked to anonymously send copies of *Atlas Shrugged* to people in the public eye who he felt were being seduced by collectivist nonsense. Just a week before, he had annoyed Turnbull by telling him about how he saw a particularly dumb basic liberal tweet from intermittent actress and endlessly tiresome activist Alyssa Milano. "Someday she'll read it and come around," he told Turnbull, who replied that Casey should stop talking to him.

Schiller had a Smith & Wesson M2.0 automatic in his belt. The other operators all had various handguns. They each chose their own with no regard for uniformity. Miscellaneous long guns leaned against the walls.

Deeds picked up the monitor's remote, but paused before turning the screen off. The anchor was barely concealing a smile as she reported the network's latest scoop – not the result of a journalist digging but of an administration figure calling up the reliably obedient network and leaking the information he wanted reported. CNN was only too happy to oblige.

"Our sources close to the administration tell us that after the death toll of not less than 75 peaceful protesters murdered at the Republican white supremacy rally in Washington, the President intends to issue executive orders regarding commonsense, and what polls say are very popular, limitations on the ownership of weapons of war."

Deeds flicked off the monitor.

"What the hell happened out there?" he asked.

"Crane was behind it," Turnbull said. "I saw him."

"Why didn't you shoot him?"

"Couldn't get a clear shot. But he was there. And those assholes were his. This was a set up."

"The shooters ignored the rally," Ted said. "They were only shooting at the people across the street, the leftists."

"And the media is buying the lie," Deeds said.

"Buying it?" Casey Warner said. "They are in on it. They are trying to set the conditions to clamp down. Shit, it's right there in front of us. It's a left-wing coup!"

"No more," Deeds said. "No more. This task force is not political. Not at all. We're defending the Constitution, not for one side or the other."

"But what if only one side is for the Constitution?" Casey snapped back.

"Chill," Turnbull told him. "We don't do politics."

"Watch out," Schiller said, speaking up for the first time. "Because politics might just do you."

Turnbull stared back, annoyed at the latest version of the cliché. He never liked the guy, though the guy was highly capable in the field. Of course, Kelly Turnbull did not like much of anyone.

"We do one thing," Deeds said firmly. "We defend the Constitution, most often by taking out terrorists. That's our job. That's our only job. The politicians handle the politics. We help make it so they can settle their differences without the US turning into one of those places we were off fighting in. Does everyone here get that? Because if you don't, get out. We are not here for our own agendas. Are we clear?"

No one responded in the negative. Deeds continued.

"We need to find Merrick Crane III. It's pretty clear what he's doing – trying to provoke even more conflict. And it's working."

"If they start trying to confiscate guns...," Casey began.

"Yes, I know," Deeds said. "That could dip the torch into the gasoline."

"Do we know anything new about his organization?" Turnbull asked.

"Not a lot. He's wanted for other crimes, but law enforcement is not looking at him for the Mall massacre. We have sources throughout the IC and law enforcement feeding us intel, and he's barely even on their radar."

"Who is?" asked Turnbull.

"That depends on whose radar you are talking about. The law enforcement and intelligence communities are picking sides, and they are focusing on wrangling with each other instead of the real enemy. I have to vet anyone I talk to in the IC before I accept his intel," Deeds said. He then addressed the entire task force. "In any case, we need to jump. This safehouse may be compromised within 24 hours. Casey, weapons disposal. Every weapon that you fired today we need to destroy. No links to us."

Casey nodded, but Turnbull pondered his reporter problem. The other team members stood up and moved out.

Turnbull was handing over his fired firearms to Casey when Deeds approached.

"A word?" Turnbull left the submachine gun and SIG in Casey's hands and walked off into a bedroom with Deeds. Deeds shut the door.

"This is bad, Kelly," Deeds said.

"Yeah, I saw."

"I've been getting information from various sources. They are going to push this hard. This is the excuse some in the administration have been looking for. They are going to clamp down on guns, and on what people say on the air and on social media."

"That's going to get pushback."

"And there are discussions about how to take over certain state governments that are not cooperative," Deeds said.

"That sounds like a coup, except by the federal government. Can you coup yourself?"

"I don't have to tell you how dangerous a time this is. We have a president who is barely coherent surrounded by left-wing fanatics and a brand-new vice president scheming to take over."

In fact, recently-installed Veep, Elizabeth Warren, had only been in office for a month. The announcement of Warren as his third VP in under two years had not gone well. The President told the cameras, "And most importantly, Elizabeth Warlock is a woman of color, an Indian, like tee-pees, you know, not like tandoori." After that, he made no further public appearances.

The prior occupant of the office had been Stacey Abrams, who herself had replaced Kamala Harris after the latter suffered an unexpected allergic reaction to some brownies sent to her by the First Lady. Vice President Abrams had been found in her bed at Number One, Observatory Circle, the official residence of the Vice President, having choked on a ham sandwich.

Had Turnbull ever ventured onto the internet, he would have been baffled by the profusion of Biden Administration/*Spinal Tap* drummer memes.

"I don't know what is going to happen," Deeds said. "But we need to deescalate this. These people need to put what's coming on pause and think about the consequences."

"Sounds like they sense an opportunity."

"They need breathing room in spite of themselves. Look, Kelly, you have no politics at all. That's why I need you. You have no agenda. You just want to shoot bad people."

"So, which bad people should I shoot?"

"For this one, you need to slow your roll and not kill anyone for a while. Help me give them some time to rethink their plans. Look, the FBI is already heading out to Virginia to the NRA headquarters to confiscate a copy of the membership rolls and bring it back to DC. That's a list of five million people who own guns – they are target number one when this executive order banning privately owned firearms comes out tomorrow."

"Rounding up guns seems like a really bad idea," Turnbull said. He was not much of a joiner, but he had made the NRA the beneficiary of his military life insurance policy, albeit mostly because he thought his only relative, his brother, was a PC ass. "Do these people know any gun owners? Because gun owners are not going to like people showing up demanding their gats."

"Get the list, without killing anyone. I've got folks who will help the NRA purge its computer system once the FBI is gone so it can't come back and get another list. You just get the copy of the list the FBI confiscates. Then they won't have a road map to Second Amendment afficionados and that may buy us some time. But, and I want to emphasize this, don't kill anyone."

"So, you want me to hijack some FBI agents and take the evidence they are holding. That's quite a step," Turnbull said uncertainly. "This is nuts, Clay,"

"Yes, Captain Turnbull, it is. This is a crisis. And none of the people making these decisions have our perspective. They have never seen a country in true chaos, and COVID-19 and -21 did not count. A few months of wearing masks and bingeing Netflix hardly qualifies as societal breakdown. But this, well, this could lead to the real thing if some of us don't tamp down the insanity."

"I'll get the list," Turnbull said. "Somehow."

"I have an ID on their vehicle from my sources," Deeds said. He had contacts throughout the government, though many of them were going silent as they picked sides.

"Take Schiller," he added, "Again, I hope it goes without saying that you can't kill anyone. That is your wheelhouse, but this is not war. This is to stop a war, and these are fellow Americans, law enforcement officers, even if they are doing an intensely dumb and dangerous thing."

"Yeah, I kind of figured you didn't want me shooting a couple FBI agents dead in the street," Turnbull said, annoyed. "I'm not a particle physicist, but I am pretty clear on the not murdering innocent Americans part."

"Can't hurt to reiterate the obvious."

Turnbull paused.

"Well," asked Deeds.

"Little problem."

"And what is this little problem?"

"I kind of got filmed by this Trump News reporter killing the terrorists, who it was A-OK to shoot."

"Filmed?"

"Yeah."

"So, I'm going to see your face on cable news?"

"Not if I give her some information on what I was doing there, you know, killing terrorists."

"Kelly..."

"I was a little busy shooting those assholes when they started filming. I shot their camera too, but they upload the footage as they shoot."

"Who was the reporter?"

"Avery Barnes."

"I assume she's pretty," Deeds said sourly.

"I think they all are. It's a job qualification. Not like on MSNBC, where it's a handicap."

"So how do we handle it?"

"Let me talk to her. I'll give her a fake name and point her to Merrick Crane and try and get her off my back."

"If it was anyone else, I'd suspect you were trying to get to know her better," Deeds said. Turnbull frowned, a bit insulted.

"Can you have one of your people get me her cell number?"

"I can get her browser history if you think that would help."

"Pass. Just the number," Turnbull said. "Hey, let me handle this FBI thing alone."

"Take Schiller."

"Schiller's an asshole."

"Take him anyway."

Turnbull sighed, then left the bedroom and headed downstairs to draw his new weapon and to gather up his new partner.

A private security patrol car with its siren blaring passed by headed south on R Street NW. The security officers in the wealthy enclave of Georgetown were always both numerous and heavily armed. They were the opposite of defunded, since rich liberals funded them directly. They ensured their neighborhoods were safe, unlike in the rest of the city where Thomas Hobbes' rules applied.

Senator Richard Harrington let the drapes fall back across the window and turned back to the other guests gathered in the living room of his host's red brick townhouse. It was impeccably furnished and decorated with African art, and Harrington made a mental note of his hostess's vulnerability. What was woke today could be used as a weapon tomorrow. A very pale rich lady owning such treasures would easily be accused of cultural appropriation and racism with devastating effect, if it became useful to do so. He filed that away with his growing collection of similar mental notes about current friends who might become future rivals or enemies.

The hostess was the improbably named Amanda Van de Vere. She always regretted taking her second husband's last name, but considered it a small price to pay for inheriting his estate after he died of heart failure while in action between two Ukrainian hookers whom Hunter Biden had arranged for him to meet while they were both in Kiev on a business deal. Van de Vere was rail thin, heavily botoxed, and she sat in a chair that cost more than the average American earned in six months. She considered herself a huge advocate for such average Americans, although she had not known any personally since that mortifying summer before Yale when her self-made father had made her work for a week at a McDonald's to "learn about people who aren't rich spoiled brats like you."

It did not take.

Each of her guests had something in common besides a total commitment to the ever-evolving progressive ideology. Each person there represented a conduit of funding. Some dunned individual donors, lonely leftists out in the hinterlands who would forgo a few bong hits a week to scrape together $20 a month to fight faux fascism. Others worked the circuit of the younger second wives of Fortune 500 company CEOs who controlled their corporate giving and lavished funds on anything fashionably left-wing.

Professor Cole Mensius, the MacArthur Award winner who chaired Georgetown University's sociology program and headed the online fundraising powerhouse Blue Action, was there talking pinot grigios with actress Jane Fonda's new 27-year-old husband and personal representative, Chase Palestine. This was not his real name – that was Lloyd Tracey Purnass, and until hooking up with the desiccating starlet he had been a part-time activist and part-time DoorDash driver. His meal ticket, who had to explain to him why people would yell "Kiss my ass, Hanoi Jane!" at her on the street, mostly refused to leave her apartment anymore because, rumors held, her latest facelift failed to take. But she still directed millions from her donor network to the left-wing causes she fancied and lavished attention on her boy toy, who enjoyed the financial aspects of their relationship far more than her surprisingly rigorous erotic demands.

The House Majority Leader's chief of staff Tobias Toobin was there as well, guzzling the Mongolian yogurt liquor called *airag* that was currently all the rage among the fashionable set. Among other benefits, the buzz helped dull the constant tension he felt waiting for someone to inevitably make a crack linking him and his famous onanist namesake. It never failed – it happened on every single Zoom call he attended.

Brian Stelter had been invited, but he was a no-show. He was still smarting after James O'Keefe had released a tape of Anderson Cooper and Don Lemon giggling about his recent weight gain and calling him by his nickname "Tater." O'Keefe was himself sitting in Riker's Island for violating New York's new "Journalism Fairness Act" by releasing that video, though that small measure of justice was not enough to curb Stelter's stress eating.

"Where's our guest, Amanda?" Senator Richard Harrington asked, sounding bored. The junior senator from a tiny and marginally relevant northeast state, he was known as much for his ambition as for his progressive bona fides.

"I expect him soon," Van de Vere said, slightly annoyed at this mere senator's lack of deference. He might hold elective office, but if Amanda Van De Vere gave the word, you were a social non-entity in this town. That was real power. Someday, she resolved, she would teach this uppity first-termer that lesson.

"Relax, Rich. Have an *airag*," Toobin said, hoisting and downing another shot of the thick white liquid.

Harrington stared silently, vexed by such informality from a mere staffer. He liked titles, and like Van de Vere, he loved deference.

"It's very *goyo amttai baisan*," Toobin said, praising the drink but slaughtering the Mongolian phrase he had learned on a co-del to Ulan Bator earlier in the year. Toobin held out another full shot glass to the senator.

"I'm not sure where that hand has been," Harrington replied, dismissing the offering from the crestfallen Tobias Toobin.

Someone rapped on the front door.

Noting that the servants were out of the room fetching canapes, Van de Vere quickly assessed the occupants of the living room, calculated their respective statuses, and asked, "Chase, darling, could you be an angel and get the door?"

Unaware that he had been designated the low person on the totem pole – a term none of them would dare use lest they be accused of disrespecting the culture of America's First Peoples – Chase Palestine stepped to the front door and pulled it open. Merrick Crane III stepped inside, along with his man, Mr. Soto. It would have been *gauche* to call Mr. Soto "security," but that is what he was. Bald, silent, always watching – no one asked what he carried under his bulging black suitcoat.

Chase Palestine pushed the door closed behind them.

Crane said nothing as he took off his coat – it was getting chilly – and draped it over a chair. He wore a suit with no tie, and the grip of the Walther pistol tucked in his belt peeked out. Mr. Soto moved to a place by the wall; if the other guests had been a bit more aware, they would have realized that from his vantage point he had a clear field of fire at each entrance to the room, and at each one of the room's occupants.

"Merrick Crane, the mind behind the People's Militias, a true revolutionary. It's an honor to have you here," Van de Vere said. The rest of the guests murmured their concurrence. They stared at him, enraptured.

He was *doing* something, and not merely talking. Just being in the presence of the fugitive gave them all a tingly thrill.

"After today," Crane said, "there is no more sitting on the sidelines. You either personally commit to taking the action necessary to purge the right-wing influence from this country once and for all, or you are complicit."

"That's so true," Professor Mensius said.

"Correcto-mundo," replied Toobin, toasting with his tumbler.

"I hate complicity," intoned Chase Palestine solemnly. "It's the worst."

"Nearly seventy-five young martyrs to justice lie dead, dead because the power in this society is held in the hands of only a few reactionary racists. This country is built on a foundation made of the corpses of slaves and indigenous peoples. It is time to tear it down once and for all."

"Remarkable," Harrington thought to himself as he watched the others leaning forward, nodding and offering their support. He was both impressed by the speaker's complexion – clearly the man had a formidable skin care regimen – and also by his ability to make violence seem not merely necessary but admirable to people singularly incapable of committing any themselves. Maybe Fonda's walking sex toy had not put the pieces together, but the rest of them certainly understood that Crane and his growing guerilla band were the vanguard, and that the dead this afternoon were a sacrifice to their progressive Moloch.

Harrington correctly assessed the young man as extremely dangerous.

Toobin, his *airag* sloshing in its tumbler, spoke up.

"Tomorrow, the House goes into an emergency Monday session," he said. The room was impressed – the House working on a Monday meant it was serious. "We take up the new laws on guns and hate speech. They're already drafted. The rule will limit the debate and with luck it will all pass by noon. Then over to the Senate."

"Where it could pass tomorrow evening," Harrington said. What he did not mention were the myriad procedural tricks and tactics the GOP could use to stop it.

"And we will finally be on the way to ridding America of the scourge of assault weapons, all because of you," Van de Vere said to Crane, who she fully understood had just killed dozens of people using assault weapons.

But Crane was silent for a long moment, and he drew out the pregnant pause as the room uneasily waited for him to speak.

"Laws," he said. "I have to say that I am still surprised that you don't seem to understand. This is not about laws, or institutions, or the system."

"What is it about?" Toobin asked, visibly annoyed. "Enlighten us."

"It's about power," Crane replied, a friendly smile widening across his face.

"The Congress *is* power," Toobin said, sipping his *airag*.

Crane studied him for a moment, reached his right hand under his coat, drew out the Walther automatic and shot Toobin in the face. It was not silenced – the noise set the surviving guests' ears to ringing – and blood and chips of skull splattered across the front of a three-foot statue of a Zulu warrior that was directly behind where the unfortunate staffer had been standing.

"That," Crane said, slipping the gun back into his waistband, "is power."

The smell of the smoke spread across the dead silent room as Toobin's body twitched in the puddle of Mongolian liquor.

Crane glanced at Mr. Soto, nearly imperceptibly shaking his head "No." Soto's right hand relaxed at his side, his flat affect unchanged.

"You need to understand, to comprehend," Crane said after allowing them nearly a full minute to contemplate their new reality, "that this congressional action is just a rearrangement of the pieces on the chessboard. We are playing a whole new game. All this, this whole system, dies. And this poisonous society will be reborn antiracist, decolonialized, intersectional, and entirely reimagined. Those who can change and who play their parts now to support it will be rewarded. Those who cling to the past will be...."

Crane paused, staring at the corpse on the rug. The room was still.

"Culled," he said. After a few more moments, he continued.

"Go forward with your laws. It's a useful step, for now. But know that the only way to get to our objective is to wade through blood."

Harrington cleared his throat. Some of Toobin's brains had splattered on his slacks and he did his best to ignore the stains. Crane looked to him.

"The Senate will allow a debate as if the old rules still applied," he said. "It will give a platform to the racists and reactionaries, the Republicans. A spontaneous response by those outraged by hate speech designed to deny marginalized people justice would send a powerful message about the new paradigm."

Crane smiled again. "I will arrange for my cadres to plan and oversee a spontaneous response tomorrow."

Harrington said, "Thank you."

Crane had recently resolved that eliminating informants before they informed was much more efficient than doing so after. Now he turned to Van de Vere and gestured at the body.

"This creature was leaking to the *Washington Post*. Not about this, but other things, yet it was only a matter of time until he exposed too much. The *Post* is sympathetic, certainly, but not yet fully committed. This movement is a secret too delicious for someone like him to resist sharing. These games are part of the old way of thinking. We are building a new paradigm, and there is no room for selfish antics and selfish people. All these Washington games are done. There is no room for them in the world we are making. What happened to him was justice. Do not let it happen to you. Now, talk to me about the money."

The discussion moved to the subject of funding, the real incentive for Crane to come out of the shadows and appear in person. After all, his plan for subsidizing his operations with untraceable drug money had been disrupted when someone crippled the representative of his erstwhile partners at a rally right in the heart of New York City.

Each one of the other guests strived to assure him that his or her network of individual and corporate sponsors would continue to come through. Cash, he had reminded them, was the blood that kept the revolution nourished. Traceable money was better than none.

They each offered their pledges, running into the millions of dollars. Crane would leave it to them as to how to ensure the payments made available to him were obscured, though the idea that this administration would allow its Department of Justice to take time away from persecuting conservative groups to eyeball dubious financial shenanigans by allied left-wing organizations was simply laughable. At the end, Crane was satisfied, and he did not even bother to point out the obvious, that the group should figure out a way to dispose of the corpse they had all been pretending to ignore, and also that the penalty for failing to make good on their pledges would result in them meeting the dead man's fate too.

4.

Turnbull *really* liked his new pistol. He liked the way it felt in its holster as he drove, as well as everything else about it. It was solid, a handmade work of art. He knew he was going to like it when he finally shot it. And to think that he had almost had to make do with a lesser one.

Casey Warner was in charge of gathering up the used weapons for disposal and with issuing new, clean ones.

"What do you want?" he had asked Turnbull, opening up a briefcase with an impressive selection of weapons – Glocks, HKs, Smith & Wessons, and more. The operatives were all pros, and their weapons were their tools. They were picky. Even fussy.

Turnbull surveyed the choices.

"Take a Glock," Casey suggested. There were several.

"Maybe," Turnbull replied, pondering his options. He liked Glocks, sure, but the classic ceramic receiver pistol just did not feel right at that moment. And the only times his feelings mattered to him were when they were regarding armaments.

Turnbull's eyes darted back and forth over the options in the felt-lined case, sizing them up, considering each one in turn.

"It's like shoe shopping with my girlfriend. Come on, Kelly, I have shit to do."

"Hey, you can't rush this."

Casey sighed. "Do you want a revolver?"

"No, I'm not in a wheel gun place at the moment." Turnbull stroked his chin, and his eye caught something at the bottom, covered by felt. "What's that?"

"That's nothing," Casey said quickly. "How about the Walther? Everyone likes a Walther."

Turnbull's eyes had alighted upon what was now clearly a large bulge under the felt in the corner beneath a next generation Taurus 92F. He reached his hand toward it.

"That's mine!" Casey said.

"No, you didn't shoot anyone today, so you still have your piece. Let me see it."

"Kelly," Casey protested, but Turnbull had pulled off the felt and exposed the hidden pistol.

"Oh, I think I see why you were hiding it."

"Damn it, Kelly," Casey said, but Turnbull now had it in his hand and was not about to let it go.

"Is this a Wilson Combat CQB?" he asked, though it said so on the slide.

"Son of a bitch," Casey swore.

It was beautiful, a handmade rethink of the classic M1911A1 .45, solid black and with the eagle insignia on the grips. Turnbull pulled out the four eight-round chrome mags, each loaded with Federal .45 ACP +P Tactical Bonded LE hollow point rounds, and slid one into the well.

"Smooth," he said as he racked the heavy slide. "Oh, baby."

"You nabbed *my* gun," growled Casey.

"You mean *my* gun," Turnbull said. And he walked out of the safehouse and got into the car with Schiller.

Turnbull smiled thinking about his new pistol as he sat in the passenger seat of the 2020 Ford Fusion. It helped drown out Schiller's monologue about some blonde deputy assistant undersecretary at the Department of Agriculture he had allegedly scored with the prior evening. Schiller seemed quite proud of his conquests and frequently shared the tales of his penile prowess with anyone trapped in a small, confined space with him.

Turnbull ignored the dissertation and watched the urban Virginia terrain roll by outside the side window. Schiller was driving; it was pretty clear to Turnbull that his partner had gone through the Special Ops tactical driving school somewhere along the line. No one in the unit talked about his background before Task Force Zulu. Turnbull was unsure which black organization Schiller had come from – he did not know him in the Green Berets, and Schiller was not bulky or loud, so that excluded the SEALs. He suspected Delta. Turnbull had a beef against Delta anyway, making him distinctly unimpressed by that pedigree.

"Eastbound I-66. Five minutes out," Schiller said, looking at the text from Deeds on his burner phone. Deeds' informants were passing him real time updates on the van's progress from the NRA headquarters in Fairfax, Virginia, on its way to the J. Edgar Hoover Building in downtown Washington.

"It's a white Dodge van with 'FBI EVIDENCE RESPONSE TEAM' on the side," Schiller added.

"So, it's not actual agents. Tech guys. Probably unarmed," Turnbull said. "They have to get off I-66 in Rosslyn before the Teddy Roosevelt Bridge. Can't cross there. Some assholes are still occupying it."

"I think this time it's Asian Gender Fluid Lives Matter," Schiller said.

"That's super specific. You sure? Maybe it's someone else whose lives matter. Whatever," Turnbull said. "I bet they'll get off the interstate at Quinn, then head east on Lee to the Key Bridge and cross the river into the District that way."

Being so close to Georgetown University, the Francis Scott Key Bridge had been renamed the "Toni Morrison Bridge" because Key lived in the same era as slaveholders and was therefore evil, and because every woke college kid had been made to read some Toni Morrison book in high school. Normally, one would have likewise expected that bridge to be under permanent occupation. However, the school had gone 100% online during the cyclic flu scares and, upon it dawning on the administration that the students would still pay full freight for a correspondence college degree, the university had never truly reopened. Those few professors who advocated actually teaching the students were terminated for "literally murdering the faculty with their advocating for death pedagogy." So, the bridge, now renamed for the J. K. Rowling of mundane wokehood, remained open for transit.

"Wanna hit them at Lee Highway and Lynn Street?" Schiller suggested.

"Yeah," Turnbull replied. "I wonder when they'll get around to changing those names."

"I know who Lee was. Who was Lynn?"

"Does it matter?" Turnbull asked.

"Not really. Just follow my lead when it goes down," Schiller instructed. He turned onto Lee Highway heading east.

"Oh, I'm following your lead?" Turnbull asked.

"Yeah. I'm a major."

"Zombies don't do rank. What do you *suggest?*"

Schiller was irritated. "I *suggest* that I cut them off and that when they stop, I shoot the driver and you shoot the passenger and that we take the external drive."

"Remember the part about not killing FBI agents? That was an important part of the brief and I think you missed it."

"Screw them."

"Yeah, we're not killing FBI agents."

"They're evidence techs."

"Schiller, I think you're unclear on the basic premise. We're still not killing them. We can beat the shit out of them if they resist. I'm up for that. But no body bags."

"You were always soft."

"Yeah, that's always been one of my problems. Too soft. And caring."

"That's why I blackballed you from Delta," Schiller spat.

"What?" Turnbull said, now interested.

"You heard me," Schiller said, proud to have gotten a reaction. "I was on the board for your assessment. I rejected you because you're weak."

"Is that how it went?" Turnbull asked.

"Yeah."

"I've seen my assessment file. Deeds gave it to me when he recruited me. In fact, the board said that I was too dangerous. That I was a little too free-spirited, not enough of a robot," Turnbull said, adding: "And if they took your sorry ass, then they weren't good enough for *me*."

"You want to stop this car and settle this now?" Schiller asked savagely.

"Yeah," Turnbull replied. "But squaring you away can wait until the mission is done."

"I can't wait," Schiller said.

"And yet you will," Turnbull replied.

Something up ahead caught his eye. White, blocky, eastbound like themselves on the one-way US 29, the Lee Highway.

"It's up there," Turnbull said, switching into pro mode and pointing. "Number one lane, 100 meters."

Turning north at the intersection with North Lynn Street would take the Dodge Ram van north over the Key Bridge. On the south side of the street were a row of modern high rises, and to the north, a park full of tents and bums. The van eased into the turn lane to make the left, about three cars back.

"Come up alongside," Turnbull said.

"I know how to...," Schiller began, but Turnbull cut him off.

"Just do it!"

The Ford slowed parallel to the van, which had "FBI Evidence Response Team" printed on the side, along with the black spray-painted legend "Nazi Pigs Fork Off." Apparently, the artist had closed up what was supposed to be a "u" and screwed up the "c" entirely.

"Now!" Turnbull yelled, and Schiller spun the steering wheel hard left, skidding the Fusion to a halt in the space between the van and the blue Honda idling ahead of it.

Turnbull flung open his door and yelled, "You follow my lead!" as he bailed out of the sedan and leapt up unto the hood.

Schiller shifted the transmission into park and popped his own door, but before his feet hit the pavement, Turnbull had hopped down off the hood and raced around the front of the van to the driver's door.

The driver was more alert than expected – he shifted the van into reverse, punched it, and promptly smashed into the front end of the red Chevy Camaro waiting behind them. Turnbull narrowly dodged being clocked by the sideview mirror and darted the five feet it lurched backwards to again reach the driver's door. His Wilson was in his hand and Turnbull was in no mood for a discussion – he smashed the side window with the butt, showering glass all over the terrified driver.

"Get out!" Turnbull yelled, the big .45 looming in the young man's wide-eyed face. The tech cracked the door and Turnbull threw it open. The man awkwardly fumbled with, and finally unclicked, his seatbelt, and Turnbull pulled him out and flung him down onto the sidewalk.

Behind them, a large guy with an evident taste for 'roids and vehicular phallic symbolism was getting out of his Camaro howling with rage at his impacted front end.

"Get back in your car!" Turnbull yelled, the .45 making the case even more emphatically. Muscle Man wisely complied and Turnbull turned his attention back to the young nerd in the blue windbreaker with "FBI EVIDENCE RESPONSE TEAM" written across it in yellow. At the same moment, Schiller was arriving on the sidewalk, forcing the female tech from the passenger seat forward ahead of him.

"Get down!" he snarled, pushing her to the sidewalk. She fell and sat there with her partner, panting. In the park behind them, the bums living there were gathering to watch.

"You have a hard drive. Where is it?" Turnbull asked.

"I don't know," said the sullen male. Schiller kicked him in the leg.

"Ow!"

"My partner here wants to shoot you, and I'm keeping him from doing that," Turnbull said. "When I am the voice of reason you are totally screwed. Now tell me where to find the hard drive before I take a walk and he takes you both out."

"I'm not telling you anything," the male said.

"Fine. Shoot her," Turnbull said. Schiller smiled and lifted his gun.

"About time," Schiller said.

"Hey, it's in the back!" the female said. She looked at Turnbull dead on, and winked.

"Show me," Turnbull said, reaching down and pulling her to her feet, then pushing her back into the van. He followed her as Schiller watched the sullen male.

She moved between the front seats and into the rear, which was set up like a workshop with a bench on one side and a number of drawers marked "EVIDENCE BIN" and numbered. She went to Bin Number 4, then turned.

"You gotta be political," she said to Turnbull.

"I'm just here for the disk."

"You're one of the good guys, and there are a lot of us in the Bureau who are with you but who are keeping our heads down," she replied. Turnbull looked at her quizzically as she took the bagged hard drive out of the bin.

"Look, this is our only copy. Fry it. Without it, they can't confiscate shit," she said.

"You're pretty helpful for someone I'm robbing."

"You think we're all leftist pieces of shit?" she said, her voice low. "We aren't. There's lots of us who are actual patriots. And if that freak out there reminds me one more time that his pronouns are they/them, I might slap the shit out of *them*."

Turnbull took the bag with the drive. From outside, Schiller yelled, "Clock's running!"

"The Bureau is turning into an American Gestapo. We're moving from chasing crooks to chasing patriots, and I don't know how long I can be part of it," the tech told him.

"Stay where you are on the inside of the agency. You can help from there."

"I dunno. I figure I might head out to Texas. Our intel says the governor is forming a provisional militia to resist," she said. "America's choosing up sides, red or blue, and I ain't blue."

"I've been trying to be colorblind," Turnbull said. "Just keep your head down. And forget us."

"Two guys, short and fat," she said. "At least fifty. Probably trans."

"Thanks a lot," Turnbull replied.

"Take *their* driver's license. Tell *them* you'll come to *their* house and cap *them* and *their* life partner and *their* cats if they ID you. That'll shut *them* up."

Turnbull nodded and both exited the van. Turnbull made a show of pushing her, and the female made a show of snarling as she hit the sidewalk.

"Asshole."

Schiller raised his pistol but Turnbull swatted it down.

"Here's the deal. Hand over your driver's licenses. Come on!"

They both did, bitterly.

"Let me shoot them," Schiller said.

"Okay, Libby Capewell and Pat Cardigan," Turnbull said, glancing at their licenses. He noted that Capewell had handed him her business card as well. "If the FBI gets a good ID on us, our pals come to visit you and your life partners and your cats and they will do what my running buddy here thinks we should do right now. We knew where to find you today, and we'll sure as hell know what you tell the investigators. You got me, lady?"

Libby nodded.

"And you, dude?"

"I don't identify as..." Pat began, but Turnbull kicked him in the leg.

"Yes, I got you," Pat said. "Just don't hurt my kitties."

Turnbull nodded, took his phone and snapped a photo of the licenses. He then handed them back to their owners (but retaining her business card), and then walked back to the Ford. Schiller got in on the driver's side, put the Fusion in reverse, pulled out, then gunned it down the street.

A text containing just a phone number came through on Turnbull's burner as they pulled up at the new safehouse. It was a single-family residence on the outskirts of Arlington on a tree-lined and quaint lane. A couple blocks up the street was a big construction project, a 50-unit low income housing unit being built there at the command of the feds. The sign on the site read, "RESIDENTIAL JUSTICE IS A HUMAN RIGHT – AMERICANS UNITE TO FIGHT SUBURBAN PRIVILEGE." There were about ten "FOR SALE" signs among the twenty or so houses on the street.

"You can't get a U-Haul to Texas for under $10,000," Schiller said. "Even if you can pay the Virginia Departure Tax."

"Gimme the keys," Turnbull said, and Schiller handed them over as he got out with the hard drive. Turnbull knew the number came from Deeds and dialed it. It rang.

And rang.

And rang.

Turnbull gave people three rings and hated to leave messages. He was about to hang up when the line came alive.

"Avery Barnes."

"It's your friend from the rally."

"Oh really? I guess you dug up my number."

"Here I am."

"We should talk."

"Not on an open line." Turnbull figured folks were listening to everyone at Trump News.

"Sounds edgy," she cooed.

"Let's meet. Lunch, tomorrow. Where?"

"I better not say where, since this is an open line and all. So, let's see how smart you are, mystery man. Meet me in Alexandria where they toss commies out of helicopters."

"I hate games," Turnbull hissed.

"See ya at *once y media*," Barnes said before hanging up.

Turnbull sat at a booth in the back of the restaurant, facing the front door. He had arrived at the King Street location a half-hour early and assured himself that there was no surveillance before going inside to wait. Once inside, he had mapped his emergency egress out the back, if it came to that. He had a sweet tea. There were menus; Turnbull had already made his choice.

At 11:30 a.m. on the dot, she walked in and took off her sun glasses.

"You *are* smart," Avery said approvingly. She was in jeans and a dark top, definitely toned down from her on-camera Baptist Girls Gone Mild vibe. She slid into the booth across from him and put her purse on the bench. "So, how did you figure it out?"

"Helicopter rides, Spanish time hack," Turnbull said. "Gotta mean Chile."

"Hard Times Chili," Avery said, picking up the menu. "I haven't been here in years. Actually, I haven't been allowed to eat in years, but that's the life I've chosen."

"We all have regrets. Well, not me, but other people."

"So, what is your name anyway."

"What do you want it to be?"

"You're not going to tell me, are you?"

"We had a deal. You've kept your part. I'll keep mine." In fact, after the phone call the prior evening, Turnbull and Deeds had spoken at length about exactly what he would share with the reporter. And, more importantly, they discussed how they could use the reporter for their own purposes.

"Can you at least give me a fake name? But one that's not going to get me fired. Can you imagine coming to your editor today and telling her your secret source is named 'Deep Throat'?" Avery giggled. "That's a #MeToo felony."

"How about 'Chris'?" It was the name of a Philly-based podcast host Casey was always listening to.

"I like it. Gender indeterminate."

"I try to integrate intersectionality into all my pseudonyms," Turnbull said.

"I'm not sure your operation yesterday at the rally met your objectives," Avery said, turning serious. "You killed three of them...."

"Four, but who's counting?"

"Actually, I am. You got four, and who I presume were your buddies got two more, and it didn't matter. The story was still all about how knuckle-dragging Jesus people gunned down the Wall of Moms."

"That's bullshit."

"I know, Chris. Remember, I was there. But that's the story everywhere else but on Trump News and what few conservative social media accounts haven't been banned yet."

"It was a set up. We know who organized it. Merrick Crane III. A rich asshole gone rogue. Google him."

"Do you have any proof?"

"Besides seeing him there?"

"If you saw him, why didn't you shoot him?"

"Because you damn civilians got in the way. Next time though...."

"I believe you, but unlike the *Times* and the *Post* and CNN and the rest, we don't go with one-source, anonymous stories."

"Just my luck," Turnbull said. "I happen to get extorted by a reporter at the one outlet with any residual journalistic integrity."

"Look, I'd love to dive into a bowl of red with you, but I need to get changed and get up to Capitol Hill for the debate on the gun and speech laws."

"You think they'll actually pass them?"

"They were already written and waiting for something like yesterday. They'll try to ram them through, but Cocaine Mitch is pretty wily."

"If they try to confiscate guns...."

"I wasn't born in the big city. I know what happens if they try that. By the way, I've been hearing some rumors that the FBI grabbed the whole National Rifle Association member list last night, but that someone ambushed the forensics flunkies taking it back to the FBI headquarters. You know anything about that?"

"NRA? Never heard of it."

"Yeah, I'll bet." Avery leaned in. "Who are you people anyway? Some kind of special ops thing? Deep State stuff?"

"I'm whatever the opposite of the Deep State is. We're just trying to keep the whole thing from exploding."

"Which side are you on?"

"No side. Like I said, just trying to keep everything cool."

"Well, good luck with that, Chris," Avery said, sliding out and standing up. "I actually believe in this country and its principles, and right now this whole country is on the edge of going off like we haven't seen since Fort Sumter." She pulled her bag around her shoulder. "I'll be in touch, now that I have your number."

She turned and walked out. The waiter approached, puzzled.

"Just me," Turnbull said. "Four-way chili mac." That was chili over spaghetti with cheese and onions. It was the closest thing on the menu to his favorite MRE entrée.

He kept his eye on the front door as he ate, just in case. Then his phone rang.

Deeds.

The Capitol was in chaos. A glass bottle filled with red paint flew over their heads and shattered against the stone wall of the Rotunda, spraying shards of glass and red paint all over Avery Barnes and her cameraman Lou. Black-clad Antifa-types ran back and forth, as did terrified civilians, and the dome echoed with screams, shouts, and chants.

"No justice, no peace!"

"Burn it down!"

"Death to the fascist insect that preys on the life of the people!"

And there were a few gunshots too.

"I gotta get you out of here!" Lou said to Avery as they huddled, the spots of red congealing on their clothes. She assessed that he was mostly eager about getting himself out of there.

"Just film!" she said. Ten feet away, Lindsey Graham was grappling with a rioter and pulling his hair. Nearby, the elderly Senator Richard Blumenthal was being held and punched in the gut by a couple of Black Bloc types as he pleaded his leftist credentials.

"That's no way to treat a war hero," Avery sneered as she directed Lou to capture the melee on tape.

She caught a glimpse of Rand Paul, who had apparently decided he was never again going to come out second best in a fist fight, judo flipping a fat Antifa-type onto the stone floor.

One thing she did not see was cops. There were none.

She made her move, heading to the Senate visitor's gallery. Normally, a camera crew would get nowhere near it, but all security had vanished. The Antifa types ran up and down the halls, toppling statuary – this was one of the few places where any had, until now, remained upright – and defacing portraits. There was worse too – several were using the passageway as a latrine.

"We can't go in there!" Lou protested, but Avery pulled him and his rig into the gallery box above the Senate floor.

The rioters filled the gallery, and in fact they filled the floor too, having bum-rushed the "Senators Only" entrances. Only about two dozen senators had been allowed to remain in the chamber, all hard-left Democrats, all under the watchful eyes of the hundreds of rioters occupying the floor. The rest of the senators, all the Republicans and those Democrats deemed insufficiently woke, had been forced out. Several were badly hurt, but apparently the order was not to actually kill any of them. At least not yet.

A giddy CNN crew was taping the events below from the edge of the gallery, the hefty correspondent shouting into the microphone over the din about how this was a spontaneous expression of the people's intersectional demands for justice.

"It's so exciting to see the Senate respond to the people's desires!" he enthused. "This is true democracy!"

Below, they were tearing down the United States flag that flanked the rostrum.

Ignoring technicalities like a quorum and every other rule and procedure, Vice President Elizabeth Warren was presiding over voice votes on the various proposals. The ban on the private ownership of guns passed, with a decade in prison for violators. So did a tightening on the ban on hate speech, again with a decade in prison for violators. And then they banned prisons, excepting for those convicted of these new crimes or of "such other crimes that may impact the people." This was not defined in the law, but there was little focus on details as the festival of *faux*-legislating continued.

Lou filmed as Avery went live for the Trump News special report, "Chaos at the Capitol." Unlike her CNN colleague, she did not celebrate what was happening and attempted to report it straight. This drew the menacing stares of the Antifa-types around her, and of the CNN correspondent.

"I don't know why we are tolerating the fascist press propaganding here!" the obese CNN reporter shouted, blissfully free of the tyranny of English. He had been hired under CNN's "Looks Like America" program to promote diversity, and he apparently represented the demographic with diabetes.

The crowd closed in, angry and clearly lusting for blood. One thin, pale lad in a black shirt and helmet with a red kerchief grabbed Avery's microphone arm, and she responded with a vicious kick that sent her heels into his genitals. He screamed, loud and high-pitched. The rest of the mob paused, but then moved forward, converging.

There were two of them directly in front of Avery, each with bats studded with nails, and they seemed so focused on her that when two huge hands grabbed their heads and smashed them together, they were shocked for the split second before they went unconscious. A third pivoted and took a swing at the attacker. That was an error. Kelly Turnbull drove his pile driver fist into the punk's face, melding lips and nose into one red smear of goo.

He reached down and picked up one of the nail bats, and the game got a lot less fun than it was when they were threatening a Trump News reporter and her cameraman. They scattered.

"Turn it off!" Turnbull yelled, and Lou complied instantly.

"Chris?" Avery said, shocked, but Turnbull pushed past her, charging the CNN cameraman before he could turn the lens on the new arrival. Turnbull grabbed the video apparatus and tossed it over the side, not particularly caring if it landed on some Antifa creep below.

The CNN reporter screamed, and Turnbull punched him in the ample gut.

"Come on," he said, gathering up Avery and Lou and pushing them to the door that opened onto the corridor.

"Did you follow me?" she demanded.

"No, I was here to rescue some different folks, but they don't seem to need it. McConnell's locked in his office, and when I tried the door, he unloaded a double barrel blast of buckshot in my direction, so he's good. Tim Scott didn't need my help – he knocked the guy getting in his face on his ass. And Lindsey Graham nearly scratched the eyes out of a couple of these shitheads. My pals are hustling them out."

"I need to stay!" Avery said.

"These bastards are getting worse. They will hurt you. You need to come with me and...."

They stopped.

There were a dozen Antifa types, most with bats but one with a samurai sword, blocking their way.

"Fascist pigs," one tiny woman spat. They stepped forward.

Turnbull shrugged.

"Okay," he said and drew out the Wilson Combat .45. "When I get to ten, I start dropping you."

They stopped, unsure how to proceed.

"Six," Turnbull said.

They seemed puzzled.

"Seven. Eight."

It was dawning on the smarter ones.

"Nine."

A couple, then a half-dozen turned and ran.

"Ten." Two more bolted, leaving four, including Samurai Boy.

Turnbull blew his kneecap out first, and the cheap blade actually broke when it hit the stone floor. But you could not hear the snap over his screams, or those of the other two who Turnbull shot through the kneecaps in quick succession.

The last one dropped her bat and ran away, discretion being the better part of avoiding years of physical therapy.

Turnbull pulled Avery and Lou with him as they passed through the three howling casualties. Samurai Boy actually asked him, utterly seriously, as if it was the biggest surprise he had ever experienced, "Why'd you shoot me, bro?"

Turnbull paused.

"Because you're an asshole," he said, taking a few seconds to reload a fresh mag. He snapped it into place, and then the trio was gone toward the Rotunda.

Senator Harrington walked off the Senate floor, the Antifa mobs opening a path for him to exit into to the cloakroom. They had been instructed that he was to be treated with respect, and in addition to Mr. Soto, whom Crane had instructed to assist the senator, there were two particularly large cadre members assigned to make sure that the less experienced participants did not get out of hand and harm this most valuable resource. One young Goucher College sophomore had laid her (maybe xir – Mr. Soto did not care) hand on him, and Mr. Soto forced the unfortunate creature's paw to one of the senators' desks and smashed it to a pulp with the butt of his H&K handgun. The two cadre members nodded with approval.

This was the last time any of them had interfered with Senator Harrington.

Harrington had watched the discipline be inflicted with amusement. The screams made him smile.

In the cloakroom, most of the rioters were busy spray-painting slogans on the walls. But in the center of the space stood Merrick Crane III. His escort was arrayed around him. His Walther pistol was in his waistband.

"As promised," he said as Senator Harrington approached. He did not offer his hand to shake. Besides being too traditional, the COVID epidemics had put an end to such customs, at least among the elite.

"You can thank Speaker Pelosi for disbanding the Capitol Police and making this spontaneous outpouring of public outrage possible," Harrington replied.

"This is nibbling around the edges of what is to be done, Senator."

"What we have achieved here today is remarkable," Harrington said. "We have passed laws that we could only dream of just a few months ago."

"You've merely resuscitated a corpse for a little while longer. This country is going to die, and I intend to be the one who kills it."

I understand your view that all this, all these procedures and all these institutions, must go. But perhaps today showed you that they can actually help us achieve our objective."

"What is your objective, Senator Harrington?" asked Crane.

"Why, I believe mine is identical to yours."

"Do you? Really?"

"What will it take to obtain what you want, Mr. Merrick?"

Merrick gave a bitter little laugh. "Blood, of course."

"Yes, but what allows you to shed blood?"

Crane did not answer, so Harrington answered his own query. "Power."

"So, your objective is power, Senator?"

"Yes, Mr. Crane. As is yours."

Crane's bitter laugh returned. "Then very soon I will be very happy indeed, because I intend to have power that you can't imagine."

"Oh, I can imagine a great deal," Harrington said. "Together, we can realize all our objectives. But *together* – that's the key. Me inside, you outside."

"I'm a revolutionary," Crane said.

"I'm not," Harrington said. "And together we are unbeatable."

Crane laughed bitterly once more. "For now, Senator, we're allies. For now." He turned and walked out with his escort.

"Someday you must share your skin care regimen with me, Merrick," Harrington shouted at him as he departed.

All of Capitol Hill was chaos. Black-clad rioters ran across the pavement of the grounds, while others gathered on the grass. Across First Street to the east, the Supreme Court building, already marred by graffiti, was smoking. The mob had ignored the Library of Congress so far, but then again, the Library had complied with demands to purge itself of offensive books, and perhaps its groveling submission to the mob during the last few years of chaos had bought it a temporary reprieve.

A number of vehicles had pulled onto the pavement where typically only Capitol Police would have been allowed – a collection of busses, vans, and a few sedans. There were a few media trucks too, but they were all on fire. Including the one that said "TRUMP NEWS."

"Shit," Lou said, lowering his camera rig. "My dinner was in there."

"Come on," Turnbull said. "And get rid of that thing."

He pulled the camera off Lou's shoulder and dropped it on the steps.

"I need to cover this," Avery said. "America needs to see what's happening."

A black-clad figure with wild hair poking out from under his ski mask approached, shrieking something about abolishing the racist media. Turnbull punched him in the throat, and he went down.

"You need to get out of here," he said. "And America won't see anything if you two get lynched."

Most of the rioters made way for them. The ones who showed an interest were deterred by the barrel of the Wilson .45.

"Where the hell are the cops?" Lou asked as they followed Turnbull down the steps.

"Defunded and/or abolished," Turnbull said. "What flatfoot is going to put his ass on the line to suppress a riot his police chief's boss supports?"

Turnbull directed them south, toward the House side, but something caught his eye in the other direction. There were four dark sedans parked in a row, absolutely untouched, outside the Senate wing. There were maybe a dozen figures around them, but Turnbull made out one.

Merrick Crane III.

He could not believe it, but there the SOB was, and this time the terrorist was going to die.

Turnbull dashed forward, leaving Avery and Lou shouting after him. There were rioters running about in his line of sight, but they were rioters and Turnbull did not classify them as civilians. At about 50 meters, one of the goons with Crane spotted him and let out a yell as Turnbull raised the .45 to a two-handed grip and fired.

It was a long-range shot, and that first round apparently missed. Still, Crane spun around as if someone had grabbed his left arm and pulled it hard to the rear. The second shot took out the passenger window on the van directly behind where he had been standing.

It was unclear where the third and the rest of the rounds went because Turnbull was blasting out 230 grain hollow point rounds as fast as he could squeeze the match-grade trigger. One of the goons was drawing and took two center mass, flying backwards as Turnbull pivoted to engage another one who was pulling a long weapon – it looked like an M4 – out of another vehicle. The back of his target's head vanished in a pink puff and he dropped to the deck like a puppet with his strings cut.

The others were scrambling, then one returned fire with some sort of pistol. The Wilson was out of ammo, rack back locked. Turnbull had fired nine shots in about four seconds, the one in the pipe and the eight in the handmade, oversized Wilson mag. Turnbull hit the release with his thumb and the dry mag dropped into empty space even as his left hand grabbed a full one and slipped it into the well. The slide released and snapped forward as Turnbull selected his target and fired again and again. A rioter caught in-between Turnbull and his targets clutched his gut and fell. Turnbull ignored him, partly because the guy had not been in his line of fire, and partly because he didn't much care if they shot one of their own. He was too busy putting down another of the guards.

Then, nothing. Silence. No movement. Everyone in the target group was either hit or hiding by the vehicles. Turnbull reloaded, and, as he was inserting the fresh mag, a head with a gun prairie-dogged up from behind the hood of a Dodge. Turnbull engaged, and the target returned fire. The 9mm round cracked over Turnbull's head right at the same moment one of Turnbull's .45 hollow points cracked the shooter's head open. The target was gone, and Turnbull scanned the bodies piled up in front of the vehicles for Crane. Turnbull intended to dump the rest of his mag into him, just to be sure.

The overhead light in one of the sedans came on as the door on the far side opened. There was movement – there was something going on, someone getting out, or getting in.

Turnbull fired the rest of the rounds into the vehicle and the slide locked back as the sedan roared to life and sped away.

Turnbull snapped in his last mag, the short one he had used on the kids in the hall. He fired off two rounds, but it was no good. The vehicle was gone, careening across the pavement toward Delaware Avenue and escape. It hit at least two Antifa flunkies on the way out. They went tumbling through space.

Turnbull paid them no mind as he advanced on the heaps of dead anarchists.

Avery caught up to him as he lowered the pistol. People were running everywhere, except around Turnbull. They were avoiding the hell out of the guy with the big gun and fixed glare.

"What the hell was that?" she asked, breathless.

"I think that cat's used up two of his lives," Turnbull replied, as he surveyed the pile of dead goons. He had a small glimmer of hope that one of the five bodies was Crane, but alas, none of the spilled meat sacks was his quarry.

"You killed them!" a young woman with a nose ring howled.

"Go," Turnbull said, pointing the pistol at her. She ran off.

He knelt by the bodies and quickly took out their wallets, stuffing them in his jacket pockets. One had a M1911 pistol, and he took the dead man's spare mag.

He was standing and peering into the one vehicle that still had its glass intact.

"This has keys, so we're taking it," Turnbull announced.

"It's a crime scene," Avery said.

"We can walk over to the Cannon Office Building and catch the Metro there instead," Turnbull said, opening the driver's door. Avery and Lou considered the idea of going down into the subway tunnels and wordlessly got into the car.

Turnbull hit the gas and the rioters generally got out of the way. One guy with a homemade shield slammed it into the passenger side as they passed him, but otherwise getting off the Capitol grounds was relatively easy. Once to Constitution Avenue, Turnbull turned west and they put the riot behind them.

The building housing the Trump News studio on North Capitol NW was surrounded by barriers and heavily guarded by big, armed security officers, most of whom had been cops before most cops pulled the plug during the last two years and went into the rapidly expanding private security markets. The security services the government refused to provide they sold to the highest bidder. Those who could not afford to pay were prey.

Lou got out, but Avery lingered.

"What happened there tonight?" she said. "It's crazy."

"I facilitated some dead terrorists. Not really a big departure for me."

"I don't mean to you. I mean to the country. A mob went in and forced Congress to pass the laws it demanded. We aren't a democracy anymore, Chris."

"I thought we were a republic...."

"I'm serious!" She was visibly upset.

"This was all coming for a long time," Turnbull said. "I'm not political, but I could see it happening even from overseas. It was inevitable. And it's only getting worse."

"How can it get worse than this, Chris?" she asked.

"Trust me, it can. I've seen it worse. I know what worse looks like. You need to be careful. They'll come for you."

"I'm going to keep reporting," she said. "I'm going to tell what I saw tonight. People need to know the truth."

"That's why they will come for you."

Avery paused. "And what are you and whoever you work for going to do?"

"We're going to try to stop it."

"Do you really think you can?"

"I don't want to think about what happens if me and my people can't."

Avery got out, but leaned back into the door.

"I'm supposed to be objective too, but I'm afraid before this is done, we'll all have to pick sides," she said. "Most everyone else in the media did years ago. You'll have to too."

Turnbull shrugged, and she shut the door. As he eased away from the curb and into the street, Turnbull wondered if he already had.

5.

He had pulled the car to the side of the road near Judiciary Square, not far from where the National Law Enforcement Museum had been until a few months before, when the city government remade it into the Museum of Colonialist Oppression. The crowds had been sparse ever since, so one day a mob just burned it down, citing the structure's "residual racism." The D(formerly known as)C municipal government had left it untouched, and as Turnbull watched, the junkies and bums living in the ruins warmed themselves around barrel fires.

The cell at the other end of the line rang twice, and Turnbull resolved to give it two more rings. He was using a burner, of course, and the number would come up as unknown. These days, people didn't often welcome the unknown into their lives. The known was bad enough.

Another ring, and his thumb was moving to hang up when a woman's voice came up.

"Yes?" she said. It sounded like she was driving.

Turnbull placed Libby Capewell's card back in his pocket and said, "This is your friend from earlier."

"I thought so. But this line is clear."

"I'm using Vocoscram," Turnbull said.

"Vocoscram's okay, if we keep it short," she replied. That was a Finnish app, recently banned in the US but ubiquitous, that gave a reasonable level of eavesdropping protection to cell phone calls. It would not stand up to the ponderous number crunching super-computers of the NSA – which was not supposed to be listening in domestically yet totally was – but it was good enough to maintain security against most people who might be listening in.

"I need some help."

"You understand the shit storm I've been in because of you?"

"It's not your fault you got jacked."

"Well, they figure it's got to be someone's fault," she said. "They started on me about not holding out and me giving up the hard drive, but I told them I was feeling unsafe because of their sexism and that got them to back off."

"What did your pal say?"

"He said you were short and fat."

"Good. I need something."

"You said that. I'm afraid to ask what."

"Names. Bad guys. I need you to run them, tell me what you can."

"I'm inbound to the Hoover Building. All hell broke loose at the Capitol tonight. A bunch of dead people and assaulted senators. We're cleaning up the mess, but we're standing down from clearing them out of the Senate chamber. They'll keep occupying it."

"Well, these bad guys might have been those dead guys."

"Who the hell are you?"

"I need to find their boss. I need a clue where he might go. His name is Merrick Crane III."

"I've heard of him," Capewell said. "You're asking a lot, especially for someone who stuck a gun in my face this afternoon. If they find out I'm helping you, I'm toast."

"If you don't, we all may be toast."

"Send what you have. I'll call you back." She clicked off. Turnbull texted her photos of the documents taken from the dead men's wallets, then used a rag he found under the seat to wipe clean the steering column, the ignition button, and the door handles. He left the door open after he got out of the car, leaving it running with the key on the console, and walked away quickly. Before he turned the corner onto 5th Street NW, a couple of the local transients were already getting into their new ride.

"We need to meet," Turnbull said into his phone. "Somewhere no one is watching."

Deeds was at the other end, and he agreed. "Fine. I know where no one is watching."

Turnbull accepted the suggestion and hung up. It was about a two-mile walk through the deserted city to the rendezvous. Lots of eyes sized him up. The denizens assessed the burdens inherent in crossing him as substantially outweighing the benefits of interfering with the big, confident-looking guy walking through the dark, so they let him be. It took him 30 minutes to get to the rally point.

"Why here?" he asked Deeds when his handler reached the top of the steps. Behind Turnbull, the seated figure of Abe Lincoln loomed. From where he stood, Turnbull could see the Capitol at the far end of the Mall, the Washington Monument halfway between them, and to the northeast what had been a crime scene following the previous day's massacre. The cops were long gone.

"I know no one is watching here," Deeds said, as he handed over a gift from Casey – several loaded mags for Turnbull's .45. "There's intentionally no surveillance. They would love nothing more than someone to come and destroy this statue and this whole memorial."

"I was not a great student, Clay, but I do recall that Lincoln was the guy who freed the slaves. I'm a bit confused about why he's now a bad guy," Turnbull said, pocketing the ammo.

"Do you admire him, Kelly?"

"I never really thought about it like that."

"Think about it like that."

"Okay, sure. He was tough as hell and he held the country together when a bunch of people tried to tear it apart."

"*That's* why Abe Lincoln is a bad guy. You and others admire him. And they want to destroy everything you admire then remake this country in their image, with them in charge."

"'They' being the ones who want to tear things apart today?" asked Turnbull.

"Yeah," Deeds said. "And like back then, a lot of them are Democrats. Many are straight-up socialists, communists, anarchists. The whole left-wing menagerie."

"That sounds political, Clay."

"I know." He walked past Turnbull and stared at the stone president. The graffiti slanders and curses the ralliers had cleaned off it had not yet been replaced. Lincoln stared straight ahead, his gaze fixed.

"Or have we in Task Force Zulu been political from the beginning?" asked Turnbull.

"That's what you called me here to ask, isn't it, Kelly?"

"I guess it is."

"In a lot of ways, not being political and opposing these leftists are the same thing. You want to know if we are on a side? We are. We're on the side of the United States of America, and Kelly, I can't tell you that today that is still the same side as much of the United States government."

"So, all the shit we've done is unauthorized?"

"Depends on how you define 'authorized.'"

"Well, I'd like to think there's some generals up there giving orders to us Army guys, so we're not just making this all up as we go along."

"Some are, some aren't."

"So, we're semi-official." Turnbull shook his head. "Us Zombies are just another faction?"

Deeds pivoted to look in Turnbull's eyes. "We're the patriotic faction. We're the good guys. We're trying to stop the bloodshed."

"Yes, by shedding blood. That's what we did overseas."

"We do the hard things that need doing."

"This isn't overseas, Clay. This is home."

"Yes," Deeds replied. "It's even more important that someone be willing to do the hard things here."

"Some parts of the military and civilian leadership are supporting us," Turnbull said. "I assume other parts are against us."

"Yes. Or are neutral, for now. And there are also private citizens. Rich ones who give money or do other things. Elon Musk is financing his own private militia in that county in Idaho he bought."

"Are we coup plotters, Clay? Is that what you have gotten us into? I trusted you."

"I've told you never to trust anyone, Kelly. Except yourself. So, where do you stand?"

"I think I'm going to go stand out in the middle of nowhere away from all this bullshit. Maybe Elon has an opening in his personal army."

"No, Kelly," Deeds replied firmly. "You don't get to check out now just because it suddenly got a little too ambiguous for your tastes. You've been killing bad people for years and you've been telling yourself it's all for God and Country. Well, sorry to disappoint you, but God and Country have a side. I'm on it. So are you, unless you quit."

Turnbull pointed at him as they circled each other on the memorial. "Clay, if I ever want to quit, you and Schiller and the whole bunch can't stop me."

"Oh, Kelly, far be it from me to get between you and what you want to do. I like breathing a little too much to do that. No, I'm not going to try to make you do anything. You're going to stay, and you'll do it because you know only you can do what has to be done."

"Kill more people?"

"Yes," Deeds said. "Starting with Merrick Crane III."

"I almost finished him tonight," Turnbull said. Deeds' eyes brightened.

"You got him?"

"I think maybe I winged him. Maybe. But I don't think he's dead."

"That's too bad," said the disappointed Deeds. "Because if you don't kill him, I have no idea how many people he'll be responsible for putting in their graves. I just know it will be a lot."

"Just one guy?"

"But a key one. This, all of this, is part of a bigger plan. We don't know exactly what yet, but we know he's building toward something."

"What is it?" Turnbull asked.

"You know," Deeds said. "Go on. Say it."

"Say what?"

"Say it, Kelly. You've seen it before over there. He wants it here. He has the connections with the establishment to make it happen. And all this over the last couple days is designed to provoke it."

"What?"

"You damn well know. Say it."

Turnbull paused. He paced back and forth, feeling suddenly caged, wanting to bolt down the steps but being held back by something he could not completely explain.

"Say the words, Kelly. Two words."

Turnbull stopped and glared. Some voice in him piped up that he should draw the Wilson, take aim, and send Deeds to hell, but that voice was drowned out by another one, urging him to answer.

"Civil war," Turnbull whispered.

"Not just riots. Not just political chaos. A civil war. A real one. Here, in America. That's what Crane wants."

"Why?" Turnbull asked.

"Why does anyone want a catastrophe? Because he thinks that at the end, he's the last guy standing."

"So, we smoke Crane and it's all better?"

"No," Deeds said. "Crane's just a part of what's happening, but he's the match that's lighting the fuse. In the last month, the People's Militias he helped organize have taken over a half-dozen big cities and are fighting to take more. Yesterday, he got dozens of his own people killed and blamed it on the constitutional opposition. Today, his thugs took over the Congress for the left and they essentially enacted their wish list in a parody of democracy. It's going to ignite a response and he wants nothing more than to let it get out of control."

"You sure it's not out of control already?"

"The lights are on at the Pentagon tonight. I don't know what's being planned, not yet anyway, but it's not good."

"I'd volunteer to go find out, but I've made it a point of pride to stay out of the Pentagon."

"You really should stay away from the Pentagon," Deeds said. "Regardless, Kelly, we're here in DC and out there in America, all hell is breaking loose."

"If that's so, shouldn't I be out there?"

Deeds laughed a little, and bitterly. "Good point. You find Crane, wherever he goes, and after you figure out what he's doing, you make sure he's terminated. You know, with extreme prejudice."

"Communist lives matter," Turnbull said. "Just not to me."

"But we can't be sure of our own situation. We all have the idea that there's one government, but after the Russia nonsense under Trump, it's clear that there are factions. Some for us, most against. The Deep State and all. The parts of the agencies that are against us are looking for us. They know there are rogue elements like Task Force Zulu out there. We can't count on our friends to keep us safe. So, watch out."

"We're trying to save the same government that will be hunting us? I'm not at all confused or anything."

"In the Civil War, there were clear lines. North, South. Here, there are two big groups and only tenuous geographic distinctions. You have Texas, whose governor seems to be nearly ready to declare it the Texas Republic again, and it's got Austin in the middle of it like a malignant tumor. Oregon has freedom supporters in, well, pretty much all of Oregon that's not Portland."

"Seems like we are sitting on a couple tons of TNT smoking Marlboros."

Deeds nodded. "We have to keep it from spinning out of control. But to do that, we have to understand that we have now chosen a side. And it's not the left. So, are you in?"

Turnbull sighed. "I hate politics."

"Politics hates you back. Time to choose."

"I'm in. But one thing. Are you sure we're fighting for the United States as it's supposed to be and not just for some different set of assholes to be in charge?"

"Well, Kelly," Deeds said. "How would you react if I screwed you over like that?"

"I'd be *very* unhappy with you, Clay."

"And you know I've seen the results of Unhappy Kelly. So, to the extent you can trust anything, you can probably trust my instinct for self-preservation."

"Okay," Turnbull said. "Now to find Crane."

"One thing, though," Deeds said. "You keep that cynicism, Kelly. Never trust anyone not to choose power over principle."

"Except me. I just want to be left the hell alone."

Turnbull's burner rang. He pulled it out and looked at Deeds.

"That's a bad omen for me being left alone," he said, and then he answered it. "Yeah?"

"What the hell did you get me into?" Capewell said almost in a whisper, as if she was trying not to be overheard.

"I'm guessing additional trouble."

"Damn right. Those IDs, those really are from some of the dead guys at the Capitol."

"Well, they were bad guys."

"Well, that's what their records said, except the word going out from here to the media is going to be that they were choirboys murdered by Republican white nationalists."

"And Merrick Crane?"

"I couldn't run him. He's on an alert list – any searches about him are routed to internal security immediately."

"The FBI is protecting Crane?"

"Are you shocked?" Capewell asked.

"At the FBI being a corrupt political weapon? No."

"Look, there was one thing they all had in common. Gopher Antifa."

"Like, some animal rights assholes?"

"No, Minnesota."

"I'm lost."

Capewell sighed. "The Gopher Antifa is the nickname of the People's Militia in Minneapolis. Ultra-radical. They're pretty much the new cops in the city since the real cops got abolished. Hell, they are pretty much the whole city government. We're not supposed to interfere with them. But we still get info on them, and we're hearing someone big is coming to town. It's got them scrambling."

"Who else is big besides Crane?" Turnbull wondered.

"I don't know the who's who of assholes. I do know the dead guys all came from there and they were with Crane, and I've seen intel previously that indicates that Crane has used it as a base of operations before. He knows he's safe there. Makes sense to check it out, unless you got a better lead. You got a better lead?"

"Nope."

"Okay then. But you have to get there first and it's a long trip."

"There are still airplanes."

"I wouldn't risk it," she said. "Hold on." She put the phone down and it was another minute before she picked it up again. Deeds was visibly annoyed, but Turnbull motioned for him to wait.

"I gotta go. But you need to know that the Pentagon sent over a bunch of names and some targets. One of them is General Scott. And there are supposed to be rogue military elements plotting treason, they say."

"Well, that totally sounds like me."

"They are hitting a place in Northern Virginia in an hour. I don't know where, and I don't know whose name is on the warrant – I can't get a look at the info without blowing my cover. Sorry."

"You've done plenty. Thanks."

"Thank me by not rolling over on me when they catch you."

"I'm not the 'taken alive' type."

"Good luck," she said and the line went dead.

Deeds looked at him expectantly.

"We may be blown."

"Who was that?"

"A source at the FBI. The FBI is hitting us in an hour, unless there's another group of SOF operators with a safehouse in Northern Virginia. We may all be burned. She didn't know for sure."

Deeds frowned. "Then we don't have until tomorrow to bug-out of the safehouse."

"Gets better," Turnbull said. "Your Pentagon pals are moving on General Scott. Seems they are charging him with treason for plotting against the government."

"That's a helluva escalation," Deeds replied, thinking fast. He began dialing.

Turnbull turned away and looked east across the Mall at the Capitol. A wisp of smoke was rising from the Senate side – it was hard to tell if the building was burning or if the fire was in the city to the east.

Deeds spoke quickly and curtly, then hung up.

"I need you to grab General Scott."

"I need to go to the Gopher State."

"What?"

"Minnesota. Its mascot is a varmint for some reason. But that's where our boy Crane might be headed. And if I'm blown, then I need to drive."

"You spirit Scott out of their crosshairs first, then I'll arrange a pick-up on the way to Minnesota. I'll text you Scott's location."

"I need your ride." Deeds handed over the keys to his Lexus and pointed to Constitution Avenue where it was parked.

"Schiller and Casey will meet you there."

"How about I do this alone?"

"How about you play nice with others? This is critical. General Scott is a national hero. He's one of the few people with enough support to make a deal that resolves all this. If they arrest him, or kill him, that's all the spark his supporters will need. You have to keep him safe."

"There's just one problem."

"And what's that, Kelly?"

"I hate generals."

6.

"No OPs," Casey said as he slid into the back seat. Turnbull and Schiller were watching the street from the Lexus, and Casey had gone and walked it on foot, looking to see if the house was under surveillance. He had detected no observation posts.

"Let's go," Turnbull said. "Roll up front and we'll get him."

Schiller shifted the idling sedan into drive and accelerated down the leafy residential lane. It was dark and the street lights were on. 1324 Carthage Court was a white and blue Cape Cod with a Dodge Jeep parked in the driveway, and it was totally indistinguishable from the other suburban Virginia houses around it, with one exception. At 1366, there was a beige house with a Prius out front that had a large sign in the front yard listing exactly whose lives mattered, with the lives of those absent presumably not mattering much at all. There was also a hand-rendered sign suggesting that Republicans perform a logistically challenging sexual act upon themselves right next to another one reading "HATE HAS NO HOME HERE."

Schiller pulled to a fast stop as Turnbull and Casey bailed out. When the doors shut behind them, he took off to pull a U-turn to face out of the cul-de-sac.

Turnbull got to the porch and rapped on the door with the back of his knuckles. Casey faced outward, watching the street. Their weapons remained hidden. The interval before the door opened, probably 30 seconds or so, seemed eternal.

The man inside was perhaps fifty, with close cut hair and a definite military vibe. His right hand was out of sight.

"I'm here for the general," Turnbull said.

"There's no general here."

"Open the door and don't shoot me," Turnbull said. "We need to get him out of here, now."

"There's no gen–," the man began but Turnbull slammed his body into the door, knocking the man backwards. There was a Beretta 92F pistol in his right hand. Turnbull was on him even before he had finished staggering backwards and tore the automatic out of his paw. The man stared back, furious.

Turnbull dumped the mag and jacked out the round in the pipe, then tossed the weapon onto the couch.

"Get rid of that as soon as we leave," Turnbull said. "They'll be here in a few minutes."

"Who?"

"The feds. They want the general in custody. We're here to get him out of here."

"There's no general here."

Casey came in and shut the door behind him.

"We do not have time for this," Turnbull growled.

"I told you," began the man, but he looked over Turnbull's shoulder and stopped.

"It's okay, Dan," Lieutenant General Karl Martin Scott said, silhouetted in the entry to the hallway. "You gentlemen are here for me, I presume?"

"Yes, sir," Casey said.

"Are you here to rescue me or kill me?" asked the general. He gave off the air of being indifferent to either option.

"Rescue," Turnbull said. "This time. The folks on the way have a different intent."

"I guess my bail is being revoked," the general said, a faint smile crossing his weathered lips.

"They're charging you with treason."

"Well, that certainly makes sense," the general said thoughtfully. "I am guilty as sin. And I am not surprised to be proscribed. Kind of ironic, considering my historical mentor."

"We need to go."

The general nodded and walked over to Dan with hand extended. Dan took it and they shook, a slightly jarring sight in the wake of COVID-21.

"You've always been loyal, Dan," the general said. "You were the best operations officer I ever had. I'll need you. Find me."

"No better friend," Dan said. "No worse enemy."

General Scott smiled.

"Come on," Turnbull said impatiently. "Get your shit, general."

Dan glared at the impudence, but the general was serene.

"I have no shit, gentlemen," he said.

"You got a cell phone?" Turnbull asked.

"I'm a general," Scott replied. "Not an idiot."

"Those aren't mutually exclusive," Turnbull said. "Let's go"

Casey opened the door and scanned the street. There was Schiller out in the middle of the road, idling in the Lexus, and nothing else.

"Clear," he said. Casey went first, then the general.

"Lose the piece," Turnbull said to the irritated staff officer. "And anything else that might show Scott was ever here." Then Turnbull followed the pair out the front door.

They did not speak much before they crossed into Pennsylvania on Route 97. They had agreed that driving late at night would be too conspicuous, so they pulled off down a deserted country road and slept, with one awake on security at all times, until it was after 9:00 a.m. Then they got moving north again.

The general was seated in back with Casey, and Turnbull sat in the passenger seat watching the farmland go by. Deeds had called earlier and set the pickup. The location was at least ironic, if not a calculated statement.

"It will make a good story," the general said. "The story is always important."

A sign read "GETTYSBURG - 12 MILES."

"Sir," Schiller said, "I guess your story is just beginning. I got to say, it's an honor to be part of what you are doing."

"We're part of a team," Scott replied. "We all do our part."

"I was in an ODA in Syria when you were there. Killdozer 6, no better friend, no worse enemy," Schiller said.

"Sulla," Casey said. "That was Sulla's epitaph."

The general smiled. "It was indeed. Sulla has been one of my historical mentors since West Point. A great general."

"Didn't he pull off a coup, occupy Rome, and kill all his enemies?" Turnbull asked. He had tried to ignore the conversation, but it was grating on him. "Not that I'm against killing all one's enemies. I just prefer to do it in a semi-fair fight."

"He restored the Republic after it was undermined by morally inferior men. And he was harsh when it was called for. He would proscribe his enemies, put their name on a list and post it in the forum. The lives of those on the list were forfeit. Anyone could kill them, even a slave, who would win his freedom on top of a bounty. The state would inherit their property."

"Seems very efficient," Turnbull said.

"Kind of like that old *Star Trek* where bizarro Kirk has that machine in his quarters that makes people disintegrate?" Casey said. Turnbull turned around in the seat to give him a baffled look.

"Field expedient justice. Sometimes that's necessary to do harsh things to do what's right," the general said, ignoring Casey and looking at Turnbull. "I'm sure you understand that, given what I expect is your record. I didn't catch your name, soldier."

"I didn't give it, general," Turnbull said, turning back to facing front.

"That's an O-9, Turnbull," snapped Schiller. "You address him with respect."

"Are we doing rank here?" Turnbull asked innocently. "Because I thought this was a wanted fugitive whose ass we just saved. I think here, the chain of command concludes with the general, not begins. No offense, general."

"None taken," said Scott. "I always believed that special operations forces needed more...flexibility when it came to good order and discipline."

"Say the word, sir, and I pull this vehicle over and square him away," Schiller said.

"You're totally going to make 0-5 below the zone with that kind of ass kissing," Turnbull said. "Except the general whose ass you're kissing doesn't really belong to the Army anymore. Again, no offense, general."

"I admit I'm getting a little offended. Turnbull, was it?"

Turnbull said nothing. The general continued. "You seem to have a beef with senior officers. You don't like them very much."

"Don't take it personally, general. I don't like anybody very much."

Scott laughed a little laugh.

"What happens to you after your pickup?" Schiller asked.

"I believe I am headed south. And Turnbull here – what's your rank, son?"

"I'm a fourth level elf." Turnbull was not sure what that meant, but he had heard Casey say it.

"He's a captain," Schiller said.

"The captain," Scott continued, "is wrong about my ass not belonging to the Army. Or, rather, *an* army. Things are moving quickly and dangerously. It appears I will be leading a new army."

Turnbull turned in the seat and looked at the general.

"Dan is not my only contact in the DoD," Scott said. "I have a whole network of leaders who have worked for me over the years. And they share our driver's –"

"Major Joe Schiller, sir."

"Major Schiller's faith in me, which I greatly appreciate. And they tell me the military leadership is gearing up to clamp down on our own American people. A response is inevitable. The people won't stand for it. And those who desert the military that they are unleashing on the people will need a banner to rally around."

"So, you're just forming an insurgent army?" Turnbull asked.

The general chuckled. "This is not a typical insurgency. In some places, the blue areas, it is disorganized and decentralized. In red areas, there are existing governmental structures."

"State governments," Turnbull said.

"Multiple state governments, working in tandem," Scott replied. "And their National Guards, with loyal active units, will form a preexisting structure to build out a conventional force."

"So, they're going full stop civil war?" Turnbull said. "And you're our...Sulla?"

"More like Ulysses Grant, in this case. I don't have any political ambitions like Sulla."

"I partied a lot in high school, but I do recall Grant became president."

"It was forced upon him, really. You disapprove?"

"I'm not sure what I think, except everyone seems intent on driving this runaway train right off a cliff."

"Having a credible, organized force is the best deterrent to war," he replied. "That's why the Roman model of every citizen serving has always appealed to me. Don't you agree?"

Turnbull did not reply, because he did agree. Scott's logic was sound, and even a general could be right occasionally. Sometimes the only thing to bring people to their senses was the possibility of a fist to the nose. But that did not always work. Sometimes you had to throw the punch. And that was the rub. He let Schiller and the general continue talking as he went back to gazing out the window.

There was a surplus store outside town, boarded up but open, and Turnbull made a quick run inside to get the gear and provisions they needed. He paid with cash. Farther up the road, at the edge of Gettysburg itself, there was a police checkpoint that Schiller could not avoid without a dramatic and attention-drawing 180 turn.

It looked like an established checkpoint, not one just thrown up as part of a manhunt. That made sense – the Gettysburg riots and the conflicts between patriots and protesters had received extensive coverage in the media. Still, Turnbull pulled the .45 out of his holster and kept it low but ready.

The officer, older, heavy, and in a tan uniform, came to the car window and looked them over.

"Welcome to Gettysburg," he said, not particularly hospitably. "What's your business here?"

"We're here to see the park," Schiller replied.

"The park is closed to...," the officer began, but he was interrupted.

"Officer, we really need to go see the park," said the general, leaning in from the backseat. The cop froze upon seeing Scott, and he looked around nervously. There were three other officers at the checkpoint with their cruisers parked alongside the road. He turned back to the general.

"There's a back-way in. Just follow me." The officer stepped off and motioned over another cop. They huddled, with the other cop looking at the Lexus with some level of puzzlement. Then the officer walked over to one of the parked cruisers and got in. He waved from the window for Schiller to follow.

Much of the main street area was still boarded up, with only a few of the windows having been replaced in the six months since the troubles. Most of the graffiti had been scrubbed off. There was a statue of Abe Lincoln, who had been there with stovepipe hat held aloft. The arm with the hat and Abe's head were gone. In the center of town, the middle of the round-about that was Lincoln Square was still charred from the bonfire the rioters had set before being driven out of town by patriots. Several people, out-of-towners, had been killed with buckshot and deer rifle rounds. The local police had declared themselves unable to find the culprits. The Department of Justice had arrived to investigate what Rep. Eric Swalwell had labeled "the Gettysburg Racist Massacre," but the locals denied any knowledge of any riot, much less any killings.

They followed the police car through the town, with the citizens all taking note of the strange Lexus with DC plates bearing the city's new motto, "Born of Slavery – 1619."

"I recall it more welcoming when we came here for our War College staff ride," the general said. "But it appears the second invasion of rampaging Democrats was no more effective than the first one."

They passed what was apparently one of the main entrances. It was blocked off with Jersey barriers and signs reading "PARK CLOSED." Someone had spray-painted "DEATH TO RACIST UNION AND CONFUNDERATES" on the white concrete.

"What's a 'confunderate'?" wondered Casey.

"Looks like our boy is taking us around the back way," Turnbull observed as the police cruiser turned off on a private road and headed toward the park. Turnbull had been there before and vaguely remembered the lay-out. They were now clearly inside the park – there were monuments every hundred meters or so. Often, they were damaged or destroyed. Most had obviously been scrubbed of painted epithets.

After a few minutes, the cruiser pulled over at the side of the deserted Emmitsburg Road. The cop got out, and so did the four men. The officer came back to them.

"General, it's a damn honor to meet ya," said the policeman. "I was a tanker in First Cav in Desert Storm."

"I was with the Twenty-Fourth Division over there. Thank you for your help, trooper."

"The BOLO came out an hour ago and said you were wanted for treason. We just laughed, sir," the policeman said. "Like we would turn in General Karl Scott if he ever showed up here. And sure as shit, here you are. You're a hero. There're millions of us behind you. You just call on us, sir, and we'll answer."

"I may do that."

"They call this 'Pennsyltucky,' sir, because PA is Pittsburgh and Philly with Kentucky in between, but even the ones here who aren't vets know their way around a deer rifle. We showed those sombitches from the city when they came out here. We fought back, and they never came back," he said proudly. "We're ready for whatever they got for us."

"I know. You people are the heart and soul of America."

The officer beamed. "You'll be safe in the park. No one is allowed in here anymore, except us."

The general extended his hand to shake, but the officer saluted. General Scott returned it, and the policeman made a remarkably adept about-face before returning to his car and driving away.

"You got fans," Turnbull said.

"If you offer to lead, men follow," the general replied.

"I'll follow," Schiller said.

"I'll do my own thing," Turnbull said. "Let's get where we're going."

Between them, they knew how to get where they were going. Little Round Top was a hill at the southeast end of the battlefield. There were several monuments to the units that fought there, particularly the Union units that had held the end of the Union line and kept it from being rolled up by the Confederates.

One of the monuments was what looked like a small castle, complete with a turret. A wide arch opened out toward Devil's Den, the rocky outcroppings below the heights that had been the scene of particular carnage.

They parked the Lexus out of sight under the trees – they were bare, but at least there was some concealment. The foursome got the camping gear from the surplus store out of the trunk and walked up the hill to the castle. It had been built as a memorial to the 44th and 12th New York Infantry Regiments, and a plaque indicated that it had been dedicated on July 3, 1893, thirty years after the battle.

"The tower is 44 feet high, and the inside space is 12 feet square," Scott said.

"Like the units," Casey replied, standing on the stone floor and looking around. A circular staircase inside went up to an observation deck.

"I got first watch," Turnbull said, putting down his sleeping bag but taking one of the MREs he had bought. He saw it was shredded beef in barbeque sauce and grimaced. Once at Ranger School, he had eaten some of that and spent his whole patrol retching.

"Three-hour shifts," he said over his shoulder as he went to the stairs.

General Scott's pickup would be in 13 hours.

7.

Taking first watch meant also taking last watch, and at dawn Turnbull was walking around the castle, partly patrolling, partly stretching his legs. It was cold, and he had on a light jacket. Below him, over Devil's Den and the rest of the far left of the battlefield, it was still. Hard to believe that this peaceful Pennsylvania countryside was the site of the largest battle ever fought in North America.

"It happened right over there," said a voice behind him.

Turnbull was not surprised. Every few steps he stopped and listened, and he had heard stirring in the little tower a while before.

"A lot happened here, general," Turnbull observed.

"Right in those trees, on that hill, Colonel Joshua Chamberlain and the 20th Maine were holding the far end of the Union line. Out of ammo, with the Southerners coming up the hill, they were out of options. So, Chamberlain had his men fix bayonets and ordered a charge. The Confederates did not expect that. They broke and ran." Scott joined Turnbull on the path, looking over the battlefield.

"I know the story."

"Chamberlain was a college professor before the war. Imagine that. A college professor who loved America enough to take up arms to defend her. Now our college professors are at the vanguard of those who seek to destroy her," General Scott said.

"If those Maine men had not held, the battle could have gone the other way, and we might be looking at a country split in two."

"Seems like we might be looking at that soon enough," Turnbull said.

"It's called the Union for a reason," Scott replied. "Some people talk about a national divorce, but I prefer a national reconciliation."

"You don't seem the kiss and make up type."

"I'm not. When I say 'reconciliation,' I mean like Abraham Lincoln reconciled the country."

"At a cost of 600,000 dead," Turnbull observed.

"If need be. It's a small price to pay, if you think about it," Scott said. "If there had been a divided America in 1940, Britain and Russia would have fallen to Hitler."

"If we're doing the butterfly effect thing...," Turnbull began, but the general, not used to having his monologues cut off by company grade officers, continued.

"The Union must endure, whatever the cost," Scott said. "And we need leaders who understand that, who are willing to act aggressively and even ruthlessly to do it."

"Sounds a lot like your boy Sulla."

"Sulla did what had to be done, what lesser men were incapable of."

"Maybe we should let the politicians figure this all out," Turnbull said.

"The politicians got us here, captain. This country is on the verge of civil war. Law and order are breaking down. Mobs have supplanted the government in our big cities. Our Congress is being held hostage. Our rights are being trampled. We need to rise up."

"I guess you're going to help out with that part."

"I will do my duty," the general said. "But when the time comes, will you do yours?"

Turnbull looked at the general hard.

"I always have," he snarled.

"You don't like me much, do you?"

"Don't take it personally," Turnbull said, walking off. "I don't much like any generals."

The helicopter that picked up the general, Schiller, and Casey in a field near the 99th Pennsylvania Infantry Monument was a civilian Eurocopter EC175. Turnbull was a little surprised that it was not military, but who knew where any given unit stood right now on the red-blue rainbow? With a civilian pilot, you paid him and he flew whoever wherever, no questions, just cash.

When the general, Schiller, and Casey took off, so did Turnbull, hopping into the Lexus and going out of the park the back way.

The miles passed as he drove west on Interstate 70 through Pennsylvania. The land was quiet but the vibe was tense. Several signs read "STOP THE COUNTING, STOP THE CHEATING," a reference to the disputed Pennsylvania Senate seat election that headed back into a recount every time the previous recount showed the Republican ahead. Each time, some precinct in Philly discovered a big box of ballots that had somehow been ignored during each prior recount.

Other signs registered even more dire sentiments. Outside a little town called New Stanton was a billboard that read, in red letters on a stark black background, "IF YOU COME FOR OUR GUNS, MAKE SURE YOU'VE UPDATED YOUR WILL." Something called the "Liberty Corps" was its sponsor, with crossed AR15s as its symbol, and it had a phone number and website listed if you wanted to know more.

The traffic was light for every category of vehicle except military. There were more camouflaged vehicles than usual, trucks and hummers, many headed west. Turnbull noticed several OD green lowboy trailers hauling M1AI tanks. Letterkenny Army Depot, where they rebuilt and refurbished armored vehicles, was just off of I-81, but that was back east near Gettysburg. These, like many of the military convoys, were headed toward Pittsburgh.

Since Turnbull could read a bumper number, he noted that most were National Guard. However, some were from Reserve units. That meant the Pentagon had activated these forces, since Army Reserve units did not work for governors, unlike unfederalized Guard units. Which faction these forces were allied to was not clear.

Turnbull considered alternate scenarios. Maybe they were just training, but Guard and Reserve units typically did their two-week training in the summer. Maybe it was all just precautionary. Maybe the whole country was spinning out of control.

A blue minivan with a "COEXIST" bumper sticker next to a "BETTER DEAD THAN RED" bumper sticker passed him. The red it referred to was not the communists.

He flipped on the radio as he passed south of Pittsburgh.

"I am a searchlight of intelligence in a world of birthday cake candles. This is the *Teddy King Show*, maybe for the last time. Folks, it's time to panic," the host said. He sounded about twelve years old. "Do the new security orders bar us from broadcasting? I don't know. The feds may show up here and we might get arrested on the air during the show today. Who knows? They already tried to arrest my competitor Larry O'Connor in DC – I hear he's now in Texas. But I won't stop until they gag me."

Turnbull had heard of Teddy King even before the awkward incident a few months before with the clerk at the New York City Best Western. King billed himself as "the most hated heretic in the history of UC Berkeley," and Turnbull found his rants tiresome even when he agreed with them. But, in fairness, he found most people tiresome.

Yet it was the closest thing to news there was out here, at least in English. The host went on. "No one knows exactly what is happening, and it is unprecedented. Texas Governor Abbot has basically said he and the rest of what he's calling the

Constitutional Alliance will not comply with the new laws, and will not allow the federal government to enforce them. Not on speech limits, not on gun confiscation, none of them. So, besides the Lone Star State, we have most of the southern states joining him. California's governor, the guy with the great hair, is talking about seceding with Oregon and Washington. The military is all over the map, with some generals announcing they will obey the president, others announcing they won't. In the blue areas, People's Militias, which I have been saying for a year should have been stamped out, are the actual government in several cities. Provisionals and Liberty Corps units are organizing in the red areas. This is it. This is what the Second Amendment was made for. This is the worst-case scenario!"

"You have no idea about the worst-case scenario," Turnbull muttered aloud as he flipped the radio off and accelerated to 80.

He passed through the sliver of West Virginia and across the Ohio River at Wheeling. The low hills surrounding the town were covered with bare trees, and the greenish water below the long bridge just kept flowing despite the chaos among the humans on its banks. There were lots of police cars, and several exits into town were closed. Exit 0, the last one before the Ohio border, was open. He got off, filled his tank, and ordered a Whopper with cheese prepared his way, no mustard. The pimply ginger at the counter began to argue with him that the Whopper did not come with mustard, to which Turnbull replied that then his order should be easy to make.

Turnbull stepped back to wait for his meal. He noted that two of the restaurant's windows had been broken out and were covered with plywood. Few of the customers interacted in the messy dining room.

A West Virginia state police car, dark blue with a gold diagonal slash painted across the side, pulled in and parked. Two officers got out, both with long weapons over their backs. One stayed with the vehicle, and the other came inside. The ginger at the counter muttered "Pig" under his breath and took the cop's order sullenly.

The officer stepped back to wait and turned to Turnbull.

"How you doing today?" The man had a local accent, but his voice was not friendly.

"I'm fine. How about you?"

"Just great," the cop answered, clearly not great. Like Turnbull, he watched the cooks making the burgers so no one added a loogie to his sandwich. Outside, the other cop was alert and looking around.

"You need to guard your vehicle?"

"Better safe than sorry."

"And you got rifles."

The officer assessed Turnbull and decided he was unlikely to be some sort of radical. Turnbull gave off a military vibe.

"Two of our officers were shot on a traffic stop the other day. The perps used automatic weapons. Normally, that would be big news, but no one but us even noticed," he said. "It's a scary time. Bad people think they can do whatever they want. But not here. We're not having it."

"Sorry about your friends."

"Me too," replied the officer. "I guess you're passing through."

"Going west."

"The Ohio staties have a checkpoint a few miles in," the officer said. "Stopping everyone coming in, checking ID, looking for assholes. I'm waiting to be told to start doing the same."

"So where does West Virginia stand?" Turnbull asked.

The cop looked him over, considering how open to be with the stranger. "I don't see us going blue. We broke off from Virginia last time everything went to hell because of the Democrats, and we aren't inclined to go along with nonsense this time either. Anyone comes here trying to make us comply better have his affairs in order."

"Number twelve," said the ginger, sullenly.

"That's mine," Turnbull said.

"Take care."

"You too."

Turnbull went to the counter, and the ginger handed him his bag and his Coke, frowning.

Turnbull passed through the Ohio entry checkpoint with no problem, his fake credentials identifying him as a DHS agent earning him a quick wave through. The line of cars was long even though the traffic was light, and Turnbull was glad to have avoided more detailed scrutiny. He headed into the Buckeye State.

There was smoke hanging over Columbus. At the outskirts, the name had been painted over several signs, with "Genocyde City" spray painted in black. Turnbull wondered if the spelling was intentional, or evidence of a public-school education.

He drove through the city on I-70 without slowing down. A convoy of eight cop cars passed him heading east. Turnbull checked the gas gauge and decided to wait to fuel up until he hit the suburbs on the west side of town.

He pulled off at the Pilot Truck Center where US-42 crossed the interstate. In contrast to the freeway, the lot was packed with big rig trucks of all sorts. He fueled up and then parked, going inside to grab something to eat. The drivers filled all the seats in the restaurant, and many stood around nursing coffees or Cokes. There was a television on showing ABC News.

Something bad was happening in Los Angeles. And Chicago. And elsewhere. The anchor, however, was explaining that the "occasionally fiery, mostly peaceful protests" were not the cause of the disorder. That was the racist militias and white supremacists resisting the new laws and decrees issuing from the liberated Capitol, the anchor assured the audience. The audience, at least in the truck stop's restaurant, was not buying it.

"Screw these assholes," one trucker yelled. "Turn it to a local channel."

The manager complied. The Action News team was on live. There was footage of rioting in downtown Columbus. The cops seemed unable to deal with it – there were none in sight. The reporter looked scared. An auto parts place burned behind him.

"They need to send in the National Guard," one of the drivers said. "Martial law."

"The problem is half the government is on the side of these animals," another driver interjected.

"This shit is out of control. I counted four bullet holes in my trailer," said another as Turnbull stepped up to order at the counter. He asked for a BLT and fries with a large cup of joe.

There were mumbles from the rest of the assembled teamsters. Apparently, many of them had been targeted too.

"Without us, the cities starve," said the driver who had taken fire. "I don't get paid enough to get killed delivering ham."

"I had a buddy hauling a load of Budweiser. They caught him on a surface street, took it all. He's in the ICU."

"No one is putting me in the ICU," replied another driver with a large beard and a ball cap with a flag on it. He opened his blue down vest, and there was the butt of a .38 revolver that was wedged in his jeans.

There were murmurs of agreement. Turnbull sat back and listened, taking it in. Apparently, the police had ordered all commercial traffic to avoid Columbus, and those on their way into the city had pulled off and were waiting here. Several drivers announced that they were simply turning around and going back where they came. Others opined that where they came from was in a similar mess.

The waitress handed Turnbull his cardboard cup and his paper sack with his dinner. "Lucky you're getting this," she said. "I'm not sure when we'll get any more meat or produce delivered."

Turnbull grunted his thanks, and noted the Mossberg 590 12-gauge leaning against the inside of the counter.

There was a little rain, but luckily it was too warm to turn into snow. Turnbull kept heading west. He passed south of Springfield and north of Dayton. He saw no overt evidence of chaos from the interstate, but the traffic remained light on the interstate.

It occurred to him it had been a while since he had shot anyone. If things went as he hoped, that would change soon. He had no intel on Minneapolis or the Gopher Militia, and he figured he'd improvise on the ground.

It was hard for him to listen to the mainstream news, when he could pick any up on the radio. Except on the expressly conservative stations, the agenda was all pro-left. The big problem in America, the mainstream media narrative ran, was "racists" and "right-wing militias" invading the cities, if you believed the media. The propaganda was awkward, unlike in many of the dictatorships that Turnbull had served in, but they would improve their dark arts with practice.

The reporters celebrated the various decrees made via the captive Congress in the wake of the DC massacre. In cooperation with the tech companies, social media sites were taking action to muzzle "subversive" and "hate" speech. The truckers waiting at the truck stop had been complaining that half their Facebook and Twitter feeds were blocked out with "RACIST COMMENT" notifications. That included any commentary that dissented from the view that the coup in the capital was illegitimate – and any commentary supporting resistance to it.

Turnbull was crossing into Indiana when a station reported that a collection of ex-generals and admirals had left their highly-paid positions with defense contractors and as media commentators to form a "National Military Unity Council" and were urging military forces to follow the orders of the NMUC – how it fit into the actual chain of command was unclear, as was whether the Pentagon and subordinate units would obey or ignore these retired flag officers who were trying to bypass the chain of command. The media was certainly all in – the mainstream media narrative was that this ad hoc blue junta was, as Jennifer Rubin stated, "more legitimate and moral than any oath these military people took."

"Screw that," Turnbull muttered to himself. The Constitutional Alliance, which the announcer called "the illegal racist and transphobic red state regime," demurred to the authority of the has-been flag officers.

This was followed by a report that Elizabeth Warren had announced a "truth and reconciliation" tribunal that was being formed to "understand and illuminate the crimes of the racist white supremacy regime." Basically, that meant that people associated with the Donald Trump administration were being arrested, where they could be captured. But reading between the lines, many of the targets were seeking sanctuary in the red states, and getting it. The reporters' questions to what they called "one of America's preeminent voices of womyn of color" were all along the lines of "How can you be so brave?" This was especially ironic, since her DNA test had proved she was not one.

The whole issue of freedom never came up.

Turnbull was particularly amused by the order for people to immediately turn in their "weapons of war," which appeared to include any weapon designed after 1900. It was unclear who would collect the hundred million or so weapons covered by the command. Good luck with that, Turnbull thought to himself as he drove westward.

Outside Indianapolis, he listened to host Tony Katz's special report and his highly critical coverage of the American crisis.

"Are we going to take this tyranny, or are we going to stand up and be citizens?" he shouted. Turnbull listened until the station went off the air following a tumult of shouts and yelling.

It sounded like the studio was being raided. Turnbull was not shocked – you always seize the radio stations first.

He scanned the rest of the stations on the dial – most were still playing music, usually awful music, as if the country was not busy tearing itself apart.

Turnbull turned the Lexus off of I-70 at an interchange in the middle of the city, which echoed with lights and sirens in the dark. He headed north on I-65 toward Chicago.

But Chicago was closed.

A collection of Guard soldiers, police from various agencies, and armed civilians had blocked off the interstate near a small town called Dinwiddie south of Gary. It was less a roadblock to stop those going in than for stopping those coming out, as no one seemed to want to head north.

"It's a cluster in the city," a sergeant told Turnbull as he waved him onto the detour. The NCO had an M4 with its mag in the well as well as several hand grenades. "The Chicago PD has the blue flu and there's no law or order in there. It's chaos."

Turnbull noted that several of the hummers were gun trucks with mounted .50 caliber M2 machine guns. He also observed that coming out of the metroplex was a long line of regular suburban vehicles, minivans, and SUVs, many heaped with bags tied to roofs, along with kids and dogs.

"You keeping them in there or letting them go through?" Turnbull asked.

"Not if they seem okay. Families and stuff, we let out. Gangbangers and thugs, we deal with."

"Deal with?" asked Turnbull.

"You need to move along, sir," the sergeant said firmly.

"I'm a vet too, so just answer me this," Turnbull said. "Who is the commander of this operation? Who are you working for? The governor? The Pentagon? The Constitutional Alliance? This NMUC cluster?"

"Hell if I know. Now, you need to go."

Turnbull complied and took the Lexus on a long, backroad detour far south of the city. At several intersections he stopped to allow long military convoys to head north. And many other folks were moving south, escaping the chaos.

There was no place to stay the night. All the motels were either closed or full – mostly closed. He grabbed some gas, but he sat in line for a half-hour to get to the pump and even then, he had to pay the $19.99 a gallon in cash – the owner was inflating it above the $10.99 gas cost per gallon a week before, thanks to the Green New Deal's recent Phase I carbon tax.

It was tense at the Minooka Citgo off I-80, with the only excitement being when a couple of punks tried to jump the line in front of Turnbull. He gave them a chance to repent, they did not, and they regretted it. The other people in line applauded as the cutters limped away, and Turnbull quickly gassed up and moved out.

He continued west on I-80 into the prairie, turning north on I-39 at La Salle. Despairing of finding a motel, he pulled off on a remote offramp and drove out into the inky nothingness until he found a dirt road extending through a stand of trees. Pulling in, and satisfying himself that he could park on the shoulder safely, he took off his seatbelt and slept in the reclined driver's seat, his Wilson in his lap.

"Don't," boomed a loud man in his 60s with a beard and a red hat that read "TRUMP IS MY PRESIDENT." Turnbull could read it because it was light out. The man had a Remington 870 pump-action shotgun pointed at his window, and, therefore, his face.

Turnbull raised his hands, making no move toward the .45 in his lap.

"Come on out of there, careful like," said the old man, using his left hand to grab the door handle. Pulling it open was awkward, as the man discovered when Turnbull kicked the door out into him. The man staggered, his gun knocked off target, and in a split-second Turnbull was on his feet with the Wilson pointed at the man's face.

"Gun, ground," Turnbull ordered.

The man dropped the 12-gauge, grimacing. The Wilson muzzle did not move from his face.

"You alone?" Turnbull asked.

"Wish I wasn't." The man raised his hands and furrowed his brow.

"Ok, five steps backwards. Move!" Turnbull directed.

The man nodded and stepped back carefully, trying not to trip. Turnbull glanced around, confirming they were alone.

"Turn around," he said. The man did, and Turnbull patted him down, the barrel of the automatic pressed into his neck. The man had an old .38 Smith & Wesson Airweight Model 42 hammerless revolver, with worn wood grips and the bluing wearing off, in his front jeans pocket.

"Hey, I got that from my daddy," he complained as Turnbull tossed it into the brush.

"You can look for it once I'm gone," Turnbull said, turning him back around.

"That was pretty smooth. I guess you ain't some punk doing thrill-seeker liquor store holdups with a 'Born to Lose' tattoo on your chest," the old man said. "Who are you?"

"I've got the gun. I get to ask the questions."

"Well, gun or no, this is my land and you're trespassing."

"Just spending the night."

"They got things called 'motels' for that."

"Not anymore, it seems," Turnbull said. "Guess you haven't gotten out much lately."

"No, I've been staying put, ready to protect what's mine."

"Well, you don't need to worry about me. Nothing here I want, except some z's."

"You got those. Why don't you be on your way?"

"In a minute. First, what's your name?"

"Noah. Like in the deluge."

"I know who Noah was," Turnbull snapped. Sunday school had made at least some impression on him. "What's the situation?"

"All hell is breaking loose. That's the situation."

"I mean specifically, like around here."

"Can I put my hands down? I'm old. And it hurts."

"Sure," Turnbull said. "Just, you know, don't make me blow a hole in you."

"Well, I'll try to be on my best behavior," Noah said bitterly. "Chicago is gone totally out of control."

"People keep saying that."

"I mean no control at all. The cops walked off the job. The Army National Guard got called up. My boy is with the Second of the 130th Infantry in Effingham and he phoned me – wasn't supposed to, but he knew I'd be worried – and sooner or later they are going into the city and set things right. It's ugly – it's not just rioting. The People's Militia is hunting down folks. They say they got lists."

"That hat will get you on a list."

Noah sniffed. "Let 'em come. Next time, they won't get the drop on me."

"Next time, operate in a team, Noah."

"We'll be doing that. We knew back in 2020 that we'd have to be ready to take matters into our own hands sooner or later. We're organized into groups of Provisionals. The sheriff is with us. Nobody better come out here, not to loot, not to steal, and definitely not to try and take our guns."

"Well, I'm leaving you your guns," Turnbull said. "Just don't pick them up until I'm back on the main road."

"Where are you headed?"

"Nowhere good."

8.

Before Kelly Turnbull had left Washington, Merrick Crane III had gotten out of a Chevy Suburban that was parked on the shoulder of the interstate and walked back to where Mr. Soto was locking a fresh magazine full of .40 caliber rounds into the well of his smoking UMP40 submachine gun.

It was good to have Mr. Soto back, Crane mused. If keeping Harrington safe was not so vital, he never would have allowed his trusted bodyguard out of his sight.

Crane coldly surveyed the two West Virginia state troopers lying on the asphalt.

"Finish them and get their dashcam disc," he said. Soto nodded almost imperceptibly and moved toward the patrol car.

Turning toward his vehicle again, Crane got back into the passenger seat. It was an unbearable drag to have to drive to Minneapolis, but there was no other way. Even assuming that there were flights operating, to get on one would risk exposure. And while a good portion of the government was aligned with the blue and could be relied upon to cover for him, others within the government were still red and might well capture him or worse. That was the downside of the chaos he was sowing – you never knew who was trustworthy. Of course, once this phase was over, he would set himself to the task of ensuring loyalty. The thought of the camps he envisioned made him smile.

Soto returned to the vehicle silently and slipped behind the steering wheel. In a moment they were headed west again. It did not occur to Crane to ask Mr. Soto why he had decided to kill the cops instead of simply present them with their false identity documents. Mr. Soto was absolutely reliable in such things.

Crane had identified him early among the true believers, the thugs, and revolutionary role players within Antifa. Mr. Soto did not talk – he acted, decisively and deadly. That's why he had kept Mr. Soto with him. If Mr. Soto appreciated it, he never said so. He never said much at all. Crane's discreet background check gave him all the information he had about his companion's past. It had indicated that Mr. Soto grew up near Seattle and had some sort of military training – his investigator had told Crane that Mr. Soto's records were very generic, indicating that his years in the Army were either very dull or very interesting indeed.

Judging by the deft manner in which his associate dealt with the two officers, Crane was inclined to go with "interesting."

His phone rang, or rather, one of the dozen burners he carried with him. He had written "A" on it with a black Sharpie – all the others had letters printed on them too – so he knew who was on the other end.

"Darling," he said. The woman on the other end cooed and proceeded to update him. He listened carefully, especially to what she had to say about timing.

"No more than a week, and that's at the outside. There are many moving pieces to this," he said. He listened as she complained about what her mission entailed, what she was having to do. When she paused, he spoke again.

"I understand your sacrifice," he said, though he truly did not care all that much. "This is for something so much more important than ourselves. We are all victimized by the systems of oppression we are fighting to bring down."

This seemed to mollify her. She expressed how much she missed him and, feeling it necessary, he reciprocated. Then he returned to the business at hand.

"You know where I am going," he said, knowing she would understand the operational security consideration that kept him from speaking the name "Minneapolis" over the air. "I'll be only a few hours away when you are ready. Call me the moment you are."

He tolerated her telling him how much she missed him. For a progressive woman who rejected the cisnormative paradigm of this patriarchal society, she could be as banal as any rom-com heroine, though Hollywood never made romantic comedies anymore, at least not ones revolving around straight men and women.

"I feel the same," he told her. "I'm waiting for your call." He hung up. Mr. Soto's eyes were on the road, and he betrayed no interest in the conversation. Crane dug into his bag of burners for another burner, this one marked "T." He hit re-dial, and after two rings there was an answer.

"I'll be there before dawn," Crane said. "Be ready for me." He hung up and dropped the burner back into his bag.

About 24 hours after Crane had passed that way, Turnbull approached Minneapolis on I-35 from the south. There was now only one news station left on the radio, and it was only in the loosest sense of a kind of news station. "Radio Free MLAZ" it called itself, and it was nothing but incoherent babbling about the "revolutionary space" and how "liberation was at hand." The People's Militia was apparently running the show – there were also comments about "Antifa deviationism."

Turnbull smiled at the thought of the two strains of the Marxist pathology in conflict with each other. Blue on blue was awesome.

It never used the term "Gopher Antifa" except once, and that was to declare it a "racist and humanocentric" term and therefore a crime.

What was apparent was the lack of any kind of law enforcement. Turnbull knew the Minneapolis and St. Paul police departments had been "abolished," but apparently the entire state's law enforcement apparatus had disappeared too. The same with the military. And the road north was even emptier here than anywhere else he had been on his journey. The opposite was true of the other direction – there was a steady stream of heavily laden civilian vehicles heading south.

Turnbull was running through his options about entering the city when he heard an interesting tidbit. The current voice of Radio Free MLAZ was going on a long rant about the "revanchist militias" controlling Burnsville and promising to bring destruction down upon them when "we come to burn your imperialist suburbs."

Burnsville was not far ahead. Turnbull accelerated.

"Are you Provisionals or Liberty Corps or what?" Turnbull asked the apparent leader of the dozen or so armed men – and several women – whom he encountered not long after getting off the interstate.

"Does it matter? I guess Provisionals," said one of those women, her AR15 with combat optic at low-ready. She seemed to be in charge, and she wore ACU camo pants and combat boots. She saw Turnbull taking note of her fashion choice.

"I am – was – Minnesota Army Guard. The Guard kind of ceased to exist, so here I am. I'm Taylor Furness. This is my squad. We're defending our homes."

Turnbull had parked the Lexus and was openly wearing his Wilson .45 on his thigh. He figured he'd fit in better with a gun than without one. There were a lot of armed citizens here, sort of organized into small units, busy securing their town.

"Are the Antifa pushing out here?" he said. "Whoever Radio Free MLAZ is seems to dislike Burnsville in particular."

"That's because we shoot them if they come here," Furness replied. "And the People's Militia are worse than Antifa, mostly because they are organized. They took over the city government and now they are running, if you can call it that, the city. Well, now it's the MLAZ – the Minneapolis Liberated Autonomous Zone."

"They want to change the name 'Minneapolis,'" interjected a man of about 20 with a scoped Winchester 700 deer rifle. "They say it was a stolen name, stolen from indigenous people. You know, Indians."

"It was apparently Elizabeth Warren's idea," Furness observed sourly.

"She's been busy," Turnbull replied. "So, they are in charge in the city? The government just left?"

Furness nodded. "Totally, both Minneapolis and St. Paul. The People's Militia is trying to organize a government and the Antifa types are being anarchists, though both sides say they are anarchists. The damned anarchy symbol is painted on practically every flat surface in town."

"I need to get into this MLAZ," Turnbull said.

The woman smiled, and looked as if she was about to tell him he was a fool when there was a commotion that caught her and Turnbull's attention.

Another squad was surrounding a small group of perhaps a dozen unarmed civilians, mostly middle-aged with a few older kids, carrying luggage down the middle of the street. It was obvious these people were not choosing to do the duffel bag drag. The squad surrounding them and moving them along was encouraging them with curses and insults, as well as the occasional threat.

The leader of the escorts waved to Furness, who returned the gesture, and the sorry contingent proceeded along its path.

"Liberals," the woman said, as if that explained what just happened.

"What are you doing with them?" Turnbull said.

"We're not hurting them," Furness replied. "We're just moving them out."

"Out of their homes?"

"Out of our town," the woman replied defensively. "They're blue sympathizers. You can pick them out. They always have a sign out front that says 'Hate has no home here' or 'We believe in science' or some shit. Of course, hate totally lives there and they don't accept any science they don't like. They're on the other team."

"So, you're kicking them out of their homes?"

"No," the woman said, annoyed. "We're kicking them out of our town. Just like all the normal people who got kicked out of Minneapolis."

"Where will they go?"

"Their problem. They can go into the MLAZ, they can go somewhere else. But they can't stay here," Furness replied, a bit defensive. "You know, we didn't start this, but we will damn well finish it."

"I'm not here to judge you. I'm here to get into Minneapolis – MLAZ, I guess – and I need to know the best way to do it."

"Well, you don't want to go straight north, that's for damn sure. They have security all around the city, but it's heaviest against us. There's a firefight every night now. Which we win."

"Well, far be it from me to want to interfere in shooting communists. I need a way in, though. Do any of your people ever infiltrate?"

The woman paused.

"You need to talk to Scott George."

Turnbull eased the Lexus through the dark streets. Some blocks had power, others none. His passenger, a middle-aged man with graying hair and wearing an old woodland camo Army field jacket, directed him.

"It's usually pretty clear through here," the man said, craning his neck and surveying the residential neighborhood. "Usually."

Turnbull said nothing and kept driving. He did not actively dislike his passenger, which was unusual. Scott George had not pretended to be anything other than an amateur, but he had crossed into the MLAZ several times in the last couple weeks and survived inside with nothing more than his wits, an old FN Browning Hi-Power 9mm pistol, and a stack of large bills.

"The border is fuzzy – the MLAZ is not exactly strictly defined," George said. "Downtown there's no question. The People's Militia and Antifa are the law, to the extent that anarchists have law. They have a tense relationship, but they cooperate against outsiders."

"Where exactly do you think your daughter is?" Turnbull asked.

George was silent for a moment. "I'm not sure. The best information I've gotten says the group she was running with was camped out near the city hall. But there's maybe 40,000 of them in there, some cadre, some criminals."

"And the rest suburban kids with daddy issues," Turnbull said, harsher than he meant it to be.

"Yeah," George said. "And I'm getting her out of there."

"I'll drive us as close as I can. You just guide me in."

George nodded. "About half of the normals left before the MLAZ started clamping down on people leaving. I guess they want civilians as human shields in case someone decides to retake the city. Of course, the government around here seems to be on the rioters' side. There's a military truck convoy that goes in every day with free food. Our piece of shit governor has the Guard, or what's left of it, feeding the damn Antifa and People's Militia."

"I thought you said there were no checkpoints here," Turnbull said, his eyes fixed on an armed figure ahead in the middle of the road ahead, standing there casually with his hand up commanding that they halt. Several others, some with long weapons, were on the sidewalk. Like his friends, the guy in the street was wearing a white and black checked keffiyeh wrapped around his face.

They were not Antifa – that faction tended to wear all black. He was definitely People's Militia. George had briefed him that the Minneapolis branch of that group used the neck scarf as their uniform, having aped it from the fashion choices of Palestinian terrorists. This likely explained the burned-out synagogue a few blocks back.

"I said 'usually,'" George replied, concerned. "Okay, let me talk our way through."

"You want to talk to them?" Turnbull asked.

"What else can we do?"

Turnbull gunned the engine and the militiaman's eyes got really wide in the second before the front bumper smashed into his legs and he went tumbling over the hood and the roof, sprawling on the asphalt behind them as the Lexus sped away.

"What the hell was that?" George said, looking back at the twitching figure in the road that was being surrounded by his comrades. "You just drove through him!"

"Sure did," Turnbull said. There was a crack as a bullet went into the upper right corner of the rear glass. The other militia members were firing, mostly ineffectually. Turnbull kept driving and took the next left.

"You didn't have to do that," George said.

"No, I didn't," Turnbull said. "But it worked out okay. For us."

"I'm here to get my daughter, not hurt people."

"That why you have a pistol?"

"It's for self-defense."

"The best self-defense is a good self-offense," Turnbull said. He continued: "This is no game and the rules are a little looser than usual. Those guys decided they wanted to play horsey, and this is horsey."

"You can't just kill people!"

"I know. That's why I didn't put it in reverse and finish him."

"I didn't bring you along to start a war. I just want my daughter back."

"And I just need a guide downtown to wherever the People's Militia HQ is."

"Well, now we are going to have to ditch the car. They have cells and radios too. They'll be looking for a blue Lexus."

"Then we hoof it," Turnbull said. He drove on a little ways, then pulled over. They were in front of a burned-out Wendy's. Someone had written "ANIMAL GENOCYDE" on the charred ruins in red spray paint.

"Is this 'Y' a thing?" Turnbull wondered. "Are they rebelling against spelling too?"

They got out and Turnbull took out his day pack from the trunk. It held his gear, like a medical kit and spare socks. He also had his collection of helpful tools and items that might come in handy, like superglue, various phone chargers, a cigar torch, a Leatherman tool, and a shortened handcuff key. He carried his pistol under his jacket. They both looked ratty and disreputable. Turnbull hoped they did so sufficiently to fit in.

The walk into the heart of what had been Minneapolis took them through an urban wasteland. Turnbull was shocked by the number of buildings that were merely charred ruins. He had been aware of the riots over the last couple years, but the scope of the damage stunned him. He had not seen it reported in the mainstream media. Instead, on the rare occasions that what was happening in Minneapolis (and other cities) was mentioned at all, it was in cheerful terms that saluted the joyous philanthropy of the young and diverse people reimagining a new kind of society inside the ruins of the cold, inhumane cities of capitalist America.

Antifa, the primary street fighters, rarely got a mention except to deny that they actually existed – "Antifa," America was duly informed, "was merely an idea." Nor was there any talk, except in general and glowing terms, of the People's Militias that were bringing order with a human touch to the cities where the police – and even the municipal governments – had been defunded and abolished.

The closer to the center of the MLAZ they got, the fewer operating businesses there were, and at some point, there stopped being any stores at all. What was not destroyed was largely boarded up, but often the boards had been pulled off and the looters had gone inside and pillaged them. It was not just the stores that were trashed but every kind of business. Even an insurance agency lay in ruins, though it was unclear how peddling whole life had provoked the mob.

There were a small number of residences that had not been abandoned, and scared faces peered down from the few occupied apartments above the looted businesses. No normal people were out – the streets belonged to the denizens of the MLAZ. Most of them seemed to be bums or drunks, druggies or lowlifes lounging on filthy sidewalks, occasionally passed out or actively shooting up.

And then there were the authorities. The People's Militia, in their checked neck scarfs with their guns – many seemed police or even military issue – patrolled in loose bands. They would occasionally hassle people on the street. Similarly, Antifa crews would run down the middle of the vehicle-free roads, often stopping to lob a rock through the rare unbroken pane of glass or to spray-paint something on an undefaced surface.

Turnbull and George kept their heads down, shuffling along like they were just another pair of vagrants looking for a fix or a six-pack. George was good at deescalating most of the few hostile encounters with locals. The one encounter he could not deescalate involved a wild-eyed man with ruined teeth and sores on his face who demanded Turnbull's bag, and who was introduced nose-first to a brick wall by Turnbull...several times. Turnbull walked away from the unconscious man past a staring George, who said, "You don't have to keep hurting people."

"Sure I do," Turnbull replied. "And if this was overseas, he wouldn't still be breathing."

City Hall was completely taken over, primarily by People's Militia who guarded the perimeter. The US, Minnesota, and Minneapolis city flags were gone, of course. In their place flapped an anarchist flag, a multi-colored rainbow flag, and a red banner with a hammer and sickle.

Some Antifa members were actually protesting the People's Militia out front, claiming that "All government is oppression." Merrick Crane III looked out at them from an upper-floor window, annoyed. The black bloc types were useful now, despite their ridiculous stunts like this protest, but at the appropriate time those who could be taken within the People's Militia structure and organized to exercise real power in an effective way would be integrated. The rest would be eliminated. Adolf Hitler had done that with his own movement – Crane found *der Führer's* rise provided him with a cornucopia of lessons.

Crane had done a lot of thinking about who needed to be eliminated. And every time he turned his mind to it, more categories of dangerous obstacles to progress who needed to be removed came to mind. But that purification would have to wait until the struggle was complete. For now, all shades of leftism were useful.

He smiled, understanding the part he had played in bringing the situation to a head. He had reports from several cities that their branches of the People's Militia had taken over. Los Angeles was particularly successful, with Governor Newsom actually formally handing over law enforcement responsibility to the local People's Militia cadre after the dismantling of the LAPD and other law enforcement agencies in California and the opening of the prisons.

Crane was not in direct command of the individual branches, which he found annoying. The local cadres controlled the local branches of the People's Militia. This was against his Leninist principles, but he could tolerate the lack of a clear chain of command for now. Once the struggle concluded and the old order had been cast off, that would be the end of the decentralization of the movement. There would be one central authority; it went without saying who that would be. And he smiled, knowing that the means of accelerating and concluding that process was soon going to be in his hands.

Crane's eyes darted to the doorway as a young woman with half a head of long, straight green hair, and the other half close-cropped, entered the room. She wore the People's Militia keffiyeh.

Normally, Mr. Soto would have alerted to unexpected visitors, but he had already gone on ahead on a long journey of his own.

"Comrade Crane!" said Tania Cinque, who had adopted the title "Chief Facilitator" of the MLAZ after the mayor was ejected from the city a few weeks before. This was not her given name. Tania Cinque, aka Caitlin McCain, was a Connecticut grad student at Cornell whom Crane had suggested read a book on the Symbionese Liberation Army as part of her political awakening. She had adapted some of the members' *noms de guerre* as her own *nom de* revolutionary struggle.

Her face was marred by pocks and acne. She had listened carefully to his ideological instruction, but she had totally disregarded his expert advice regarding skin care.

"Comrade," Crane replied, turning from the window and using a greeting he found annoying. He noted how each collective across the country chose its own modes of address. The lack of standardization irritated him. He resolved that he would change that too once he assumed the title role in the coming dictatorship of the proletariat.

"I have so much to tell you. The work of administration is underway. We're creating a human-based, profit-free space in the MLAZ where every identity can fulfill xis, her, or his full potential. Just last night at our consensus council meeting, we guaranteed free health care, banned all expressions of racism, and validated Comrade Ilhan Omar's proposal to decriminalize and celebrate sibling unions."

Crane forced a smile. These councils were an exercise in political onanism where for several hours a procession of spotlight-seeking grievance mongers would whine, then the assembly would wiggle its fingers – applause being violence – to approve a variety of proposals ranging from inane to irrelevant to impossible.

Crane found it all tiresome. Power came from guns, guns used to kill one's enemies.

"I am curious about the status of our self-defense forces," he said.

Tania Cinque frowned. "We have been prioritizing human need," she explained.

"The war is upon us, Tania," Crane said gently. "And I told you to focus your efforts on preparing for that."

Tania Cinque's eyes began darting back and forth.

"We have over 40,000 comrades," she sputtered.

"But not all armed. And most of those are Antifa, which is not an effective fighting force. It is an effective mob."

"But there's no threat of invasion," Tania Cinque said. "The governor will not intervene, and the police agencies are gone. There are racist forces in the racist suburbs though, but they are not trying to invade us in force. We have time."

"You said 'in force.' Is the MLAZ secured?"

"There is some fighting on the south side. Several comrades have been killed. And today, someone ran over a comrade who was personing a roadblock."

"Going out or coming in?"

"Coming in."

"Then it appears we have an infiltrator. Have you alerted our forces?"

"Yes, it's a Lexus, and we found one with a dent on a grill parked several miles from downtown."

"I think it would be useful to find this infiltrator, this spy, and deal with him publicly."

"What if –," began Tania Cinque.

"What if what?" asked Crane.

"What if it's not a him. It could be a her. Or a non-binary."

Crane paused for a moment, remembering that the price of leveraging critical theory to spur the revolution was that some percentage of the resulting revolutionaries would take it far too seriously.

"The hate criminal will be a male-identifying. This kind of phallocentric systemic violence is uniquely patriarchal," he said, adding, "Once we have secured the revolution, we must redefine masculinity."

Tania Cinque smiled.

"Now," Crane said. "Find him."

They had walked quite a long way, passing mostly damaged buildings and shuttered businesses. Turnbull noted an empty pedestal of an installation dedicated to Minneapolis music legends that now consisted of nothing but ankles and feet – the statues of the performers had been sawed off at the legs. Under the multiple splashes of paint, he could still read the plaque and learn who had been deemed unacceptable. The answer puzzled him. The Replacements were notably pro-intoxicant, which should have been a plus, but were also especially cis, a negative. The punk trio Hüsker Dü was 66.667% LGBTQ, yet they had not survived this ideological purge. And Turnbull had no idea at all what Prince did to earn his statue's ignominious fate.

Scott George had his sources from coming down here before. Turnbull was both impressed and concerned by the number of folks who, upon seeing his companion approach, came over to seek a little something green. Most had nothing for him. One sketchy gentleman, however, assured him that he did.

They took shelter to talk inside a wrecked coffee shop. Inside, George handed $100 to the fidgeting man standing by the upturned counter in the ruined Starbucks. The man took the cash and jammed it in the front pocket of his brown corduroy trousers, then scratched his cheek. The guy had an Antonio Fargas vibe, if Antonio Fargas' great-grandfather had been from

Stockholm and if Huggy Bear had lost all his ladies and started snorting meth.

"I saw her in City Hall, I mean People's Hall," the junkie said. "Yesterday, and the day before. She's definitely around there."

"Is she in the People's Militia?" George asked. Turnbull, standing nearby with one eye on the questioning and one eye on the broken window they had come in through, frowned. This was not a Kelly Turnbull interrogation.

"I dunno," the junkie responded, a Minnesota accent coming through.

"Does she wear one of those stupid things around her neck?" Turnbull asked.

"Like a checker scarf?"

"Yeah, a checker scarf."

"I ain't seen her with one."

"Next question. Merrick Crane. You know him?"

"Who's he?"

"He's the big boss, the big enchilada. Is he in town?" Turnbull asked.

"Somebody important is in town, that's all I know."

Turnbull glanced at George. "You got anything more for Huggy Bear?"

George shook his head and the junkie made ready to go. Turnbull placed a meaty paw on his shoulder.

"We weren't here. If you tell someone about us, I will hunt you for sport. You got me?"

The junkie nodded.

"Go," Turnbull said. The junkie did not linger – he quickly slipped out through the broken plate glass window.

"If my guy is anywhere, he's around City Hall, or People's Hall, or whatever they're calling it. I guess we don't need to split up quite yet."

"What do you intend to do to your guy?" asked George.

"Share some love," Turnbull said. "You need to be more focused on how you get your kid out of here, assuming she even wants to go."

"I'll get her out," George assured him.

"Frankly, you got the worse mission," Turnbull said. "Rescuing people is a pain in the ass. Glad I don't have to do it."

"I'm still not even sure who you are," George muttered.

"Then I'm doing my job."

They approached City Hall, which was in the heart of downtown not far from the Mississippi River, from the south, passing the Hennepin County Medical Center. The lights were still on – for some reason, there was power, but Turnbull had no idea who was going to be paying their electric bills around here. The only activity was out in the parking lot. A painted sign said "FREE CLINIC," and there were a couple dozen people hanging around outside waiting.

"Single payer healthcare," George observed.

Turnbull said nothing – he stepped over a comatose bum and continued walking.

Approaching their target, they lingered in front of one of the high rises that surrounded the facility. The façade was riot-damaged, as it was on every building in the area. And it appeared to have been abandoned. Their position gave them a good view of the City Hall.

What was now called "People's Hall" was an ugly brown stone building with a greenish roof several stories high that opened to a large open square to the front. Turnbull noted the weird flags and the protesters protesting the other protesters. A ring of Jersey barriers encircled it, and People's Militia guards were walking the perimeter. They seemed more alert than he would expect – the ones whom they had passed over the last couple hours since the man versus sedan incident had been pretty lax and had not paid them any attention. Turnbull wondered if Crane being in town accounted for it, or worse, if they had been alerted to infiltrators.

"Maybe they have some sort of list of people in the MLAZ inside," George said. "A census or something."

"Yeah, these anarchists seem like they'd be conscientious record keepers," Turnbull sneered. "How have you been trying to find her before now anyway?"

"She kept going up into the city as the riots continued," George said. "Her mom and I tried to stop her but she's an adult. One day they declare the MLAZ and the police and the mayor get ejected and she stops even texting us. I mean, her cell still works and I keep paying the bill, but she doesn't answer my calls. She never came home and I came up here to look for her when you could still just drive into the city. Then they sealed it off and I just decided to sneak in. I've done it seven times."

"You ever find her?"

"No, but like you saw I have a lot of informants. Probably all lying to me."

"That's a good possibility," Turnbull said. "Hard to go wrong distrusting a junkie."

George looked pained. "I have to do something. It's not safe here."

Turnbull looked away from the worried father and surveyed the City Hall. Whatever answer he was seeking – there was no assurance his girl wasn't lying dead in some alley – this was not the place to find it.

"Look, there's not going to be some master list of Antifa members inside there, and even if there was, I doubt it will give us an address to her squat. I gotta go in and deal with someone. You gotta do what you gotta do."

"Can we just do a circuit around here and maybe we might see her?" George said. "She should be easy to spot."

George had shown him a photo of his kid on his Android, a nice-looking kid. Of course, now her brunette hair was dyed purple and she had a cast-iron ring through her nose that she told him that she installed to illustrate "the slavery of Christian oppression you and mom condemned me to." Apparently, there was a guy involved, of course, and the sheer cisnormativity of it was probably a scandal in her circle of comrades. Naturally, she met him at the University of Minnesota, where he was a teaching assistant in her mandatory Third World Studies 101 course.

"Sure, we'll shuffle around the circumference and see what we see. This front entrance is not looking enticing."

It was a good time to move. Down the block, a squad of People's Militia was hassling a pair of bums over something. They proceeded to beat the men to the ground with the butts of the shotguns that Turnbull suspected had been liberated from the police department's abandoned armory.

They continued on Third Avenue past the City Hall toward the ruins of the federal courthouse. That had gone up in flames very early in the rioting and after the feds had failed to defend it.

George tugged on Turnbull's jacket. "It's her," he said, pointing down the street. Turnbull's eyes followed, and yes, there was a splotch of purple above the shoulders of one of maybe a half-dozen black-clad figures clustered on a sidewalk, apparently sharing a joint.

George started to move toward them and Turnbull hesitated, glancing at the City Hall once more.

Their pal Huggy Bear from the ruined Starbucks was by one of the Jersey barriers having an animated conversation with a clump of People's Militia.

"Shit," Turnbull hissed, and he trotted after George, who was moving much faster than he looked capable of.

"Kendra!" he yelled. He was about 50 yards from the group. They did not seem to notice – people were screaming all sorts of things in downtown MLAZ all the time. So he yelled again.

"Kendra!"

The girl with the purple hair turned and squinted.

George waved, smiling. He trotted over to her, with Turnbull not far behind.

Her face registered her surprise, and then her expression hardened and she screamed, "You fascist piece of shit!"

George stopped, stunned.

"You asshole, you piece of shit fascist!" she howled. George was stricken, uncomprehending.

One of the males had an axe handle, and he stepped forward, joining in the screaming. Then the rest of the clique did too, adding their own torrent of obscenities to the barrage.

George looked at his daughter, his face pleading.

"Kendra," he said. Turnbull reached him.

"Fascist!" the male with the axe handle said, coming forward.

"Think it over hard," Turnbull said evenly.

"Come home," George pleaded to his daughter, whose face was a reddened knot of pure hatred.

"Get away from me, fascist. I hate you!" she spat.

The others were screaming louder now, and the one with the axe handle decided to move on George.

Turnbull was faster, and nastier. He grabbed the man's skinny arms as he tried to pull the axe handle back to swing, putting him off balance and exposing the side of his leg. Turnbull jammed his right boot into it hard from the side, and the crack was audible even over the man's high-pitched screaming. The ruined joint gave way and he fell, howling.

Turnbull stepped over him as another of the males pulled a chrome revolver from his black jacket.

Turnbull went into automatic mode, drawing and firing twice center mass in his chest before the shooter could get a lock. The rounds blew through him – he was skinny, probably thanks to the wonders of chemistry – and his corpse sailed backwards into the blood splatter.

Turnbull pivoted but the rest were running away shrieking, including Kendra. Turnbull leapt forward and caught her by the arm, jerking her around hard and bending close to her face.

"You're coming with us and you're not saying a damn word or I will break your neck," he snarled.

"Kelly!" George shouted.

Kendra twisted and flailed with her hands, smacking Turnbull in the face and shoulders, shouting profanities and threats.

"We're taking you home!" George said, but she looked at him with pure hatred.

"I hope they kill you!"

Turnbull saw the People's Militia coming from the City Hall enclosure, a dozen of them with Huggy Bear running along and pointing. He let Kendra loose – she stumbled, recovered and ran off with her friends – and Turnbull took up a two-handed stance and opened fire.

It was about 100 yards, but there was no more accurate .45 to be had. He targeted the ones in the front rank because he wanted the ones behind them to have a chance to rethink their notion that this was going to be easy. Blowing off the rest of the mag – there had been one in the pipe and eight in the chrome Wilson magazine – he dropped three of them. The rest hesitated and went to cover or ground.

"Come on," Turnbull said, grabbing George. "She's gone. We've got to go!"

"Kendra," the man yelled. It was in vain – she was running down the street, then she turned a corner and disappeared.

"Run!" Turnbull yelled, and George staggered forward.

Turnbull switched in a fresh mag and followed. There was return fire, high and above their heads, and Turnbull could hear their shouts and radio calls. He spun, and several were rising or coming out from behind cover. He suppressed them with four rapid fire rounds – he did not see any hit, but it disrupted their pursuit.

They ran down the street, and Turnbull had to pull George away from following his daughter.

"She's gone," he shouted again. Behind them, the pursuers were coming, and their volume of fire was increasing.

They rounded a corner, into an alley. It was packed with tents and lean-tos. Turnbull dodged a shopping cart piled high with junk, then stopped. There was an open door to a building down the alley.

"Get in," he said to George. The father, face streaked with tears, seemed uncomprehending. He could hear the shouts of the pursuers.

"In the tent, and shut the flap. They'll follow me. I capped their pals," he said.

"I won't leave you," George said.

"You're slowing me down, and you need to get away. There's something you have to do – you have to survive to get your daughter when she comes around. And I have to do something too. Get in!"

He pushed George into the nasty den.

"Pull the flap, let them go by," he said.

"Thanks," George whispered but Kelly was gone. He pulled the flap and thirty seconds later heard a herd of militia and others charging past.

Turnbull took aim from the doorway at the lead militiaman, who stopped in his tracks before the 230-grain round went through his neck from front to back. He collapsed and the others took cover. Turnbull was inside the building – it was some kind of Class B office space with lots of cubicles – before they recovered and returned fire.

Turnbull slammed and locked the door, then ran to the front of the building, but there were more bad guys out there, so he doubled back to the elevator and the door opened the moment he hit the button. He jumped inside and went to the third floor.

From there, he looked out the window. They were swarming all over the street outside, scores of them. Turnbull turned from the window and ran to the other side of the building, but a glance out the window there told him the same. He was surrounded. And he had only a couple mags left.

Not enough.

They were pounding on the door downstairs. It would not be long now.

Not a lot of options. He chose the least worst one.

He bet that guns were not the only police gear they would be using. It was a pretty risky bet.

He walked to the bathroom and rifled through his medical kit. There were several sizes of Band-Aids. He selected the 1" x 1" one and put it on the counter. Then he took out a small tube of antibiotic ointment, and also an unopened tube of super glue.

He had thought this idea through before, but never truly expected to need to use it. The pounding downstairs and the chaotic yelling made it clear this was the best of his few options – and it had the fringe benefit of also being the one that was likely to put him right where he wanted to be, face-to-face again with Merrick Crane III.

Besides the regular blade, his knockoff Swiss Army knife had a small cutting bade that he kept exceedingly clean and sharp, and that he never used. He would use it now. He left it open on the counter as he dug through his stuff for a small, two-centimeter-long metal cylinder with a small projection on the end. This he slathered in the antibiotic ointment. He did the same with his knife blade, and a patch of skin over the meat (but away from the veins) on the underside of his left wrist.

They were pounding of the locked door downstairs; not much time. He did not hesitate – the blade sliced through his skin. That hurt like hell, and it hurt even worse when he shoved the metal object into the cut, squeezed in a dollop of antibiotic, and then pinched the wound closed and sealed it with super glue.

There was a crash. They were inside.

There was blood, which he wiped off with tissue paper. That went into the toilet and was flushed. The ointment and glue went back in his med kit, which went back in his bag.

There were shouts and yelling, and the sound of feet on the stairs.

The Band-Aid went over the wound, the packaging into the trash.

He walked out of the bathroom and stood hands-up as the mob rushed into the room.

They tackled him, stripping him of his gear, handcuffing him with bracelets liberated from the police station, and roughly pulling a dark sack over his head after one of them clicked a photo of him with her cell. His only thought was that he found it amusing that there was still cell service in an area dedicated to the destruction of capitalism.

As they hustled him away, after the fifth time one of them called him a "fascist spy," he managed to lash out with an elbow. It felt like he connected with someone's teeth, but then he felt a rifle butt hit the back of his head and it was lights out.

Tania Cinque returned to Merrick Crane III's office with the good news. The infiltrator had been captured. She mentioned nothing about Scott George because none of the People's Militia leaders had mentioned him – no second spy, no embarrassing questions about the second spy getting away.

Crane was pleased, especially when Tania Cinque provided a texted photo of the agent.

"I think we've met before," he said, delighted. "I'm eager to get reacquainted."

But there were other things to do, other issues to address, so he put it off. He had calls with People's Militia leaders in other cities, and with Democrat officials in Washington. Things were moving quickly, but not quickly enough. Some of them were becoming aware of the need for decisive action now, when the chaos could be leveraged. Others were sadly unable to, or simply refused to, acknowledge that everything had changed.

Regardless, the spy was not going anywhere. Let him stew. He was doubtless some fascist flunky more valuable for the amusement he could provide than for any good information. But, after all, amusement was amusing.

And then his priorities changed completely when he got the call from the same woman who called earlier. It was the call he had been waiting for.

9.

It was the kind of problem he seemed to have all the time. Kelly Turnbull needed to get a decent amount of his own blood on the white tile floor, and he needed to get it there fast.

He had figured out he was sitting in one of the interrogation rooms of an old Minneapolis Police precinct. The new occupants had redecorated since the police force had been disbanded and the People's Militia took over. The white walls were covered in spray-painted graffiti of varying levels of artistic merit – right in front of Turnbull, it read "ACAB," meaning "All Cops Are Bastards," with the "A" the anarchy symbol. The cliché table that the detective and the suspect would verbally spar over in the movies was gone. Now there was the straight-backed chair in the center of the room that he was sitting on, and that was it except for the hood that they had kept over his head while bringing him there. It was now on the white tile floor in the corner where they had tossed it after ripping it off of his head.

There was no sparring with interrogators in the new regime. There was just confessing, incentivized however necessary.

One tormentor was right in front of him, a reedy, wild-eyed militia punk with a nose ring and bad skin, wearing a Soundgarden t-shirt and a keffiyeh around his pencil neck. He seemed volatile.

That helped make the blood on the floor problem easy enough to solve. It would just require a little pain. Turnbull looked up at the punk pacing back and forth in front of the wooden office chair that he was handcuffed to and addressed him, pleasantly.

"Hey, you know that when I was banging your mom last night, all she kept talking about was how much better I was than you. That is, when she could talk."

Simple and effective. The wild-eyed punk slugged him with all his might across the left side of his face and both Turnbull and the chair went down sideways onto the floor. The guy hit like a girl, Turnbull assessed, but his mouth filled up with blood anyway from where his molars had dug a trench across the inside of his cheek.

It was perfect. Just what he needed.

Wild Eyes was now yelling something obscene about Turnbull's mother, a pure hypothetical since she resided six feet underground, but Turnbull ignored him to focus on trying to figure out the spot on the floor that would likely be right under his wrists once the thug lifted him back up. Annoyed at the lack of reaction to the blow, Wild Eyes kicked him solidly in the gut, then shouted some more about Turnbull's mom's specialized sexual expertise. Turnbull disregarded the monologue and the pain. He was busy planning.

Turnbull chose his spot and spit out a huge glob of coppery red goo – a perfect hit, splattering nicely. The blood on the floor looked like bad art, but it was art with a purpose. Now they wouldn't notice the blood dripping from his wrist when he started using his fingernail to dig out the endpiece of the handcuff key he had slid into the cut and hid under a Band-Aid in anticipation of just this situation.

As expected, Wild Eyes pulled him and the chair off the floor and upright just about where Turnbull thought he would end up. The thug – Turnbull had not caught his name in the run-up to being dragged in here to await Crane – was breathing hard and little flecks of spittle quivered on his lips. But as much of a show as he was putting on, it was pretty clear the punk was terrified of his prisoner even though Turnbull was, for now, immobilized.

Maybe he wasn't as stupid as I thought, Turnbull considered. The guy was busy screaming incoherent obscenities. No, Turnbull decided, he *was* that stupid.

Wild Eyes' buddy, the calm one in a neat Patagonia vest – the company was a big supporter of the left and was an unofficial uniform of the punks – was leaning on the wall across the room by the bolted door, watching the prisoner carefully. He was afraid too, and it was clear that he wanted nothing to do with Turnbull. That was wise, considering what Turnbull had done to his friend's teeth even while restrained and hooded.

"You like that? You want more?" demanded Wild Eyes. He was hiding his fear behind his words. Turnbull would have been more concerned if the thug had just kept his mouth shut; silence enhances the mystery. Maybe the guy had some Irish blood in there somewhere – when he got angry, he reddened up like a Kennedy at an open bar on St. Patty's Day.

"No, that was plenty." Turnbull smiled. He didn't need the thug angry anymore. It wasn't fear that stopped him from antagonizing the goon further. It was simply that there was no sense in taking unnecessary damage.

"You think you're some kind of badass? You think you're going to be such a badass when Crane gets here?"

"Excuse me?" Turnbull replied, looking up. He hadn't really been paying attention to what the thug had been babbling about. He had been more concerned about how he was going to kill the calm one across the room once he got unhooked from the cuffs. But the mention of Crane showing up was of great interest.

"You got shit in your ears?" yelled Wild Eyes. "I asked you if you think you're some kind of badass!"

"Peter...," began the calm one, but Wild Eyes cut him off, pointing at Turnbull. As he did, Turnbull happily lifted up the Band-Aid, plunged his fingernail into his own skin and commenced digging at the cut he had superglued closed. He could feel his blood welling out of the hole.

It hurt a lot.

"Shut the hell up. I'm talking to this asshole." Peter was one of those tough guys who had never met a truly tough guy.

"We aren't supposed to talk to him until Crane gets here," the calm one said sensibly, but Peter was enjoying himself way too much. Turnbull pegged him as someone who delighted in exercising any power that might come his way. He had probably thrived on campus, with the administration behind him, hassling people for unwitting microaggressions. If the country hadn't started collapsing, he'd have probably found his calling in local government compliance work, doing things like pestering citizens for flying oversized flags off their porch.

"I want to know how this piece of shit became such a badass," Peter said, turning back to Turnbull and staring into his eyes. Wild-eyed Peter's fear had been overcome by his innate sadism. This was a grave tactical error.

"You don't look so badass now, do you?" he asked.

"No, I probably don't right this moment."

With Peter looming in front of him, the more intelligent thug across the room couldn't see the movement as Turnbull used his fingernail to work the key fragment out of the skin of his inner wrist. It really hurt.

"You look like shit," Peter declared. "You some sort of Special Forces Delta SEAL or something?"

"Delta wouldn't take me, and SEALs are Navy," Turnbull replied evenly, his cold eyes locked on Peter's. He did not mention his attendance at SERE school, the military's Survival, Evasion, Resistance, and Escape training program. It had involved a simulated interrogation exercise that was quite realistic and therefore quite unpleasant. Turnbull had nearly been dumped from the course for hurting one of the instructors, a particularly sadistic fellow who overstepped the broad latitude given SERE cadre to mimic real world scenarios, thereby allowing Turnbull to get a pass on his retaliation. The instructor would spend the rest of his life remembering Kelly Turnbull every time he put weight on his shattered knee.

Turnbull wanted Peter standing right where he was, so he was pleasant when he continued.

"I was Special Forces, sure, but that's really not where the ... talents ... you're talking about came from. I mean, it gave me some skills, but the skills are not really my secret."

"Your secret? Of how you're a military pig colonialist racist badass killer?" He said it all without irony, not imagining how stupid it sounded to normal ears.

Turnbull now had a hold of the short handcuff key he had embedded in his wrist. It was stuck in the healing tissue – he had to rip it out. He could feel pulling it out was doing a bit of damage to the meat but that was what it was. He was almost beginning to regret this scheme.

"Cuz you're a badass, right? You know some kind of special martial arts? Like mixed martial arts or something?"

"No, not really." Turnbull replied evenly. It was true. He could hold his own in a fight, but he wasn't some sort of mixed martial arts star. Too much finesse. He was mostly a "punch them until they became a bloody pulp" kind of guy. Not a lot of nuance.

The key came loose from his wrist's flesh. The pain was excruciating but necessary. Turnbull ignored it. Blood dripped out and dropped onto the floor right by where he spat the blood from Peter's punch. It blended in nicely, thereby hiding what he was doing with his wrist.

"You're like some kind of gun nut? You use exotic weapons and shit?" Peter's breath smelled of plaque and skunk weed, as well as the Axe body spray he'd bathed in that morning.

"No," Turnbull replied pleasantly as he gently maneuvered the key with the tips of his fingers. "I do prefer the classics – like the 1911A1. I like quality. You have my Wilson Combat. Top shelf weapon. I kind of like a gun that puts the target down on round one. I mean, I can pretty much use any weapon in the world, and I'm an okay shot. I know close quarter battle better than most. But there are lots of guys I've killed who were better at gunplay, technically speaking, than me."

Peter pulled up to his full 5'10 glory and regarded his captive with hands planted on his waist. Turnbull smiled, mostly because he had just worked out how he was going to kill the calm one. He had decided how he would take out wild-eyed Peter at least a half hour before. Sadly, he would have to wait around on the chair listening to this idiot until his real target showed up.

There was a noise – a cell phone in the pocket of the thug standing by the door. Peter looked over at his partner, who looked up and said, "It's Crane."

The thug put the Android to his ear. "This is Nathan. ... Okay. ... What's a Minot? ... Okay, we will."

Nathan clicked it off.

"He on his way?" Peter asked. Turnbull smiled a little.

"Nope. He's going out of town. He says to not to wait for him and to finish this one off."

As Peter started laughing, Turnbull sighed and slid the key into the lock of the left cuff behind his back, just like he had practiced hundreds of times in the past.

"Well, orders are orders," Peter said, broadly smiling.

"Wait, you're anarchists who take orders?" asked Turnbull. "You realize that makes you guys pretty shitty anarchists?"

Peter pondered this for a moment, then flushed with anger.

"The People's Militia is Marxist, not anarchist!" he said.

"Excuse me for not keeping your dipshit ideologies straight," Turnbull replied.

But, instead of getting angrier, Peter remembered that he still had the upper hand. He smiled a thin smile and leaned forward.

"Let's just take care of him," said Nathan, nervous.

"Shut up," Peter told his partner.

"Him? Your ally is assuming my gender and that makes me sad," Turnbull said, deadpan.

Peter ignored the jibe and came closer to Turnbull.

"You're pretty funny for a fascist," he told Turnbull. "What's not so funny is what we're going to do to you."

"Well, I'm pretty certain one of us is going to be laughing soon," Turnbull promised. Peter ignored him.

"Before we finish you off, I still want to know your secret for being such a badass," Peter said, smiling. "Cuz you don't look so badass right now, bitch."

Turnbull spat out some more blood, and turned the cuff key as he spoke, his voice covering the "click."

"You really want to know my secret, Peter?" Turnbull asked.

"Yeah, I do," Peter answered. Turnbull locked his eyes onto Peter's bloodshot peepers.

"My secret is that I always take the time to plan out how to kill whoever I meet."

The cuff fell open off his left wrist, and now freed, Turnbull leapt from his seat, his hamstrings powering him upward like a piston. The crown of his skull smashed into Peter's nose from below.

There was an audible crunch as the cartilage shattered, but Peter was too hurt to make any sound beyond a stifled groan as he staggered backwards, blood streaming from his face.

Nathan was stunned by the rapid assault, and Turnbull was already charging him even as the thug reached for the SIG P226 in his belt. Turnbull crossed the distance between them in about a second, swinging the open handcuff like a scythe. The pistol's barrel was almost clear of its holster when the end of the open cuff tore into the thug's throat. Turnbull completed the arc of his swing and his target's neck erupted in a cascade of red as the hook formed by the metal cuff tore out the thug's carotid artery.

Nathan went down to his knees, having forgotten about drawing his gun, both hands now desperately trying to staunch the flow of blood. It wasn't helping. Turnbull reached down and took the SIG and the extra mag, then pushed the gurgling Nathan over onto the floor.

It was looking like an abattoir in there now.

Peter had fallen and was now trying to get to his knees. Turnbull helped, grabbing him by the hair and pulling him up to his feet.

"Okay Peter, you got a weapon?" Turnbull did not wait for an answer. He patted down the punk. Clean.

"Remember how I promised that someone would be laughing? That would be me, but I'm going to put a hold on my chuckling for a bit while you stand there and bleed and not move, understand?"

Peter stood unsteadily as Turnbull removed the remaining cuff and tossed it onto the crimson-flecked tile. It clattered across the floor.

"How's your nose?" Turnbull asked. "Bet it hurts."

Peter's eyes were watering.

"Get the hood and wipe off the blood," Turnbull ordered. As Peter shuffled away, he turned his attention to his wrist. It was a mess. He pushed the bandage back over it.

Peter wiped off most of the blood. Turnbull grabbed him, pulled him close and shoved the pistol under his jaw.

"Here's how this goes, dummy," he began. "You yell, you die. You go for my gun, you die. You fail to do exactly what I tell you, you die. You annoy me, you die. Do you have any questions about what things will lead to you dying?"

Peter shook his head.

"Good," Turnbull said. "Where are we?"

"The People's Militia station," he managed to reply.

"I know that part. Where in the building are we?"

"Second floor. No, third."

"Do you want to think about it, Peter, because guess what you do if you guess wrong? Here's a hint. Bang."

"Second floor."

"Okay, which way to the elevator you brought me up on? Is it to the right?"

"To the right."

"And where is my stuff?"

"Locked in an office," Peter said.

"You got an office? And you can lock it? They just handed you over the keys when the police got abolished?" Turnbull asked.

"Yeah," Peter said, confused about why that might seem odd.

"Come on," Turnbull said, pulling the thug along roughly.

Turnbull paused to get Nathan's cell phone. It needed a fingerprint to open, and he used the corpse's digit to do it as Peter watched. Turnbull memorized the number of the last call coming in and then tossed the phone into the corner.

"Open the door," Turnbull directed. Peter walked to the door and put his hand on the handle.

"Careful," Turnbull warned, the SIG pressed against the base of his captive's skull.

Peter pulled the door open and the smell hit them, a heady brew of urine, sweat, and worse. The hallway was dingy and dark, and covered with graffiti. There were voices, but not excited ones. Turnbull held Peter by the collar and stepped out of the room, keeping his pistol out of sight. A pair of young women with keffiyehs were walking down the hall in animated conversation. Turnbull caught only a snippet – something about "that sexist whore bitch" – and paused to gauge their reaction to him and Peter.

There was none – the women walked by the pair without a second glance. The nice thing about anarchy is that disorder can be exploited – and the lack of uniforms meant necessarily that everyone *not* in a uniform was, effectively, in uniform, even if none of them looked the same.

He pushed Peter ahead of him down the hallway to the right, past a long black spray-painted monologue about how capitalism would collapse. The last word in the diatribe, "pigs," happened to fall on an office door.

"Here," Peter mumbled.

"Open it," Turnbull replied, glancing both ways. At his feet, a man in cargo shorts and with no shoes on was sleeping on the floor, his torso half-submerged in some putrid liquid. Peter dug around in his pockets and came up with a key. He stuck it in the lock and pushed the door to the dark office open.

He went in first and Turnbull followed, flicking on the light. After a couple steps toward the desk, Peter lunged forward and Turnbull lost his grip on the t-shirt. It was clear what Peter was going for. The Wilson .45 was there on the desk, beside a tall, violet glass bong and a half-empty bag of Doritos.

He almost reached the weapon, but Turnbull was faster, bringing the butt of the SIG down on the back of Peter's neck. There was another crunch – for all his posturing, the anarchist was rather fragile – and Peter fell to the ground twitching, the nerves below the severed C6 vertebra still firing.

Turnbull closed the door and went over to the desk. Peter stopped his involuntary movements as Turnbull gathered his gear. After using his medical kit to close up the wound on his wrist, he liberated Peter's keffiyeh, noting the ugly maroon welt on the back of Peter's neck where he had shattered the unfortunate punk's spinal column.

"I told you, dummy," he said as he left the office with his stuff, shutting the door behind him and gingerly stepping over the gentleman who had slept through all the recent unpleasantness. His gun was holstered; in his right hand he carried Peter's purple bong.

He got a few steps down the hall and saw up ahead a pack of four militia types approaching with long guns liberated from the cops. They seemed more focused than the average drones, and Turnbull pivoted right and pushed open an ajar door as he stepped inside. They passed by outside as he stood inside the room. There were a number of flags leaning against the wall, American flags and Gadsden flags, and a variety of gear, including tan plate carriers with Punisher skull patches, "Molon Labe" shirts, and a couple of faded "Make America Great Again" hats. Despite feeling quite at home for the first time since entering Minneapolis, Turnbull wondered why the People's Militia had a storeroom full of right-wing clichés.

KURT SCHLICHTER | 155

He put it out of his head – the hallway was clear and it was time to go.

He made his way to the front of the first floor. Since he looked like shit, unshaven, unkempt, and battered, he fit right in with the occupants of the deserted police station. The militia crew was trying to present the image of order and discipline, with the cadre instructing the amateurs and trying to instruct the street criminals. There was a desk up front where citizens could come in and petition the militia for the redress of grievances. Mostly, the few community members who came by hoping the People's Militia would keep order as promised ended up being lectured about their greed for not being grateful over having their stuff stolen or for their racism, sexism, and/or transphobia demonstrated by their not wishing to be assaulted.

Turnbull walked through the middle of teeming masses occupying the squad room. He noted that most had very bad skin. No one paid him much mind at all. That is, until he got near the front door, where a bleary-eyed gentleman with no shirt stepped in front of him and asked, "Hey, smoke me out, man?"

Turnbull handed him the bong, and the stoner held it in his hands, a purple glass object of wonder. When he looked back up, the stranger had gone. He looked back at his gift and treasured it.

Outside, it was getting dark. In front of the precinct, the buildings up and down the road were largely burned out or boarded up. Antifa members walked to and fro, with a fat woman in a black tank top and jeans shorts screaming into a mic across the street. The amps were cranked and her voice distorted, but apparently, she had some beefs with her dad. He apparently did not get her and therefore had to die. A couple teen-aged girls sat listening and nodding, but it was unclear if they were moved by the orator's passion or merely stoned out of their gourds.

There were a fair number of armed People's Militia types milling about, one with a rainbow Punisher skull patch on his tan plate carrier rig. He had an AR15 and several tattoos of a sexually ambiguous Mickey Mouse on his arms. It was, apparently, a theme, though why it was his theme Turnbull neither knew nor cared to find out. He assessed the Mouseketeer as a target, made a plan on how to kill him if he became an active threat, and moved on down the street, quietly whistling "M-I-C, K-E-Y, M-O-U-S-E."

Getting out of the MLAZ was not that difficult. It was certainly easier than getting in. He walked to the suburbs, talking his way through People's Militia checkpoints. They saw the keffiyeh, and they saw he did not look like someone to mess with, and they did not dig deeper into his allegiance. Outside the ring of leftist checkpoints, he paused by a traffic light to assess his transportation situation. While he waited, he called Deeds and gave him the cell number from Nathan's phone.

"The only info I have is that there's something going on in Minot," Turnbull said. "I think that's in North Dakota. Unless there are other Minots out there."

"The location on the phone number is coming back," Deeds said after nearly a minute. "That cell call came as the phone was moving north on State Route 52, right toward Minot, North Dakota." He did not need to add that the phone and cracked SIM chip probably went out the window right after the hang up.

"The only thing I know about Minot is that there's a big Air Force base there," Turnbull said.

"A nuke base, Kelly."

"What, is he going to launch a Minuteman ICBM?"

"We don't know. That's the problem. Get up there. Find out. Stop him."

"I'm on the way," Turnbull said, eyeing an SUV pulling up to the stop light. "I think I have transport."

He hung up and stepped into the street. The gray Toyota idled, the driver a pink-haired twenty-something with a putative male in the passenger seat. In the back seat were ten overflowing grocery bags. There was lots of soda, chips, and beer, the kind of carb-rich treats the state was not delivering to them.

Turnbull tapped on the window, and instead of gassing it, the woman rolled down the window.

"People's Militia, requisitioning this vehicle," he told her.

"Oh, we're People's Militia too. This is a food run," the woman said, smiling. She had a keffiyeh on, as did her partner.

"We requisitioned it from the pigs in the suburbs," the one in the passenger seat that probably identified as male announced smugly. Their MO was to go to the grocery stores in the liberal suburbs – the ones in the city having been looted and destroyed – and demand "reparations" under the threat of the People's Militia paying them a visit. Most paid the tribute.

"I'm still requisitioning this ride. Get out," Turnbull said.

"But...." the driver began and then Turnbull's pistol was in her face.

"I'm decolonializing this vehicular paradigm," Turnbull said. "So don't make me shoot you because then your buddy is going to have to clean it up and if you saw *Pulp Fiction* you know you don't want to be Travoltaing it out here tonight."

Their expressions were blank – the movie was released long before they were born and they never watched traditional movies anyway – the male actually had his iPhone in-hand and had been watching a YouTube video on how liberating children from the oppression of age of consent laws was the next great rights struggle.

"Get out or I will shoot you," Turnbull said, rephrasing his command. They complied.

"Keys," Turnbull demanded. The crying female handed them over, as the crying male looked on.

"But it's my parents' car," she said miserably.

"You should probably call the cops," Turnbull said as he slipped behind the wheel and slammed the door shut behind him. "Oh, right. Minneapolis abolished its police. Bummer."

Then he pulled the keffiyeh off over his head and tossed it out the window at their feet. With them both looking on slack-jawed, he hit the gas.

Minot was about eight hours away.

10.

Even on the empty plains, it seemed tense.

Turnbull was very much alone on I-94 as he tore across the cold, windy flatlands. The power grid was on in some places, off in others. Traffic was very light, lighter than he would expect even at night. It was the missing trucks that he noticed. There were so few now, and there should have been more, many more.

He considered the consequences. Once the trucks stopped rolling, the food stopped getting delivered. Normal people would run out of food. With nothing in the grocery stores to "requisition," the People's Militias were certain to get even more vicious as they got hungry and rub up against the suburbs and countryside. And the Provisionals would push back.

There were about two million members in the US military. And 100 million Americans owned guns. No one was keeping the peace if the people didn't want the peace kept.

"Great," he muttered. On the upside, it was not snowing.

At 9:00 p.m., he flipped on the radio and ran through the stations looking for news. It took him a while. He hit four country stations, two Spanish stations, a Somali one, he guessed, and finally some guy just talking in English.

"We apologize for not having the Trump News feed, but it's not coming through the satellite," the announcer – who was probably a board operator having to talk on-air on the fly – said. "And we have no *Teddy King Show* today either, for some reason." The station abruptly shifted back to ads for local farm supplies and bankruptcy lawyers for several minutes, as if people were buying farm supplies and hiring bankruptcy lawyers right now. It was like hearing a message from the past.

Turnbull glanced down and saw that he needed gas. There was a town improbably called Fergus Falls ahead. He saw some lights back off of the freeway, and he took the Exit 54 off-ramp. There was a Comfort Inn just above the interstate, but its sign was not on.

Turnbull braked. Two cop SUVs with flashing red and blue lights, and several pick-ups, blocked the road at the top of the rise before the intersection with West Lincoln Avenue, which ran perpendicular to the freeway and was apparently one of Fergus Falls' main drags.

This was no surprise. Several, if not most, of the off ramps on along the way north from Minneapolis had been posted as "EXIT CLOSED," sometimes with trucks or police vehicles blocking them.

Turnbull slowed approaching the checkpoint as an Otter Tail County sheriff with a tactical vest and an AR15 slung across his chest approached, right palm up and a flashlight in his left hand. There was another deputy with another long weapon by one of the SUVs, and at least a half-dozen men with varying degrees of tactical gear and various weapons – hunting rifles, shotguns, and even one guy with a FAL rifle tricked out with an optic and a rail.

Those weapons were not slung.

Stopping, Turnbull switched the vehicle off and put his hands on the top of the wheel nice and slow as the deputy walked up and knocked on the window. Slowly, very slowly, Turnbull took his left hand off the steering wheel and dropped it to the window button. As the window opener whirred, a blast of cold air hit him in the face.

"Evening, deputy," he said.

"You need to slowly back up down the off-ramp and keep going," the deputy said.

"I need gas."

"You can get gas on down the road. Barnesville, Fargo."

"I'm not going to make it to Barnesville, much less Fargo."

"You go on and give it a try."

Turnbull sighed. "Look, deputy, do I strike you as Antifa?"

"You strike me as a stranger." The cop flashed his light into the cab and it settled on the Wilson .45 in Turnbull's holster.

"Gun!" he yelled, stepping back.

Turnbull's hands went into the air as the better part of a dozen weapons pointed at him.

"I'm a federal officer on duty," Turnbull said calmly. The deputy was pointing a Glock at him. "Can I show you my ID?"

"I need you out of the vehicle," the deputy said. "Slowly."

"Left hand to the door latch," Turnbull said.

"Slooooowly," the deputy reiterated, dragging out the vowel.

"Like pond water," Turnbull said. He very carefully opened the door and, keeping his hands plainly in sight, stepped out of the car and into the cold.

"Hands on the roof."

Turnbull complied. The deputy removed the Wilson from his holster.

"There's a SIG in my waistband too," Turnbull said. He had kept Nathan's piece.

"Lou," the deputy said. The other sheriff's deputy moved forward and took the .45.

Now, the deputy removed the SIG and Turnbull's wallet too.

"Turn around." Turnbull did so, hands up.

Lou was admiring the 1911. "Wilson Combat CQB," he said, whistling. "Damn Jesse, this guy's got a fine gun." He sniffed it. "Been fired recently."

"I've been busy," Turnbull admitted.

"Looks like it. Who hit you in the piehole?"

"A guy who is sorry he ever met me. Or would be, if he wasn't dead."

"Christian Collins, DHS," Jim read off of an identification card from the wallet. He confirmed that the photo and description matched Turnbull.

"That's not really my name," Turnbull said. Jim looked up. Lou's radio crackled and he cupped his earpiece.

"It's not his Toyota either. It's registered to a Mike and Holly Hampton of Eden Prairie, Minnesota."

"Yeah, I requisitioned it from a couple of People's Militia punks in Minneapolis," he said. "They were on a food run. I guess it became a food walk, except I kept the food, so it became just a walk."

Deputy Jim's flashlight illuminated the backseat and the sacks of stolen groceries.

"That's a lot of carbs," Jim said. "So, what's your story?"

"Can I put my hands down?"

"No. Why are you here?"

"I've got to get to Minot ASAP."

"Why?"

"Well, I can't say, but I wouldn't be going to Minot if there wasn't a damn good reason, would I?"

"He's got a point," Deputy Lou said, still examining the Wilson. Deputy Joe ignored him.

"How do we know you're for real? You already told us this is a fake ID."

"I told you it's a fake name. It's a real ID. Run it with Homeland Security. If anyone can run anything right now."

Joe considered it for a moment, then passed the ID to his comrade. "Give it a shot," he said.

Lou shrugged and walked off to the cab of his SUV, talking into his mic.

"Can I put my hands down now?"

"Sure. Just be cool."

"Yeah. Tell your buddies here to be cool and not point their weapons at me."

"They're Provisionals, all sworn in by the sheriff," Deputy Joe said. He cocked his head, never taking his eyes off Turnbull. "Hey, fingers off the bang switch, guys."

The Provisionals relaxed just a bit.

Turnbull relaxed just a bit too, but kept his movements slow and deliberate. He noted that it was getting really cold.

Lou returned from his Explorer. "There's a Christian Collins in DHS and this same picture is in the system as this ID."

"So, if I can have a fake ID from DHS, I'm probably something echelons above DHS. Now can I get some gas?"

"Why did you tell me it was fake?"

"Because you local guys have common sense and intuition, unlike most feds, and you would have pegged me as all kinds of wrong. I mean, I am splattered with blood and I have a high-speed .45. So why not go with the truth?"

"You are wrong as hell," Jim said, handing back the wallet. "Lou, give him his ID." Lou proffered the card, which Turnbull took.

"My pieces?"

"On your way out of town," Joe said. "Just so everyone stays cool."

"Fair," Turnbull conceded. Down below on the freeway, a big rig roared past, the first vehicle in several minutes.

"You follow me to the Cenex up around the corner and fill up. We still have power but who knows for how long," Joe said. "You got a credit card or is that fake too?"

"Uncle Sam is my sugar daddy. He's good for it. At least, I think he still is."

"You sure?" asked the deputy. "Everything is going to hell."

"That why you've blocked off the town?"

"We're a good two-and-a-half hours out of Minneapolis and they hit us here once. Seven or eight carloads of them, People's Militia and their friends. There was a shootout. After that, we mobilized, formed a Provisional unit. We have lots of vets and deer hunters. Then they came back for another go 'round. That went badly for them."

"How badly?"

"We got a lot of remote corn fields here in Otter Tail County," Deputy Joe said. "No outsider will ever find you."

"It was a good day," Turnbull said, recalling a popular *Twilight Zone* episode that involved consigning offenders to a cornfield.

"But I did have to use my AK," replied Deputy Joe. "Love me some Ice Cube, especially after he went for Trump."

"I'll take that gas now," Turnbull said. Fifteen minutes later, fueled up and with his weapons back in hand, he was back to rolling up the endless plains toward Fargo and, beyond that, Minot.

"I'm 30 minutes out," Turnbull said. He had mated the phone to the Toyota's Bluetooth and was talking to Deeds while watching the road. North Dakota in the dark was not significantly different than western Minnesota in the dark, except it was colder. There were now patches of snow on the ground – it had been an unusually warm fall so far, which meant it was merely cold as opposed to cold as hell.

"I reached out through official channels to the base commander, General Gough. He's expecting you. Use your real name – no time for games."

"Is he one of us?"

"He's reliable."

"You mean red?" Turnbull said.

"That's right," Deeds said. "He's Constitutional Alliance, and he's ignoring those NMUC guys. We're lucky – not all generals are."

"Notice how we slipped into having a side? I've noticed."

"I think the restore the status quo option was nixed by popular demand," Deeds replied wearily. "The situation is deteriorating."

"Yeah, I noticed. How bad is it elsewhere?"

"It's not just Minneapolis. Seattle, San Francisco, LA, all under People's Militia control. Governor Newsom signed an order to do it in all of California. He's allied the state with the National Military Unity Council generals. There's pushback though – the loyal Army units out of Ft. Irwin and Marines out of Pendleton are alerted to move into the LA basin."

"So some places it's sort of an official thugocracy? That's bad. How's New York City? Is it out of control too?"

"New York is always out of control. De Blasio won't leave office. He declared himself 'Comandante' and he's fortifying the city. The media is thrilled," Deeds said. "And that's not all. The red states are mobilizing."

"This General Gough – what's his deal?"

"He's got a few thousand nuclear weapons and his deal is to ensure none go off while we settle this crisis."

"Seems weird to be saying this over open lines."

"I don't think anyone is listening anymore. Everyone is either at home huddling with their families or at home cleaning their guns," Deeds said.

"No, a lot of folks are out and in motion. Trust me."

"Get to Minot and stop whatever the hell that sonofabitch Crane has in mind."

"With extreme prejudice," Turnbull said, hanging up.

11.

The front gate at Minot Air Force Base was back somewhere behind a gaggle of Humvees and armed guards in ACU camouflage and carrying M4s. They seemed agitated.

Turnbull drove up to them, very slowly.

A security police sergeant, identifiable by the stripes on his jacket, approached him.

"Base is closed. Turn around."

"I'm expected."

"By who?"

"By your general. Call him."

"What's your name?"

"My name is a long story. Just tell him his guest is here. He'll know me."

The verification process took about five minutes, and he got a hummer escort to lead him through the empty streets of the dark, frigid base.

Total lockdown. Nothing was moving except the occasional SPs on patrol in a hummer or a blue and white SUV with a light bar.

The headquarters was guarded as well, with miserable airmen out front stamping their feet in the cold. Turnbull was met by a lieutenant and walked directly upstairs to the general's office. It was warm inside, which was nice.

General Gough seemed frazzled.

"Have you found Colonel Sykes?" he shouted at the LT escorting Turnbull. It was probably the general's aide-de-camp.

"No sir," the young officer replied. He was awkwardly wearing a pistol. "He's not answering his cell either."

"Find him!" the two-star shouted, and the lieutenant turned and fled. The flag officer turned toward his guest. "Well?"

"You understand what I'm here for?" Turnbull said.

"Some commie terrorist asshole is trying to get on my base? Not happening." The general had a weird badge that looked like a rocket above the "U.S. AIR FORCE" nametape on his ACU uniform. He was missile qualified. That meant he spent a lot of time on the buried Minuteman III ICBM command posts out on the prairie that he now oversaw as the unit commander.

"If I were you, I'd send a car around to your Colonel Sykes' quarters and make sure Merrick Crane hasn't gotten to him," Turnbull said.

"Sykes is my executive officer, and he lives off-post. I'll have it done. Though I'm not really concerned. I'm relieving him."

"Why?" asked Turnbull.

"I don't trust him. He's been sleeping with a subordinate and he's been going downhill since his latest pass over for promotion. Perfect is our standard, and he's not."

"Your HR issues are your problem. Merrick Crane is a terrorist leader and he's headed here and your base is the only thing that is here, so I need to find him. And this is where he'll be."

"No one's getting into my base. It's locked down tight," replied the general.

"You've got a lot of fence line to watch."

"And I have the highest security you can imagine. Like I said, perfect is the standard. You know what we do here. Nukes, and lots of them. Gravity bombs, cruise missiles, Minuteman ICBMs. Every inch of ground is monitored and observed and we have a boatload of security police. No one is getting in here. Not your terrorist, nobody."

"Anything else around here he might be interested in?"

The general looked at Turnbull as if he were mad. "You saw Minot coming in. There's nothing here for miles except used car dealers and chain restaurants. And cold. They call this base 'the Frozen Hell.'"

"Charming," Turnbull said. "The missile silos are out on the prairie. Can he get into one?"

The general laughed. "Besides video and other monitoring, the launcher closure door, the cap for the silo, is about 110 tons."

"I don't think Crane has that kind of upper body strength. He wants something here, and it's got to be something to do with a hot rock. But what the hell is it?"

"Roger, sir," the sergeant said, passing the ID back through the window. He recognized the officer but always asked for identification. In the nuke world, perfect was the standard. "Let him through!" the NCO shouted to his men, and then turned back to the driver. "They have been looking for you."

"And here I am," the officer grunted.

Colonel Ulysses Sykes accelerated his Honda Civic through past the security police Humvees and through the gate into Minot Air Force Base. The headquarters was ahead, but he did not turn into its parking lot. He kept going down the road, directly toward the 5th Support Squadron's complex near the airfield.

Two phones sat on the passenger seat. One was his personal phone, and it was off. No doubt the general had had his minions calling him and the voicemail box was probably full of increasingly desperate pleas that he report for duty. The other phone was his burner. He had had it for a while, plugging it in nightly from 2100 to 2200 hours in his off-post condo just in case the call would come.

It came, along with his opportunity to strike a blow against the racist paradigm that he had served for so long before his new girlfriend – a 25-year-old captain, gorgeous by Air Force terms, and wise enough to see the merit in the 47-year-old colonel that the Air Force had not – had helped him become woke. His whole career had been serving a lie based on white supremacy and – what was the word she used? – "cisnormativity" – and that phone call had led him here to tonight, when he would make amends for his twenty-six years of complicity.

Who would have thought that when he walked in on his wife – now ex-wife – with the plumber and watched for a while, it would have led here? Sure, his former wife had mocked him, but this action would show her and the USAF and everyone else that Ulysses Sykes was not some pathetic clown. Then, after this was all over, he and his 25-year-old paramour would be together, the Air Force a vague and fuzzy memory.

The parking lot was silent when he got out of his Civic – in fact, the whole base was as quiet as a tomb, other than the wind. Usually, you could count on hearing the roar of one of the 5th Bomb Wing's giant B-52H bombers lumbering down the runway. But not tonight.

Instead, a trio of Stratofortresses stood silently on the airfield side of the 5th Support Squadron's building. More were parked down the tarmac.

He collected his phones and got out. Sykes shivered a little in his flight suit and adjusted the Beretta pistol on his belt as he walked back toward the trunk.

A flick of the button on the key opened the lid. Merrick Crane III rose from the trunk and climbed out onto the asphalt.

"How do you tolerate this icebox?" he growled. His skin was suffering terribly from the frigid conditions.

"If we hadn't stolen it from the indigenous First Peoples, we would not even be here," Sykes replied, awaiting acknowledgment from Crane.

Crane rubbed his arms and considered his response to the colonel's expectant gaze.

"Of course," he replied. "And we will be happy to give it back, once we have defeated the right-wing fascists."

"It's in here," Sykes said, shutting the trunk lid and pointing toward a side door under a lonely, bare light. A sign read "SPECIAL SECURITY AREA – ABSOLUTELY NO ADMITTANCE TO UNAUTHORIZED PERSONNEL. DEADLY FORCE AUTHORIZED."

"Did you confirm that everything is underway?" Crane asked.

"Yes, on the way here. Everything is according to plan so far. The alert actually made it simpler. The civilians are not allowed on post, and all non-essential personnel are restricted to quarters. So, it's only the people on the duty roster here, and I prepared the duty roster."

They got to the door. Sykes took off his left glove to punch in the access code on the key pad. Crane's hand fell to the Walther's butt, just in case the colonel had not fulfilled his end of the arrangement.

The door opened, and they left the cold to enter a long, white hall lit by fluorescent lights. At the far end, decorated with more signs warning dire consequences to those violating the sanctity of the space, was another door and a guard post. The guard inside, an airman with an M4 leaning against the wall, smiled and simply buzzed them in, not asking for ID or why the suave civilian was accompanying the colonel into one of the most secure facilities in the United States of America.

The support operations center was a large room with several monitors and many desks. There were about 15 people inside, all uniformed, some armed, and all smiling as Sykes and Merrick Crane entered.

"Thank you," squealed a short and stocky lieutenant, a female whose nametape read "GANZ." "This is the most impactful thing I've ever done."

Sykes scanned the assembled personnel for one face in particular, and he found her. She was in a flight suit, and when she saw his eager smile she smiled back.

"Ashleigh," he said.

"Uly," she replied. "I knew you would validate yourself and bring us this ally." Sykes overcame the urge to run to her and take her in his arms.

"Hello again, Ashleigh," Crane said, and she smiled shyly. Sykes involuntarily felt a pang of jealousy, but he understood that Ashleigh and Crane had met while she was a cadet at the Air Force Academy doing an independent study semester focused on diversity issues in military leadership. He had been her mentor in developing a revolutionary consciousness, Ashleigh had explained, and nothing more.

"Time to do what we came to do, don't you think, Ulysses?" Crane said pleasantly.

Sykes nodded. "All right," he said, eager to take charge, to be seen as taking charge. "Flight crew, prep zero-zero-nine but no engine start until loading is complete."

"It's fueled up," said the master sergeant in charge. "We ran diagnostics. Turn the key and it will go."

Sykes nodded and continued. "Loaders, stand ready and ordnance, you come with me into the Pit. Remember, when we cross the threshold, the alarm goes off. I will make the false alarm call, but we'll have maybe ten minutes to do what we have to do. Then we all load up."

Crane was watching a thin sergeant who seemed to be nervous. As Sykes spoke, the sergeant was whispering to the master sergeant with increasing intensity.

"You," Crane said. "Do you have a problem?"

Sykes, and the rest, were silent. The sergeant stared back.

"No," he mumbled.

"I think you have a problem," Crane said.

"This is crazy," the sergeant blurted out. "You can't do this."

"So, you think we should let this racist, sexist Nazi regime just go on oppressing womxn, blackx and latinx peoples?" Crane said gently, pronouncing the terms.

"We can't do this!" the sergeant said.

"You mean *you won't* do this?" Crane replied evenly. The audience was transfixed. "You just aren't committed."

"I am, but not like this."

Crane, delighted by this turn of events, turned to Sykes. "What does this person do?"

"He's part of the maintenance crew."

"And I gather from what I heard that the plane is already maintained?"

Sykes nodded.

"Good," said Crane, drawing out the Walther and shooting the sergeant in the gut. The man fell to the tile floor moaning, clutching his abdomen. Crane walked over to him.

"He was not committed," Crane said, shooting the man again in the forehead. The moaning and the movement ceased. "Now, you are all committed. Accomplices, to what the prison-industrial state would call murder, but what in a just society would be considered an act of political hygiene."

Sykes stood there, staring at the body of the sergeant. Like all the personnel in the 5th Support Squadron ops center, Sykes had personally recruited him into their clique. At Ashleigh's urging, he had carefully sought out like-minded thinkers, gauging their commitment, bringing them slowly around until they were willing to throw in with a plan that went against everything they had been trained to do as Air Force airmen in general and Personnel Reliability Program-cleared personnel in particular.

And this sergeant had betrayed him, *embarrassed* him. He was not unhappy that the man was dead, but he was very unhappy that Ashleigh had seen that he failed.

"Follow me," he told the technical crew, reasserting his diminished authority. "We're going into the Pit. Move, everyone."

Crane holstered his pistol, and the airmen gingerly stepped over the heap on the linoleum. Some went out toward the door marked "FLIGHT LINE" while the rest filed along behind Sykes. Crane followed.

The Pit was the secure underground storage section of the Support Squadron building,

There were multiple key pads for entry, and multiple guard posts, but since Sykes had manipulated the duty schedule the guards were all part of their little team. At a cargo elevator, a dual validation process became necessary. Lieutenant Ganz and Colonel Sykes, standing at terminals over twelve feet apart, simultaneously used their access keys to enter. Six people went down into the depths, plus Crane. It was the first time in over sixty years that a civilian not connected to the United States government had taken that ride.

The enormous cargo elevator was 30' long and 20' wide, and 15' tall, with double doors at each end. The doors on the opposite end opened once it stopped in the basement – there were only two floor buttons – and it opened into and underground chamber with concrete floors and cinderblock walls. They stepped out, none bothering to take the radiological badges that rested in a basket under the sign warning their use was mandatory.

Sykes glanced up at the cameras. He knew the feeds were going to empty guard posts. He smiled for the benefit of the analysts who would be poring over these tapes soon enough.

Directly before them was a dark gray AGM-86B air-launched cruise missile resting on a motorized cart with a tech sergeant fussing over it. It was about 21 feet long and two feet wide, with two stubby swept-back wings poking out about six feet at the middle. The front was rounded off, and at the rear end was a tail and a jet engine intake nozzle.

The tech sergeant, whose nametape said "BETTS," was sweating as he looked over the visitors to his dungeon.

"I picked BGXM472," he said. "All its diagnostics are good. It's not one of the fueled ones though. You said it didn't need to be fueled."

"It doesn't," Crane said. The tech looked at the civilian, still unnerved that he was in here in the Pit, where two dozen immediately ready ALCM's were kept right below the flight line in the event that they needed to be loaded on the B-52s fast. The rest were miles away in other bunkers.

"If I have to arm it," Arnold Betts said, "that's another 30 minutes."

"No," Sykes said, stepping in to take charge. "Just bring the terminal." The portable terminal that plugged into the missile underneath an access panel was in an OD green backpack on the floor. "Let's move."

His people knew their job. They had practiced it again and again and knew exactly how to get the weapons down here up there to the planes and mounted on the wing hardpoints quickly. And since there was no need to fool around with targeting, it was simply a move-up, hook-up job.

One airman grabbed the control pad for the motorized cart – the missile weighed about a ton and a half – and rolled it slowly into the cargo elevator. Betts grabbed his backpack and joined them.

As the double doors swooshed closed and the elevator began hefting its heavy load up to ground level, Sykes turned to Crane, who was watching with some interest as the crew inspected the cruise missile for faults or damage, just as they had been trained to do. It amused him, as he had no intention of launching the rocket.

He was only interested in the passenger nestled inside the front few feet of the fuselage.

"When we push this out of the elevator upstairs," Sykes said, "There is an automatic notification at headquarters. I can't cut it off or stop it. They'll call here to confirm it's not a false alarm. We'll answer and say it was a mistake, but there will be another one when we cross out to the flight line and that one, they'll definitely investigate."

"Then I guess we should hurry," Crane said pleasantly.

"He was hours ahead of me," Turnbull said aloud. "Meaning he's been around here for hours."

The general looked over. "We know he's not infiltrating into my base."

"Did you find your missing colonel?"

"We sent some SPs to his house off-post. He was gone. But then we got word from the front gate he came on post a while ago. Probably banging the EWO he keeps flirting with." The general meant "electronic warfare officer." He knew the forbidden relationship for what it was – a potential career ender. He had brought in Captain Ashleigh Curry and personally asked her if she was the victim of harassment by his executive officer. She had replied that his statement "invaded her personal sexual autonomy and made her feel unsafe." He let the matter rest, and silently cursed the social justice-aware product that the Academy was putting out into the field. He decided he could at least can Sykes, but that had been delayed by the growing crisis.

"Your guys sure it was him? Maybe Crane whacked him and used a fake ID."

"No, they know him by sight. They would have caught him if he tried to use Sykes' ID, or even a fake one with a different picture. Sykes is just a worn-out BUFF pilot on the way out to pasture." The acronym "BUFF" stood for "Big Fat Ugly Fellow" – though the last "F" could stand for something else.

The aide was at the door.

"Sir," he said, panting. "Something is up at 5th Support. We've had two threshold alarms on BGXM472. They said the first one was false, but then we had the second alarm go off."

"What's a threshold alarm?" Turnbull said, but General Gough was pale.

"What's a threshold alarm?" he repeated.

The general turned. "There's an internal locator in every ready-alert cruise missile. Once, they accidently loaded six of them on a B-52 heading to Barksdale. After they fired everyone even remotely involved with that screw-up, we installed the alert devices so we could always account for every W80 and never have one accidentally go missing again. When it crosses various thresholds from the storage area – the Pit – and the flight line, it trips an alarm."

"What's a W80?" Turnbull said, but the dread was building before the general could answer.

"It's a 'dial-a-yield' nuclear payload package that can be set up to 150 kilotons."

"You mean an H-bomb?"

"Yes," said the general.

"Tell your SPs to get to wherever that place is now!" Turnbull yelled. "Come on, let's move!"

The cart under the wing of aircraft 009 holding the cruise missile that contained W80 serial number BGXM472 was slowly lifting its load up to the hardpoint. The missile would attach there. The aircraft's black paint scheme made the wing above them look like empty sky. Over 150' long and with a 185' wingspan, the B-52H was massive. Eight Pratt & Whitney turbofan engines, recently upgraded, also hung beneath the wings. Most of the 60-year-old bomber had been upgraded over the decades. Between service in Vietnam, Desert Storm, Kosovo, Iraq (multiple times), and Afghanistan, serial number 009 had had so much of itself rebuilt that it was like the apocryphal axe whose owner alternatively replaced the handle and head over time. Pretty much all that remained of the original aircraft Boeing delivered to the Air Force in 1960 was its serial number.

The crew locked the ALCM into place for transport, avoiding the longer process required to attach it for launch during flight. As the cart returned to the ground, Crane turned to Sykes.

"I want to speak to the heroes of the crew who are not accompanying us," he said. "I want to make sure they know where to meet with our comrades once they get off this installation."

"Okay," Sykes said, nervous and breathing heavily. They were about five minutes from the last threshold alert. "I'll start the aircraft."

"Don't leave without me," Crane said, smiling. Sykes nodded, and followed by Betts he ran to the crew access ladder. Captain Curry was already in the cockpit – she would act as co-pilot.

Crane turned to the stocky lieutenant. "Come on, Lieutenant Ganz, let's assemble your people in the ops room."

There were about a dozen airmen in the ops room plus Crane. He looked at them proudly.

"You have struck a blow for real freedom from the racist, sexist paradigm that prioritizes human greed over human need," he said, walking around the assembled group. They were all nervous and fearful, and the dead body reminded them that they were in this for murder as well as stealing a nuclear weapon – oddly, their concern over the consequences from the death of one person was greater than their concern for the consequences of stealing a device that could kill hundreds of thousands.

Crane found that interesting. Human nature was strange. And so were humans. Strange, and unreliable under pressure.

That fact required harsh measures to ensure security. Sacrifices had to be made.

He walked to one of the security policemen and said, "Can I have that weapon?"

The SP handed over the M4. Crane charged it, confirmed it was loaded, and opened fire, targeting those with weapons first but eventually shooting everyone in the room. He ran out of bullets from the 30-round magazine and had to finish several with headshots from the Walther. It took about 90 seconds to kill them all.

He tossed the rifle down and ran out toward the B-52, which was starting up. There was no chance Sykes and the other two onboard heard the shots.

"Get the damn door open!" Turnbull yelled. He swore he heard shooting inside the 5th Support building, and there was now a huge and unmistakable roar from the airfield.

"Damnit!" the general yelled, punching buttons. The door finally opened and Turnbull rushed in, his Wilson up and seeking targets with five security police following behind him. There were no targets, but there was another door ahead. He grabbed the general and ran him through to the key pad.

The general punched in numbers, and the door opened.

The ops room was silent, and Turnbull saw why – corpses were everywhere, many finished off with headshots. Someone wanted no witnesses.

"The flight line," shouted the general, leading the way across the operations center to the flight line door.

Turnbull beat him to it and ran through to the tarmac. Two hundred meters away, the BUFF was picking up speed down the runway.

His Wilson was up and firing, blasting off one clip, then a second. But the aircraft kept going, faster now, accelerating down the runway, and taking wing near the end in a thunderous roar.

Turnbull, the empty, smoking .45 hanging limply in his hand, watched as the bomber disappeared into the northern sky.

BOOK TWO

12.

Major General Kelly Turnbull rolled up to the headquarters of III Corps in a Humvee from the Texas Army National Guard's 36th Infantry Division and got out. The building sat in the midst of the Fort Dukakis cantonment area – during the Great Renaming, someone with a wry sense of humor had chosen it as the new name for Fort Hood, the largest active duty post in the United States Army and famous for its tank units.

The fort's commanding general was using the III Corps building as the command post for the installation and the tens of thousands of combat troops stationed there during the Crisis, as the media was now labeling the chaos engulfing the United States. Some smartass in the 36th Division's G3 section had, in fact, named the building OBJECTIVE WHATABURGER, and Turnbull had thought the structure kind of looked like the Texas institution's logo in the Google Earth shots he had examined.

Turnbull wore no jacket in the drizzle and ignored the chill. Twenty-four hours before, he had been freezing on a runway in Minot, North Dakota. That was true cold.

There were armed military police out in front of the HQ, nervous and a bit baffled about the entire situation. They had weapons, with mags in their wells, but there was no concertina wire up around the perimeter. Their vehicles were parked on the dirt off the circular driveway. They paid no attention to the arrival of the convoy of Texas Guardsmen – the Guard used Fort Dukakis all the time and even had some facilities at the far end of post where a brigade of the event, newly federalized Guard was assembled. The MPs had been briefed that the main threat was from "so-called Provisionals and other right-wing terrorists," but also sympathizers within the ranks. Fort Dukakis' commander had pledged their loyalty to the National Military Unity Council. It was unclear whether the troops shared that commitment.

The base, other than the MPs on patrol and standing their posts, appeared deserted. All troops had been ordered to remain in their quarters except for essential personnel, and the gates on and off post were closed except to military traffic.

Brigadier General Patterson of the 36th, a banker in civilian life, much older than Turnbull, and actually a general, got out too and joined Turnbull on the sidewalk. Turnbull wore dark glasses and had his soft cap on, but pulled low over his face. There were two stars on its front.

"Well, general," said the real general to the fake one. "You ready to brief the corps commander?"

"I am all about the PowerPoint," Turnbull replied, scanning the building. No one on the roof – that was good.

There were about forty Guard soldiers unloading, mostly officers and senior enlisted soldiers. They all wore their battle gear, but with soft caps, and there were no mags in their weapons, whether M4s or SIG Sauer pistols. Many had black civilian backpacks, and others carried rolled papers and the like. The MPs noted the guns, but they paid the reservists little heed – this was clearly some dog and pony show for the three-star by these weekend warriors.

It was no doubt related whatever the hell was going on, what the media was calling the Crisis.

Two days before the mobilization order had come from Washington. Fort Dukakis was on alert, and the III Corps commander, who was dual-hatted as installation commander, was directed to take charge of all installation units – some were not organic III Corps units – and prepare them for operations. But it was initially unclear on whose side.

The commander duly issued the alert, and hundreds of troops deserted. Whether they were deserting from their active duty units, or to something – like the Provisional units popping up all over the country – was unclear. The commander sealed the gates before the trickle could become a flood, ordered the all but essential troops confined to their barracks, and put the various weapons rooms under guard by the military police. And then waited, because those reaching three-star level rarely do so by taking unnecessary risks, to see who whether red or blue looked like it would be the winning side in whatever the hell was going to happen. When it seemed that the blue might have an advantage, the commander committed to the NMUC, which was thrilled to add the critical units located there to its tally of forces supporting the blue junta of retired generals.

Turnbull and the real general started moving toward the building entrance, and the rest of the staff followed. BG Patterson had an aide-de-camp, a perky female lieutenant who seemed nervous. Turnbull had an aide too, a smart staff sergeant from Lubbock he had borrow a first lieutenant's rank, since real aides were officers. The NCO, SSG Kruger, had a combat patch from Afghanistan, so he knew his way around in a fight. The last thing Turnbull needed was some West Pointer with two years in who'd never been shot at covering him in as audacious a mission as this one.

General Patterson, lanky and from Houston in civilian life, pulled the door open himself and smirked as Turnbull went inside. There were a few III Corps staff officers running around in the foyer trying to look busy. All corps staffs were bloated with straphangers, and while the worker bees noticed the two-star and one-star, they worked for a three-star and ignored the reservists. No doubt the weekend warriors were here for the corps commander to set them straight about their mission in support of the blues.

They were wrong.

There was a desk in the foyer, with a lieutenant who had to have been a superstar because only the achievers got to ride a desk greeting visitors to HQ. In fact, 2LT Rizzo had been an armor platoon leader until he got caught in a turret firing his main gun downrange toward a chubby female tank driver, so to speak. Even the new Army frowned on lieutenants having sex with specialists, and the LT found himself in this new and crappy job.

"Hey," 2LT Rizzo shouted, rising. "Where are you going? Do you have an appointment?"

"You better sit your ass down," SSG Kruger said, stepping between the camo *maître d'* and his general. Turnbull, not a particular student of protocol and no fan of generals, noted that one never truly could take the stripes off a sergeant.

2LT Rizzo stopped, his aggression terminated and his aspect now imploring. "I don't have any briefings listed on the schedule."

"Oh, your general clears all briefings with you?" demanded Kruger. "Maybe you should call upstairs and ask them to help pull your head out of your ass while my two-star waits?"

Rizzo did not want that, and he was not meant to.

"Third floor," he said, defeated.

"I know where our damn briefing is," Kruger said before stalking off.

Some stayed behind. This group, less about ten folks who had stayed in the lobby, were making a great show of digging through their backpacks.

The other two dozen or so members of the 36th packed into several elevators. Most would get out in the staff area on the second floor. Turnbull himself hit "3."

General Patterson looked on as Turnbull drew out his Wilson Combat CQB and slid a magazine of eight 230-grain Federal hollow points into the well.

"We're supposed to do this peacefully," the general said gently.

"Supposed to," Turnbull replied.

"That's not a standard sidearm either."

"I'm not standard either," Turnbull said, letting the slide go forward and slipping the black handgun back into its holster.

Turnbull was there to assist the Guard in its critically important operation; Clay Deeds had selected Turnbull of all the Zombies for it.

"General Scott wants the fort taken. He does not care how," Deeds said when Turnbull had landed back in Dallas after traveling from Minot via an Air Force jet. Luckily, he had slept on the plane.

"Weapons free?" Turnbull asked Deeds. "Sounds like him. I'm not excited about killing other soldiers even if they are flirting with the blue."

"That's why I picked you. Schiller will turn it into a blood bath," Deeds had told Turnbull. "You *might* not. Plus, you'll like Texas."

"I don't like anything," Turnbull snapped. Then he headed straight out to Killeen and Fort Dukakis.

Kelly Turnbull had grown up in Southern California and had zero interest in the Lone Star State. But he'd been there a few hours and was already enjoying it. He also surprised himself at how much he liked the laconic Texans who made up the 36th Division. They had been watching things going to hell on television – and sometimes the media showed their own neighborhoods burning. Sure enough, they had been mobilized by their governor, who was emerging as the leader of the red resistance, the Constitutional Alliance of red states. But then the federal mobilization order had come – instead of their own governor commanding them from Austin, it was the Pentagon taking charge, and they were ordered to become part of III Corps. They had a collective decision to make, and Turnbull was there to help them make it.

"Fort Hood – I cannot bring myself to say 'Fort Dukakis' – is critical. If it stays blue, and if it takes the Texas Guard out of the equation, that's huge. That's the Southwest," Deeds had said. "You have to keep them red."

"I'm one Zombie," Turnbull said.

"One fort, one Zombie," Deeds had replied and sent him south.

Patterson knew he was coming and had leveled with him.

"My governor says we remain for Texas. My men will stay loyal to their state. But no one wants a fight. Not with other Americans."

Turnbull did not say what he was thinking – that the peaceful resolution horse had left the barn, which struck him as something one would say in Texas.

"I need to go in," he said.

"I got some guys who can take you. Pretend you're doing a supply run or something, anything but recon."

Turnbull nodded, and the leader of the group Patterson had provided was SSG Kruger. Together, they had scouted the whole cantonment area, the small city on the edge of the vast training ranges where people lived and worked on the sprawling base.

"It's too big to take over with your forces. They would see you mobilizing and react," Turnbull said. "It's got to give up."

"Only one person can give it up," BG Patterson replied, understanding Turnbull's assessment.

"Then I guess we need to figure out how we persuade the commanding general to do that."

"You want to rethink that, general?" The muzzle of Turnbull's Wilson was looming in the three-star's face. His own disguise had worked. Brigadier General Patterson probably would have been blown off, but the corps commander had agreed to make time for the astonishingly young-looking new Guard two-star, who had shown unannounced and turned out to be a distinctly unwelcome guest.

Lieutenant General Francis Orme was terrified. A quartermaster officer before being promoted to flag officer, Orme had been profiled on CNN by Jake Tapper as "a new kind of general." That was true. Orme rejected gender identity and had ended traditional physical training in their corps, substituting a "nonthreatening, welcoming regimen of stretches, noncompetitive sports, and holistic eating." The media was gaga over the progressive new commander; the troops were largely baffled.

"I order you to...." Orme began. Kruger, whose M4 now very much had a mag in it, burst into laughter.

"Ma'am, sir, whatever, but my boss is not in a 'taking orders' kind of mood."

"Here's how this goes," Turnbull said evenly. "You are going to order the staff in this building to stand down and you are going to call every battalion and brigade commander on post and tell them to stand down too. General Patterson is assuming command. The 36th is in-bound and it will be occupying the base. And then you are going to a nice, comfy GO quarters under guard and wait this out."

"And if I don't?" Orme said with more courage than Turnbull had been expecting.

"Oh, then I kill you and we announce your suicide by two .45 slugs to the forehead," Turnbull replied pleasantly, before shifting into not-so-pleasant. "If smoking some general is the price of a bunch of soldiers not dying fighting over this fort, don't think for a millisecond I won't lay my money down."

"You better listen, general," Kruger said. "I don't know this guy well, but I know he'll cap you and then go out for tacos and Shiner Bock."

"What's Shiner Bock?" Turnbull asked, neither his eyes nor his handgun's barrel leaving Orme's face.

"Once this is over, I'll show you and we'll pound a few, sir."

"See, now I have something to live for," Turnbull said to Orme. "Do you?"

The purported "staff officers" of the 36th, who were mostly enlisted troops wearing company and field grade rank, disarmed the MPs and took over the HQ building without a hitch once LTG Orme had directed cooperation with the Guardsmen.

Kruger took the former corps commander away, and Turnbull walked out of the ornate office.

"I guess this place is yours now," he told Patterson. "Lots of pictures with Obama on the wall, though, and lots about whose lives matter."

"I anticipate redecorating," Patterson said. "Our troops are entering the cantonment area now. They will sweep through the locked-up units and give the troops a choice. Stick with us in the red, or go home."

"How many do you think will stay?"

"You mean join the red?" asked Patterson. "Most, I imagine. The troops don't want to fight, but I think they will. More senior officers than you might think will leave."

"Kind of like the Civil War, with the Southerners departing their Army units for the Confederacy."

"Yeah, and again it's the Democrats," Patterson said. "Thanks for the help."

"You guys did the work. I just provided some persuasion."

Off 761st Tank Battalion Avenue there was the Candlewood Suites Hotel that operated as the bachelor officer's quarters. Turnbull had taken a room under an alias he had already forgotten and had been there 12 hours, hoping Task Force Zulu and its leader had forgotten him.

He was cleaning his .45 when the knock came.

"Just a sec, I gotta get dressed," he shouted, reassembling the pistol. That took 35 seconds, and he closed the slide on a loaded mag as he walked to the door.

"I heard the slide, Kelly," came a voice from outside the door.

Turnbull opened it. Clay Deeds smiled. He held a computer case.

"Nice work," the spymaster said, coming inside unbidden.

Turnbull shut the door as Deeds walked to the dining table at the far end of the suite, near the balcony that overlooked the cantonment area. There was more activity down there now that those remaining on post were all on the same team.

"So, what's happening?" Turnbull asked. They both sat down at the round table.

"Chaos," Deeds said. "It's even more out of control today than yesterday. You must have seen it on the television."

"I don't do TV."

"Then the internet."

"Or the inner webs."

Deeds sighed. "You know the Texas governor and other southern states declared themselves outside federal control. The Constitutional Alliance is not answering to anyone."

"Sounds like something my new Lone Star friends would do."

"And the old blue states are busy declaring themselves, if not independent, then doing their own thing. The West Coast is a mess. The People's Militias in LA, San Diego, and the Bay Area are in charge. Red units are mobilizing to try and retake control."

"Do they understand that these leftist forces want to kill them?"

"There's no real understanding in much of the military of exactly what's going on," Deeds said. "They are treating this like a big civil disturbance."

"I think we're way past riots. Are they aware that BGXM472 is still out there somewhere?"

"The idea of a missing nuke is too much for them to process right now. They are too busy trying to keep a lid on this Crisis so it doesn't turn into a full-fledged civil war."

"Good luck," Turnbull said.

"I need you to help make some luck," Deeds said, even more serious now. "Zombie style."

"Oh, so someone needs to die?"

"Not someone. Several people. You know the composition of the leftist militias?"

"Cadres, spoiled brats, and crooks."

"Without the cadres pushing them, the rich kids' live-action role-playing revolution can't handle planning or logistics, and the criminals run wild. So, we have to target the cadre. And we have a very good idea of who they are from mapping these organizations, the Antifas, BLMs, People's Militias. But there's no one to arrest them. The FBI and the DOJ are falling apart – half of senior federal law enforcement is blue and sympathizes."

"So, just assassinate them?"

"Well," Deeds said. "Yeah."

"Seems like a bold step."

"Last night, Antifa barricaded a precinct of cops in a Seattle station house, brought up a tanker of jet fuel, and burned 34 of them alive," Deeds said. "I have drone shots of the People's Militia in Los Angeles executing 'enemies of the people' in front of crowds in Echo Park. Still got moral qualms?"

"My qualms were always rhetorical anyway," Turnbull said. "Targets?"

"Key leaders. You got SoCal," Deeds said, pulling his laptop out and setting it up on the table. After he turned it on and opened the file, he continued: "Jake Eggers, a former B-movie actor turned warlord in the Valley. He has 2,000 militia. Felix "Tang Devil" Pounder, a nondenominational gangbanger from South Central. Thousands at his command. And there's Taylor Soames, who used YouTube to get 4,000 in Santa Monica and the Westside."

"Oh, you got me killing girls now?"

"Don't worry – Ashleigh does not identify as female."

"Oh, well that's convenient."

"And Martin Rios-Parkinson, a UCLA assistant professor of oppression studies or some such nonsense. A real piece of work. He formed the original LA People's Militia and now walks around trying to look like Che. Those were his hangings in Echo Park."

"And you want me to take them out?"

"All four of them. Our assessment is that without them their little band will fall apart." Deeds handed over some files. "The logistics are in here. We have Operation GLADIUS assets inside the blue cities planting weapons caches, just in case. They can provide you with whatever you need."

"So now the Zombies are straight up assassins?"

"Think of the Zombies as mechanics. And shooting Marxist sons of bitches is just part of your toolkit."

"When do I fly to LAX?"

"You don't. LAX is closed – planes flying in on approach over South Central get shot up. Plus no one in their right mind is traveling now anyway. No, you go to Victorville and infiltrate in. it's about 75 miles west along the I-10 corridor."

"I know LA," Turnbull replied.

"Of course you do. The Army is on the ground there, though I hear there's no joy."

"I just need to get as close as I can and then I'll slip in and do your wet work for you."

"I knew I could count on you, Kelly."

"Too bad. I was getting to like Texas."

13.

The B-52 did not benefit much from the last six decades of technical advances in noise-proofing, and the aircraft was very loud as it flew over the darkness. Crane sat in the cockpit, in the electronic warfare officer's seat where Captain Ashleigh Curry would have normally sat. She was in the co-pilot's seat for this very special flight. The pilot, Colonel Ulysses Sykes, was wearing night vision goggles, as was Curry. Crane could not sense their altitude from peering out the window, but he knew it was low from the instrument panel.

Flying low would keep them off of American and Canadian radar screens, assuming anyone was looking for them right now. The maintenance crew had carefully disabled all the transponders and satellite links that would have provided a fix. And they activated some of the secret electronic warfare gear designed to scramble any random radar beam that might glimpse them.

Crane smiled, knowing that the only things that might hear the low-flying bomber passing above them were the occasional polar bear and random Eskimo. Crane caught himself – he meant Inuit. Or maybe First People.

He shook his head. Even he too was poisoned by his upbringing in a colonialist, capitalist culture.

The plane flew on for hours, northwest over the vast nothing that made up most of Canada. By then, they were over the

Northwest Territory, the sparsely populated wilderness between temperate Canada and the Arctic. They still had a long way to go.

The Inuvialuit Lands are the Canadian equivalent of a reservation, occupying over a million square kilometers and with a population of only about 15,000 humans. The snowy landscape is dotted by hundreds, perhaps thousands, of lakes, so many that even some of the bigger ones have no name.

One of those lakes, lying at the 68th Parallel, was an oval about 6,000 feet long and 3,000 feet wide. Nine miles east was a small exploratory oil drilling station authorized by the Inuvialuit Regional Corporation and one of the few petroleum extraction facilities not yet closed in the name of global warming – the First People's financial interests had trumped Gaia's displeasure, at least for the moment.

The small base was on the tundra off an unpaved road 137 miles long that crossed the nearly featureless flatland to the tiny settlement of Inuvik. The east-west dirt track passed close to the oblong lake, just one of countless lakes it passed close to along its course. The track turned to mush during the short spring/summer thaw, but it was now frozen as hard as concrete. To the west, Inuvik itself straddled the Dempster Highway, which was likewise largely unpaved but was somewhat more improved. The Dempster Highway ran north-south, and it was the route of the long drive south to what the uncharitable would call "civilization."

The drilling base consisted of several austere but functional buildings and a heated garage for the construction equipment. Sixteen people lived there, at least until some unexpected visitors arrived led by an unsmiling, silent, and bald man. After a few brutal moments, only one still lived, and then only long enough to show the visitors where the keys to the equipment were. Soon he joined his friends in the trash ditch scraped into the tundra just outside the camp. The visitors then set to work on their task.

Colonel Sykes picked up the faint navigation signal on the agreed frequency and made the slow turn toward it. The B-52 was flying at under 300 feet and the pilot slowed it to about 250 knots. They remained radio silent – their presence would be announced only by the jet's eight Pratt & Whitney engines. Merrick Crane watched as Sykes brought the jet to 200 feet and slowed it to 200 knots – stall speed was about 150 knots.

It was black as coal out the window. Sykes, still wearing his night vision goggles, flicked a knob on the control panel.

"Gear down," he said.

The plane jostled almost imperceptibly as the landing wheels deployed. Crane sat back in his seat, unhappy to be powerless but fascinated by the process.

"I see the markers," Curry said. It still looked black to Crane, who did not have the benefit of NVGs, but slowly yellow dots in two parallel rows appeared ahead.

The plane continued descending. The bump surprised him, and Crane – had he been a religious man – might have taken that moment to offer a prayer of gratitude that his confederates had read the ice depth correctly and accurately calculated its load bearing capability.

They were still moving fast across the surface of the frozen lake.

"Deploying drogue," Curry said, manipulating the controls. From the rear of the aircraft a small parachute popped out and inflated. Its task was to pull the large drag chute out to provide the necessary additional stopping resistance. If there had been light, the people waiting on the ground would have seen that it was olive drab in color.

The plane was slowing fast now, and there were no awful cracks or buckling from the ice below them. Ahead, as the jet rolled to a stop, there were vehicles waiting, a half-dozen at least, judging by the headlights. The plane halted.

"I did it," Sykes said with pride.

"Excellent work," Crane said. "Anything more to do?"

"No," Sykes replied, flipping up the NVGs attached to his flight helmet. "Sad to see this happen to old 009 though."

"You're quite sentimental, Colonel Sykes," replied Crane. "Ashleigh?"

The lieutenant drew her Beretta and shot Sykes through the right temple, splattering his brains on the inside of the windscreen and leaving all their ears ringing. The now-retired colonel slumped forward in his seat over the yoke, his eyes under his helmet wide with shock.

"Pig," Curry said, putting away the smoking automatic.

Technical Sergeant Betts had come to the cockpit doorway, and his face was flush white.

"Don't worry, Betts," said Crane. "You are my bomb whisperer."

"Why?" was all the young man could say.

This amused Crane. The sergeant had helped him steal a nuclear weapon that could incinerate hundreds of thousands, maybe millions, and he was mooning over the corpse of a dead liability.

"He wasn't fully committed," Crane said.

"And he was a sexist pig," added Curry.

"I appreciate your commitment to Me Too," said Crane. He turned to the sergeant. "Now Betts, you need to get out there and help dismount BGXM472 without damaging it. And then you need to remove the warhead. Go on."

Betts nodded and went, carrying the backpack with the control terminal.

Curry took off her helmet and put it on the cockpit, then looked at him beaming. "I did good, didn't I?"

"You certainly did," Crane said before he shot her between her saucer-wide eyes.

There were about a dozen men out on the ice in addition to Betts, who was fussing with the warhead that he had removed from the cruise missile. They had used a loader from the oil camp as a field expedient way to get it off the wing and to move it away across the ice to where the vehicles were. There, under the supervision of Sergeant Betts, they separated the warhead from the missile. The fact that it was well below -20 degrees Fahrenheit out, and the wind was picking up, made it twice as hard to do anything, but they still made good time.

The W80 itself, a pug-shaped, silvery contraption that resembled a fire hydrant that one might find under the domes in *Logan's Run*, weighed in at about 300 pounds. Betts needed help to lift it into the back of one of the trucks the visitors had ridden in coming up to the base, a mid-sized, ironically-named Chevy Tundra with a four-man cab.

The guy he picked to help heft up the bomb was named Gary Kelso, and Kelso had worked as a driller in Alaska before wandering into Seattle and meeting a girl and getting wrapped up with Antifa. He enjoyed the fighting part of the movement, and distinguished himself because he was one of the few of the non-street criminals in the disorganized organization who had actually been in a fight before. The college students and alienated twenty-somethings had, for the most part, never given or taken a punch.

Kelso had gotten noticed by the anarchist organization's hierarchy – if anyone had detected that conundrum, they never mentioned it – and one evening after a victorious clash with the remnants of the Multnomah Sheriff's Department, which the rioters had won, a cadre member had taken him aside. He had heard something about Kelso and now asked if he had done work on oil rigs. Kelso confirmed it reluctantly, a bit worried that his past would be held against him – defiling the Earth and all.

"There's someone you need to meet," was all Kelso was told.

That someone was Merrick Crane III, and Kelso felt he was a minor leaguer being pulled up into the majors. Crane was a legend, the uncompromising man in a world of half-steppers.

"How far are you personally willing to go to tear this whole shitty paradigm down?" Crane had asked after quizzing him further on his background.

"However far I have to," he said. Apparently, this response was satisfactory. He was relieved of his cell phone and driven away that evening to a remote cabin in the Oregon wilderness where about a dozen men began training for their mission. He never saw the girl who he had joined Antifa for again.

Now, out on the frigid Canadian tundra, Kelso watched as Crane descended alone from the big aircraft. The scary guy named Mr. Soto, who had led the visitors to the oil camp, greeted his boss with a coat and gloves. Kelso was not normally fearful, but he had kept out of Mr. Soto's way – the man reeked of trouble.

After they had eliminated the oil workers – Kelso was glad he did not have to be one of the shooters – the team had set to their tasks. It had been planned meticulously. First they used the 'dozers to cut a track from the oil camp road to the lake and then to plow the snow away down to the ice. Luckily, the weather had held while they worked.

Kelso had been one of the guys who did the test drilling through the ice. Someone else did the math and confirmed that it could hold the plane's massive weight. Later, he did some more plowing of the runway and helped set-up the landing lights. Finally, he helped drill the 40 holes around the spot where the plane would be parked – where it was at that moment. Other guys, experts in their field, took over work on the holes after Kelso finished digging them.

Then they waited, expecting it to be several days. It turned out the plane landed just two hours after they finished their work.

Crane approached as he and Betts finished securing the warhead in the back of the idling truck.

"It's safe, isn't it?" asked Crane, though he knew the answer.

"There's no short-term radiation hazard for the occupants in the cab," Betts said, still shaken by what happened in the cockpit.

He had noted the absence of Captain Curry but did not inquire about it because he did not really want to know the answer. He continued: "If there's an accident, the big problem is the conventional explosives, or more likely the fissile material spilling. But it would have to be a big accident to crack the case."

"It can't go off, right?" Kelso asked. Crane frowned at the intrusion, but Betts responded.

"No, you have to set it and authorize it, which I could do but I haven't yet. I'm going to attach a timer system when I get some parts. Maybe the shaped explosives could go off, but in an accident, they would be deformed and they have to be perfect to set off the hot rock."

"Good," Kelso said. Then he went on – he was not particularly sensitive to nuance. "What are you going to do with this?"

Crane smiled. There was no reason not to tell him.

"I intend to use it to ensure that no one can stop the chaos until we get what we want."

"What do we want?" Kelso asked, fascinated and horrified.

"We want to abolish the United States of America. And we are starting by setting this off in Texas."

Kelso nodded, but he was chilled to the core as he walked away from them, the snow crunching beneath his boots. It looked like work was finishing up. Some of the other guys were moving the equipment underneath the aircraft now. They would be departing soon.

He decided he needed to take a leak. The thought of having to sit in a truck in the cold holding it for hours horrified him almost as much as the bomb. He walked off across the lake to make it happen, dreading the cold on his junk. But that was better than squirming in a truck for miles or trying to piss out a window with his wang in the wind.

Crane directed Betts to the backseat of the cab of the bomb truck, which the tech sergeant was delighted to enter – all the vehicles' engines were always kept running so they would not freeze up, and it was toasty warm inside. There were a couple more personnel trucks to take them all back home parked nearby and idling. Everything else – the loaders, drillers, earth movers and plows – were now parked under the plane.

"Time to say good-bye to 009," Crane said. The head of his team seemed baffled at the reference. He held a black box with red switches.

"That's the aircraft number. Gather your men and let's finish this."

The man put the black box on the hood of the truck and called his men over. As they assembled, Crane glanced at Mr. Soto, who glanced back.

"All here," said the supervisor.

"Everything wired?"

"Tested and ready to go. Should we load up?"

"No," Crane said, pulling out the Walther and shooting him in the face. Mr. Soto's submachine gun was roaring and Crane began picking off those who tried to run across the featureless lake surface in a fruitless attempt at survival. It took about sixty seconds to kill them all. Crane finished a couple with head shots, which he considered a kindness.

"Sergeant Betts, get out here and help!" he commanded. The terrified airman slowly got out of the truck.

"Don't worry," Crane told him. "Like I said, you are my bomb whisperer."

The three dragged the bodies to among the vehicles under the B-52. As they walked back, having dragged over the last of them, Mr. Soto suddenly pulled up his MPX40 and fired off most of a magazine into the darkness.

Crane and he then stared into the dark.

"If there was someone, he'll die out here," Crane said. "He should have chosen a bullet."

Betts and Mr. Soto drove the last two vehicles over to the aircraft and left them there underneath it.

Kelso rolled on the ground, trying to stifle his groans. What was the chance that one of the rounds would find his left side? He should have run the other way instead of coming back to investigate the noise.

He packed snow into the hole, hoping the cold would numb the pain. Then he looked back at the aircraft. In the dim light, he could see that three figures got in the one remaining vehicle, the bomb truck, and drove off about 150 yards farther away, then stopped. It had to be Crane, the bomb guy, and that freak Mr. Soto.

Damn, bullets really hurt, he thought. This was a lot worse than the non-lethal rounds the pigs had shot him with at demonstrations.

The figures got out again and were just standing there.

"What are they doing?" he said to himself. "Oh, right. Disposal."

There were muffled explosions and huge geysers of snow and ice all around the B-52 and the vehicles. He had drilled the holes. Other guys, guys now lying ventilated inside the circle of explosions, had packed them with explosives. It was all planned out – the depth of the holes, the distance, and the explosions. They worked hard to get it right, and they did.

The explosion sounds faded away and there was now only a massive groaning. This groan became a crack, and the left wing of the bomber suddenly dipped. The cracking was now impossibly loud, and the B-52 shuddered once, then dropped, disappearing in seconds. One moment, the plane, the trucks, and the people were there, the next they were all gone beneath the surface. Kelso had heard the other guys say that the water was 190 feet deep there. And he had heard that a storm was coming that would re-freeze the hole and cover up the evidence that they had ever been here.

Now the trio were back in the truck and they were departing, heading toward Inuvik.

And Kelso realized that he was alone in the cold.

14.

The Walmart parking lot in Hesperia bordered I-15, which ran north past Victorville a mile up the road and then continued on northeast to Las Vegas a few hours across the desert. The store itself was a burnt-out shell, looted long ago for reparations, and the parking lot was packed with military vehicles, mostly light wheeled ones in desert camo paint. There were maybe five hundred troops in the lot, all busily engaged in various preparations for the incipient operation. Turnbull made his way through the soldiers assembling there, looking for the command post. He got directions from some soldiers with 40th Infantry Division patches from the California Army National Guard. Apparently, some of its units had abandoned their blue governor and gone over to the red. They all looked exhausted.

Turnbull knew the force here on the ground 75 miles from LA was not enough to stop what was coming. But he had his own mission.

The MPs at the main command post scrutinized his ID – Turnbull had not had time to get a new fake one and it was his real Army identification card. The young sergeant looked him over, taking in the large, stubble-faced man in civilian tactical gear and dark glasses with a tricked out M4 over his shoulder.

"You're, like, special forces or something?" the E-5 asked.

"We're all special in our own way," Turnbull said. "Didn't you pay attention during diversity training?" Not far off, two female specialists guarded three disarmed males in uniforms sitting on the asphalt with their hands flexi-cuffed behind them. In a few hours, as morning turned to afternoon, they would bake if their captors did not get them into the shade.

"Blues," the sergeant said, noticing Turnbull was looking at the prisoners. "Gathering intel."

"What are you going to do with them?" Turnbull said, and the sergeant looked puzzled.

"I don't know," he said. "Wait here." After about two minutes, the NCO was back, and he ushered Turnbull into the tent that housed the command post.

The one-star had bags under his eyes, a Blackhorse patch on his shoulder, and a mug of coffee in his hand that read "World's Greatest General." He looked Turnbull over and sighed as various troops around him in the tent converged over maps and shouted into ringing phones. Brown-rimmed Styrofoam spit cups sat next to the guys who chewed tobacco.

"You're going to be a pain in my ass. I can tell," the general said.

Turnbull, by now extremely over dealing with generals, simply replied with the code phrase Deeds had given him to repeat to the commander: "Sierra Tango Foxtrot Uniform." It was appropriate since Turnbull was not in his happy place regarding flag officers these days.

The general sighed again. "I figured that choice of code phrases was a subtle message that I should shut the...," he paused. "Up, and then give you whatever you want. Am I right, captain?"

"That is my understanding, general."

"I'm a little busy trying to stop the tsunami coming out of Los Angeles, so what do you want? A boat to float up the Nung River, take out some fat rogue colonel?"

"I'm always up to smoke an O-6, but right now I just need to pass through your lines without your boys smoking me. I'm headed into LA."

The general laughed. "You think so, huh? That's where we just came from. We fought our way out and all the way back here. This is where we hold them. Cajon Pass.

"You're an armored cavalry regiment. They pushed *you* back?" Turnbull was genuinely surprised. The general's Blackhorse patch was the 11th ACR out of Fort Irwin. They ran opposing force operations for units rotating through the simulated brigade battles at the hi-tech National Training Center and had a reputation for being very, very good. The unit had rejected the orders of the National Military Unity Council and was firmly red.

"Look," the general said, pointing to the S-2 section. The intelligence staff had several monitors going. "That's People's Television, used to be KTLA Channel 5 in Los Angeles. All propaganda now."

The station was showing footage of a gaggle of lumpy individuals marching in something approximating a military formation while the chyron read, "Hollywood Stars Join People's Militia To Fight Racizym." It was unclear to Turnbull whether "Racism" was spelled with a "zy" by accident or if it represented some new social justice affectation.

"Is that Rob Reiner?" Turnbull asked, squinting. "When he does a right face, he needs to go to his other right. And I'm glad to see Chelsea Handler's getting work again."

"Unfortunately, we aren't just facing tubby Tinseltown has-beens and aging tramps. We sent in two combat squadrons and a few companies of Cal Guard, with none of our armor or arty because they said we wouldn't need it," the general said, laughing bitterly. "And no air power either. They have fighters and bombers too, and both sides are holding off bombing each other. For now."

"So you have to do things the hard way?" said Turnbull.

"Yeah, that's one way of putting it. We're up against probably 20,000 People's Militia pouring out of the city. That's about a five to one ratio. Like I said, it's not just a bunch of washed-up actors acting. The blues built a real force, not well-trained but armed and in large numbers. A lot of them are gang members or anarchists, and many of them are drugged up. PCP, meth, all brewed up in China. Most just don't care if they get shot or not. The ones who do care move forward because they have units following the main body shooting anyone who retreats. Penal units. We got drone footage of it. Just like the Russian front. We fought a running battle with them all the way from East LA over the last 48 hours. That's who you need to go through to get into Los Angeles."

"Just get me to the front line. I'll do the rest."

The general smiled bitterly and stepped to a map, pointing to what looked like the empty Mojave Desert. "Back here, about an hour-and-a-half from where we are, is Fort Irwin. That's their objective. It's packed with ammo, weapons, and combat vehicles. Enough to fuel World War III, or at least Civil War II. It's also got all our families, so we have a personal stake in stopping them. A mile south of here is Cajon Pass, which is a long canyon where I-15 lifts up from the Inland Empire outside San Bernardino eleven-hundred or so meters to the high desert plateau where we are now. It's narrow, thanks to the San Andreas Fault, and defensible."

"You'll need more troops than you got to hold it, general, not that it's my problem."

"No, it's my problem. We're flying infantry units into the Victorville Airport from Hood and Carson. We need 24 hours to build up our force. That's why Ironhorse, our first squadron, is deployed at the base of the pass, to hold it until we can complete the defenses. I can get you down to 1st Squadron and they can see you through the lines, if that's what you really want to do."

"Nobody ever asks me what I really want to do," Turnbull replied.

"I'll get you down there then. Alpha Troop is probably the best place to cross the LD/LC." He meant the line of departure/line of contact, the border between friend and enemy. "It's at the southern edge of the front."

Turnbull looked at the map. There looked like a mile of flat, open dry wash to the front of the Ironhorse line. Good for defense, bad because he'd have no cover crossing it trying to infiltrate west.

"Okay, sir. Just remember that I'm dead."

"Dead?"

"Yeah," Turnbull said. "Meaning I was never here."

The general nodded and Turnbull took two steps out when he heard the general and turned around.

"Hey captain, any word from the real world? What the hell is going on out there? Are we in an all-out civil war, or is this just a skirmish?"

"I have no idea, general," Turnbull replied. "But if you don't hold them back at Cajon Pass, that's going to be a pile of bricks on the all-out civil war side of the scale."

There was a Humvee heading down from the plateau to bring some medical supplies to the forward units, and Turnbull hopped in for a ride. About a mile south on I-15, the wide freeway dived downward at a steep decline, winding broadly around in a long, looping arc so it would not be such a precipitous grade. The rocky, chaparral-covered slopes of mountains on each side – the San Gabriels to the west and the San Bernardinos to the east – loomed over the pass as it narrowed into a slot barely wide enough for the freeway and some train tracks. It was a good defensive position, but the enemy had the advantage of an endless horde of stoned cannon fodder. Those reinforcements had better arrive soon or the bad guys would force the pass and the road to Irwin would be wide open.

They got off the largely deserted stretch of I-15 at the Glen Helen exit. Back in the 1980s, forty years or so before, the US Music Festival had been held there – Turnbull was unsure why he knew that, since it was before he was born, but he was pretty sure U2 had played there before Bono had become unbearable. A couple months earlier, Turnbull had read that the rocker had broken his hip falling in the shower.

The exit led to a street, and the street led to a large subdivision off to the south of I-15. Since I-15 was right up against the base of the mountains, the subdivision that ran a mile or so south was a blocking obstacle to forces moving west toward the entry into Cajon Pass. The houses themselves were regular suburban homes, packed neatly into well-ordered, carefully planned streets. It seemed word had gotten out that something bad was in-bound, as the streets were largely deserted. A few hold-outs remained, mostly middle-aged men with rifles and shotguns stalking the sidewalks in packs who refused to abandon their little castles and whom the cavalry squadron's patrols ignored.

The vehicle dropped him and the med supplies off in front of a house on White Ash Road that had apparently been turned into the Alpha Troop command post. A few dozen Humvees lined the street with "11ACR" painted on their bumpers in black. Each also had a three-digit number preceded by "A," for Alpha Troop.

Turnbull walked up to the first trooper he saw. The young trooper was petting what looked like a black lab with a red collar.

"I need to see whoever is in charge." He was not in a uniform and his eyes were behind dark glasses, but he gave the order in a tone that said he expected to be obeyed.

The young specialist he had spoken to told him to wait and whispered into the tactical radio mic on his shoulder. Turnbull dropped his ruck and stood in the sun – it was warming up – then alerted at the sound of rifle fire to the north. Single rounds, controlled. That was good. You wouldn't want to blast off all your ammo too soon. He looked at the specialist who looked back at him, suspicious. Also good. Outsiders to a unit should be treated as suspect until proven otherwise.

"You the spook?" someone yelled loudly. The man approaching was short but nearly as wide as he was tall, and he wore a black Stetson hat with crossed sabers and a gold three stripes, three rockers, and diamond insignia on the front face.

"Hello, Top," Turnbull said. "I guess I am. And I'm also not here."

"Sir, I really don't have time for this shit, captain or not." He stopped in front of Turnbull, but offered no salute. Turnbull, perfectly happy to not be pointed out to any local snipers, paid what would otherwise be a breach of military courtesy no mind.

"I just need to lay low until nightfall and then I'm moving out west, First Sergeant Hernandez," Turnbull said, reading the nametape on the man's plate carrier. The senior noncommissioned officer of the cavalry troop had a 1st Cavalry Division combat patch on his camo uniform's right shoulder.

"Out west?" The first sergeant laughed. "I'd like to see that. Follow me. I'll orient you to this cluster fark." He did an about-face, and Turnbull followed him around behind the house where the senior NCO laid out the situation for his unwanted guest.

Alpha Troop – a cavalry company is called a "troop" – was positioned at the southwest corner of the subdivision. Directly south of the housing development was a huge open pit a hundred feet deep with steep gray embankments where they used to dig stone for concrete back when the economy was such that anyone might consider building something. It went on south for another three-quarters of a mile and provided a formidable obstacle, so the squadron had only a light force covering it.

Behind the houses lining the west side of White Ash Road was an endless face of fences. In the yard Top took Turnbull through, the men had simply knocked down a ten-foot hole in the wood barrier so they could pass through it. On the other side was what looked like a 20' black asphalt bike path with a white line running down the center and a row of sandbags creating a wall about three feet high along the west edge that the troopers could rest behind out of sight. To the south a hundred meters, the bike path bent east around the subdivision, skirting the concrete quarry. It ran north as far as he could see, under and beyond the I-15 bridge and into the towering mountains that marked the northern edge of the subdivision.

The key terrain feature was the dry wash. It ran north-south across the face of the whole subdivision, a half-mile or so long. The wash itself was at least a half-mile wide from east to west, and on the far side of it was another subdivision where the enemy could assemble out of sight. The floor of the wash was gray dirt and light sand, and it was dotted with a few low bushes. There was some uneven ground, but it was generally flat – no real cover. It lay about 20 feet below the level of the bike path. The angle of the embankment up from the bottom to their level was a little steep, but not unclimbable. The men of Alpha Troop were strung out along the top, behind their sandbags, oriented to the west.

To the north were the other units – Bravo and Charlie Troops. Bravo held the center and Charlie held the north, including the freeway bridge that crossed the wash. They likewise lined the bike path oriented west.

"Lucky you, getting this frontage," Turnbull told the senior noncommissioned officer. "This is where I'd hit you with my main effort." If you hit Bravo, all three units would fire on you. Charlie had the mountains preventing a wide swing north. But here, in the south, they could come and swing south, then come up along the concrete quarry, break through there, then roll up the whole line from the flank. He noted a platoon and a machine gun position down at the far south edge.

But that was the only machine gun.

"Where are all your M240s, Top?" Turnbull asked.

"In our vehicles, sir," the NCO replied. "I got enough ammo left for one, and it's right where it'll do the most good."

That was true – it was the best place for the weapon, able to engage south and sweep anyone coming north. But Turnbull realized the first sergeant had buried the lede.

"You're out of 7.62?"

"We burned through it fighting our way out. We're low on 5.56 too."

"Hard fight?"

"They kept coming, sir. I saw scumbags like them growing up in Compton. Druggies, gangbangers. We were ordered in, told to be gentle, we come in peace, you know? And then they hit us. Got close and just came at us. We had to shoot our way out, then fight our way back, leapfrogging units left in contact. We burned through most of our ammo pretty quick," the first sergeant said, pulling off the Stetson and running his hand through his short-cropped salt-and-pepper hair. "I've been to war. I never expected to fight one in America. In my hometown. This shit is messed up."

"Sure is, Top."

"You the spook?" came a booming voice from behind them.

"Our CO, Lieutenant Faith," 1SG Hernandez said. Faith was tall and big, even bigger and taller than Turnbull, who assessed him quickly. West Point ring on his right hand. No combat patch. And he was a second lieutenant.

"I know you," Turnbull said. "John Faith. You were the linebacker at West Point a couple years ago who almost signed to the pros."

The lieutenant stopped and looked hard in Turnbull's eyes. His uniform was filthy, like everyone else's, and his weapon was hanging over his shoulder. "That's right," he said, his voice a booming bass.

"I always root against West Point," said Turnbull, who was commissioned through the Officer Candidate School at Ft. Benning before they changed the base's name to "Ft. Patton" because whoever Benning was was a confederate. Then, immediately after that, it was again renamed, this time to "Ft. Walter Mondale," after there was an outcry and it was determined that General Patton's reputation for aggression made him no longer suitable for emulation and honors from the new Army.

The lieutenant seemed unsure how to reply. He knew the stranger, despite his civilian kit, was a captain, and after four years at West Point, Academy grads were very conscious of rank.

"I won't hold it against you, and I won't interfere with your unit," Turnbull said. "When night comes, I just need to slip into that wash and I'll be out of your hair forever."

A flurry of shots from the north echoed over the positions, probably from Charlie Troop to the north.

"They probe the squadron's positions," Faith said. "Not so much ours. I got OPs out a few hundred meters. They smoke most of the infiltrators before they get into range."

"What do the bad guys have?"

First Sergeant spoke up. "AKs. New ones. We think Chinese. Must have shipped in thousands and then the People's Militia got issued them. They can't shoot worth shit though. They just shoot a lot."

"Captain Tran got killed outside Diamond Bar," Faith said. "We were trying to hold them from high ground on I-10. We had to fall back. The XO got wounded at Ontario Airport and got evaced. So did a platoon leader." He didn't mention that the other lieutenant assigned to Alpha Troop had defected to the blue even before they left Fort Irwin.

"So you assumed command?"

"Yep," said the young officer.

"The LT got us back here mostly intact. But we left Irwin with 127 on our battle roster and we got 87 boots on the ground now," First Sergeant said. "Plus some civilians."

"You ready for this, LT?" asked Turnbull. A company command for an inexperienced officer in combat could easily be a disaster even with a top-flight first sergeant.

Faith started to answer but 1SG Hernandez jumped in. "LT is squared away, sir. We're homies. He grew up about a mile from where I did, though I got out 17 years ago when he was what, six?"

"Seven. You'd get killed three times by the gangs walking between my house and yours, Top," Faith said. "This isn't my first time getting shot at. Just my first time shooting back. I was a preacher's kid. I studied and played football at Compton High. I didn't get in trouble like Top here did."

Hernandez smiled. "I was bad news. The judge told me, 'Son, you can wear green or you can wear orange,' and I figured wearing green at least I had a shot at getting it on with girls, so here I am. Cav to the bone. Garry Owen!"

Turnbull recognized the cavalry cry, taken from the name of an Irish tune that George Custer adopted for his ill-fated Seventh Cavalry and which all American cavalry units subsequently embraced, one of their many peculiar idiosyncrasies, like the black Stetson hats they insisted on wearing. Top was clearly wearing his hat as a morale builder, a way to let the tired troopers know the most experienced soldier in the unit wasn't worried so they shouldn't be either.

"Well, you seem to have your shit together," Turnbull said. "Where can I rest up until dark where I'm out of the way?" He meant, "Where none of you regular Army types will bother me while I crash."

"We've taken over the houses along White Ash Road," Top said. "Pick one, find a bed, rack out. Just don't pick one with one of these civilian guys in it. They'll shoot you."

"I'll be careful."

"And look out for dogs."

"Dogs?"

"Yeah, some of these people didn't take their dogs when they *di di mau'd*, so there are hungry dogs running around. They don't bite – they're all pets. They just beg for food. My guys keep giving them their damn MREs."

"American troops love dogs," Turnbull said. "Not me, though. Never got the appeal."

"Got me some huskies back at Irwin," Top said. "Anyway, it's the civilians you gotta watch for. We got about 20 that agreed to help us out. Most of them have ARs or AKs, all illegal as hell in Cali but they got 'em and they got bad attitudes about the People's Militia too."

"How bad?"

"When we got here, there were some bodies piled up at the entrance to the subdivision," Hernandez said. "A warning."

"Don't screw with suburban dads," Turnbull said, not caring a whit. "I've seen a lot of that round the country. You can't build up hate and expect it not to go somewhere."

"Any news from the real world?" Lieutenant Faith asked.

"None good," Turnbull replied.

"Sir, let's...," Hernandez began, but he was interrupted by shouting from the south. The trio walked quickly down the bike path to the machine gun position. All the troopers were standing-to, looking down at something on the floor of the wash.

Turnbull, Faith, and Hernandez moved down the line of troops huddling behind the sandbag wall until they reached the machine gun position. Turnbull noted only about ten belts of 7.62mm ammo – not nearly enough. But what he saw below the position was even more noteworthy. It was at least a dozen troops in two ranks with a short, sturdy leader out front. The man was in camo, and built like a fire plug.

"Who are you?" 2LT Faith shouted down to them.

"Who the hell are *you*?" came the reply.

"You believe this?" Faith said to Turnbull and Hernandez, shaking his head and not quite believing this. "Okay, I'll play."

The big officer looked down and shouted, "This is Alpha Troop, 1st Squadron, 11th Armored Cavalry Regiment, United States Army. Now, who the hell are you?"

"We're United States Marines!"

Turnbull, Faith, and Hernandez looked at each other.

"How do we know for sure?" asked Hernandez quietly.

"They *look* like Marines," Faith said.

"And they are very annoying, so there's that," Turnbull added. "Okay, let me try a test."

Turnbull looked down over the edge at the group, which he noticed was assuming a 360-degree security posture.

"Who is John Basilone?" he shouted down.

"Gunnery Sergeant Basilone, John, United States Marine Corps. Medal of Honor, Navy Cross, killed in action, Iwo Jima 1945."

Turnbull turned back to the other two men.

"Either he's a Marine or they've really changed up the syllabus in his gender studies class."

Faith leaned over the side. "Bring your men up!"

The Marines scrambled up the side of the wash and assembled in two ranks on the bike path. The leader turned and faced Turnbull, Faith, and Hernandez.

"I'm Sergeant Betley," he said. "We're Alpha Company, 1st Battalion, 1st Marines."

"You only got 19 guys, sergeant," 2LT Faith observed.

"We're what's left," said Betley. He put his unit at ease.

"You walked all the way from Camp Pendleton?" said Turnbull. "That's got to be 80 miles."

"Fought them every step. Made them pay."

"What happened?" Turnbull asked.

"Most of the force was deployed trying to unscrew the Crisis. We had a few companies left on post to secure the weapons and equipment. They hit us hard out of San Diego. Shitheads, druggies, convicts. We held for a while but there were too many. We had to retreat, and lost all the officers, but it was a fighting retreat." The 1/1 Marines were used to fighting retreats – they had been at the Chosin Reservoir in Korea.

"Glad you're here. I'm Lieutenant Faith. This is First Sergeant Hernandez."

"Who's this guy?" Betley asked, gesturing at Turnbull.

"I'm not even here," Turnbull said.

"Oh, you're probably some brand of Army special ops," Betley said, with not a little disdain. "You're definitely not a SEAL. We've been talking for almost two minutes and you haven't mentioned that you're a SEAL yet."

"Top will take you back to refit and rearm, then we'll integrate you into the defense," Faith said.

"Hell, sir, we need to go link up with a Marine unit."

"While you sort out your order of battle, I'm going to crash," Turnbull said.

"Definitely special ops," Betley said, before returning to his debate with the company commander.

Turnbull and Hernandez walked back to the company command post. There were perhaps 20 local civilians around with all manner of weapons, from ARs to Remington and Mossberg shotguns to a particularly sweet jet-black Henry lever action rifle with a scope.

"Auxiliaries," the first sergeant said.

"They are calling them 'Provisionals' elsewhere," Turnbull replied. "It's happening all over the country."

"We need every swinging dick," Hernandez said. "I guess I can say that again and not get relieved."

"I'm thinking diversity and sensitivity programs are a low priority right about now."

"Well," the first sergeant said. "At least some good has come out of this cluster."

The company command post was in one of the houses, in a breakfast nook attached to a vaguely dated kitchen with granite surfaces and a brushed steel Samsung side-by-side refrigerator. The place was a mess. There was water on the floor, the power being out and the freezer having melted. A dirty blender sat on the counter surrounded by smoothie fixings. A 5-kilowatt generator hummed from the porch outside.

There were a couple admin clerks in the CP, working on laptops with attached printers on the dinner table. Even in combat, the Army ran on paperwork. There was a map tacked to a wall, and a white board that had once memorialized the owner's schedule had been repurposed to show the platoon sectors. In the next room, the living room with windows facing out to the street, there was a large, OD green tarp covering something on the tan carpeted floor.

"C4," Hernandez said. "I got a bunch of it."

"What for?" Turnbull asked.

"No idea. The engineers dropped off a thousand filled sandbags, and I knew what to do with them, but they dropped this off too and I have no clue what to do with it. Charlie can blow the I-15 bridge, I guess, but we got nothing to blow."

"You could give it back."

Hernandez looked at Turnbull like he was insane. "Sir, you don't give stuff back," he said slowly, as if Turnbull was an idiot.

"I'm racking out," Turnbull said.

"There are a couple bedrooms upstairs."

"No, I sleep better when I'm not above several hundred pounds of plastic explosives. I'm going to that house across the street. It looks abandoned. Come get me if you need me. Knock first."

Hernandez nodded, and Turnbull went out the front door. Apparently, the supply room was being run out of the open garage, and platoon sergeants were lined up on the driveway getting cases of water and MREs for their men. There was arguing and bargaining going on – NCO business – and the noise was another reason to rack out across White Ash Road.

Fortunately, the house across the street was abandoned. Turnbull had taken no chances, opening the door and yelling that he was coming in and anyone inside should make himself known. The last thing he wanted was some angry homeowner with a Kel-Tec dumping a tube of buckshot shells into him for invading his castle.

A fat, yellow sausage of a dog waddled out into view and started barking at him. He paused, listening. Satisfied he was alone, he approached the barking pet, M4 still ready just in case.

He could see its bowls on the floor, both empty. There was a bag of dog food that was folded closed. Maybe the owners had left so fast they forgot their corgi. He went over, opened the bag and filled one of the bowls. Then he noticed the sliding glass door to the fenced-in back yard was open. That was good – otherwise the house would be an outhouse by now.

"Stop barking," he said. The corgi did stop, but only because it was eating. He filled the water bowl out of the tap, which was still working, and left the animal to its meal.

Weapon ready, just in case, he went up the carpeted stairs.

The master bedroom was nice but it faced the front of the house, and it was noisy even with the windows shut. Across the hall was a bedroom that was more suitable. It faced the back and had a twin bed underneath a large poster of the cover of Billie Eillish's latest album, *My Parents Make Me Sad*. Looking around the décor, Turnbull assessed it as the room of the owners' beloved daughter or greatly disappointing son.

A family had lived here once. Who knew if one would again?

Families. Turnbull sighed.

He took out his cell and looked at it. Though the power was out, the cell service was still on. First sergeant probably had a hell of a time making sure the younger troopers weren't twittering or facebooking or texting Mary Jane Rottencrotch back at Fort Living Room and focusing on their job.

He considered the phone for a long time, before deciding to dial the number. It was memorized, not on speed dial – Turnbull did not have that many personal numbers to remember. It was a 415 number, the Bay Area.

It rang. It was a new phone, and after two rings he figured his half-brother Jim would not be answering the strange number, but a soft voice did answer.

"Hello?"

"It's me."

"Who?"

"Who do you think? Are you and what's her name all right?"

"Oh," Jim replied, disappointed. "You. And my girlfriend's name is Tiana."

Turnbull ignored him. "Listen, this is all going south fast. You're near San Francisco. It could get ugly. Is there a place out of town you can go to?"

"Why would I leave, Kelly?"

"You do watch the news, right?"

"I watch enough to see what racist assholes like you are doing to hurt mostly peaceful protesters. I assume you're still in the Army. That you haven't come over to the Resistance tells me all I need to know about you."

"Jim, you were always stupid and weak, and you need to break out of your MSNBC bubble and listen to me. This is for real. Get out of there."

"We're not going anywhere," Jim snapped. In the background, a woman's voice said something indistinguishable. Jim replied to her, "My asshole half-brother wants us to leave town. Says we're in danger."

Now, she was clearer. "Only from racist fascists like him."

"Jim, get your stupid booty call under control and get out of Dodge. This is the last time I'm warning you."

"We're not going anywhere!" Tiana shouted – now Jim was letting her listen in.

"You aren't even married yet and your balls are already community property."

"We're not going anywhere!" Jim repeated. "And don't call me again. I'm done with you. Antiracism requires purging racists from our life and I'm purging you. I don't want to ever see you again."

"I'm so proud of you, Jim," cooed Tiana. Doubtless his bro had just earned his monthly quickie.

"No, you really don't want to see me again," Turnbull snapped and hit the hang up button.

He sat there for a moment, then he put it out of his mind. He had tried. Jim had always been a fool, and now he was Tiana's problem – and vice versa. Turnbull walked out of the room and used the restroom off the hall then came back and shut the room's door behind him. He put his head on the pillow under the dead-eyed gaze of whoever Billy Eillish was, willed himself to forget his half-brother, and shut his eyes.

Scratching at the door.

"Are you kidding me?" he said aloud. "Go away!"

More scratching.

He rolled out of bed and opened the door, and the corgi rushed in and leapt up on the bed and lay down.

"Move over," Turnbull said, shoving the hefty animal over so he had room to lie down. Then he went to sleep.

15.

He had slept for a couple hours and was watching the door when the doorknob to the bedroom turned. Before it was all the way open Turnbull's black .45 was up and in the shocked face of one of Top's admin clerks.

"My security system picked you up as soon as you came in the house," Turnbull hissed, the growling corgi standing on the bed with its back hair up. "And Mr. Wilson prefers you knock." The young trooper's eyes were fixed on the silver barrel nestled inside the black slide of the Wilson Combat CQB.

"Sorry, sir," the trooper replied. Turnbull put the pistol back in his holster. After a long moment, he spoke.

"Yes?"

"Um, Top needs you."

"For what? We under attack?" Turnbull did not hear any firing.

"The SCO's coming."

"What's a SCO?"

"Squadron commanding officer," the clerk explained, as if Turnbull should have known it instantly.

"Oh, well why does he want me?"

The admin clerk's face contorted in agony, no doubt fearing that he would have to go find the first sergeant and explain that the strange officer with the civilian clothes didn't want to come when summoned.

Turnbull checked his watch – 1400 hours, so he had had about two hours of sleep – and decided to have mercy. "I'm on my way. Make sure the dog's got water."

There was a crowd on the driveway in front of the storeroom, half troopers and half Marines, in a circle cheering and yelling. A fistfight? Maybe – these horse soldiers and the naval infantrymen had all manner of strange customs and maybe pummeling each other into pulp was one of them.

Turnbull edged his way through the crowd to the front and saw the cause of the commotion. Both 2LT Faith and SGT Betley were on the driveway in the front leaning rest position doing push-ups.

Betley was slowing; Faith was going steady, one-two, one-two. Turnbull marveled at the sight. After another thirty seconds, Betley's muscles failed and he fell onto the oil-stained asphalt. Faith just kept on going.

The Marines groaned, and Betley got to his feet, winded.

About thirty seconds later, enough to erase any doubts about who had won, Faith stopped and hopped to his feet. Betley smiled, and put out his hand.

"Okay, sir, I guess you can lead Marines," he said. "On a temporary basis."

Faith smiled. "Well, sergeant, I am honored."

"SCO!" 1SG Hernandez yelled. He had been watching from a distance, and when he hollered the crowd scattered – not chaotically but in that unique way enlisted troops have of getting out of the blast radius of senior officers while looking as if they have a purpose instead of a mere desire to be elsewhere.

The SCO's hummer was coming down White Ash Road from the north – he had been next door with Bravo Troop. Hernandez, Faith, and Turnbull walked down to the edge of the driveway to meet him.

"You think now was the best time for PT?" Turnbull asked.

"Gotta win them over, sir."

"Good thinking," Turnbull said. He liked this guy's style, but as a second lieutenant, Faith was far too young to be commanding a company in combat. "Not my problem," Turnbull told himself.

The squadron commander's vehicle pulled up and stopped. He stepped out, tall and thin with a shoulder rig for his desert brown SIG Sauer pistol. An M4 lay inside on his seat. The window in front of him was pocked with three bullet holes.

No one saluted.

"John," he said to 2LT Faith. "Good to see you. Top, you too. I'll need you to walk me around your position. But give me a minute with our guest here."

Faith and Hernandez left them, and the lieutenant colonel motioned Turnbull a few steps away from the vehicle so the driver would not hear.

"The general tells me you're a captain," he said.

"I'm not even here," replied Turnbull.

"Yeah, yeah. That special ops shit. I get it. You're still a United States Army officer though, and an experienced one I take it."

Turnbull shrugged. He hated dealing with the regular Army.

"John – Lieutenant Faith – he's a good officer, but he's too new to have this job. If I had anyone else to spare, I'd put him in command, but I don't. You can see as well as I can that their main effort is going to be Alpha's sector."

"Colonel, I'm not really good at nuance. What are you telling me?"

"I'm telling you – I'm asking you, because you guys don't do well being told stuff – to keep an eye on the situation for as long as you are here and to step in if shit goes south."

Turnbull sighed. "I have a mission."

"And I have about 90 of my guys and a bunch of add-ons here who I don't want to send home in bags. If you need to take charge, do it. And I'll talk to Faith about it."

"Like I said, colonel, I have my mission."

The colonel looked him over. "If I thought I could order you to and you'd listen I would. So, I'm asking. Do what needs doing."

Turnbull said nothing.

"Good luck, captain," the colonel said and then walked over toward the driveway.

The gunfire woke him up. Turnbull checked his watch: 1530 hours. It was clearly M4s with a smattering of other makes and models, and emanating from the direction of the dry wash.

They were coming.

He rolled out of bed – he slept in his boots – and grabbed his web gear and rifle and ran out of the room and out of the house, leaving the corgi barking.

There were a few troopers in the garage/supply room across the street gathering up ammo and piling boxes on what looked like a kid's wooden wagon. Necessity is the mother of invention, Turnbull remarked to himself silently as he picked up the pace to a trot and went around into the back yard. There was more firing from ahead of him.

He passed through the hole in the fence and stepped onto the blacktop of the bike path and beheld the wash.

The floor of the wash was moving.

It came into focus. The wash was packed with running People's Militia. A wave of them. A tidal wave, all across the whole frontage of the subdivision. And it was about 300 meters away.

Turnbull charged his M4 and surveyed the situation. Top was at the north end trying to slow down the rate of fire – the guys were blowing off way too much ammo. Faith was down at the south end near the machine gun, which was already cranking. The Marines were deployed along a narrow section of frontage and Betley was controlling their fire. The Provisionals were next to them covering about 50 meters of front and firing their collection of weapons with no real coordination.

"Shit," he muttered as his eyes swept over the chaos. A flight of bullets cracked over his head. A few meters up the line, a trooper caught one in the face and spun around and sprawled on the bike path. A couple of medics ran to his aid.

Now the howling and yelling of the militia was rising above the noise of the gunfire. One trooper backed off the wall and Top threw him bodily back in line. The return fire was disorganized and haphazard. The guy with the Henry repeater was at least using his optic to carefully select a target, take it, and move to the next one – the .44 magnum rounds the carbine took were on a bandolier around his torso.

They were at 250 meters, and they were not slowing down. If the cavalry had had some artillery and air power, this would not have been an issue. But that wasn't happening. This was rifle work. And that meant the bad guys had a chance.

"Shit!" Turnbull said loudly. "Lieutenant Faith! First sergeant! On me!"

They both heard him, and they sprinted to him. In those seconds, Captain Turnbull made his plan.

With the two in front of him, panting, looking for leadership, Turnbull spoke, clearly and firmly and as calmly as he could muster.

"Gentlemen, I am senior and assuming command of Alpha Troop," he said. Neither Faith nor Hernandez reacted – they just listened.

"LT, you get the Marines and form a flying squad. You plug any holes. Move!" Faith turned and ran, shouting to Sergeant Betley. Turnbull pivoted to the first sergeant.

"Top, get the platoon sergeants to hold fire and prepped to take my fire commands!" Hernandez turned and was shouting to the acting platoon leaders as Turnbull ran forward to the wall. A scared Provisional in a Foghat concert t-shirt and cargo shorts was blowing off rounds from his Mossberg 12 gauge. Turnbull put his hand on the man's shoulder.

"Save it for when they get closer," he said. The man stopped shooting. He was scared shitless.

They were at 200 meters and coming fast. There was no real rhyme or reason to the charge. They were just coming, without any kind of uniform – many were shirtless in the sun except for a bandolier of AK mags – and in no coherent order. Behind the wave, in a second, more orderly but thinner line a few hundred yards farther to the rear, were the motivators. Except no one was turning and running away – they could smell blood.

The shooting from the cavalry line died out. It had been nearly ineffectual anyway with only a few dead or wounded militia lying still or wriggling on the wash's bottom in the wake of the wave.

Behind him and south, Faith shouted to Sergeant Betley, who pulled his Marines off the line and formed them up in two ranks behind the lieutenant. The NCOs spread out their troopers to fill the empty space.

"First sergeant!" Turnbull shouted. 150 meters. They were coming faster now, some even running, amped up not only by whatever they had smoked but by the lack of fire from Alpha Troop.

Hernandez ran over. "Sir?"

"At one hundred meters, volley fire."

Hernandez broke into smile. "Hell yeah, captain," he said before turning and bellowing out the new commander's order.

"Stand-to! At 100 meters, volley fire!"

The younger troops looked at each other baffled, but the NCOs got it. Volley fire would serve three purposes – control the ammo, make sure the people they hit had enough time to fall so they weren't wasting bullets on people they had already shot, and break the enemy's morale when they watched their pals die in waves in front of them.

The rounds were coming fast and heavy from the charging militia, most all going high and snapping over the troopers' heads. The cavalry soldiers and their Provisional auxiliaries leaned over the top of the sand bags. Turnbull watched the enemy come and estimated the range.

"First sergeant!" he yelled.

"Present! Aim!" the first sergeant shouted – not a common command, one rarely given in the last century, but the squad and team leaders had figured it out. The men leaned into their weapons and selected their shrieking targets at the crest of the wave of euphoric humanity.

"Now!" Turnbull ordered.

"Fire!"

The firing line erupted as if letting loose a single thunderous round upon the charging enemy. The wave seemed to halt for a moment, but it was an illusion. Only those in the front of the line who had been hit stopped, or staggered, and then fell. The faces of the next rank were confused by the dozens ahead of them suddenly dropping, but they kept coming, and the firing line took aim again.

"Fire!" first sergeant said, perhaps seven or eight seconds after the first command.

The troopers and auxiliaries along the wall of sandbags fired again down into the wash, and the front rank of charging militia wavered and fell in a rough row of still and twitching bodies.

"Fire!" The firing line fired as one, the rounds tighter in timing as the men fell into the steady rhythm of a volley every eight seconds. Turnbull, who joined in the firing with his M4, lost count of the volleys. He selected a target, squeezed on first sergeant's command, then moved to a new one, his red dot landing center mass and holding until he squeezed.

The mob was close now, depleted but at the foot of the incline up to the sand bags. About half the wave was wavering, the other half trying to scramble up the embankment to close on the cavalry troopers. Turnbull glanced at the penal units a few hundred meters back. They were firing now, trying to turn back the swelling ranks of those who had turned tail in the face of the scythe that was Alpha Troop's merciless volley fire.

The north of the sector was holding well – the wave was weakest there, with only a few trying to claw their way up the dirt wall. To his immediate front, in the middle where the Provisionals were, the attack was heavier, but its heaviest blow came at the south end, by the machine gun, which was now roaring non-stop. A quick glance and Turnbull confirmed that Faith and his flying squad were on it, and when the first head poked over the sand bag wall right where the Provisional with that sweet Henry repeater lay dead, shot through the face in an ugly row of red pocks, the last thing the owner of the pioneering noggin saw was the muzzle flash of Turnbull's carbine.

"Independent fire!" Hernandez yelled. The entire sector echoed with shots as the single fight by force devolved into dozens of independent battles, some hand-to-hand.

"Ready?" shouted 2LT Faith, standing to the right of the two ranks of Marines that made his flying squad. In front of him across the bike path the line of cav troopers at the sandbag wall was wavering. Militia was cresting the embankment and clambering over the wall. Four or five troopers lay on the ground among the attackers.

"Now!" Faith yelled.

"First rank, fire!" Betley bellowed.

The first rank was nine Marines, and the volley leveled most of the attackers on the bike path.

"Second rank, fire!"

The next nine, with Betley and Faith joining them, dropped most of the rest.

"Second rank, forward and kneel! First rank, stand!" None of it was SOP, but the Marines got it. Joke all you want about jarhead mental acuity, they were instinctive killers. The rear rank fired, then it moved up. The second rank rose and fired, and by now all the attackers who had made it to the bike path were lying dead or wounded on the black asphalt. The Marines closed on the sandbag wall and proceeded to fire at point blank range into the swirling mass huddled below.

A round slammed into the lower receiver of Turnbull's M4 and tore it from his hands. He looked up and the wild-eyed militiaman who shot at him, and who was dressed in a white sweatsuit top and jeans for some reason, charged him. Turnbull's hand dropped to his .45 but he did not get it out of its holster before Hernandez collided with the attacker at full speed from the side, sending him sprawling. The Wilson was out by now and Turnbull put Sweatsuit Guy down with a round to the face, then shot another militiaman who was climbing over the sandbag wall. The target flew backward into the wash, the three 230-grain rounds ensuring his day was ruined.

Hernandez was up on his feet. Around him, there were attackers clambering over the wall, and a mix of troopers and Provisionals fighting them. Some of the soldiers had bayonets. Others, apparently out of ammo, used their weapon as a club. It was medieval.

"Sir," Hernandez began, but Turnbull shot over his shoulder and put a round in the forehead of a guy trying to use the AK he had just reloaded to ventilate the NCO.

"Now we're even," Turnbull said. He fired a few more rounds at the attackers before the slide on the Wilson locked to the rear. He reloaded fast, by instinct, and slipped the weapon back in its holster as he sent the slide forward. Looking around, he saw what he needed. He grabbed the Henry rifle and slipped the bandolier off its dead owner.

"That's some Wild West shit right there, sir!" the first sergeant said, sliding a fresh mag of 5.56mm into his M4.

"Yippee ki yay, first sergeant," Turnbull said as he pumped the lever and ejected a spent round, then fed .44 magnum rounds into it until it was full. He surveyed the sector. The bike path was strewn with dead and wounded militia, along with soldiers and Provisionals.

The machine gun was out of ammo belts, but the Marine counterattack had crushed the assault on the southern end of the line. Organizing the remaining soldiers, whom he stopped from firing on the retreating attackers – "Save those rounds for when they come back!" – into a defense, 2LT Faith took his flying squad and moved north toward the company commander and the embattled middle of the line.

Turnbull popped over the sandbags, then took aim through the optic at the closest attacker, a redhead who looked like the son of Carrot Top and who was clambering up the dirt embankment. The .44 magnum round hit his target center mass and threw him backwards into the wash, where he landed on a pile of bodies. Turnbull saw movement right and another enemy was firing at him, high as usual. Turnbull levered three quick rounds into him and shut him down for good. He was really starting to like the Henry.

There was a lot of firing to his south, and his eyes darted over to where he saw Faith and the flying squad moving up along the wall, unleashing their deadly rifle fire on the hapless attackers stuck at the bottom of the embankment.

The attack broke. One moment it was a seemingly unstoppable, indistinguishable wave of humanity, and the next it was hundreds of frightened individuals fleeing the killing ground heedless of the penal units waiting to their rear.

Turnbull watched as the tide turned, and pivoted to Hernandez, who did not need to be told what to do.

"Cease fire!" Hernandez bellowed. "Cease fire!"

The shooting stopped, and for a moment there was silence along the line. Farther north, in the Bravo and Charlie sectors, there was still some shooting, but it too was dying out as the attackers turned tail and tore back west across the corpse-strewn wash.

It was then that another noise replaced it, groans and occasional screams of men shot and lying in the burning sun. There were certainly wounded on the bike path, but most of the cries came from below, down in the wash where the repeated volleys had blown holes in the advancing front line, and in the individuals as well. The 5.56mm round – contrary to the bizarre myths promulgated by the disarmament crowd whose hatred of the AR15 matched its hatred of their owners – was not a large round. It did not necessarily kill. Instead, it caused horrific wounds, and while the medics rushed to treat the wounded soldiers and Provisionals, the wounded enemy was a different story.

"We're short medics and Class VIII," Hernandez said to Turnbull, referring to the logistics category that included medical supplies. Implicit was the question of what to do with the wounded enemy.

"Evac the wounded, reallocate ammo," Turnbull said. "And toss the enemy into the wash. If they come again, they can do it over their buddies."

Hernandez nodded. So far, he had counted eight more dead among his troopers and scores of wounded. He gathered a detail to heave the enemy off the bike path.

"That's old school," Lieutenant Faith said, eyeing the Henry as he approached Turnbull.

"Does the job," Turnbull said. He looked over the young officer. "Good work."

Faith nodded. "Thank you. For everything, I mean."

"It was no hit on you, LT. It's just...."

"The troops come before my ego, sir. You were the right guy at the right time."

Turnbull looked out over the wash, at the dead littering the floor – had to be several hundred of them – and at the retreating remnants fleeing back to the subdivision across the way. A few minutes before, the penal units had stopped firing and allowed the retreat.

"I still can't believe it's come to this," 2LT Faith said quietly. "Americans fighting Americans. I had a great-great-great grandfather in the 54th Massachusetts. But that, that always just seemed like history to me, like it could never happen again. But it has."

Turnbull was not sure what to say, not sure what he wanted to say. These people tried to kill him, so he killed them first. That was how it worked, right? But these dead men, on both sides, were Americans. That had to matter.

Enough.

Nothing he could say or do would change the reality of the situation the country was in, so he instinctively focused on the mission.

"They'll be back," Turnbull said.

"When it gets dark?"

"A night attack is hard enough for trained troops," Turnbull mused. He tried to remember what phase of the moon it was and drew a blank. "My guess is dawn."

"We're red on ammo. We'll go black if we have another attack like that one."

"They'll probe us tonight, try to keep us awake, make us waste bullets. You've got to make sure the men preserve their rounds."

"I'll cross-level ammo."

"Top's on that. Let the NCOs do their thing. Fifty percent security. I've had my nap. You go get some z's."

"I'm not tired, sir."

"Yeah you are. You haven't slept in days. The adrenaline is just telling you you're not tired, and it's a lying ass bitch. That was not a suggestion. I need you sharp when we stand-to at 0430."

2LT Faith nodded, and looked out at the battlefield one last time.

"Sir," he said with a hesitation that seemed incongruous for someone so physically large and imposing. "Will I ever get used to this?"

Turnbull was looking at the battlefield too, and he did not take his eyes off it.

"You're a praying man, right, LT?"

"I am."

"Then pray you don't."

16.

Martin Rios-Parkinson – he occasionally used the rank "colonel" not because he knew what it meant but because he thought it sounded impressive – listened glumly to the radio reports from the faltering attack. He was no military man, and the one actual veteran in the command post was a former Air Force Reserve Judge Advocate General major who had only gotten that far for having been a protégé of a fellow JAG, Congressman Ted Lieu. But he understood defeat, and this was a defeat, even if only a temporary one.

"The forces are coming back," he said, searching for the military term. "Retreating, I believe it is called." A Smith & Wesson .38 revolver hung in a holster to his side, and Rios-Parkinson still walked with a limp after having accidentally shot off the tip of his little toe cleaning it not long after the assistant professor had been presented with the weapon in recognition of his role as founder, organizer, and generalissimo of the People's Militia of Los Angeles.

Using his collection of addicts, criminals, committed cadre, and pierced, bitter college students acting out their rage at their parents, his mob had effectively become the only organized armed force in the Los Angeles area after the LAPD had been dismantled, though in some outlying areas there were still uncooperative and reactionary forces in control. He recalled the ill-fated attempts to enter Simi Valley and Castaic and intimidate the locals; the People's Militia, or more aptly, the survivors, had staggered away after meeting determined resistance from the organized locals who had apparently not received the memo that their personally owned firearms were to have been turned in.

They would be dealt with all in good time. Now, it was essential to reach Fort Irwin and its storehouses of arms and ammunition. To do that, they had to break through the Army forces holding the bottom of the Cajon Pass. It would cost lives though, many lives, and as a Marxist, if there was one thing that Professor Rios-Parkinson was it was conscious of class. The privileged college students who had been his original shock troops, intimidating other faculty and soft bureaucrats first at the colleges and later in the city government, were not here. That caste, segregated into the Patrice Lumumba Battalion, was better suited to bullying civilians back in Los Angeles. And, educated and woke as was Rios-Parkinson, they were his own kind and, therefore, their lives had value to the cause. These others – the ones out here fighting in that dry wash – could serve the cause either alive, or through their deaths.

Rios-Parkinson was utterly indifferent as to which.

The fighters at the foot of Cajon Pass were neither pampered nor schooled in social justice, nor particularly interested in it beyond the most superficial level. They were the disaffected and dispossessed, some recently released from the prison-industrial complex where they had been incarcerated unjustly, whether they had committed their alleged crimes or not. Others were homeless. Many were young men, and a few women, from the blighted parts of the blue city with no prospects thanks to the Los Angeles School District's chronic malpractice, who were handed a Chinese assault rifle, a packet of meth or PCP if they wanted it (also provided by Beijing), and pointed at the people they were to kill.

But even the joy of violence, the prospect of loot, pharmaceuticals, and the *frisson* of ideological fervor was not always enough to incentivize these amateurs to run into the blazing guns of the professionals. So Rios-Parkinson reached back to Soviet history – Stalin was an endless cornucopia of tactics, techniques, and procedures for the likes of Martin Rios-Parkinson – and implemented one of the Red Army's most notorious motivational initiatives.

"Tell the penal units to cease firing on those who are retreating," Rios-Parkinson said. The former major, named Lou Carper, was wearing a camouflage shirt and tan Dockers, and he was surprised. After all, it had been Rios-Parkinson who had come up with the carrot and stick approach to urging the force forward. The carrot was the ability to loot and pillage the racist suburbs they swept through coming east from Los Angeles along the I-10 corridor. The stick was groups of more reliable cadres manning machine guns following behind the main force shooting anyone going the wrong way.

"Let them come back. Gather them together here," he directed. "More forces are coming from Los Angeles and up from San Diego. We will reorganize here and attack again tonight." They did not know that what they were setting up was an "assembly area," but what they lacked in a familiarity with military nomenclature they made up in sheer number of bodies and cheap Kalashnikov knockoffs helpfully smuggled into the Port of LA by Chinese intelligence inside CONEXs that were supposed to contain coffee mugs and sweat shirts destined for Walmart.

"A night attack"? Carper asked. "Those are challenging even with trained troops. It will be hard to control them, and hard for the penal unit to see them to motivate them. Maybe we should wait until first light?"

Rios-Parkinson considered the advice. Carper's pronouns were he/him, at least for now. He had famously accused the Air Force of systemic racism in a blistering congressional hearing overseen by Ted Lieu and had been immediately offered a full professorship at the UCLA School of Law. As a JAG, he had little actual experience in combat operations, and as an Air Force officer, ground operations were not in his wheelhouse. But he had been in some form of the military and he was certainly politically reliable – his main teaching assignment at the law school was a class titled "Racism, Rap, and Resistance: Critical Theory and Copyright Law" – so Rios-Parkinson brought him on board to assist in organizing what had grown into an army of over 40,000, many of whom were still in Los Angeles, maintaining order, such as it was.

And they had done remarkably well so far. They had successfully surprised the military forces entering Los Angeles, taking advantage of the Pentagon's rules of engagement that tied the soldiers' hands and allowed Rios-Parkinson to get his hordes close enough to launch a devastating surprise attack. The military had retreated backwards, but with its hands untied it made the leftists pay for every foot they took crawling through the successive cities along the Inland Empire toward Cajon Pass.

"Dawn it is," Rios-Parkinson said. "We will overwhelm the racist forces, and we will kill them all."

Except for the enforced rest for the lieutenant, who had not slept for two days as he led his men on their fighting retreat, there was no rest for Alpha Troop. Wounded had to be cared for, the bodies of soldiers and Provisionals carefully removed, and the bodies of the enemy not so carefully removed. Ammo had to be cross-leveled, spread evenly among the remaining troops. The magazines from the dead and wounded were policed up and handed back out. The remaining loose ammo was loaded into empty mags. And all the time they watched the wash, trying to grab a swig of water or quickly down a packet of whatever MRE entrée was handy.

Alpha received some resupply, a little 5.56mm ammo and some boxes of MREs. They also got crates of bottled water, mostly Dasani, even though the water, unlike the power, was still on. A LOGPAC, basically a convoy of trucks, had come down from the logistics base miles to the rear. First Sergeant Hernandez, who was in charge of beans and bullets, had overseen it. Turnbull finished walking the perimeter when Top pulled up in a hummer leading a five-ton. Hernandez got out and opened the back door. A frightened private in a fresh uniform stepped out, awkwardly cradling his M4 and looking around with very wide eyes.

"Got us a replacement," Top said, grinning.

"One?" asked Turnbull.

"Well sir, I'm sure he's a badass."

Turnbull looked over the eighteen-year-old. The private did not know what to make of the civilian garbed, scary man, but he caught the "sir" and saluted.

"Hey!" Top shouted. "You want to get the CO sniped? Be a badass, not a dumbass."

The lad looked petrified.

"Come on," Turnbull said.

Turnbull and the first sergeant walked the nervous new soldier over to one of the squads from third platoon. They were reloading mags and shooting the shit. The group of eight got quiet as the commander and Top approached.

"New guy for you, Sullivan," the senior NCO said. The squad leader gestured for the private to take a seat and when he did, the staff sergeant handed him a bottle of Dasani from an open, half-empty case. The trooper sat, nervous, cradling his bottle and his M4.

"You guys set?" Turnbull asked.

"Garry Owen," replied the squad leader. His eyes were bloodshot and there was a smear of red on his uniform – whose it was unclear.

"You got any questions?" Turnbull asked them.

"Do we have any fire support?" asked the squad leader.

"Does throwing grenades count?" Turnbull asked. The squad, less the new guy, laughed bitterly. They had not been issued grenades because no one expected full-scale war against other Americans. The new guy looked around, confused.

"How long we gotta hold here, sir?" asked a team leader, a buck sergeant with a bandage stuck to his forehead.

"Until they tell us to move out," Turnbull said. "They're trying to fortify the pass, so after they do that, they'll pull you out. My guess is tomorrow morning." He said "you" because he still intended to infiltrate west. He still had some roaches to exterminate.

"The bad guys will at least probe us all night," the squad leader said.

"Try and get your guys some z's," Top said. "No less than 50/50 on the line. Stand-to at 0430." The squad leader nodded. He would not let more than half his guys try and catnap at any one time in their positions during the night. At 4:30 a.m., everyone would be up and ready to fight – the pre-dawn light would be a good time to attack.

"Anyone else got any questions?" Turnbull asked. Normally he avoided conversation, but the men needed to know he cared, and so far, all the questions had been good ones. So far.

"Sir," the new private said after taking a swig from a bottle of Dasani. The whole squad looked at him askance, since his job was to shut up and learn. But he had not learned *that* yet, and so he asked his question.

"You've done this before, sir. How does it feel to kill another human being?"

Turnbull paused. It was an awkward query only a freaking new guy would ask the old man, but he had asked it and now the whole squad was watching to see how Captain Turnbull answered.

"I don't know," Turnbull said. "I've only ever killed *jihadis* and communists."

The squad, again less the new guy, broke into laughter, and the staff sergeant said, "Badass, sir, I straight up love that internet meme!"

Turnbull squinted. "What's a meme?" he asked, genuinely puzzled. Then he moved on with Top behind him.

"Damn," said the squad leader, watching the command team walk off. Then he turned to the new guy. "And you, new guy – keep your dumbass mouth shut!"

There was very little moonlight, and the wash was pitch black. During the night, there had been some shooting – most of it bursts of fire from militia crawling up within a hundred meters and unloading a mag at the embankment. One guy caught a slug in the arm from a lucky shot; the rest of the rounds flew off into the interior of the subdivision. The squad leaders made sure that the return fire was from designated marksmen aiming at the bursts. Most of the return fire probably missed, but occasionally they would hear a moan and a collective cheer would go up along the line.

Turnbull's first concern was that he was short about 20 men. The Provisionals, who lost seven of their guys in the first attack, were pulling out.

"I need you," he said.

"Our families need us," said a bearded man with a full battle rig and an FN SCAR. He was a high school coach before all this and the unofficial leader of the Provisionals. "They are going to come back tomorrow and you don't have the ammo to hold them off."

The coach was right, and Turnbull had no good counter argument. "Get your families out of here. Get up the pass. If they break through that, drive out into the desert and hide out."

The coach nodded. "Sorry to do this to you."

"You got your mission, we have ours." The coach left with his men, and Hernandez strung the troopers even more thinly across the frontage.

Leaving Top on the line, he went back out to White Ash Road to the home that housed the aid station. About two dozen troopers sat or lay inside the living room as the medical platoon sergeant worked over a wounded young trooper. He glared at Turnbull as the new commander entered. Turnbull ignored him.

Who could blame him for fury at the perceived author of this butchery? Then Turnbull proceeded to speak to the men.

"I know you're hurt. I need every one of you who can fight."

The men were silent for a moment, then they looked at each other, and most all of those who were not lying on stretchers – and a couple who were – struggled to their feet.

"Where do you need us, sir?" said a sergeant with his left arm in a field expedient sling.

"Report to Top," Turnbull said. "And thanks." He watched as the men limped out the door behind the NCO.

He did not sleep at all but walked the sandbag line back and forth all night. The new trooper was snoring as he lay against the wall. SSG Sullivan shook his head.

"Well sir, there's at least one thing the new guy is good at," he said.

Turnbull paused to look over the battlefield. Mercifully, most of the moaning from the wounded had stopped.

"Reminds me of *Zulu*," the squad leader said. "You know, Rorke's Drift? You ever see that, sir?"

"Of course. I identify as male," Turnbull replied. "Except there's a big difference. The Zulus were proud, tough, and brave warriors, and these are criminal assholes."

"True, but they are American criminal assholes. It probably shouldn't make a difference, but I kind of think it does. Some of our guys maybe have brothers or sisters or whatevers in the blue. I don't – my people are from Nebraska and we don't put up with that shit."

"How's your family?" Turnbull asked, then he regretted it because it reminded him of his own.

"They're Provisionals," SSG Sullivan replied. "It's hardcore back there. There's one group of Provisionals out there that they say Larry the Cable Guy commands. They say they spelled out 'Git-R-Done' with the heads of Antifa that came out into the country looking for trouble."

Turnbull looked at him skeptically.

"That's what I heard, sir."

"I don't care who ya are, that's funny right there," Turnbull replied before continuing on down the line.

At 0430 hours, when it was still dark and the sun was not even yet hinting at peeking over the San Bernardino mountains to the east, the first sergeant called stand-to. Every soldier and Marine was awake and on the line, looking toward the wash and waiting. Turnbull, Faith, and Hernandez were in the center, also looking west, thinking about their plan.

"That's a bold strategy, Cotton," Lieutenant Faith said to no one in particular.

"I know that movie," replied Turnbull. It was one of the ones they had played over and over on deployment, and it had ingrained itself in his mind. "If you can dodge a wrench, you can dodge a ball."

"It's risky as hell, sir," said the first sergeant.

"If you've got a better plan, I am all ears," Turnbull said, and he was serious. He desperately wanted a better plan, but he couldn't think of one, not under these conditions. His recent visit to Gettysburg had kept running through his mind. And finally, it was clear what they had to do. "We've got under a hundred bodies and almost no ammo. We do have the terrain, though, so we use that."

"I don't have a better plan," Top replied. He was still for a few moments. "I'm going to go make sure everyone is clear on everything and make sure they pull that car around into the back yard."

Turnbull nodded. The car was key. Everything depended on that.

They waited. Behind them, the sun was starting to rise. At least it would be in the enemy's face when they came.

The wash was still dark and murky, the rays not yet probing into its darkness, as Turnbull walked the depleted line of sandbags. He did some spot checks along the way, confirming everyone had at least two 30-round magazines. A few had some more magazines, but none had less. Sixty shots each and ammo would be black.

Not enough. Hence the plan.

The rays of the sun rapidly filled the wash. It was dark one minute and the next it was light, and they were there, thousands of them, having snuck out as close as they dared in the early morning and waiting for dawn. Exposed by the sun, they stood and they shouted, a guttural, hateful roar that was meant to inspire terror. But the cav troopers were too tired to be scared. They stood on the line, impassive, and watched.

Turnbull walked down the line until he was in the midst of the Marines.

"That's a lot of assholes," SGT Betley said, spitting a disgusting wad of chew over the sandbag wall. It was the last of his Copenhagen, but judging by the sheer number of People's Militia out there, he figured he probably wouldn't have much use for any more.

"Sure is," Turnbull replied. It was the same collection of mostly young men, hopped up on goofballs and screaming incoherently. There were very few of the little princes and princesses who enjoyed their bespoke rebellion while on sabbatical from college. Apparently, they were excused from cannon fodder duty. It amused Turnbull that the class war had finally come and it was the damn Marxists who rigorously observed class distinctions. In the dictatorship of the proletariat, it was the proles who were getting dicked.

They were starting to move forward, though with some trepidation. The human debris from the prior afternoon was out there rotting on the floor of the wash, and now that it was exposed by the light the carnage killed some of their buzz. They were out at 300 meters. Turnbull knew that precisely because he had ordered some troopers to break up a white picket fence in the neighborhood and go down onto the floor of the wash among the corpses and plant a white picket at every 50-meter interval out to 300 meters.

Turnbull moved back toward the center of the line.

"Steady," first sergeant yelled.

The militia started to pick up speed, and their shouting picked-up volume. It was as if the enemy was collectively talking itself into the idea that charging the cavalry was a good idea.

Turnbull entered SSG Sullivan's sector. The NCO was peering over the wall at the charging, roaring enemy, and Turnbull stopped beside him.

"We should have got a stereo out here and cranked some music of our own," Sullivan said.

"There's no power," Turnbull mumbled, watching them come.

"We could sing," Sullivan replied, as if the answer were obvious. "*Men of Harlech* would work."

"Welshmen will not yield," Turnbull muttered.

"Or cavalrymen," added the sergeant. Turnbull appreciated the sentiment. He declined to remind the squad leader of how, at Little Big Horn, the outnumbered and outgunned cavalrymen died with their boots on.

To a man.

The enemy crossed the 200-meter line, then the 150-meter line. They seemed giddy now, barreling forward without resistance.

"Come on," Turnbull said quietly. They approached the 100-meter picket, a wave of angry, riling humanity, now firing bursts of 7.62 x 39mm rounds at the sandbags.

"First sergeant!" They crossed the 50-meter mark. "Now!"

"Volley fire, present, aim!" Top shouted. The 50 or so men along the wall stared down their rifles and selected targets.

"Fire!"

The line of rifles roared. Dozens of the enemy staggered and fell, engulfed by the mass of bodies rumbling forward.

Hernandez silently counted eight and yelled, "Fire!" He yelled loudly – their ears were all ringing.

The men had not needed to be told to select their targets. They just did it, and another four dozen fell.

Turnbull was firing along with his Henry, trying to pick out leaders. There did not seem to be any among the mob, so he tried to shoot those who seemed the biggest and the bravest.

By the time they fired three more volleys, the mass of militia was at the foot of the embankment, its momentum stalled by the hundred or so just shot down as well as the bodies of those killed the day before. Still, they began to scramble up the dirt hill.

Turnbull was already back across the bike path at the hole in the fence. In the back yard of the headquarters house, there was a Ford Explorer that one of the guys had hotwired and driven around the side to park on the turf in back. The hood was propped open. A young trooper sat in the driver's seat, door open, eyes wide.

"Now!" shouted Turnbull. "Now!"

The trooper looked at Turnbull, baffled.

"Now!"

The trooper furrowed his brow, and Turnbull understood. The soldier couldn't hear him after shooting all afternoon. Turnbull made the "honk" gesture with his hand.

The soldier saw and understood, and he hit the horn, a long and sustained blast that everyone across the front could hear despite the ringing in their ears.

The 50 or so troopers along the sandbag wall turned and bolted back across the bike path to the foot of the fence line, where they turned back again, then knelt and took aim. Above them, the rest of the cavalry troop stood up over the fence, perched on lawn furniture, boxes, or whatever else was handy to provide a step. They too took aim.

The enemy was climbing up in front of a 100-man firing squad.

At the gap in the fence by the headquarters stood Turnbull with his Henry. Top joined him, his own M4 ready.

"Volley fire!" Top yelled as the first wave came over the top of the sand bags. "Aim! Fire!"

The first volley cut the initial wave of attackers to pieces, strewing them across the bike path and draping them over the sandbag wall. More took their place.

"Fire!"

The volley shattered the attackers who had gotten to the top. More scrambled up and over.

"Fire!"

It went on and on, volley after volley, with only a few militiamen managing to stagger as far as the white line down the middle of the bike path before being killed. But some managed to fire their weapons and there were several cav troopers hit, some kneeling, some shot through the wooden fence that provided concealment but not cover.

The kneelers who had fired the first volleys from the sandbags ran dry first and changed mags. Five volleys afterward, the fence rank did the same.

Hernandez did not call for another volley, not yet. There were no live targets left on the bike path.

Lieutenant Faith bellowed, "Forward!" and the men lurched back across the bike path to the sandbags. The entire troop was now positioned above the roiling mass of trapped militia below. The enemy could not advance up the embankment, and the penal units were melting their barrels driving them forward. They were caught among hundreds of their dead comrades, and many tossed their rifles away and focused only on getting out of the death trap.

Turnbull looked north. Bravo was in desperate trouble. Charlie too. If they fell, Alpha would be swept away by the enemy hitting its northern flank. With Ironhorse gone, the pass would fall, and then Irwin.

Turnbull knew what he had to do. He didn't want to, but it was necessary. And they started this civil war.

"Do it," Turnbull said.

"You sure?" asked the lieutenant.

"Do it."

"Fire!" commanded Lieutenant Faith, and the troopers did, again and again, shooting down into the hapless mob. Nearly 100 men fired fifteen volleys into the mass of attackers below. But the enemy did not break – they cowered in place.

For the plan to work, they had to run. They had to be routed.

"Time to get our Joshua Chamberlain on," Turnbull told the lieutenant.

"Bayonets!" boomed Faith's deep bass voice. "Fix bayonets!"

The troopers paused from the slaughter to pull out their M9 bayonets, ugly green-handled knives with a serrated blade that snapped onto a lug on the end of their M4s.

"Here you go," the first sergeant said to Turnbull, handing him an M4 with an M9 attached to the barrel. The blood splattered on it told him its former owner would not be needing it. Top's own carbine already had its blade mounted.

Turnbull put down the Henry and checked the M4's mag – about half-full – snapped it back in the well, then turned to Faith. "Now!"

Faith yelled "Charge!"

The entire cav troop and the Marines hopped the sandbag fence and rushed down the embankment. The men caught at the bottom were utterly baffled at what they saw – a hundred soldiers with spear points gleaming charging *them*.

And when what was happening finally registered, their reptile brains took over. Those knives produced exactly the terror that Turnbull had hoped for. The machine guns of the penal units were much preferable to being gutted by these fiends and their blades.

The vast majority of the enemy broke and ran west into the penal units, which kept the machine gunners from firing on the troops. But some of the militiamen fought. A few got rounds off and some soldiers fell. The chaos swirled – there, Faith was throwing a militiaman over his head into another one, here,

Sergeant Betley was smashing in the face of another with the butt of his carbine, before turning it around and plunging the knife into the man's gut. Even the new guy was trying to pull his blade out of the shoulder of a screaming man who was waving his fists impotently at the trooper.

Turnbull jabbed the left eye of a guy trying to brain him with an empty AK. The man dropped the rifle and put his hands to his face as Turnbull jammed the knife up under his rib cage and ripped it back out, the serrations along the top of the blade leaving a horrid gash. The man keeled. Turnbull was suddenly knocked down from the right, falling on top of two corpses, the M4 still in his hand. He twisted and saw his attacker, a guy with bloodshot eyes and snot running out of his nose. When the man tried to leap upon him, Turnbull pivoted the M4, and the attacker impaled himself. His corpse hung in the air for a moment, then fell over, wrenching the weapon out of Turnbull's hand.

Another guy, this one wearing a black t-shirt that read, in white letters, "BURN THIS MOTHER DOWN," staggered forward with an AK, firing from the hip. The rounds stitched the corpse to his right. Turnbull managed to pull the Wilson before the man could acquire him and fired three times, one of the hollow points dotting the "I" in "THIS" and blowing the target backwards into a heap of bodies.

Turnbull got to his feet, pistol in hand. To his right, Hernandez slashed open the abdomen of another enemy, who shrieked as his innards spilled. A direct thrust through the sternum silenced him. A few yards away, mixed in with his own men, a militiaman was pulling back the charging handle on an AK. Turnbull dropped him with a single shot through the left temple.

And that was about the end of the fight. Here and there, a trooper was thrusting his M9 into one of the laggards, but the rest of the mob had fled, utterly broken. As the southern flank of the People's Militia attack disintegrated in panic, so did the center, and then the north.

The attack failed. Ironhorse had held the subdivision.

"Back up top!" Turnbull yelled, gulping for air. "Let's go!"

The cavalry turned and climbed back up the embankment, and the enemy fled back to the west.

"You all set, First Sergeant?" Turnbull watched some of the troop's tactical vehicles pulling out, driving slowly and trying to keep down the engine noise. It was hot, about 1400 hours, and it was starting to stink something fierce. Out along the line, there was still a squad manning the perimeter. But there was also a long line of helmets set there on the top of the sandbag wall. Their owners would not be needing them, but they were useful to give the impression that the line was still fully manned.

"I'm all set, sir. And I got laid up some surprises for them when they do come," Hernandez said, grinning.

"No surprises until I cross over," Turnbull replied. Hopefully, they had bloodied the enemy's nose well enough that they would not try again before dark. If they came during daylight, Turnbull would have little choice but to try to hide out in the subdivision, then escape and evade west after sunset as the bad guys fought it out with the few remaining homegrown Provisionals and occupied it.

Lieutenant Faith trotted over, a bandage around his upper left arm. His radioman was with him.

"They want you, sir," he said, handing Turnbull the mic.

"It's your troop now, John," Turnbull demurred. "I'm back on mission."

"They said you specifically." Turnbull sighed and took the mic.

"Yeah," Turnbull said, ignoring proper radio procedure. Whatever this conversation was going to be, it was not going to be standard operating procedure.

"Your mission is scrubbed," said the voice on the other end. It sounded like that one-star Turnbull had talked to before coming down.

"Scrubbed?"

"Roger, scrubbed. You come out with the unit. They have other plans for you."

"I can't do that without authentication."

"Your boss said you would ask for it. Is your authentication code really 'Pretty in Pink'?"

"I didn't choose it," Turnbull growled into the microphone. "I never choose the codes."

"See you soon. Out," Turnbull handed the mic back to the RTO and looked at Faith.

"I guess I pull out with you guys. Like I said, this is your unit now, LT. I'm going to go sit in the back of a hummer and sleep."

2LT Faith nodded and turned to his first sergeant.

"I want to make sure we have one hundred percent accountability, Top. Everyone goes home, alive or dead." Top nodded. The wounded had been evacuated first. He had already made sure that the troop position, as well as the dry wash below, was totally swept, and that not a single cavalry trooper's or Marine's body would be left behind. One of the five-tons held nothing but the honored dead, their bodies carefully wrapped in tarps and gently placed feet-out on the steel floor of the truck.

"We ain't going anywhere until we have accountability, sir," Hernandez replied. He held up a three-page printout he got from the admin section, which was now typing again instead of fighting. It was the unit battle roster, the list of each soldier in the troop by position. His handwritten notes indicated who was present for duty, wounded, and dead.

Satisfied that 2LT Faith had this under control, Turnbull walked over to a hummer and got in the back-passenger's seat. He was met by barking.

"Stop barking," he told the corgi, exasperated. "You're first sergeant's problem now."

The troops had gathered up a half-dozen of their animal friends and were taking them out of there with them. It was probably against some regulation, but Top knew that if he told them not to do it, they'd just focus on doing it without him catching them instead of focusing on their mission, so he said nothing. American soldiers, he knew, loved dogs.

Not Turnbull, though. "Really?" he said as the animal stepped gingerly onto his lap. He gave up, shut his eyes, and leaned back in the seat to try to drop off to sleep.

An hour later, they were turning up onto the Cajon Pass grade on I-15. The helmet ruse had fooled the bad guys for a while, but it became pretty clear as the last elements of Alpha Troop were loading up that the Army forces were abandoning their position. Small clumps of attackers sniped and probed, moving cautiously forward through the bodies of their predecessors that littered the sandy floor of the dry wash. Those who got too close had met a hail of well-aimed rifle fire from Sergeant Betley's Marines, who had insisted on taking the dangerous rearguard mission. Top had consolidated most of the remaining ammo with the detachment left in contact, and now more enemy bodies joined the hundreds lying dead from before. But the bad guys kept coming, and eventually the last troopers and the Marines pulled back, mounted up and rode off toward the rear.

First Sergeant Hernandez was in the passenger seat and turned around to Turnbull. He offered him what looked like an OD-green cell phone.

"You want to do the honors, sir?"

Turnbull shook his head.

"Seems like NCO business to me," Turnbull replied.

"Damn, captain, some sergeant trained you right," said the smiling NCO. He looked down at the device and pushed the blinking red button.

The Jeep Wrangler bumped and jolted as it crossed the wash heading east. Rios-Parkinson silently cursed the driver. Ahead of them was a line of armed men who made up the penal unit. They were not employed at the moment, since their warriors were advancing as ordered. The subdivision a quarter mile to the front had been abandoned by the Army. The mass of the People's

Militia had run forward eagerly and was now entering the line of subdivision, assured of whatever spoils its members could take from the houses. Cash, appliances, jewels, money. Maybe some women who had not fled. No, now the problem was not urging them forward but holding them back.

The jeep shuddered, and there was a wet sound. Rios-Parkinson looked out the window. The bump had been a body, now flattened by the tires, and there were more and more of them as they got closer to the battle line.

Rios-Parkinson turned toward Carper, who sat in the back seat looking at a map.

"Our militia will want to waste time taking their reparations," he said. "But we need to immediately move up into the pass and secure it, before the racist forces can build another line of defenses."

"If they haven't already," Carper said. "There's a very good chance that is why they held us here, to give the rest of the force time to build up a defensive line in the pass."

Rios-Parkinson scowled. A second big fight, in a long canyon, would be bloody, but in the end that did not matter as long as there was a victory. Another several thousand People's Militia had arrived coming north from San Diego with heavy weapons from Pendleton, though there were not enough veterans among them who knew how to put the armor and artillery to use. No matter. He had numbers. There were thousands more from the City of Angels being transported out to the fight using old Los Angeles Unified School District buses. Plenty of angry, motivated fighters. And he had plenty of Chinese AKs to provide them.

He smiled. His army would roll over whatever resistance the imperialists presented and seize Fort Irwin and all the treasures it held. And then he could afford the time to allow his fighters to avenge themselves upon the families of those who chose to fight for fascism. #MeToo did not apply to them.

"I believe our victory is cert–," he began, but then the entire line of suburban houses facing the wash along White Ash Road, along with the People's Militia that had just occupied them, detonated in a massive fireball. The jeep skidded to a stop, and a blender blasted out of the kitchen of one of the houses landed on the Jeep's hood with a terrifying crash.

Rios-Parkinson just stared forward, wide-eyed.

"I appreciate what you did, Turnbull," the general said. They were in the command post. Outside, Turnbull had seen the difference a day had made. Many, many more soldiers had arrived in the last day, along with equipment like 105mm towed artillery. Cargo planes were circling overhead waiting for their tight slot to fly into the Victorville Airport and disgorge even more men and material. And on the drive up I-15 to the high desert plateau, it was clear that the combat engineers had been at work. Trenches, barbed wire, mines. The People's Militia would come, and a kinder person would have prayed for them.

Turnbull was not a kinder person. They would get what they deserved.

"Good unit. Good young LT," Turnbull said.

"They'll get a few hours to refit and rearm and then back on the line."

"One more thing," Turnbull said. He handed the general a three-page printout, stapled in the upper left-hand corner. "Awards. For valor."

The general took it and examined it.

"This is the Alpha Troop battle roster," he said, confused.

"Yeah," Turnbull said. "They all deserve a medal. Every damn one of them." He turned to go.

"Your name's not on here," the general said, looking up. Turnbull pivoted back to answer him before walking out.

"I'm dead, so I was never here."

17.

Kelly Turnbull and Clay Deeds were standing in the red states' main command post outside Dallas, ID badges clipped to their shirts. There were many big-screen monitors mounted on the walls, tables with computers linked to bundles of wires, and a collection of uniformed and civilian-attired personnel scurrying about.

The monitors displayed various news channels, like Trump News, which had abandoned New York City and Washington for Dallas – as well as maps. They were situation maps, with standard military forces symbols Turnbull recognized – divisions, brigade combat teams, and battalions – in red and blue, and many more that were annotated "P" (always red) or "PM" (always in blue).

"Lots of Provisionals and People's Militia," Turnbull observed. The People's Militia forces were primarily within the cities and the Provisionals mostly outside of urban areas in the suburbs or countryside. "There are a lot more of them than professional soldiers."

"Yes, the Constitutional Alliance ordered all healthy adult citizens between 17 and 60 into service as Provisionals. About 50% appeared for duty. Of course, a bunch of older guys showed up too. A lot are veterans, and they took charge organizing their own local units. It being Texas and Oklahoma and such, most had their own rifles already," Deeds said.

"I'm sure there are some sissies even in the red states," Turnbull said.

"We have a lot of folks coming in here from blue areas, and a fair number flowing out," Deeds replied. "We were preparing to storm Austin but we gave the liberals a chance to leave."

"So, basically a herd of pumpkin-infused IPA drinkers with skinny jeans and not much upper body strength is heading north?"

"You've never seen so many Priuses packed with luggage," Deeds said.

Turnbull examined the maps. "The red forces are surrounding the cities," he said. "But not going in."

"Exactly," Deeds said. "Your pal General Scott wants to clear out the People's Militia, but the consensus is we don't have the forces to take and hold the cities."

"I saw that at Cajon Pass," Turnbull said. "They held the pass but there just aren't enough red bodies to go in and take and occupy LA."

"It's the same almost everywhere," Deeds said. "Instead of assaulting them, if they are in the red, we're going to let them leave, and if they are in the blue, we're going to starve them out. Notice how our forces are cutting off the highways and waterways into urban areas?"

"When the blues run out of kale, they are going to be sad," Turnbull observed. "I bet their community urban gardens are won't quite cut it."

"They were so busy being smug they forgot who grows most everything," Deeds said. "The other scary stuff is international. The Chi Coms are active, the Russians too. And the UN is talking about a peacekeeping force for North America."

"That would be a bad idea," Turnbull said. "Not that fighting the UN would bum me out. Other Americans, not a good thing. The United Nations, count me in."

"The point is that right now subduing all the blue areas is impractical, militarily and politically, no matter what General

Scott thinks. Our professional military forces, after desertions, are at about 65% strength, and there were never enough soldiers to forcefully occupy the country even before. Counting cops, and they tend to go red or blue depending on their locality's color, we still don't have the numbers. Cops are designed to arrest criminals, not take and hold territory like the infantry. The Provisionals' heart is in the right place, and while they are okay for local security and defense they are just not organized, equipped, or trained for offensive military operations."

"I am, though. I could be whittling down the opposition brain trust in sunny Southern California. I hear some of the other TF Zulu guys are doing that elsewhere," Turnbull said.

Deed shrugged.

Turnbull frowned at the evasion. "Why did you pull me back, Clay?"

"You're not in LA stalking blue bigwigs because we got incredibly lucky," Deeds said. "We have a line on Crane's location."

"You know where he's taking his hot rock?"

"Not for certain. But the guy who may know is in Texas Health Presbyterian Hospital."

"What's he got? Lead poisoning?"

"Yes, plus frostbite."

The hospital had been taken over by the state of Texas under an emergency decree by the governor. It was treating the wounded from the violent suppression of blue forces in the Dallas-Ft. Worth area over the last week. As the designated capital of the red states, there was no leeway for rioting or the establishment of autonomous zones in the metroplex. Combined police, military, and Provisional forces had moved in on the few areas of resistance, responding to any violence with overwhelming force. Outside town, on the plains, there were large encampments for the prisoners. The morgues were full of those who were not so lucky. Regardless, Dallas was secure.

Turnbull's and Deeds' access badges got them inside the prisoners' ward. Security was provided by what had to be retired corrections officers with 12-gauge shotguns and no sense of humor. One mouthy prisoner, cuffed to his bed, was screaming obscenities at the bulls until one butt-stroked him a few times in the gut with his Mossberg.

"I guess we're not worried about police brutality anymore," Turnbull observed as they walked past down the ward hallway. "It's like I'm back in Baghdad."

"Remember, you're in America, Kelly," Deeds said. "Still, I don't know if we ever go back how it was."

"We'll see what happens in St. Louis," Turnbull replied. The word of the peace conference in the city on the edge of red and blue America had broken while they were driving to the hospital.

"Jaw jaw is better than civil war war," Deeds said.

Turnbull grunted noncommittally. The politicians had gotten the country in deep, and he had doubts that the politicians could pull it out.

"This is him," Deeds said, stopping at a room. There was a man in his twenties on the bed, fingers and feet wrapped in bandages, an IV line running into his left arm and a red, weathered face. His nose was reddish to dark purple. Deeds was not kidding about frostbite.

A chain connected the prisoner's right arm to the bed frame.

"Gary Kelso," Deeds said, standing by the bed. The Canucks had called the Americans – luckily red ones – about this injured man near the Arctic Circle babbling about a bomber in his delirium and Deeds had immediately sent a plane. He had briefed Turnbull on what little had been gleaned from the captive so far, so Turnbull was prepared for Kelso's attitude.

"Who the hell are you?" the man croaked.

"Be polite," Turnbull growled back. "I've been informed that the rules against beating the shit out of people have been temporarily lifted. Keep that in mind."

"Oh, I'm used to psychopaths."

"Is it a psychopath who shot you or just someone random you pissed off running your mouth?"

"I don't have to say anything. I have rights."

"That's not really technically true," Turnbull said, strolling around to Kelso's bedside. "In the sense that there's an H-bomb you helped steal out there and no one, but no one, is going to be particularly fussy over a few more injuries showing up on your chart."

"I don't know about any H-bomb," Kelso said.

"That's not what the Eskimos who picked your ass up stumbling down an ice road in the middle of the Arctic said you told them."

"Don't call them 'Eskimos.' It's racist."

"How about I shut the room door, and call them whatever I like as I start cracking your very brittle toes? Now, you mentioned a certain atomic weapon to the Eskimos. Elaborate."

"I was delirious."

"If a plane with a stolen nuke hadn't flown off in your general direction, and if you weren't a known Antifa asshole, and if you weren't lying here with a bullet wound, I might believe you."

"What do I get if I tell you what I know?"

"You get to spend the rest of your life in federal prison if you *don't* tell us, so I think that's a pretty good incentive to tell me."

"I only got into Antifa because of a girl," Kelso said bitterly.

"I hope she was hot," Turnbull said. "But she was a leftist, so I'm thinking maybe – what? – a five?"

"Kiss my ass."

"How about I kick it? Enough of *Fifty Shades of Kelso*. What happened?" Turnbull demanded. He paused. "I'm running out of patience, patient."

Kelso considered his position, and it dawned on him that nothing good was going to happen to him personally if Crane lit off that bomb somewhere. From the minute the Eskimos had turned him over to the Mounties and the Mounties had gone around their bosses to call in the Americans, who whisked him back to the US, he knew he was in a world of hurt.

"They picked me because I had worked on an oil rig and knew how to use construction equipment. They took us out to the National Forest and we trained, but no one would say for what. This Crane guy –"

"Merrick Crane?"

"Yeah, him. He's a monster. And he has that bald psycho with him. A real sicko. He kills people, but he never speaks."

"Well, you can't paint anyone all black."

"We go up to Canada, drive forever and finally get to this oil station and they kill all the workers. We start setting up a landing strip out on a frozen lake. This big Air Force bomber lands and I help take this missile off the wing. By then, everyone knows it's a nuke, and we're all a little freaked out."

"So, what next?"

"I go off to drain my dragon...."

"To what?" asked Deeds.

"Take a piss, man."

"Got it," Turnbull said. "Pick up after you sheathed your meat machete." Deeds shook his head.

"Even before that, I'm going in the snow and I hear shots. I can't see what's happening – I thought maybe a polar bear was attacking but that it couldn't be that because climate change killed all polar bears – and so I start back and I get closer and then I get shot. I fell into the snow. Then I see them take all the dead guys and drag them under the plane. Then they put the vehicles under there too."

"Where's this lake?"

"Oh, I don't know, but the plane's gone, if that's what you're looking for. We drilled holes in the ice and they filled them with explosives. When they blew it up, the plane and the equipment and the people sank. Then they drove off in the one remaining truck."

"Did Crane give any indication about what he was going to do?" asked Deeds.

"Yeah, he wants to abolish America by blowing up Texas. And something about a timer."

"Did he say where in Texas?"

"No, just Texas. Texas is a big state, right?"

"Kind of. Did he say anything else?"

"I don't think so."

"Well, think harder. Remember, you're in Texas too."

Kelso swallowed.

"I'm going to make some calls. They'll need to activate NEST," Deeds said as they left the hospital. The Nuclear Emergency Support Team was a part of the United States Department of Energy. Turnbull had trained with them once long ago.

"Is there still a Department of Energy?" Turnbull asked.

"Great question. But I would think it's in everyone's best interest that a hydrogen bomb not go off in Texas right now."

"Crane doesn't seem to think so."

"No, he wants chaos," Deeds said.

"Well, if I wanted chaos, I'd nuke St. Louis and fry the peace conference."

Deeds stopped, as did Turnbull.

"The conference was only announced today, Kelly. But you're right. It's a better target than anything down here. Closer to Canada too."

"You thinking Crane might call an audible?"

"Maybe," Deeds said, descending deeper into thought.

"Glad I could help. Sounds like NEST's problem now."

"Kelso said Texas. If NEST even still exists, when the politicians hear that, they are going to order every resource be used here in the Lone Star State," Deeds said. "We need boots on the ground at the peace conference."

"I hear that subtle undercurrent of 'Kelly, go somewhere and break things,'" Turnbull said sourly.

"You're it. Most of your fellow Zombies are on other missions. I can send Schiller and Casey."

"What about Dave McCluskey?"

"McCluskey's at the Circus Circus siege in Vegas. And Ted Hiroshi is in Miami trying to keep the Cubans there from tossing any more communists out of helicopters into the Caribbean."

"Why would Ted want to do that?"

Deeds snorted. "You go on ahead and meet me in St. Louis."

"No."

The Indian – a Cheyenne, Crane speculated, since the roadblock was at the boundary of the Northern Cheyanne Indian Reservation – had a well-worn Mini-14 rifle with a scope in his hands. The other dozen men manning the roadblock on I-90 were armed with their own semiautomatic rifles too.

"I need to get through," Crane explained patiently. "I respect and support the struggle of indigenous peoples."

The Indian burst into laughter and looked around to his cohort.

"You hear that? He supports the struggle of indigenous peoples!" This was greeted with torrents of laughter.

Crane rubbed his hands together. The Montana wind chilled his fingers into numbness and it was certainly going to be hell on his skin. Back in the idling truck, Mr. Soto was waiting for the signal to take action, but even his considerable talents would not overcome better than a dozen of these warriors.

"It is important that I get through here," he said, letting slip a bit of the menace that he usually found so effective against soft liberals and elite dilettantes.

The Indian stopped laughing.

"You ain't coming through. The res is closed until further notice. So, you need to turn your truck around and get the hell off our land or you'll never leave it."

Crane considered, then spun about and met Mr. Soto's eyes. He shook his head "No." They would backtrack and go the long way.

The slow trip from the Northwest Territory south had taken them through much of Canada, which was undergoing its own Crisis, if in a much more restrained and polite form. The rupture was even more urban versus rural than in the States, and the rural areas they drove through revealed many fewer armed groups than they had seen in the States. It was a very Canadian rebellion. One crowd of protesters was carrying signs reading "Please Respect Our Rights." They were handing the police watching the gathering cups of coffee.

The trio and their cargo had crossed at an abandoned border post into Montana – apparently, the US Customs and Border Protection personnel just stopped showing up a few days before and people now slipped into the States with no trouble. True to form, the Canadian customs officers continued to show up for work and pretended that everything was normal.

The absence of the US officers made Crane's life much easier. He had been concerned that radiation monitors might catch the W80 coming home, but the power was out for the station so they simply rolled into the United States with their cargo in the back. Mr. Soto had been planning on eliminating the staff, which would have caused a commotion.

Betts sat in the back seat alone, putting together his project with the electronic components they had bought at Hoot's Hobbies in suburban Calgary. The parts for the timer to set off the nuclear bomb cost 47.25 CAD. Crane accompanied Betts in his purchasing expedition while Mr. Soto bought coffee and some chocolate glazed Timbits at the Tim Horton's next door.

Thanks to the militant Cheyennes, they had to backtrack north up I-90 to I-94 and then head east through the accursed wasteland of North Dakota toward Fargo at the far end of the rectangular state. From there they would head south, through Omaha to Kansas City to Oklahoma City to Dallas, where he would lance the boil that was the red states and get the inevitable and necessary Second Civil War truly started.

It amused Crane that his personal nuke technician was sitting in the backseat fabricating a hydrogen bomb timer out of under 50 dollars (Canadian) of parts bought in a strip mall. Arnold Betts, if he was aware of how absurd that seemed, made no mention of it. Instead, he kept tinkering with his timer assembly. It took real skills, but he had those skills. Nuclear weapons are more than just big bombs. They are actually complex machines that require constant maintenance, and Betts was the honor grad of his Air Force Specialty Code 2W2X1 course. He had also passed the Personnel Reliability Program that allowed him to work with nuclear weapons – but then all the conspirators had passed their PRP background check. The Air Force, bowing to the times, had actively avoided vetting the politics of their applicants, especially when those politics included a flirtation with the growing American hard left. Though it made eminent sense that a socialist might lack patriotism, the establishment decreed that this could not be said or acted upon even where the fiery consequences of such willful naivete would be measured in kilotons.

Betts was always more comfortable with wires, fuses, and solenoids than with other humans. Minot was a pretty lonely post even in the best of times, and when a small group of fellow airmen invited him inside their circle, he eagerly accepted their acceptance. That the focus of their group was the kind of socialist leftism that had formerly only infected college campuses did not bother him – he was never interested in politics as such before. He went along because he found the faux moral authority holding those views conferred, and the excitement of doing something covertly, made the ideology attractive. But the most attractive part of it was that for the first time in a long time, Technical Sergeant Betts had real friends, not just online chat buddies.

But as vulnerable as he was to the temptations of friendship and belonging, Betts was not stupid by any means. It certainly occurred to him, while this had all gone so far out of control, that perhaps he had not just randomly fallen in with that crowd. Perhaps they had actively targeted the lonely technician precisely because he was able to do things like jury rig a timer for a W80 warhead out of off-the-shelf civilian parts.

"How's it coming along, Arnold?" Crane asked, turning toward the backseat. Through the windshield, the road stretched off into the distance.

"It's fine," Betts replied.

"And you have the codes you need?"

"Yes, still," Betts said, irritated. How many times was Crane going to ask him that? He was the weapons tech – it was his job to activate the weapon, and to do that he had to have access to the codes. And when the guy approving access was a co-conspirator – Colonel Sykes had allowed him access – that circumvented the checks and balances designed to keep the bombs inert until some foreign enemy needed to be scrubbed from the surface of the earth.

"That's good," Crane said politely. He found the sergeant tiresome but also necessary, which was why he was still breathing.

"You know, we can make our point without actually setting it off," Betts said. "We can negotiate for the progress we want without setting it off."

"Are you a strategist or a technician?" asked Crane, and Betts understood this was not truly a question. He turned his attention back to his work.

The endless miles continued to stretch out ahead of them, and Mr. Soto's eyes were fixed on the freeway. Crane reached to the dash and flipped on the radio, scanning AM stations until he reached someone talking about the news instead of singing about his horse or preaching about Jesus.

The litany of chaos the announcer recited was welcome. The fact that red and blue would meet in St. Louis to negotiate and end the crisis was not.

Politicians from across the spectrum were gathering to reverse the rapidly deteriorating situation and somehow end the Crisis. Crane instantly assessed the summit as a threat. And then it dawned on him.

This was actually an opportunity.

He smiled broadly, then pulled out a burner and checked his signal. It was weak, but the wait until he reached five bars again would give him time to plan.

Turnbull drew a nondescript Nissan Sentra from the motor pool – it was actually one of a hundred Hertz rental cars the provisional government had requisitioned – and headed north on Highway 69 until it hit Interstate 44 in Oklahoma. There was lots of military traffic, and a fair amount northbound – including some Volvos and Priuses packed with the livelihoods of liberal families escaping the red. But the real traffic was southbound, the red families leaving the blue before everything broke apart.

"It's already war," a caller insisted to Larry O'Connor on one of the FM stations. "We all know about Cajon Pass and Philadelphia and all the rest. This is the Second Civil War and I say we fight it and win it again." O'Connor had had to relocate his syndicated show to Texas when armed blue law enforcement had shown up in his studio in DC, only to find he was broadcasting remotely. A lot of conservative media types had had been forced to head to the red – Trump News, Turnbull heard, was reconstituting in Dallas after its DC and New York facilities had been raided and shut down by federal agents for "sedition."

Now, the host was talking about the growing hunger in New York City – apparently very little cargo was getting in past blockades in the outer boroughs. Ditto Los Angeles.

Turnbull accelerated past a company of infantry in trucks convoying in the slow lane. There were a half-dozen civilian buses, charters, in the midst of the tactical vehicles, and the occupants were outfitted in civilian gear. Provisionals. Governor Abbott, the leader of the Constitutional Alliance, had ordered all fit and able men into service, along with female volunteers, and they were being deployed. Turnbull had no idea where they were headed, but they all had guns.

Above him, three A-10 fighters passed northward, navigating using the highway.

"This is just great," Turnbull grumbled.

The rest area parking lot was full of cars, many of them with families and most with possessions lashed to their roofs. They headed to the bathrooms and walked their dogs and kids ran around on the grass while their parents watched, silent and grim.

Crane came back to the truck pleased, both by what he saw and what he had just heard. Mr. Soto was standing outside of the vehicle, and Betts had returned to his backseat, having been escorted to the remarkably clean bathroom and back while Crane was away on the phone.

Crane reached for the door of the cab, but Mr. Soto's gaze fixed on him. Mr. Soto put his hand to his ear, and Crane remembered. He took the burner phone, put it to the curb and kicked it several times. Its face plate cracked. Satisfied, he tossed the debris in a nearly empty garbage can, and then considered how odd it was that the country was falling apart yet the Nebraska highway department's maintenance people were still emptying trash cans at its roadside rest outside of Omaha. It seemed strange that they would still just go on with their mundane tasks as if nothing was happening that would totally change the world they once knew.

The trio got back into the truck and headed south again – until Crane told him different, Mr. Soto was headed to Dallas. But since Crane's phone call, their destination had changed. They would be taking a left to head east to St. Louis instead of staying on a southward course toward the Lone Star State.

And they had a friend meeting them in St. Louis. A very useful one. But first, using another of his burner phones, he needed to invite some other friends to the party. He would not be telling them that they would be the guests of honor.

It was raining, but luckily it was not cold enough for snow. Turnbull offered a silent prayer of thanks for global warming as he pulled off the interstate on North Franklin Street in Cuba, Missouri, to fill up his tank. There was a line at all of the gas stations adjacent to the interstate along Franklin, and at all the many drive-thrus. And there were lots of local armed civilians in groups – identifiable by a bolt of red cloth tied around their upper right arms – patrolling their town to keep order among all these people passing through. Someone at the Sonic with Illinois plates had apparently gotten mouthy because a half-dozen of the Provisionals were kicking the shit out of him as his girlfriend screamed at them.

Turnbull let nature take its course and drove deeper into town, finding a Phillips 66 on the other side of town and stopping at a place called Missouri Hick Bar-B-Cue on old Route 66, which ran parallel to the interstate through the south side of town. It was a rustic looking place, and he sat in the corner inside and got an open-faced pulled pork sandwich with coleslaw and sweet ice tea.

There were a fair number of people in there, all locals. And all were armed – a couple AR15s, a Mini-14, and one guy had a SOCOM 16 that Turnbull admired from a distance. There was a TV over the bar showing the news, and for once people were paying attention. Nothing like your country falling apart to make you start caring about current events.

It was tuned to Trump News, the only major network not all in on the blue. CNN and MSNBC were busy lauding the armed struggle against the "white supremacist" red states. Trump News got most of its staff out of the northeast one step ahead of the blue feds. Sadly, Tucker Carlson, who not long before had left Fox for Trump News after a blistering monologue about blue tyranny infuriated the management and especially their liberal wives, had been arrested by the FBI for sedition.

There was footage on the screen of the aftermath of the fighting at Cajon Pass. The People's Militia had been turned back. Then General Karl Scott appeared, and the chyron said "Operation Anaconda Commences." Turnbull paid attention.

"First, we will cut the cities off. And then, if they fail to surrender to lawful authority, we will defeat the unlawful combatants in them, including Antifa and the so-called People's Militias," he said. The map on the screen showed red forces outside Los Angeles, New York, Philadelphia, San Francisco, and some other cities. But Chicago, Seattle, and others had no red forces near them.

There were just not enough soldiers, even including the mobilized Provisionals, to retake the whole country without a long, bloody slog.

Which is exactly what General Scott was promising.

"As Lincoln said, a house divided cannot stand," he told the reporters he was briefing. "The United States will suppress this leftist insurgency no matter how long it takes and no matter what the cost." He left the podium. The network cut to Avery Barnes.

"Even as the factions agree to commence peace talks in St. Louis, the official position of the red states' Constitutional Alliance remains that the United States must remain united under the Constitution, and as we saw at Elizabeth Warren's press conference today, the blue states' position is that the

Constitution is obsolete and must be dramatically rewritten. And the costs that General Karl Scott mentioned are now estimated at over 15,000 dead or wounded around the country in small scale fighting up to full-scale battles like Cajon Pass. America's last chance may be the peace conference that begins tomorrow. This is Avery Barnes, reporting for Trump News, St. Louis."

"Screw the blue," a gentleman with a tan "DESERT STORM VET" ball cap and a Colt Python on his hip shouted. "I fought for this country and damned if I am giving it up to those bastards." There were murmurs of approval.

Turnbull finished his sandwich and left cash on the table before walking out. In his drive back to the interstate, he passed a Baptist church with a sign out front that read: "He that hath no sword, let him sell his cloak, and buy one – Luke 22:36"

18.

"It's like the *Star Wars* cantina with uglier people," Turnbull said as Avery Barnes spun around on her barstool. Her mouth dropped open as she recognized him.

"Chris," she said, using his alias. Turnbull had remembered it, and made sure he was a "Chris" again when he got his new fake credentials, including a "Level A" security officer pass that allowed him to wear his Wilson Combat CQB .45 on his hip inside the secure area of downtown St. Louis.

Don Lemon sat next to her, frowning at the interruption. He was working Avery hard – Turnbull had seen it as he entered the Live! By Loews hotel lobby bar and figured that maybe the rumors were true and that the CNN anchor was actually straight, just on the down-low.

"Chris the security guard," Lemon sniffed, taking a sip of his *airag.*

"Yeah, that's me. Who are you?" Turnbull replied, and Lemon looked like he was about to cry.

"Come on," Barnes said, hustling him away. "That was mean. He's very insecure."

"He should be."

They made their way across the crowded, noisy room toward a fortuitously empty two-top by the back wall while drawing remarkably little attention to the Trump News anchor. The hotel was the premier one inside the secure zone, the two-mile circle around the America's Center Convention Complex where the peace summit was being held. Everyone relevant or with delusions of relevance was vying to be housed there.

There were celebrities, semi-celebrities, non-celebrities, and unknowns all mingling together. The politicians abounded, but so were the media types, along with a rogue's gallery of Hollywood stars, Instagram influencers, rappers, sports stars, tech titans, and Twitter-famous blue checks. During their short walk across the floor of the bar, they passed Sean Penn, Paul Krugman, YouTube sensation Yippo the Ween, and the My Pillow guy, who was holding a Fresca and chatting amiably with Rachel Maddow. Also, Ted Lieu was sitting in a chair along the aisle drinking a Tab and Smirnoff, making eye contact with everyone passing by, vainly hoping someone would both recognize him and choose to stop. Turnbull did not count him as a celebrity.

"Welcome to the St. Louis circus," Barnes said, sitting down first. "How do you like it so far?"

"I've been in worse places."

"Did you like the Gateway Arch?"

"Looks like a big arch," Turnbull said, sitting down, back to the wall so he could see anyone approaching.

"Always the conversationalist," Barnes said, smiling.

"I hate this place and all these people," Turnbull said. He watched as a wrinkly Bette Midler hugged Chris Wallace and grabbed a handful of butt. The Fox anchor giggled.

"Don't ask," Barnes said, shaking her head and turning back to Turnbull. "But I would expect you to hate this. This is the hottest hotel in the secure area. If you moved early or have heat, you got a suite in here or in one of the other hotels inside the downtown. If you waited, you got a room outside the area and have to cross into the area through security every day, which is a pain. Everyone who is anyone is in town for the conference. This is history happening right in front of us, and the whole world is watching."

"Any idea how the summit will go?" Turnbull asked.

"I don't know," Barnes said. "The country is on the edge. My info is the blue is demanding a new Constitution, amnesty for the differently documented, reparations, gun bans, all sorts of things. And the red wants its God and guns and likes the current Constitution just fine."

"It's ugly out there," Turnbull said. Barnes noted the bandage on his left wrist.

"You get hurt?"

"I'm okay," he said. He paused. "I was at Cajon Pass."

She gasped. "Was it as bad...?"

"Yeah," Turnbull said, nodding. "I don't have a problem fighting foreigners. But fighting other Americans is something I'm still not used to."

"Don't get used to it," Barnes replied. "We can't get used to it."

"I'm trying not to."

"I don't know what happened to our country," Barnes said. "But I want it to be like it was. I won't be part of changing it into something I hate."

"I think that might be out of our hands," Turnbull said. "It's gone pretty far."

"No," she replied. "I refuse to accept that. I refuse to change ourselves into something else. We have to honor the old rules, and not give in to this new brutality."

"Aren't reporters supposed to be objective?" Turnbull said.

"Oh, well that rule, that's done and gone," she laughed. "They took that idea out and buried its body in the woods."

"I'm just glad to see you're not locked up in Scranton," Turnbull said. Scranton was the location of the just opened prison camp for "seditionists and wreckers" arrested under the myriad new laws the hijacked Congress had been passing since the night they were last together when the leftists seized Capitol Hill.

"It was close. They hit the bureau with about 100 blue feds, but we got tipped off and we were already on the move," Barnes said. "I guess I should have expected to see you here, Chris, if that's even your name."

"It isn't," Turnbull said.

She squinted at the badge he wore on a lanyard around his neck. It had his photo and the words "SECURITY – LEVEL A" in large letters. It had a red background – he was with the red side. Blue security agents had their own similarly color-coded identification.

"Chris ... Hayes? Really?" Barnes asked.

Turnbull furrowed his brows. "Wait, was he the 'stop the hammering' guy?"

"No, that jerk was just in here yelling at the bartender and insisting that a Gibson has an olive. Chris Hayes is a different jerk. I think your people like screwing with you."

"Yeah, but I'll get my vengeance," Turnbull promised, before leaning toward her intensely. "Avery, I need to know if you have heard any rumors."

"I've heard a million rumors. This is ground zero for rumors."

Turnbull ignored that uncomfortably apt phrasing and continued. "Rumors about threats? Any kind of threats to the conference?"

"Well, you know that parts of both the red and blue want to let this keep going and play it out to the end. General Scott wants to conquer the blue, and AOC and the left want to liberate the red. Nobody knows how this process is going to go. It's just becoming more obvious that if this crisis doesn't get talked out it's going to get fought out."

"You have the best sources out there. Has anyone told you about any kind of plot or scheme to disrupt or stop the conference?"

"What do you mean? We got tipped off that 100 plus-sized womyn with a 'y' from Heavy Handmaids for Justice are going to show up tomorrow at the convention center as the conference opens at nine and whip off their robes in a nude protest of the patriarchy or something."

"It's never the hot ones," Turnbull said, shaking his head. "No, that sounds terrifying but I mean more like terrorism."

"Is there a threat, Chris?" Barnes asked. "You would tell me, right? Like, on background, anonymously?"

"You know I can't say," Turnbull replied. "But you hear things, and even the blues talk to you. If you hear something, you call me."

There was a scuffle across the bar, and they both looked over, squinting in the dark at the imbroglio.

"I think Hannity just punched Leonardo," Barnes said, standing up and taking out her iPhone. "I gotta go."

There was a joint security center inside the convention center manned by sullen personnel from both the red and the blue. The federal three letter agencies had all fractured, and members were now openly allying themselves by color. There were red FBI and blue FBI, red Secret Service and blue Secret Service. It did not make for smooth cooperation.

The joint security center was tense, and the majority of its efforts consisted of coordinating access to the secure area of downtown and routine patrolling inside the area (mostly conducted by National Guard military police units), and at least attempting to cooperate on larger threats. But the distrust was palpable, and Turnbull spent about 30 seconds inside the command post before being convinced that being there was a waste of his time. He headed toward the red security center located on the top three floors of an office high-rise on Clark Avenue near Busch Stadium.

The red security center was unmarked on the outside but was heavily defended, with plainclothes officers with M4s and dark glasses posted on the ground floor and at the entrances and exits in and out of the command post itself. Turnbull got inside and then into the internally secure area where Deeds had located the Task Force Zulu operatives. Besides Deeds, there were several Zombies present, including Casey Warner and Joe Schiller.

"Thanks for the alias," Turnbull grunted. Casey smiled.

"Yeah, I enjoyed that," he said. "Next time don't steal my gun."

"Anything on the bomb?" Turnbull asked, getting down to business.

Deeds shook his head. "No. We're pretty well set up here and we're monitoring everything electronic inside the secure area – web traffic, cells, landlines. Nothing yet."

"I assume the blues are doing the same."

"Yeah, they have their own center on the other side of the secure area. They're doing the same thing we are. If it's not scrambled, assume they have your comms."

"Clay's right," Casey said. "It's a freak show." The operative had his laptop open on the folding table set up along the wall. He continued. "We intercepted Jeffrey Toobin Zooming with Governor Whitmer. Or, as he calls her, 'Mistress Gretchen.' Want to see?"

"Pass," Turnbull said.

"Well, if that's how you feel, don't read through Adam Schiff's browser history. Man, that guy's not right."

"Casey, get back to looking for the H-bomb," Deeds said. He pivoted toward Turnbull. "Obviously, only a few of us know about the warhead, just the red leadership and us. Minot is sealed tight and commo was cut off so word is not getting out that one of our nukes is missing."

"Not that I particularly like those bastards, but blue intel might be able to help us find Crane if we told them to look for him," Turnbull said.

"And then they'll ask why. And if we tell them, they might let it out that there's a missing nuke and panic everyone and have them call off the peace conference. There are blues who want that. We are under strict orders – the peace conference has to succeed," said Deeds.

"General Scott won't like that either," said Turnbull.

"General Scott was never elected anything. The civilian leadership is in charge," Deeds said.

"You know Scott's right, as much as it pains me to say that about a general and a jerk. We're going to have to resolve this sooner or later."

"That's neither your call nor mine, Kelly. We have our chain of command. That's how we do things."

"You know, I keep hearing about how we need to honor the norms, and yet I feel like only we are," Turnbull said. "So, how do we find the bomb?"

"We keep monitoring the commo. We're putting it all through AI to find keywords and patterns."

"I thought we weren't supposed to be able to monitor all civilian electronic traffic," Turnbull said, smirking. "You know, norms and stuff."

"That practice has been the norm since long before the crisis," Deeds said. "We're also trying to make the access to the downtown secure zone tighter. It's already very tight around the convention center where the summit is being held, but obviously they don't need to get inside the convention center to blow it off the face of the Earth."

"That is the key advantage of a nuke," Turnbull observed. "So, we can't even put out a photo of Crane, can we?"

"No. Again, it'll raise questions. We'll tap into surveillance cameras around the downtown and run our facial recognition, but that's all we can do. Remember, he's a hero to much of the blue. Even with all the blood on his hands before Minot."

"Because of it," Turnbull said.

"Um, Beto is surfing an online dating website called 'HotFurryFriends.com,'" Casey called out from his table. Deeds ignored him and continued with Turnbull.

"Did your Trump News friend have anything?"

"No, but she's dialed in. Even the blues talk to her. She has this weird notion like you about norms, so they know they'll get a fair shake. If there's anything out there on the street, she'll pick it up."

"That's something," Deeds said.

"That's not enough," Turnbull replied. "Do we have a NEST team?"

"Not yet," said Deeds. "Only about 40% of the NEST personnel are in red areas and only a quarter of the equipment. Priority is to Texas because that's where the threat was aimed. But the more I think about it, the more I agree that he'll change the target to the summit. The whole world is watching, and if he prevents an agreement it's full-scale war. That's a two-fer for Merrick Crane."

"I guess if Dallas goes up in a big orange fireball, the pols don't want to have to explain how the one surviving witness to the H-bomb heist told them it was aimed at Texas but they decided instead to go protect a bunch of political hacks, movie stars, and internet idiots."

Deed nodded. "We get no nuke hunting assets until we get some evidence."

"I got something," Casey said.

"Casey, if it's more about Lisa Murkowski's personal life, I'll have you walking patrols on a sandbar in the Missouri River."

"No Clay, we got some interesting MIND FLAYER hits."

"What's that?" Turnbull asked.

"It's a program," said Casey. "One of the few truly useful things to come out of Silicon Valley. It ties in multiple data sources and picks up anomalies that might indicate a relationship to our assigned parameters."

"You need to translate your English into English."

"I tell it to look through everything to find stuff that indicates someone might be bringing an H-bomb to St. Louis. In so many words."

"It looks through everything?"

"Everything."

"What do you have?" Deeds asked.

"A bunch of possibles – the problem is it gives too many possible hits and you have to use your intuition and experience to screen them for truly useful info."

"The point, get to it, Casey," Turnbull growled.

"The key event is a cell phone that has never been used before and has never been back on the grid again called Senator Richard Harrington, who is coming to St. Louis, and who we expect is super-tight with the radicals and who we know has met Crane before at least once, the night Capitol Hill got seized."

"I don't remember him. But who cares? I bet that schmuck gets lots of burner calls."

"From rural Nebraska? Within the time parameters it would take to drive the bomb south from the Arctic? And it was within two hours of when the summit was announced."

"Do we have a tape of the call?"

"We don't. They probably Vocoscrammed it. I bet even if somebody does have a good recording, that somebody is back in Maryland and that's all blue."

"Maybe we need to pay a visit to Senator Harrington," Turnbull said.

"He's untouchable," Deeds said. "He's a senior negotiator for the blue."

"Then Casey here should go bug his hotel room. I'm guessing he'll be at Live! By Loews. I'm told it's hot."

Casey was typing furiously, and Turnbull gave him a moment. Casey looked up.

"He was going to be at Live! By Loews. He canceled. Now he's actually at the Ritz-Carlton," Casey said.

"Well, take a walk on over there," Turnbull said.

Casey shook his head. "I can't. It's not in the secure area. It's about ten miles west of here on the other side of town."

Merrick Crane III and Senator Richard Harrington were standing in an alley – the first alley Harrington could remember stepping into in perhaps decades – with one of Harrington's security men at each end. It smelled of urine and cheese. The Chevy Tundra, filthy and bug-splattered by its lengthy trip from the Arctic, was parked a few yards away. Betts was inside, having been told to lie down in the back of the cab. Mr. Soto stood by the driver's door, waiting.

Harrington eyed the stone-faced man he recalled from the Georgetown party nervously. His own men were farther away than he would have liked.

"Don't worry about Mr. Soto," Crane said. "He's absolutely reliable. He does odd jobs for me."

The sun had been down for several hours, and it was cold enough to deter most pedestrians from venturing outside. Harrington's security guards had been baffled when their boss had announced promptly at seven that he would be taking a walk, and that they were to keep 30 feet to his rear at all times. He left his cell in his room.

Crane had stayed at the Ritz-Carlton in 2020 when he was facilitating the riots there over that summer, so he knew the area. Harrington was right on time coming out for his walk. His one call to the senator from the road in Nebraska had been very brief and to the point, despite the Vocoscram program he used.

It went like this: "Hello again. I have what I need to wipe out the summit and most of St. Louis. Walk out of the Ritz-Carlton at precisely seven on Tuesday night or you will die with everyone else."

Knowing that Crane did not make idle threats, all Harrington said in response was, "Yes."

Crane gestured to the senator, who saw the alley and deployed his men, both to defeat outside threats and to defeat the threat from Crane should that manifest. Once inside the alley, Crane had explained what had happened starting in Minot, and it took all of Harrington's considerable power of sangfroid not to exhibit any kind of reaction to the news that just a few yards away was a live nuclear warhead.

"Do you want to see it?" Crane asked, smiling so that his sharp white teeth were fully displayed.

"I'll trust you," Harrington replied. "I simply find it interesting that there is nothing in any media about one of our hydrogen bombs being missing. Though, I have seen some raw intelligence that Texas is concerned about some type of WMD threat there."

Crane chuckled. "Texas was the original target for my weapon of mass destruction, but this is much, much better."

"You would not want to waste your one chance to nuke something on a bunch of backwoods cretins," Harrington observed. "I agree with your strategy. If you eliminate the summit, you decapitate both the red and the blue, and the Crisis intensifies."

"And you and I will both be able to capitalize on that," Crane said.

"I appreciate you allowing me to fill the resulting leadership void," Harrington said.

"Of course, I need your help here and now."

"Of course."

"I need to get the bomb inside the secure area. They may have radiation detection gear – I need to avoid that. But I have an idea how to do it. And I need your help."

Crane explained his plan. Harrington was listening, but in the background – he was a multi-tasker – he was evaluating his other option. That would be turning Crane and his bomb in to the authorities. The plus side would be that Richard Harrington would be a hero, though that would be marred by the nagging question about why the terrorist mastermind had come directly to him in the first place.

On the con side, it would mean that all his rivals would not be vaporized in a fireball many times hotter than the center of the sun.

He smiled, and nodded as Crane outlined his plan and his requirements.

"That's a significant ask," Senator Harrington said.

Merrick Crane III shrugged.

"Everything worth doing is hard," he replied.

"So true," Harrington said, smiling.

19.

"It's for the cause," Crane said. He was standing in the corner of a parking lot at Herman Park, behind the cover of the Chevy Tundra. Mr. Soto stood not far off, watching as the woman in a suit scowled at Crane in response to his benign smile.

"Yeah, well I don't appreciate getting calls like that," she snapped.

The call had come in late the prior evening. The Assistant Circuit Attorney was not busy – there were few trials to prepare for since the current Circuit Attorney's policy was to dismiss almost every charge, except in the most egregious and publicized cases, or in cases of a normal citizen exercising his right of self-defense. Those the Circuit Attorney's office prosecuted with a vengeance.

No, the call had been a demand clothed as a polite request that required her to go into the office and review files late in the evening, and this she did not appreciate for several reasons, including being halfway through an episode of a Netflix series about victims of microaggressions overcoming systemic racism by flaunting statutory rape laws – another crime her office no longer prosecuted. She was also halfway through a bottle of a mediocre Washington Pinot Noir, but that did not bother her much since they rarely charged DUIs either, unless a check of the arrestee's political registration came up "Republican."

She had complied because the people who had invested the outrageous sums required to purchase her boss's election expected to be repaid with favors upon request. She was a key assistant to the Circuit Attorney and such requests – demands – flowed through her so the boss remained untainted. The man calling on behalf of Senator Harrington had been clear that she was not to mention this request to her superior, but she knew not to do that without being told.

It was still a tremendous pain in the ass, and she had no hesitation in letting the man she was meeting to deliver the information to know it.

"This was very inconvenient," she sniffed. "Why did you want to know about a commercial chop shop anyway?"

She handed over the piece of paper, which Crane took and perused while ignoring her question. This annoyed the Assistant Circuit Attorney even more.

"And why couldn't I just email you the info? Why did I have to come out here in person?"

Crane looked up at her as he slid the paper into his pocket.

"Because email is not secure," he said. "And because you aren't either."

She began to say something harsh but Mr. Soto's arm was around her neck choking her to death before a word could escape her lips.

The convention center was awash in activity. The main negotiation session was taking place well out of the public space, but in the hallways and the various presentation rooms there were hundreds of people – government officials, politicians, movie stars, and support personnel, as well as hundreds of accredited media.

Avery Barnes and Lou the cameraman occupied a space by the corner of the main drag through the exhibit halls and the central walkway. She proceeded to grab anyone interesting passing by for comment. A woman from NBC had tried to infringe on her space, and Barnes had driven her away with a flurry of obscenities, like a momma eagle defending her nest.

It was worth it – she had spent a few minutes with red negotiator Ric Grenell, who characterized the blue's opening position that the Constitution must be "completely reimagined" as "a total non-starter." Lou uploaded that to Dallas immediately, as Barnes looked for fresh targets.

Bill Kristol stopped and greeted her, a half-eaten jelly doughnut in his hand. "Keep walking," she told him. He seemed crestfallen.

"Senator Harrington!" she shouted upon seeing the politician stroll down the walkway with one of his security men – the other bodyguard's presence back at the hotel had prevented Casey from bugging the room. For Barnes, Harrington was a real get – one of the main blue negotiators. He had provided her with info in the past on Democrat Party infighting, quality stuff, always self-serving, but always devastating.

"Mx. Barnes," the senator replied, using the "mix" prefix Nancy Pelosi had decreed that all Democrats would use from then on after her granddaughter – who identified as her "grandbeing" – had come home from Berkeley for Thanksgiving the previous year and announced that using any other prefix was a legacy of patriarchal oppression and cisnormativity.

He stopped in front of her and, knowing the drill, waited as Lou put the camera on his shoulder and began taping.

"Senator, can you tell us where the blue states stand on the key issue of Constitution reform? We understand that's one of the major sticking points for the negotiations."

"It's agreed among scholars and by the people that the current so-called Constitution is a racist document that enshrines systemic oppression of people of color, of womynness, and of genderfluidity, and it is time to completely reimagine what a constitution with a commitment to anti-racism, anti-sexism, and anti-cisnormativity looks like."

"The red position is that the blue states want to eliminate the Electoral College in order to allow California, New York, and the rest of the blue states unrestricted control over the red areas. How do you respond?" Barnes asked.

"The red position on democracy is clear. You can see it in the footage of the protesters murdered by the so-called Provisional death squads at Cajon Pass and in Philadelphia, and in the strangleholds on major cities. The people will not submit to this fascism," Harrington said. It came out smoothly, for he had had plenty of practice with that narrative giving it to eager anchors at CNN, ABC, and MSNBC earlier in the morning.

"Are you saying that the blue states will choose civil war if their demand for a new constitution is not met?"

"The people, including loyal military forces and the People's Militias that have spontaneously arisen around the country, will continue to take to the streets to protect the rights of the people."

"Thank you, Senator Harrington." Lou lowered the camera.

"Anything off the record, Senator?" Barnes asked.

Harrington looked around theatrically, then fixed his gaze on her face.

"There is something, on background, of course."

"On background," she reiterated. They understood that Harrington would not be named as the source, but she could report the information.

"There is a security alert that racist militias, Proud Boys or something of that ilk, are coming to St. Louis to disrupt the convention. The security forces are looking into it."

"Is this some sort of specific threat?"

"No," Harrington said. "But the talk is that they may have access to WMDs."

"I was just in the can and it smelled like death and then Eric Swalwell comes walking out of a stall," Casey Warner said. "Nasty."

"Come on," Turnbull said impatiently. Before Casey's pit stop, they had been walking through the exhibition hall, trying to get a sense of the layout. As security officers, they were both armed. People steered clear of them, which was fine with Turnbull. They were human wallpaper to the swells and celebrities packing the summit.

But Turnbull was assessing each of the attendees as they passed. And none seemed to have the hardness he was used to seeing in terrorists.

Barnes saw them first, and leaving Lou to hold their prime ground, she approached.

"I know you," Casey said, delighted. "You're on Trump News."

"Go away," Turnbull said, and Casey sullenly shuffled off.

"So, Chris," she said. "What do you hear about right-wing terrorists coming to St. Louis with WMDs?"

"Nothing," Turnbull said truthfully. "Where did you hear that?"

"Where didn't I? It's all over the blues. They're all talking about it." Several people besides Harrington had passed her nearly the same information.

"I've heard zero on our side, but I'll check it out. What have you specifically heard?"

Barnes shrugged. "You now know everything I know."

"No specifics?"

"Provisionals, Proud Boys maybe, definitely right-wing, definitely trying to disrupt the summit, and weapons of mass destruction. That's it."

"What kind of WMDs?"

"No one says. Nerve agent in the vents maybe?" she said, then someone caught her eye. "Speaking of noxious gases, that's Eric Swalwell. I gotta grab him for an interview. Give me a call if you hear more."

She was gone before Turnbull could respond.

The joint security center was a confused mess, and the first thing Turnbull and Casey saw upon entering it was two FBI agents, one with a red badge and one with a blue badge, arguing over the priority threat list. The guy in blue was refusing to erase the text next to "#1": "Racist right-wing terrorists."

Turnbull went to the intelligence fusion cell, a group of people supposedly working together to gather, process, and assess intelligence from all available sources into useable information. Except the red and the blue intel officers were refusing to talk to each other.

Turnbull recognized a face among the reds and sat down beside her.

"Libby Capewell," he said.

She smiled. "You again? Figures." She squinted at his ID badge. "So, you're now Chris?"

"Sure," Turnbull said. "I'm looking for threat info. What do you have?"

"Remarkably little. They got this summit up and off the ground so fast I doubt any of the usual bad guys had a chance to plan anything."

"I've been hearing about a right-wing WMD threat."

"Oh, that's such bullshit. That's all the freaking blues want to talk about. There's not one bit of actual hard intel on that. I mean, none. Nada. Zip. But they won't shut up about it."

"Anything else?"

"No. Except that we might start killing each other. I mean in here, literally. A couple agents got into a fistfight yesterday and everyone drew. We finally got everyone to stand down, but it's a powder keg."

"Just like the whole country."

"You know, if they can't put this country back together at this summit, we're going to go into full-scale civil war," Capewell said. "And I'm on the verge of saying 'Let's go.'"

"You don't want that," Turnbull said, standing.

"You sure about that?"

"Yeah," he said. "I am."

Mr. Soto slipped into the Washington University in St. Louis North Campus military staging area without being challenged. The facility had been requisitioned as a military staging area primarily for logistics supporting the secure area operations about ten miles east. The college itself had been closed since the crisis had begun in earnest, and the college administration was only too happy to recoup some of its losses renting its unused property to the feds at a grossly inflated rate.

The parking lots were dominated by rows upon rows of camouflaged military trucks, HUMVEEs, five-tons, tractor-trailer rigs, HEMETs, LMTVs, and MTVs. There were a dozen large white "fest tents" – massive commercial tents the Army contracted for. They got their name during the Army's 70 years in Germany, where such tents were often used to hold beer-fueled *volksfests* in the spring and fall.

Each fest tent had a purpose. Some were sleeping quarters with orderly rows of cots for the exhausted troops to rack out in when off-shift. Others were massive supply points. Some provided services. That was where Mr. Soto headed, and he wore a blue t-shirt that said "Sunrise Industries," which he had picked up for $1 at a nearby Goodwill. He had also bought three ACU pattern caps and three pairs of used brown suede combat boots, probably donated by the wives of some veterans who were sick of them cluttering up their husbands' closets.

With the t-shirt, Mr. Soto seemed like just another civilian contractor, and the few soldiers out and about were focused on their own tasks and paid him no mind. Most of the soldiers were actually inside the main building in a classroom receiving their annual transsexuality/gender identity policy briefing.

Part of the services tent was given over to the laundry. There were long tables heaped with folded camo uniforms wrapped in clear plastic with tickets showing outward. The soldier wrote in his name, rank, and the size of the unform he was having cleaned – some of this seemed redundant, as the nametape and rank on the uniform gave much of that info, but regs were regs, and if you wanted clean clothes you filled out the label in full and in triplicate.

Signs marked the tables: A-C, D-F, and so on down to the letter Z. Mr. Soto walked down the aisles, knowing what he was looking for. He gathered up three packages – besides the uniforms they also had brown t-shirts, skivvies, and socks. No one thought to say anything – it never occurred to anyone that someone might want to steal someone else's ACUs. After all, the name of the owner was right there on the front of each top.

Carrying his loot, he walked out to the parking lot and began searching for a very specific vehicle. There were many types, but he was looking for a Medium Tactical Vehicle (MTV) variant called the M1091 Fuel/Water Tanker. He found one after a few minutes, a camouflaged, ugly apparatus whose front cab looked like the head of a grasshopper. Behind it on the bed was a 1500-gallon tank with the word "FLAMMABLE" printed on it. Six large tires carried it, one axle under the cab and two axles under the back.

The door was not locked – military vehicles did not have external locks (though they can often be combat locked from inside). Nor did it have an ignition lock – keys would inevitably get lost in the field, and there was instead an "ON" switch. But there was a chain running from a ring welded into the floor of the cab through the steering wheel and secured by a government issue brass lock. This way, no one could steal the vehicle. That is, unless they could cut the lock, which Mr. Soto did with the small bolt cutter he carried in his pocket.

Shutting the door behind him, he noted the sticker on the dash in front of the passenger seat – the "shotgun" seat. It read "DIVERSITY = READINESS," and in a smaller font underneath, "Everyone contributes," with a picture of a black male, a white female, and an indeterminate person with a moustache and a pink bow in xir hair.

Mr. Soto ignored this and broke open a package, then slipped on one of the ACU tops. From the outside, it looked like a soldier was at the wheel. The M1091 started right up when he pressed the ignition, and he began driving toward the rear driveway, which he noted did not have a gate, only a sign taped to a pole that read "EXIT NOT AUTHORIZED USE FRONT GATE."

He headed out onto the street and on toward his destination.

Crane took the bag from Ethan Gold and opened it up. There was a lot of money in it. Gold and his three friends had probably liberated a few dollars for some kush on their short notice trip from Minneapolis, but that was fine. The physical volume of the cash in the bag was what was important. No one would be counting it.

"You're all ready?"

"Absolutely," Gold said, his breath smelling like a Phish reunion tour.

"You do exactly what we discussed. You cannot slip up."

"I get it," Gold said. He had worked with Crane before, including on hitting that National Guard armory to steal weapons, and he was aware of Crane's insistence on flawless performance by his underlings. And that scary Mr. Soto guy was not too far away, which made him edgy. Even prime dope could not fully numb Gold's survival instinct.

"Your house is secure?"

"Yeah, it's fine. I mean, shitty neighborhood but, you know, that's because of systemic oppression."

"Absolutely sterile. No electronics. Nothing left in it that can be traced to us. Leave behind only the items we discussed. It's important you play your role perfectly."

"I understand," Gold said. "They'll only find what we want them to find. And by the time they do, we will be back in Minneapolis."

"Of course," Crane replied, not correcting his subordinate's misunderstanding of the role he was to play. "In the meantime, be sure the locals see you, but don't make it too obvious."

"You got it. I just can't wait to kill some pigs, fry 'em like bacon."

"You might want to go sleeves down until then," Crane said.

Ethan Gold looked at his forearm and smiled sheepishly as he pulled his cuff down to cover his anarchy symbol tattoo.

Merrick Crane III got out of the truck and looked around. Betts stepped out of the back door as Mr. Soto climbed down from the cab of the M1091. Lemmy's Muffler and Machine Shop looked like a large establishment from the street, but it looked much smaller once you got just inside. Clearly, there was more to the shop than a casual observer would see – just the way the proprietor wanted it.

The door of the garage had been open to the street and the immediate interior was empty, considerably simplifying the process of entry. They had simply driven in uninvited and parked. Then they waited.

But they did not wait for long. An angry older man stormed out of a door leading to the back – there was a second, closed garage door on that rear wall – and he bellowed, "What the hell are you bringing that in here for?"

"Close the garage door," Crane directed Betts, who moved toward the control panel.

"I ain't gonna ask you again," Lemmy said.

Betts hit a button and the door to the street came down, the electric motor whining.

"I need considerable work on this truck," Crane said, gesturing to the M1091 tanker. "I need it now and I am willing to pay well."

"I don't work on that kind of truck," Lemmy said. "You know, stolen trucks."

"Of course you do," Crane said, reaching into the cab of the beaten-up truck that had carried them south from Canada. "Behind that wall you have an entire chop shop disassembling stolen cars. Let's not waste time. Look at this."

Crane held open the bag. Lemmy stepped over and looked in the bag, then at Crane's face.

"It's $100,000. I need you to drop everything and make some modifications to this truck right now."

"Are you a cop? You have to tell me if you are a cop, you know."

"I assure you my hatred of the police is much deeper and more profound than yours will ever be."

"What do you want done?"

"I need you to beef up the suspension of this truck."

"Its suspension is pretty beefed up already. It carries one, two thousand gallons of gas."

"Fifteen hundred. And you'll need to drain the fuel in there because you are cutting a hole in the tank for access and putting several thousand pounds of lead in there."

"Why the hell am I doing that?" asked Lemmy.

"Because I'm paying you $100,000," Crane said.

That was good enough for Lemmy.

20.

"I'm sorry I'm late," Avery Barnes told Kelly Turnbull as she approached him in the main hallway of the convention center. "I had to help Senator Mazie Hirono find her lost ID tag. Again."

"Did you find it?" Turnbull asked, not actually caring.

"It was hanging around her neck under her coat. Again," Barnes sighed. "She's dumber than Ted Lieu."

That impressed Turnbull.

Barnes was wearing a blue dress and walking remarkably well for wearing heels that high. Turnbull was in his typical civilian business casual, except the big pistol on his hip made it clear what his particular business was. Both wore their ID badges outside their clothes, as did everyone except morons.

"What have you heard? Particularly from the other team."

"*Your* other team. I'm a reporter. I don't have a team."

"You keep telling me that, but I'm not sure you can be a reporter without a team anymore. Regardless, what are the blues saying?"

"You should be talking to their secret agents about things like security, you know?"

"We're not exactly on speaking terms."

She shook her head, annoyed at the ridiculousness of the situation. The most important people in the country were packed into one place in one city negotiating a way to prevent a full-fledged civil war, and they couldn't even agree with each other about how to keep the whole circus safe.

"The blues are all convinced that right-wing militias are coming to disrupt the conference. You'll probably see that hit the mainstream news tonight. You look skeptical. Is it true?"

"I have nothing on right-wing militias coming here," Turnbull said truthfully.

"Of course, you wouldn't tell me if you did."

Turnbull shrugged.

"How's the peace conference going?" he asked, changing the subject.

"No progress. No movement. The blues want to remake the whole country and the reds like the country just fine as it is."

"I'm not sure about the blues' thought process."

"Well, if it comes to choosing the Founders' vision or Mazie Hirono's, obviously you want to go with Mazie," Barnes said with mock solemnity.

"I thought you didn't take sides."

"I'm objective," Barnes replied. "Not stupid."

"You let me know if you hear anything," Turnbull said.

"I'll try, but I'm busy interviewing a lot of the key blues today and tomorrow," she said. "I'm apparently the Trump News liberal whisperer."

"I'll stick to close quarter combat."

"Combat beats being up close and personal with Jerry Nadler, especially after he eats chili."

Turnbull did not seek elaboration and took off down the hall, walking past Brad Pitt talking intently to Nikki Haley about trade agreements with China.

"We're watching Harrington closely and nada. I got zip from MIND FLAYER about right-wing militias," Casey said. "Not here in St. Louis, at least."

"They'd be coming in from out of town," Turnbull said. "Maybe get them moving, buying gas, making a call, something."

"The parameters are assessing everyone we know who might fall into that category, at least before all this started. Now a couple million more people are Provisionals, which the blues would call a right-wing militia, and you just can't sweep that broadly and get meaningful results, Kelly."

"Try," Turnbull said, turning to Schiller, who entered the Task Force Zulu room and tossed his coat on a table.

"The entrances are pretty standard," Schiller said. He had just been checking them out. "One main gate is for civvies, one for security support – military and such. The MPs run them both. The civilians mostly come through on foot, except real players. They can drive in. And the main gate got a radiation scanner, like a big Geiger counter, and everyone coming in gets checked on that as well as going through a metal detector. Cars too. They check bags by hand. It takes forever. No one checks anyone going out though. I told the commander on scene they ought to account for people leaving and he told me to get the hell out of his area."

"Maybe the warhead is inside already," Turnbull said. "They only sealed off the secure area a couple days ago, but there was some time between the summit announcement and then when they sealed off the secure area. Someone could have moved the bomb in and hidden it then."

"Thought of that," Casey said, not looking up from his laptop. "I calculated they would have to drive at an average 97.3 miles per hour to get here in time. If you're carrying a bomb, you'll drive the speed limit. So, unlikely."

"But possible," Deeds said, joining them. "I requested NEST support again. No dice."

"I'd blow this place up if I were them," Schiller said. "That's the play, not Houston or Dallas. It's all about strategic effects. It would create the chaos Crane wants. And vastly improve America."

"They still think it's Dallas," Deeds said, ignoring Schiller's opinion. "At least, that's what the politicians think."

"I have a new idea about something to check," Casey said, sounding pleased with himself.

"Check it and stop talking about it," Turnbull snapped back. Casey started typing quickly.

"Any word from your source?" Deeds asked.

"She says the blues are all talking about right-wing plots. Seems pretty convenient."

"It's easy enough to start a rumor like that," Deeds replied. "It establishes a narrative."

"And when St. Louis goes poof, well, we have some pre-identified culprits. Our side," Turnbull said.

"Crane's pulled a false flag in DC," Deeds said. "It worked there. Why not here, on a much bigger scale?"

"This is the target, Clay. I can feel it."

"I thought you didn't have feelings," Casey piped up.

"Do your computer thing," Turnbull ordered testily.

Turnbull spent the next fifteen minutes watching Trump News on one of the monitors. The chyron read "CRISIS: Deadly Deadlock." Another monitor had Anderson Cooper on it. His guest was Cory Booker, who was dressed in a camouflage uniform after appointing himself the commanding general of the New Jersey People's Militia. His buttons were half undone and he wore a general's star where his nametape should have gone.

Turnbull paid CNN no mind. A few minutes later the team reconvened.

"Interested in what a confidential informant told his St. Louis PD detective handler?" asked Casey, smiling broadly. "I got into their tip log."

"I'm interested," Turnbull said. "Good job hacking. Nice to see your tweeting came in handy."

"Those are different things, Kelly," Casey replied. "And while I love the props, the department's password was 'password.'"

"That's government efficiency for you. What's the info?"

"There's supposed to be a bunch of rednecks that just moved themselves into a townhouse on the north side. That's the bad part of town. The informant thinks they're a drug crew trying to carve out a piece of turf. Not clear how many of them. And he says they put a snake flag up in the living room."

"A snake flag?" Turnbull said aloud. "Did he mean a Gadsden flag?"

"The guy told his handler a 'snake flag.' I'm pretty sure he's not a flag and pennant expert. But that's a good guess."

"I'm down with people not treading on me," Turnbull said. "But it seems a little too on the nose."

"Maybe they wanted some attention?" Deeds speculated.

"What are the cops doing about it?" Turnbull asked.

"They aren't doing shit," Casey said. "There's nothing in their warrant database for that address. The cops barely bother patrolling the North Side anymore. They just roll in to pick up the bodies and roll out again. It's a drug gang free-fire zone."

"What's the blue situation around there?" asked Schiller. "Are there People's Militia units?"

"From the CI files, it looks like the blues tried to organize in there early on. You know, the army of the impoverished shit they always try? Except the locals ran them off. Apparently not nicely."

"Gotta love that community spirit," Turnbull said. He turned to Deeds. "We need to go in and find out what the hell is going on."

Deeds nodded.

"Gear up, gentlemen," Turnbull said.

Schiller drove the gray Ford Fusion through dingy streets that were lined with leafless trees and decaying townhouses. His blocky, black, Czech-made CZ Scorpion EVO 3 A1 submachine sat on the console next to him.

In the passenger seat, Turnbull racked a round into the chamber of his Beretta PMX submachine gun. He had only fired one once before, out on a range while training with some Italian *Carabinieri* on duty in Iraq. He was very interested in their weapon – he liked its balance and compact size, though the 9mm round was a bit small for his taste. The Italian paramilitary policemen, in contrast, were very interested in finishing their day of training and getting out that evening for coffee and trying to meet some Iraqi women in the more cosmopolitan establishments of Baghdad.

His Wilson Combat .45 was at his hip.

In back, giving Schiller directions off his phone, was Casey. He had an Israeli IWI Tavor TS12 bullpup shotgun that looked like something Bill Pullman packed in *Aliens*. It was semiautomatic and carried 15 12-gauge 00 buckshot shells plus another in the chamber. They normally would have considered taking M4s or other platforms that fired rifle rounds, but a quick computer recon of the address using Google Earth had confirmed that the townhouse was in a crowded neighborhood, and they all chose weapons where the projectiles would be less likely to tear off down the street and take out collateral civilians.

They all wore black tactical plate carriers with the word "POLICE" in bright yellow on Velcro patches affixed front and back.

"Remember, we need them alive," Casey said.

"That's their call," said Turnbull. He looked through the Holosun optic mounted on the Beretta's receiver.

"I like their vibe," Schiller said. "But if they get frisky, they are going out of there feet first."

"Check one, two, three," Turnbull said into the mic and earpiece he wore. A wire drooped down to a radio in his vest.

"You're good," Casey said. Schiller checked his comms and Casey checked his. All good.

Their plan was simple. They would roll up around the corner and move fast in the front door screaming about serving a warrant. There was no time for more detailed recon. None of them particularly liked it, but they hoped to make up through speed what they lacked in hard info on the target.

The red brick, two-story townhouse was up one house from the corner – they had passed by its front once, getting a view of the place. There was something yellow visible through the front window that opened onto the porch.

"That might be the snake flag," Casey said.

Schiller made an immediate left, went down the street, then pulled a U-turn and came back, parking back from the corner behind a Chevy that rested on a milk crate where the rear driver's wheel should have been.

They piled out, weapons in hand, and stopped when a high voice said, "You ain't cops."

Though three big guns pivoted onto him, the skinny kid on the sidewalk – he was maybe 12 – did not flinch.

"What?" Schiller said. "Can't you read? Now get out of here."

Instead, the kid repeated himself.

"You ain't cops."

Turnbull confirmed that the townhouse on the end of the block was hiding them from observers in the target residence, and then said, "Kid, see these vests? What do they say?"

"They say 'POLICE,' but you sure as shit ain't cops. And I ain't a kid. My name is Lukas."

"Come on, we need to move," said Schiller. "Kid, go home."

"This neighborhood is my home. And you ain't cops, so why are you here?"

"Why do you think we're not cops?" asked Turnbull.

"Because the pigs don't come around here anymore," Lukas said. "And when they do, they ain't strapped with top shelf gear like you got."

"We're going to get made," Schiller said, keeping the Scorpion ready.

"We already have been," Turnbull said. "So, why do you think we're here, Lukas?"

"Those four cracker assholes squatting in 2520. You're going to go hit them. They got some heavy artillery though. But that's okay. You're mafia or some shit."

"Well, let me make you an offer you can't refuse. You know how to get around back of – what is it – 2520?"

"Yeah, I do."

"Can you bring me around back?" Turnbull asked.

"I'm going to need to get paid."

"Of course. After all, we're not communists."

"They shouldn't be around here anyway so no one's going to care."

"And you'll forget who we are, right?"

"Do I look like a snitch?" Lukas demanded, a bit indignantly.

"Nope," Turnbull said. "Let's go." He nodded at Casey and Schiller to drive on with their part of the original plan.

Lukas led him back to a wood fence, and he pushed it so that a space opened up that he could fit through easily, but Turnbull, with his gear, had to carefully navigate it. Once in the overgrown back yard on the other side, they moved across to the next rotting wood fence.

"After you're done, can I shoot your piece? It's sweet," Lukas said.

"How about you try to keep your nose clean and you join the Army or Marines and then you can shoot whatever you want?"

"No, I don't take orders very well," Lukas explained.

"Never stopped me," Turnbull said. "How do we get in the back yard?"

"You hop the fence," Lukas said.

Turnbull sighed and peered over. There was a woodshed on the other side that created some dead space for him to climb up and drop down unobserved. That was good, assuming the fence didn't disintegrate under him as he was shimmying over.

"Okay, Lukas, it's payday." Turnbull pulled out his wallet and took out a $100 bill. Lukas was not pleased.

"That's bullshit," he said.

"You always talk like that?"

"Only when people try to rip me off."

"If I give you two hundred will you shut up and go home?"

"I will for three hundred."

"You know, I only used to make two hundred a month delivering newspapers."

"Just cuz you're as old as shit doesn't mean I shouldn't get paid what I'm worth," Lukas said.

Turnbull, defeated, handed over three $100 bills. "You didn't see nothing, right?"

"No one will see nothing around here," Lukas said. The kid stood there, expectantly.

"Go home," hissed Turnbull. "I'm paying you to leave."

"But I can help. Let me carry that .45."

"Go!"

Lukas turned, and Turnbull did not hop the fence into 2520's back yard until the kid disappeared through the break in the fence back onto the sidewalk.

Dropping down behind the decrepit woodshed, he listened for a few moments to what sounded like a TV on inside, then slowly peered around the shed at the house. There was a cement patio with a rusty grill and an overturned trike with weeds growing up through the wheels. The townhouse itself had three windows across the second floor, and a door that was up three steps plus two more windows on the ground floor. There was movement in one of these – a young man with stringy hair was walking through what had to be the kitchen.

The occupant disappeared from view, and Turnbull keyed his mic.

"Moving up, hold position."

He carefully made his way to the door, the submachine gun trained on the kitchen windows. One building over, an old woman's face appeared in a second-floor window. She seemed distinctly uninterested in the man with an automatic weapon closing in on the neighboring residence, and she disappeared behind her gauzy white drapes.

Turnbull went up the three cement steps to the flimsy door – it had last been painted with its now-peeling white paint sometime in the twentieth century, and the wood underneath was delaminating. From there, he could peer into the house and get a vague understanding of its layout.

The kitchen ran across the back, and it was filthy. A door went out toward the front, through a dining room and a front room. Someone – maybe more than one – was watching daytime television in there. From the dining room, a staircase up to the second floor peeled off. Turnbull surmised there were two or three bedrooms up there.

Someone had tacked a Blue Lives Matter blue-stripe flag to the wall of the kitchen over the table.

Taking his left hand off the foregrip of his weapon, he gently tried the door handle. It was locked.

Okay, then it would have to be the hard way.

"I'm set. At least one tango up front," he whispered into the mic. "I'll take high."

"Roger. You'll hear us," Schiller said back.

Schiller and Casey sprinted around the corner and took the ancient wood steps to the front porch in two bounds, Casey setting right and Schiller left. The occupants had clearly heard the noise of their footfalls, because there was frenzied scrambling inside in the front room.

"Police!" Schiller bellowed. "We have a warrant! Open the door!"

There was a clunk-clunk sound, and both men instinctively leaned away as a blast of buckshot blew through the middle of the front door.

Upon hearing Schiller announce the raid, Turnbull threw his full weight against the flimsy back door and it buckled – partially. He was slamming his shoulder into it a second time as the shotgun went off inside.

Easy was never in the cards.

The door pushed back off its hinges into the shabby kitchen and Turnbull stepped through onto the yellowing linoleum floor, the Beretta PMX up and aimed at the interior doorway.

A youngish man wearing a tan chest rig with a Punisher skull patch affixed to its front ran into the kitchen, but it was his rising AR15 that caught Turnbull's eye.

"Police!" Turnbull shouted, but the weapon kept coming up and Turnbull unloaded a long burst that started with several rounds slamming into the chest plate and Punisher patch, then several more hitting his target's throat and face. The man fell back over the table, under the pro-police flag.

There was more shooting up front. Turnbull did not pause at the doorway, instead charging into the dining room. It was clear of targets, but there was a guy with an FAL rifle by a love seat pivoting from shooting out front back toward Turnbull.

He never made the pivot. The front window blew glass and shredded drapes all over the front room while the three shells of buckshot Casey pumped through took the FAL guy out of the picture before the man could zero his 7.62mm fire on the sprinting Turnbull.

Turnbull jagged right onto the stairway, which wrapped back along the side wall of the house, rising toward the back. He had seen more movement in the ground floor front room – the shotgunner was still in there, but that was his partners' problem. He bounded up the stairs as Schiller stuck the Scorpion EVO through the hole in the front door and proceeded to splatter the target holding the Remington 12-gauge all over his Gadsden flag.

Turnbull was at the top of the steps, and there were three bedrooms, one left, one in the middle of the wall, and one to the right toward the front of the house. He glimpsed movement in there and charged down the hall as Schiller and Casey both yelled "Clear!" downstairs.

He hated that there were now two uncleared upstairs rooms to his rear, but if Lukas was right and there were just four tangos, he'd be fine.

If not, he'd be dead.

Ethan Gold, wearing an ACU camo top under a tan vest with a US flag on the front, lifted up the tricked-out Arsenal SLR AK47 he had taken from a Provisional he had shot in the back outside St. Paul and fired as Turnbull rushed inside the room. Gold panicked and his rounds went high as Turnbull dove low, stitching the wall with three fast shots and probably blowing the trio of rounds through the next three or four townhouses in the row.

Turnbull pivoted on the rug he landed on, bringing the PMX up and firing a long burst into Gold's legs. Gold collapsed screaming, his thighs a red mess, dropping his rifle, and falling into a heap.

Turnbull was on him, the Beretta pressed to his forehead, and he tore the wounded man's Glock out of its holster and tossed it into the corner.

"Hey!" he yelled over the man's cries. "Listen!"

From the back of the upstairs, he heard Schiller and Casey announce that the other bedrooms were clear.

Gold's eyes were wide and his face was a mixture of terror and agony. Turnbull put aside his weapon and lifted him into sitting position.

"You hear that?" he shouted. The man stopped screaming. There was silence, except footsteps as Schiller entered, Casey having returned to the front room to sweep for intel and keep watch. Turnbull continued.

"You hear that? That's the sound of *nothing*. No one is coming. Not the cops, not an ambulance. You will bleed out in five minutes unless I put on tourniquets and take you to help, and we aren't going anywhere until you tell me what the hell is going on with you assholes."

It sounded to Turnbull like Gold said, "We're poor boys."

"What are you doing here? What's your target?"

The man groaned. "Main gate," he managed to say.

"When!" Turnbull demanded.

"Main gate," he repeated. Turnbull shook him. The blood was pouring out of the holes in his legs.

"Come on!" Turnbull said, shaking him.

"Tomorrow. One o'clock."

The man gasped. Turnbull let him fall backwards and opened the medical pouch on his vest. He carried two tourniquets and several pressure bandages, which he began to pull out.

"Don't bother," Schiller said. "I think you made Swiss cheese out of his femoral arteries."

"Shit," Turnbull said.

Ethan Gold lay there still, his face pasty. Turnbull closed and zipped up his med kit, then stood and retrieved his PMX.

"Too bad they were assholes," Schiller said, not sounding much like he thought it was too bad. "They could have been fighting blues."

"Look," Turnbull said as he bent down and pulled back one of Gold's sleeves, revealing in full what had only been partially visible before.

A tattoo of the anarchy symbol.

"These assholes *are* blues."

21.

"The electronic fingerprints are coming through," Casey said to Deeds as Turnbull and Schiller looked on. He had carried a scanner and got reads off the paws of all four dead stiffs before the Zombies took off. They were there for ten minutes after the shootout, looking for electronics – they found two unused burner phones, both turned off, but nothing else – and anything else of interest. They did find a folder with photos of the civilian front gate to the secure area, along with a notation that some unspecified event was going to happen the next day at 1:00 pm.

"Who are they?" asked Deeds.

"A bunch of arrests and dropped charges for rioting and such in Seattle, Portland, Denver, DC. Yeah, they were all Antifa."

"And yet now they're right-wingers?" said Schiller. "I don't buy it."

"Teddy King can be super persuasive," Casey said. "Maybe they read my @FullAutoGalt Twitter timeline and got some Jesus."

"So, let's review," Turnbull said. "Just as the narrative is right-wingers are threatening the summit, four Antifa assholes do everything they can to tell the world they are right-wingers via their crash pad, which is conveniently out of reach of the bomb blast even if it's dialed up to max. And I bet afterward we would be supposed to find that plan they conveniently drafted for us."

"It's like a James Bond villain who spills the whole plan to him," Casey said. "I mean, before they made Bond sensitive. I hate the new Bond."

"I assume that they would actually have gone and shot up the civilian gate at 1 p.m.," Deeds said. "The last report before the bang would be right-wing terrorists attacking."

"And that the bomb would have vaporized all four of them and, therefore, the evidence that it was a set up," Turnbull said. "Killing his confederates to make sure that no one can talk is Crane's signature move. Just like false flags."

"It's 2035 hours now. The bomb goes off at 1300 or so tomorrow," Deeds said. "Sixteen-and-a-half hours. That's not much time."

"You need to evacuate the summit," Turnbull said.

Deeds shook his head. "That will never happen. The peace conference is too important. This evidence is all circumstantial, so the reds won't buy it. The blues won't buy it because they would have to admit one of their own is behind it, and we know their capacity to deny the truth. Plus, Crane will just move on with his toy to the next target."

"Can we at least get some NEST support now?"

Deeds took out his phone. "I'll make the call."

The C-17 jet landed at the Missouri Air National Guard facility at St. Louis Lambert International Airport at 0742 the next morning and rolled toward the hangers. A dozen pasty-faced civilians disgorged from the huge gray aircraft as Air Force personnel worked to unload the three nondescript white Ford Transit panel vans and the Bell 206 Jet Ranger helicopter, also white and without insignia, but with many strange saucers and panels bolted to the fuselage and facing downward.

Turnbull was there to greet them with his Ford Fusion. The leader rode with him as he led the three vans back to the secure area, which Turnbull estimated would be a 25-minute drive with another five minutes spent getting through the security forces gate. The helicopter needed to be unloaded and set up for flight – it would follow as soon as they could get it airborne.

When Doctor Drew Long was not working as the leader of the Texas-based Nuclear Emergency Support Team 3 – it was a part time job, with team members assembled only for training or in an emergency – he was a physicist from the University of Texas, Austin. Or, rather, at least he had been until he was fired when he stated during a class that science did not allow for the possibility that Newton's Three Laws of Physics were "structurally racist and fail to reflect the experiences and vision of oppressed people." Thirty of his students had staged a die-in during the next session – conveniently, when he was holding the midterm – because his "racist hate speech is literally murdering us." The Crisis began not long after he had filed his lawsuit against the university and since it started, he had devoted himself full-time to his NEST job. He had a Thermos and poured himself some coffee into its red lid/cup. Almost as an afterthought, he turned to Turnbull and said, "Oh, would you like some?"

"I'm good, Doc," Turnbull said. They were on I-70 heading toward the downtown. Doc Long slurped his coffee, which was exactly 9% cream. He lowered the cup.

"It's kind of exciting to get a real one," he said. "We've practiced for so long and now it's finally for real."

"Yeah, it's been fun," Turnbull said. "Here's my question. Can they set it off? I mean, you'd think it would have all sorts of safeguards to keep that from happening."

"The problem is that if you have the people responsible for the safeguards all working together to end-run around them, you certainly can. I read the files you sent me on the flight up. The technician they took is trained to do it, and the officers could give him the access to the codes he needed. I mean, I guess they murdered the other accomplices, but if they want the bomb to go boom, they keep the technician alive."

"And can you find it?"

"Sure, given enough time. But if it's supposed to go off at 1300, that's cutting it close. Any idea where it might be?"

"None."

"Then we do an air/ground pattern search of the whole secure area, everything within the max blast radius of a W80."

"And what's that?"

"Well, it's a dial-a-yield and assuming they set it to the max, about a five-kilometer radius. I did a quick calculation with my software. It looks like about 60,000 dead."

"That means no more summit?" asked Turnbull.

"Oh," Doc Long said, raising his red thermos cup to his mouth again. "The whole convention center will be a glass parking lot."

"You killed them," Betts said.

"You mean Lemmy the motorhead and his band?" asked Crane. "Technically, Mr. Soto killed them. I would have given the order if he was not so good at anticipating my intentions. Now get your uniform on."

Mr. Soto emerged from the back area where the chop shop was. It was now an abattoir with five dead mechanics lying in there. And they had done a magnificent job on the M1091. They had reinforced the suspension with new and thick steel springs so that it could support the weight of the two tons of lead that they had placed into the emptied fuel tank. The lead shielding surrounded an alcove reachable by a hole cut into the tank, fashioning a door that was able to be fully covered by a large hanging sign attached by chains to the tank that said "DANGER FLAMMABLE." The alcove was just large enough for the warhead.

They used a battered but still serviceable manual scissor lift on a cart they liberated from Lemmy to lift up the bomb so they could stow it inside the fuel tank. They then used the cart to put into place a large chunk of lead that challenged the cart's weight tolerances to complete the interior lead capsule. That done, they shut the door and covered it with the sign. They strapped the cart to the tanker in the space behind the cab. It looked like just so much more equipment.

The three donned their ACU uniforms. Mr. Soto wordlessly adjusted Crane's so that he did not look as though it had been thrown at him. Crane got into a van of Lemmy's that had been in the back; Mr. Soto drove the tanker with Betts riding shotgun. The two-vehicle mini convoy left the shop and headed toward the secure area.

Crane parked the van on the street not far from the main exit from the secure area. He then hopped into the tanker. Mr. Soto drove them back northwest toward the logistics base and there they waited.

They did not wait long. Another supply convoy was heading into the secure area. There was a space between trucks, and Mr. Soto slipped the tanker into it. The driver of the LTV behind them, a specialist E-4 with just five more months on his enlistment, figured that the tanker driver had screwed up and was trying to get back in the mix, and not being a blue falcon, let the tanker in and paid no mind to it.

The convoy got to the security gate and paused as the lieutenant in charge of the two dozen – plus one – vehicles got out and spoke to the gate personnel. It was all utterly routine. No one seemed on any higher stage of alert, no one was anything other than bored by the routine they had settled into over the last few days. While history was happening in the convention center not far from where they were, to the MPs at the gate this was just another miserable duty for personnel in a military occupational specialty where miserable duty was a given.

The LT climbed back in his cab and drove forward. The whole camouflage-painted snake of vehicles began to slither forward, and they passed inside the secure area without further inspection. Inside, the vehicles followed their usual route to a supply depot for the security forces on the far side of the Dome at America's Center. But that was not Mr. Soto's destination. He took a right where the rest of the column took a left.

The specialist at the wheel of the LTV saw the tanker go the wrong way. He briefly considered taking action, then remembered the code of the E-4 Mafia.

"It's your ass, not mine," he said as he continued along with the other trucks.

"The streets are laid out in a grid pattern, which makes it easier," Doc Long told Turnbull. The NEST crewmembers were parked by the green space in front of the Soldiers Memorial Military Museum, and they all had their iPads out with interactive maps. "The grids will help us do a coordinated sweep."

"Will you be able to find it?"

"Theoretically. It's about the size of a bread basket – a 300-pound bread box – so it's almost like a needle in a haystack, if the haystack was the secure area. Anyway, it's got a plutonium physics package that's pretty robust, and Air Force bombs tend to be hotter than Navy ones because if you're in a sub, you are working in closer proximity to the warheads day in and day out. The Air Force can put them away in bunkers so there's relatively less exposure."

"So, that was a yes?"

"Well, unless they're shielding it but that much lead is pretty heavy so it's kind of impractical."

"He'll know that," said Turnbull.

"We train assuming our opponents are smarter than the average criminal or terrorist," Doc Long said. "If it can be found, we'll find it."

"Besides an escort for your guys into the convention center, what do you need from me?" Turnbull asked.

"Intel," Doc Long replied. "And back-up if we find something."

"If you find something – I don't care if it's a tritium watch face – you let me know and my guys will handle it," Turnbull said.

"I'd like to see that," Doc Long replied.

"No, you wouldn't," Turnbull said. "Just tell me you can defuse it once I find it."

"That's not really how they work," Doc Long said. "It's not going to be ticking. They would probably have to rig up a detonator and trip it. Of course, the guy pushing the button would have a really bad day."

"Crane mentioned a timer."

"I bet you could do a timer," one of Long's men piped up. Turnbull noted the man was unironically sporting a pocket protector.

"Oh, well of course," Doc Long said. "I mean, you'd have to tie in the auxiliary power line and the accentuator cable."

"Sure, but –"

Turnbull rolled his eyes, and muttered "Nerds" under his breath. "Can you stop it from going off?"

Doc Long seemed a little hurt at the interruption of what he found a fascinating hypothetical, but he answered.

"We can render it safe. There are a number of ways to do that."

"I don't need to know the specifics, just that you can."

"We can. But we have to find it first."

While Doc Long set his vehicles to cruising the streets in their assigned grid patterns, Turnbull took two of the physics nerds with him to the convention center. As they cleared security – they were supplied by Deeds with red Level A security badges – Turnbull heard a *whomp-whomp* low in the sky and saw the NEST Bell 206 flying its own pattern. It had taken a lot of coordination by Deeds with the blue security command to get it permission to fly in the zone. Turnbull wondered what cover for its true purpose Deeds offered them, but gave it no more thought as the guards waved them in.

In the main hall, the physics nerds activated their backpacks and began walking through the hall. They looked like dateless wonders, with ugly glasses and those dorky packs. That was partly inevitable considering who they were – physics grad students – but also partly intentional. The guys nobody ever noticed would, hopefully, be guys nobody noticed sniffing around for a rogue thermonuclear bomb.

They had briefed Turnbull on the likely false positives they might detect, including cancer patients whose bodies still held radioactive isotopes. But they assured them that the plutonium in a W80 would be quite distinct. Turnbull left them to their task with instructions to get on the phone the second they found anything interesting.

Walking through the hall, Turnbull passed Rep. Ilhan Omar screaming at OAN reporter Jack Posobiec, who had apparently asked her if it was true that she had demanded that any new constitution include a provision allowing people to marry their brother. Nearby, Alexandria Ocasio-Cortez was explaining that there could be no agreement unless the police were abolished, and that legislators who failed to do so must be imprisoned. She was not clear on, and none of the mainstream media reporters asked her to explain, exactly who would do the arresting in her scenario.

Avery Barnes and Lou were ahead, and Turnbull went straight to them.

"Chris," she said. "You look stressed."

"Avery, you ought to take off."

"What do you mean 'take off'?" she asked, laughing.

"I mean take off. Get out of here."

"Chris, that's crazy. This is the biggest news story in two hundred fifty years, and it's coming to a head today. I'm not going anywhere, at least until my big interview later tonight."

"It isn't safe," he said. "Get out of the secure area now." Lou, for his part, seemed considerably more receptive to the idea of getting out of there than his reporter.

"Then you better protect me," she replied. "What do you know?"

It was hopeless to argue – she was not going anywhere and telling her more would only make her more intent on finding out even more.

"I have to go," he said.

"We should listen to him," the cameraman said as Turnbull disappeared into the crowd.

"Don't be such a wuss, Lou," Barnes snapped. Then she heard a deep voice bellowing, "Give me a break, you French-looking half-wit."

"Oh look," she said. "John Kerry's trying to argue with Seb Gorka. This will be good. Come on."

The tanker came to a stop in a parking lot off North 2nd Street. They had not been molested as they drove the largely deserted streets. Several times, unmarked white vans had passed them, but they did not notice the NEST crews and, thanks to the lead shielding, the NEST crews did not notice them either.

The three of them got out of the cab and took down the lifter cart from behind the cab, setting it to the side under the door cut in the side of the tank. Removing the "DANGER FLAMMABLE" sign, they opened the door and pulled out the lead shielding that covered it on the side and let it drop to the pavement with a loud clang.

Normally, the bums living around there would have noticed the commotion, but they had been bum-rushed out of the secure area a few days before. There was no one around.

They then moved the cart under the warhead, and used it to lower the bomb on the scissor jack. They then covered the warhead with a military tarp.

"Time to go," Crane said. His watch read noon.

22.

"You've got to get them all out," Turnbull said into his secure cell phone.

"That can't happen, Kelly," Deeds replied. There was noise around him – he was inside the convention center. "Not now. Not with the negotiations so close. The hammer is cocked and if they don't agree, it comes down. If Crane takes them out, you know what happens."

"Cajon Pass times a thousand."

"Find the bomb, Kelly. The NEST guys are the best. Use them. Find it."

Turnbull pocketed his phone and jogged up to the NEST agents in their van parked next to the wide, red brick sidewalk outside the white marble Old Courthouse on Broadway. Someone had spray-painted "Die Racist America" on it, and someone else had spray-painted, in red, "Shoot a Blue."

"What do you got?" he demanded of Doctor Long, who sat in the front seat drinking from his Thermos. Behind him, in the back, a couple other techs were hunched over their equipment and paid Turnbull no mind.

"Nothing," Long said.

"It can't be nothing," Turnbull said. "He is here. The bomb is here."

"We have three vehicles inside the secure area," Long said. "We've covered every inch of the area and outside it. We have foot teams in the buildings. If we get within 100 feet of the W80, the detector goes off unless it's buried in lead. A lot of lead. It's not here."

"It's here," Turnbull said, looking around at the high rises to the north and south, and at the empty park across the street.

Long shook his head. "We've been past every building, twice. We can read a bomb from 150 feet away. If it's here, we'll detect it."

"The river?"

"We got our chopper with sensors – even the Mississippi isn't so deep here that we couldn't detect it sitting on the bottom."

A three-Humvee convoy of military police gun trucks rolled by on patrol. The security forces paid no mind to the NEST van.

"Shit," Turnbull said, and shook his head. "We're missing something."

"No," said Long. "Look."

Long took his iPad and showed Turnbull his nuke blast app. A red pin hovered over their current location.

"I can calculate the blast radius for any location, so we know where the bomb could be if he wants to take out the convention center," he said. Turnbull took the iPad. There were concentric circles of various colors around the pin, indicating greater damage as they got closer to Ground Zero.

"The blast radius seems smaller than you'd think," Turnbull said.

"You can adjust it on the app for yield. The W80 can dial up to 150 kilotons, so I have a 150 kay-tee ground burst set as the yield."

"Wait, ground burst?"

"Yeah, ground burst. Obviously, an airburst would be optimal for blast effects – gives a wider radius."

"Shit, Doc, why doesn't he just fly it over?" Turnbull asked. "He's stolen an aircraft before."

Long laughed, gesturing skywards with his thumb. "Because the four F-22s on combat air patrol up there will shoot down anything that even looks like it's going to fly into the St. Louis

Aviation Exclusion Zone. He can stick the warhead in a Cessna, but even if he made a suicide run to get close enough, he would die before he could get within range."

"Then where the hell is it?" Turnbull said. "We have less than an hour."

"If it were here, we'd have found it."

Turnbull grunted and pivoted, his mind running double time. His eyes fell on the courthouse, and then upwards. There was a graceful curve above the roof. He stared for a second.

The Gateway Arch.

"I found the bomb," he said.

Mr. Soto and Arnold Betts were both veterans and understood how to wear uniforms. Crane, not so much. His hair was too long and he walked with the slack, slumpy posture of the American upper-middle class.

Crane was a major, Betts and Mr. Soto were sergeants first class. The patches on the left shoulders of their ACUs were from the 102nd Training Division of the Army Reserve, which was a large unit based in Missouri that included Military Police and Chemical Corps elements. This fit perfectly – thanks to another expedition by Mr. Soto, they all wore MP brassards on their arms. They had briefly considered using the patches of a Missouri National Guard unit, but everyone knew everyone in the Guard and they would no doubt get spotted as frauds.

Each carried an M4 and SIG Sauer M18 issue pistol in a thigh holster. Betts just had no ammo. The MPs Mr. Soto took them from – all listed by their commander as AWOL and suspected of being off somewhere on a bender – would not miss them.

"We can't do this," Betts said.

"Shut up," hissed Crane.

They were pushing the cart, with an OD green tarp draped over the W80. There were three troops at the foot of the north leg of the enormous monument at the entrance, with signs for wrangling the tourists that were piled against the wall and with the X-ray machine shut down. A buck sergeant was in charge of the security team at the Arch's base, and he was a bit puzzled at why a field grade officer and a senior NCO were doing manual labor hauling around whatever they had on their cart.

The buck sergeant saluted and Crane returned it.

"Good afternoon, sir. Can we help you?"

"This detection equipment needs to go up top," Crane said.

"To the observation deck?" asked the sergeant. He noted the major's hair was out of regs.

Crane nodded.

The top of the structure was 630 feet high, making it the highest memorial in America. The curving structure narrowed at the top to 17 feet per side, while at the base it was 54 feet. The legs were hollow, to allow for the trams that carried people to the observation deck, along with emergency stairs of over 1000 steps. The skin of the structure was stainless steel, and the monument was designed to withstand 150 mile per hour winds as well as earthquakes.

The monument had been closed to the public for the last few months, it being "a celebration of the genocyde of First Peoples and colonialism" according to a fading sign. Before the Crisis, there had been tentative plans to paint its entire span in multiple colors to celebrate the rainbow of sexual and gender identities.

The MP team leader was not privy to the history or scheme involving the Gateway Arch. He was solely concerned with his orders to secure the area.

"No one told me, sir. I gotta call my CO."

Crane nodded as the NCO walked into the entrance way to call in to his commander. The slug hit him in the back of the head. Mr. Soto finished off the other two with a silenced Heckler & Koch USP. He immediately set to dragging one out of sight, as Betts and Crane took their own.

The bodies concealed, Mr. Soto and Betts pushed the cart to the tram entrance and Crane went to the operator's station. It was already on, but the tram was at the top. With the benefit of his instructions, and the intuitive nature of the system, Crane brought the tram down. It would take three minutes to make the trip.

"Are we clear on the plan?" Crane said. Mr. Soto nodded. Crane looked at Betts.

"Your timer had better work or you'll activate it yourself."

"It'll work," Betts said. "But look, this is insane. We can use it as a bargaining chip, like you said you were going to. This will kill thousands, tens of thousands. Both sides will blame the other, and it'll probably cause a full-scale civil war."

"That's a feature, not a bug," replied Crane. "The time for talk is over. That's what you revolutionary dilettantes never understood."

"I won't do it," Betts said.

"You will, either voluntarily or because you beg Mr. Soto to stop and let you."

Betts' eyes flashed to Mr. Soto, whose face was the same granite visage as ever, except he had a long knife in his hand.

"Mr. Soto, if he hesitates in any way, start with his toes and work north."

Betts swallowed.

"Set the warhead, and then come down and go wherever you please – as long as it's several miles from here," Crane said amiably.

"You're not coming up?"

"I need to take care of other things. You two take it up, clear the observation deck, set it, and then...," Crane said, making the walking gesture with his fingers.

Betts nodded. Crane hit a button, and the tram doors opened. The tram had five benches and sufficient room. He and Mr. Soto both pushed the cart inside.

Mr. Soto gave Crane a faint smile as the doors slid shut.

Crane turned and quickly departed, making for the main exit across the secure area. He knew he had time.

Inside the compartment, Mr. Soto gestured at Betts to move to the side of the tram, out of the line of sight through the doorway. HK USP in hand, he waited as the tram made the four-minute transit to the apogee of the arch.

The tram stopped for a moment, and nothing happened for a moment, about enough time for Betts to take a breath. Then the doors slid open.

Mr. Soto raised the pistol and fired twice, then twice more, then stepped out. There were three more shots, all the same. Betts peeked around the corner. A female MP lay dead on the industrial carpet of the observation deck about five feet from the doorway. She had probably been coming to meet the unexpected visitors when Mr. Soto had dropped her with two headshots.

Farther up the slope – the observation deck was, after all, the top of the arch – the other two MPs lay where each had been killed. None of them had had a chance to draw their SIGs from their holsters.

There were an Army radio and a couple pairs of binoculars. The observation deck had been an observation post. A line of small, rectangular windows in vestibules every few feet along the length of the deck provided a glorious view of not just the secure area, but 20-30 miles east and west.

Mr. Soto came back inside the tram car, and Betts understood what was next. He got behind the cart and helped push. They got the heavy cargo out of the tram and onto the carpet. There, Mr. Soto stopped and left Betts straining to support the weight of the warhead on the slope as he dragged the dead MP into the doorway. The sliding door tried to shut but could not. It kept closing and bouncing back off the corpse. The tram was not going anywhere.

Mr. Soto rejoined Betts, and they pushed it to the apogee of the curve, the exact middle of the observation deck, past the door with the sign reading "EMERGENCY STAIRWAY – AUTHORIZED PERSONNEL ONLY." There, they locked the cart's wheels so it would not roll. A dead soldier lay nearby, but Mr. Soto paid him no mind.

Instead, Betts looked at Mr. Soto imploringly.

"We can't do this," Betts said. "Let's just go."

Mr. Soto's hand tightened on his pistol. Betts sighed, and after considering his limited options, he opened the backpack, took out the laptop terminal with the codes, and began working on setting the timer.

Mr. Soto left him to check the other end of the deck. Betts went to work, adjusting wires and connectors. He was actually proud of the red analog numbers of the countdown timer. It looked like something out of a James Bond movie.

Mr. Soto returned and looked at Betts expectantly. Betts was on his knees next to the device; the clock read "30:00." There was a switch.

"Set, 150 kilotons, the max," Betts said.

Mr. Soto did not react.

"Once I flip this timer," Betts said, "there's no going back. You can't stop it."

Mr. Soto's face betrayed no emotion or even interest.

"Are you sure?"

Nothing.

"Okay, fine," Betts said. He flipped the switch.

29:59.

29:58.

29:57.

"Let's go," said Betts, standing up.

Mr. Soto shot him in the gut.

Betts bent forward and fell to the floor, rose on his arms for a moment, and then collapsed. He groaned and then was quiet and still.

Mr. Soto sat down in one of the vestibules, took out his phone and sent a text to the only number in the burner's memory – a volcano emoji. After that, he dropped the mag from his pistol and loaded a fresh one.

Then he stared out one of the east-facing windows at the dark brown bulk of the Mississippi.

29:13.

29:12.

29:11.

Turnbull didn't wait for the back-up he had summoned through Deeds, especially after his handler had told him that the executive session was on the verge of a breakthrough. Instead, Turnbull had sprinted at full speed the nearly 500 meters down Market Street and through Luther Ely Smith Park, past a weird sculpture of a head lying on a pedestal and another of a headless pink suit. There had been a statue of Pinocchio raising his arms to the heavens, but it had been removed by the mayor – the marionette's desire to one day become "a real boy" was deemed "actual violence towards the trans and gender-flex community."

Interstate 44 ran under the park under a north-south tunnel – of course it was empty now. The Gateway Arch was just ahead, enormous, impossibly high. Too high for NEST equipment to read the plutonium from the ground.

Turnbull was sprinting at full speed, sweating despite the chill in the autumn air.

He had no idea what he would do.

Turnbull did not hesitate at the entrance and security checkpoint – he burst inside, his Wilson .45 ready and seeking targets. No one. He cleared the area quickly, discovering and following blood trails to a heap of three dead MPs heaped behind the control panel. Scanning the instruments, he figured out the situation. There was a tram.

He identified and hit the call button. But the screen reported "MALFUNCTION – DOOR OPEN." The tram was out.

He studied the diagram on the panel.

Stairs.

He bolted across the space toward a door with a sign that read "KEEP OUT – EMERGENCY ACCESS ONLY." Saying a silent prayer, he pulled on the handle.

Not locked.

Stepping gingerly inside, weapon ready, he saw stairs winding upwards at an alarming angle. A bulb every few meters provided some dingy light. He could not begin to see where it ended.

"Are you kidding me?" he muttered, and started upwards two steps at a time.

At 200 steps he began to slow. Conveniently, there were small metal signs indicating every 100-stair increment. At 400 steps, he paused to catch his breath, leaning against the metal sheath insulating the emergency stairway. Ahead of him, the stairs kept going.

He considered taking a full minute, but instead gave himself 30 seconds before launching into another batch of two-at-a-time strides up the steps.

500.

600.

He was breathing very heavily now, and his shirt was soaked through with sweat. And he was aware that at any second, he could be incinerated inside an enormous fireball – the only consolation was that he would never know it.

700.

800.

"How high is this damn arch?" he wondered, panting and pausing by the 900-foot mark. Was that the top ahead?

He grunted, and started upwards again.

The stairs stopped a few dozen steps past the 1000th stair at a metal push-bar door with a sign reading "OBSERVATION DECK." Turnbull was breathing heavily but he forced himself to be quiet as he placed his ear against the cold metal.

Nothing.

He listened for 20 seconds, aware that if the bomb was in there and went off with his head pressed to the door, the radiation and heat would beat the sound waves and tear him molecule from molecule before he heard anything.

It was not reassuring.

He readied the Wilson and confirmed what he already knew – there was a hollow point in the chamber.

Taking a deep breath, he set his right shoulder against the push bar. Turnbull figured the layout of the observation deck was perpendicular to the door, and that he was going to be at one end. The door would swing out left, and block his view of the length of the deck unless he got past it quick.

Unless the bomb and the bad guys were at the end of the deck and behind him. Then this visit was going to be over quick and Turnbull would do something he always swore he would not do.

Die tired.

Turnbull pushed the door open fast and threw himself out from behind it. He saw he was right about the layout – he was at one end and the deck stretched out before him, curving upwards to the apogee where a cart with some big silver bomb-looking thing sat.

There were shapes on the ground he identified as bodies and disregarded. What he did not disregard was the surprised man sitting on the vestibule by the device.

Turnbull fired twice as he bolted across the deck, the rounds smashing into the concrete vestibule dividers in puffs of vaporized cement.

The other guy was good – really fast and able to send two rounds from his USP back just a split second after Turnbull was able to dodge behind a vestibule divider wall of his own on the other side of the deck.

Turnbull spun back and returned fire – high, because he had no idea if a .45 slug slamming into the bomb was going to light that candle.

The other guy came out from his divider and took cover behind the device – apparently, he figured Turnbull wouldn't dare take a shot.

He was wrong. Turnbull unloaded three just over the top of it and swung back behind cover before the other guy returned three shots of his own.

Turnbull thought he saw something on the warhead. Red, analog numbers.

01:59.

01:58.

"Shit," Turnbull said, dropping his mag to the floor and sliding in a freshie.

"Kelly?"

The voice was the shooter's, and he did seem familiar. But Turnbull could not place him.

"That's you, isn't it, Kelly?"

It clicked for Turnbull.

"Leon?" Turnbull said, back against the divider, the Wilson in a two-hand grip. "Leon Soto?"

Mr. Soto laughed.

"It's been a long time, Kelly Turnbull!"

"Kandahar, I think," Turnbull replied, his mind pedal to the metal seeking a solution to his situation.

"Maybe. Or Raqqa. Do they all blend together for you too?"

"Nah," Turnbull said. "I remember and savor each op."

"Kind of funny that we will end up dying together after all, doesn't it?"

"We weren't exactly pals. This is the most I've ever heard you talk."

Turnbull swung around and unloaded three shots, but Mr. Soto had ducked down behind the bomb and the bullets went high, flying down the length of the deck. As Turnbull pulled back behind cover, three rounds followed and impacted on the wall.

Turnbull had glimpsed the clock.

01:33.

01:32.

"Actions, not words," yelled Mr. Soto. "That's my code."

"Oh, you got a code? That's fantastic."

"A man needs a code, Kelly. Do you have one?"

"Of a sort," Turnbull said. "So, uh, why are you doing this, Leon?"

"Why not, Kelly?" he asked, and he sounded like he really wanted an answer.

"Do I have it right – your boy Crane has you sitting here and running out the clock? You know you die at the end, right?"

"So what?" replied Mr. Soto, again sounding like it was an actual question.

"Leon, I gotta level with you," Turnbull said, breathing hard. "I always thought you were a little nuts."

Mr. Soto laughed from up the deck.

"You know who was nuts, Kelly? That guy who taught us demolitions."

Turnbull laughed in spite of himself. "The NCO who kept talking about how to take down the Golden Gate Bridge?"

"Yeah, him. You think he might be able to disarm this, Kelly? Because even if you manage to kill me, you can't stop it. And you can't kill me."

"Bet?" Turnbull said as he rolled out from cover, bringing the Wilson around.

But Mr. Soto was there, pointing the HK pistol from a few feet off to the left of where he had been, just enough to get the edge.

There was a shot, and Mr. Soto's right side jerked down and he yelled, his attention now directed behind him.

Turnbull acquired and fired, slamming round after round into Mr. Soto's shoulders and chest. The nice thing about the Wilson was its tightness and smoothness. One has to try to miss. And Turnbull did not miss.

The man staggered and looked at Turnbull, his USP coming up for a shot.

Turnbull adjusted up and took a final shot that blew the back of his head out, and Mr. Soto fell backwards to the floor.

He dropped the mag and slammed another home as he charged up the curving floor past two dead soldiers.

The clock read "01:01."

01:00.

00:59.

Turnbull reached the device, and beyond it were a dead soldier and a dead Mr. Soto. Beside him, gut shot and covered with his former comrade's brains, was Betts, the loaded SIG he had taken from the holster of the dead MP in his hand.

Turnbull saw the wounded man in an Army uniform and lowered his .45.

"Thanks, sergeant," he said, turning his attention to the bomb. Maybe if he shot the timer...

In about 50 seconds he would be gone regardless. Turnbull raised the pistol

"Don't shoot it!" shouted Betts. He winced.

Turnbull ignored the wounded man. It was the only option.

"It's my bomb!" Betts managed to say. "I was with him. I set it!"

Turnbull looked at him, baffled.

"I'm an Air Force bomb tech," Betts said. "I helped steal it. I'm so sorry."

The hulking .45 was now leveled at Betts' face.

"So, stop it," Turnbull ordered.

Betts coughed up a glob of blood. "It's okay," he gasped, his lips crimson. "It's okay."

Turnbull pointed the pistol back at the timer.

00:32.

00:31.

"If you shoot it that might make the conventional explosives go off and trigger it!" Betts gasped. More blood erupted from his mouth.

Turnbull's pistol stayed steady on the device.

"I wanted," Betts began. "I wanted to make up for what I did." He groaned. His eyes were widening. "Remember what I did. You tell them. You tell them what I did in the end."

Betts groaned and again and curled into a fetal position, then gasped and was still.

00:11

00:10

00:09

00:08

Turnbull considered his options.

00:07

00:06

00:05

00:04

"This is about where James Bond manages to stop the clock," Turnbull thought.

00:03.

00:02.

00:01.

He chose his option.

00:00.

23.

"No," Schiller told Doctor Long. "*My* team is taking custody of the bomb. No one's getting a hold of it again." Several of Schiller's guys, with various assault rifles, stood nearby. This was not a debate Doc was going to win.

Turnbull leaned against the wall ignoring the jousting between Task Force Zulu and the NEST crew.

Deeds stepped gingerly over the corpse of Leon Soto.

"Your boy certainly went off the reservation, Kelly."

"Not my boy. He was always a weirdo."

"Why do you think he threw in with a lizard like Crane?"

"Why does anyone choose to be a leftist? Stupidity. Liked to hurt people. Maybe daddy issues. I don't know or much care. Piece of shit." Turnbull said adding: "And don't insult lizards."

"We got an ID on your bomb tech," Deeds said, gesturing to the sheet-covered body of the airman. "Technical Sergeant Alvin Betts, from Minot. I guess Crane kept him alive until he didn't need him anymore."

"I figured if they shot him, he was unreliable. Took a chance he wouldn't go through with it."

"I guess he was," Deeds said.

"Play stupid games, win stupid prizes."

Doc Long stepped over and interjected: "If he had connected the timer, we would all be radioactive slag."

"He was a traitor," Turnbull said. "A blue falcon. You don't get to go all the way and at the end shrug and say, 'Sorry.'"

"We missed Crane, though," Deeds said. "He's still out there. And after today, he's going to have plenty of opportunity for mischief."

"What do you mean?" asked Turnbull.

Deeds looked him in the eye. "The agreement, Kelly. The summit. The United States is splitting in two."

Turnbull was too stunned to respond instantly. Finally, he just asked: "Are you kidding me?"

"Not about that. No, they made a deal to end the Crisis. The country is splitting in two, red and blue."

Another pause. Then: "That's such bullshit."

"You aren't the only one who feels that way. Your pal General Scott is the big voice against what they're calling The Split. The blues get the coasts and the Midwest. Hawaii too. The reds get everything else. They are keeping current state lines."

"That's going to be trouble."

"There are lots of details to iron out, of course, but they'll sign the Treaty of St. Louis tomorrow between the United States of America and the People's Republic of North America."

"The what?"

"You heard me, Kelly."

"Assholes," Turnbull said. "So, what about us?"

"Us? We gotta choose sides, Kelly. Just like everyone else."

"What are you choosing?"

"I've served the USA for nearly 40 years. I'm too old to start again. Off to Texas. Looks like Dallas is the new DC."

"I guess I'm red too. Not that the blues would have me. I know which bathroom to use."

"The whole team went red. All of the Zombies. Which is good, because we still have to find Merrick Crane. Any ideas?"

"I assume he noticed that St. Louis didn't cease to exist, so normally I'd expect him to *di di mau* outta Dodge," Turnbull said.

"Normally?"

"It's easier to spot someone moving. Maybe he stays put. This place is going to be the center of the world, I suspect. America breaking in two is probably a big story. Maybe he wants to be where the action is."

"Where are you going to start?" asked Deeds.

Turnbull thought for a moment, then he practically kicked himself. He walked over to Mr. Soto's body, knelt, and patted him down.

He stood up with a cell phone, the facial recognition working to unlock it even with the large hole excavated courtesy of Turnbull's .45 out of the middle of Mr. Soto's forehead.

He handed the open text app to Deeds.

"Find out where that cell phone is."

"He might have ditched it."

"Or he might not have," Turnbull said as he walked toward the tram. "Call me and tell me when you know where I'm going."

Deeds smiled and picked up his own phone.

Senator Richard Harrington wore his Ritz-Carlton bathrobe as he stared out the window of his penthouse suite looking toward the east. The Gateway Arch was still there, and the Senator was mightily displeased.

"I missed a huge historical moment because of you," he snapped.

Merrick Crane III was not used to being spoken to in that manner, but he was also not used to failure. Now he was alone, without his henchman and, apparently, without the ability to inspire fear in loathsome functionaries like Harrington.

The Walther was in his belt under his shirt at the small of his back, and Crane briefly considered shooting his host in the throat.

No, the senator would still be necessary in the future. And gunplay would raise awkward questions and require more shooting to take out Harrington's two security men in the hall.

Instead, Crane smiled.

"I understand your disappointment," he said.

"You do?" Harrington scoffed. "You understand that I was absent from what was the most important moment in American history because of you?" Harrington had sent his regrets to the peace conference that morning. He said he had a cold – not COVID-22, thank you – but a regular cold, and would not be able to attend. And, at the appointed time, he had arranged for his security men to take him to visit a baffled third cousin who happened to live in a suburb about 30 miles away from the proposed Ground Zero. The awkward coffee with the long-lost relative had ended when Harrington realized he no longer needed an alibi for his absence, which was about two minutes after the appointed time when the eastern sky failed to light up like a million suns.

"History is not over yet," Crane growled.

"Have you thought that it might be for you?" Harington asked. "Of course, one of the key provisions of the treaty is a general amnesty for all crimes committed during the Crisis, so I suppose you have that in your favor."

"I don't need a pardon. They have no right to judge me."

"Always the revolutionary," Harrington said, the mockery in his tone not even hidden anymore. "I have an interview in a few minutes. Stay in the guest bedroom and do *nothing*. We will see about smuggling you away later."

Crane revisited his throat shot option, but again rejected it. Time enough for that later. Once the revolution came – and this irritating setback did nothing to shake his confidence that it would come, and that Merrick Crane III would be at its vanguard – the likes of Senator Harrington would be among the first to die.

The phone rang on the suite's ornate writing desk. Harrington listened for a moment, sighed, and replied, "Send her up." He hung up and looked at Crane.

"Bill de Blasio? Trying to be president?" he grunted. "Can you imagine? Warren's going to be furious." He had almost said "going to go on the warpath" but checked himself.

Harrington stalked off to the master bedroom – renamed "the primary bedroom," though that indication of hierarchy was itself problematic – so he could continue to get ready.

Crane went into the guest bedroom and shut the door behind him. He smiled just the hint of a smile, both from the joy of imagining the harrowing death that awaited Harrington once he stopped being useful, and because the hint of a new scheme was taking shape in his rat-like mind. But first, he had to attend to his face.

Five minutes later there was a knock at the front door and Harrington, properly attired in a $6,000 suit with a crisp white shirt and a subdued blue tie, strolled out of the primary bedroom and turned the knob.

His two security men, in dark suits with blank expressions, flanked Avery Barnes and Lou the cameraman, who held his gear on his shoulder. She wore an orange dress that was arguably too short but was nonetheless right in the Trump News wheelhouse. Lou was dressed like a hobo.

Harrington gestured the pair inside and shut the door behind them.

"Good to see you, Ms. Barnes. Your man can set up over there. I suggest a two-shot out through the window over the city?"

Lou went ahead to arrange things. Avery stood in front of him.

"Senator, I was not expecting you to look so healthy."

"I improved dramatically this afternoon," he said smoothly. "But, of course, I have access to healthy food and excellent free health care, things I expect the People's Republic of North America will guarantee its citizens."

"So, you support this Split?"

"I can only be sorry that about half of America will have to live under the kind of regime we have seen developing in the reactionary red states."

"You know I and my whole network had to move to Texas because leftist mobs tried to kill us?"

Harrington sighed. "Maybe your network should stop provoking the justified wrath of the people."

"Maybe we should save this for the interview?"

Turnbull was digging around in the sidewalk garbage can when he found what he was looking for – a cracked iPhone 12 resting underneath a sauce-stained Hardee's bag. He stood upright and noticed an older man and woman standing together on the sidewalk, staring at him.

"Poor man," the woman said, offering him a $20 bill. "When we split off the red fascist states you should come to blue America where your kind will be treated with caring."

"Why don't you roll that twenty up real tight, light it on fire, and shove it up your hubby's ass?" Turnbull said as he walked past them.

It looked like Crane had cracked the phone on the metal garbage can rim, but he must have been in a hurry and he apparently didn't count on the fine work of the Chinese slaves who made it. The display might be out, but it was still generating a signal. Yet, why would Crane come there? Turnbull looked around, then picked up his own phone.

"Clay, guess who is big in the blue and is staying at the Ritz-Carlton?"

He crossed the street and went toward the entrance.

"We will have a new constitution, one that actually gives rights to the people instead of throwing up obstacles to progress," Harrington said, looking across at Avery Barnes. Like him, she was seated in one of the suite's ornate chairs, and together they were silhouetted against the window, which looked out over St. Louis. The Gateway Arch was there in the distance, mocking Harrington, while Barnes was completely ignorant of the significance of its continued existence.

"Your proposed People's Republic constitution will grant rights? Aren't natural rights given by God?"

Harrington laughed. "The PR will be built on a foundation of science, not superstition, Ms. Barnes. And if you are wondering, we will grant the right to free expression, but with the understanding that rights bring responsibilities."

"So, the PR will allow Trump News back in to report?"

"It's clearly a fascist mouthpiece, but it is welcome, despite its legacy of lies, racism, and apologetics for dictators like Donald Trump. I expect we will be seeking the extradition of the members of his clique to hold them to account for their crimes. We are already preparing to formalize the truth and reconciliation process."

"I bet you are," Barnes replied. "What about due process?"

Harrington scoffed. "Due process is whatever serves justice."

"That seems like a dangerous premise."

"Only for those who would abuse rights to impede progress."

There was a knock at the door. Both Harrington and Barnes looked over, and Lou stopped shooting.

"Go get it," Harrington told him. He looked to Barnes, who nodded. Lou walked over and opened the door.

"You?" he said as Turnbull burst inside, Wilson Combat .45 up, covering the room and shutting the door with his foot. It closed, blocking the view of the two prone shapes lying still on the hallway floor.

"Quiet!" he hissed quietly, as his aim point settled on Harrington's face. The senator was too stunned to speak when Turnbull burst in, and was now too smart to speak when the intruder had his pistol leveled at him.

Barnes made to speak but Turnbull shushed her. Her eyes were like dinner plates. He turned his glare back to Harrington. His gun had never left.

"Where is Merrick Crane?" he whispered.

"Crane is here in St. Louis?" Barnes gasped.

"Yeah, he and Senator Dipshit are pals."

"I don't –," Harrington began but Turnbull cut him off.

"Where?" Turnbull whispered, with more emphasis. The chrome barrel lurking in the black slide hovering in front of his face unnerved the senator. His eyes involuntarily went to the guest room door.

"When I nod, you call him out. You mess up, you die with him. Got it? Nod."

Harrington nodded, and Turnbull moved to the guest bedroom door, taking a position to its left. He nodded.

"Merrick?" Harrington croaked. "Merrick, come out here."

Nothing.

Turnbull's pistol was at head level as Barnes and Lou watched, fascinated. Turnbull nodded again.

"Merrick, I need you, damn it!" Harrington said.

The door opened and Crane emerged, his face flushed scarlet at being summoned like a servant while he was performing his skin care regimen.

That insult became the least of his worries as Turnbull's Wilson ran up against the back of his skull.

"Good to meet you, asshole," Turnbull said. He noted that his quarry's complexion was absolutely radiant.

The revolutionary froze, then he slowly took stock of the situation.

"You got me," he said quietly. Turnbull pushed him into the center of the room. Crane staggered, his hands high, and he turned to face his captor.

"What now?" he asked.

"Now I shoot you in the face," Turnbull said evenly. "I just wanted you to know it's coming."

"You're just going to kill me?" Crane asked, risking a fey smile. "No trial, no jury, no lawyers?"

"No nothing, just 230 grains of justice."

"Should I move, since the splatter will mess up the senator's expensive suit and this Trump News propagandist's slutty orange dress?"

"Good point. Could you step off to a bit to your left?"

"Chris!" Avery Barnes shouted, standing up, and using the fake name she knew him by. "You can't just shoot him!"

"Avery, sit down," Turnbull replied calmly. "You don't know what this son of a bitch has done."

"It's pretty bad, Avery, what I've done," Crane said, smiling more broadly. "I'd shoot me, but then I'm not bound by all your procedures and processes. They are supposed to guarantee justice and they just end up denying it. That's what this thug truly thinks, but he won't act on it."

"You want to bet your life on that?" Turnbull asked Crane.

"It seems I'm doing just that. You are not going to shoot me. Not just because there are witnesses – I mean, shooting me in front of the Fourth Estate, really? But because you care about all the ridiculous nonsense you were taught about America. My rights and such."

"It's a bad bet," Turnbull growled. His pistol never wavered.

"Then why am I not dead yet?"

"Maybe if I let you run your fool mouth, you'll say something that will help me hunt down more of your pack of assholes."

"No," Crane said. "You're soft. You're still bound by the rules. But I'm not. I'm free, as you've seen. I took the rules and threw them away. Even this miserable creature, this senator, loves the rules because they give him his piddling power."

"Are you done? Because I am finding you tiresome?" Turnbull said.

"He's right," Barnes said. "You can't shoot him. It's wrong."

"Stay out of it, Avery," Turnbull warned.

"Here's how this goes. This ridiculous trollop will convince you to let me live because, beside your dedication to the rules that enslave you, at some level deep inside you think that doing so will please her enough to perhaps allow a mook like you access into what dwells under that mid-thigh hemline. And then I will sit in a cell for a while, planning and converting prisoners to my cause, and then I will be released as part of the general amnesty that goes along with this idiotic Split." Crane paused, then continued. "And then I will get out, continue my fight, and along the way take a tangent to kill everyone you ever loved."

"That won't take long," Turnbull growled. "I guess this is it. Let me ask you something, Crane."

"Yes?"

"You like movies?"

"Movies?"

"You heard me."

"I'll play. Yes, though not the fascist consumerist fantasies with magical superheroes that you likely find amusing."

"You like darker fare?"

"More sophisticated fare."

"You ever see that Brad Pitt movie, *Se7en*?"

"Yes." And as Crane thought back to it, his smile vanished.

"What's in the box?" Turnbull growled as he raised the pistol, and Crane's face went pale.

Then, in a flash, Barnes was in front of him, between Turnbull and Crane.

"Chris, no!" she pleaded.

"Get out of the way!" Turnbull yelled, but Crane was behind Barnes, grabbing her, the Walther out from under his shirt and at the base of her skull.

No shot, not without going through Barnes. The hollow points would dump all their energy in her.

"You should have shot me," Crane mocked. He pulled tighter on Barnes and she squealed.

"Chris!" she said.

Turnbull aimed, but he had no shot – not without almost certainly taking her out.

"We're leaving and I'm bringing her along, and if I see one of your pals in my way she dies. Remember, amnesty, so I have zero to lose."

"Keep in mind that I get amnesty too," Turnbull replied, still seeking a kill shot.

"That won't bring this bitch back to life, will it?" said Crane. "Senator, would you be so good as to get the door for me. I assume our friend here took care of your security guards."

Turnbull kept Crane covered as he talked; the two security men were unconscious on the hallway floor. Avery Barnes looked frightened, but not panicked. This would make a great story.

Harrington stood up, and Turnbull said, "Don't move, asshole."

"Let him go, Chris," Barnes said. "It'll be all right. I'm all right, Lou," she added for her cameraman.

"You should listen to her, Chris," Crane said from behind her. Still no clear shot.

Harrington slowly walked to the suite's front door and opened it. The two knocked-out bodyguards were sprawled on the carpet.

"Slowly," Crane said, as Barnes began the walk out of the suite with him crouched behind her.

They passed Turnbull but his aim never left them. He waited for just enough exposure to take the shot, but Crane was too careful. His mind was running through scenarios. He doubted his Task Force Zulu back-up would have arrived in the lobby yet.

It was him or no one.

Crane backed out into the hall, pulling Barnes with him while shielding himself with her orange-clad body. Turnbull followed their progress, his weapon ready for any opportunity.

"Shut the door," he told Harrington. "I will see you around, Chris."

"See you in my sight picture," Turnbull corrected him.

"Not today," Crane said and his weapon appeared and he fired several shots into the room.

Harrington and Lou scattered, while Turnbull dropped to his knee as the rounds went high. The door shut. The last thing Turnbull saw was Barnes' eyes.

Turnbull pivoted to Lou, who was terrified and on the floor.

"Call for help now!"

He leapt to the door and threw it open. They were at the elevators down the hall, and Crane took two shots. Turnbull dodged back as and the slugs slammed into the doorjamb. He banked out and fired twice, his shots pinging off the closing elevator door.

Lou was on the phone behind him as Turnbull took off running for the elevators. He was 12 stories up, so he was too high to use the stairs. He hit the call button.

The LOBBY button was illuminated. Crane stood on one side of the car, Walther in hand, and Barnes on the other. Crane reloaded a fresh magazine.

"Where are you taking me?" she asked.

"Shut up," he snapped, letting the slide go forward.

At the seventh floor, the car stopped and a door opened. A laughing man and a woman began to step into the car.

Crane's gun dissuaded them. The door shut and they continued their descent.

The light on the "2" button went on, and Crane stepped over and grabbed Barnes roughly by the collar as the elevator continued to drop.

"You know what to do. Do anything else and I'll blow your blonde head apart all over the lobby." He roughly pulled her in front of him as the door opened to the lobby.

At floor seven, the door opened and a terrified man and woman looked him over and screamed. Turnbull figured it must have been his gun. He hit the "DOOR CLOSE" button as they ran off down the hall.

The lobby. That was the only way out.

He slid in a fresh magazine.

No one seemed to take note of the man ungently maneuvering the pretty blonde who looked somewhat familiar across the lobby to the other bank of elevators. Crane paused to look behind him at the main bank of elevators – no pursuer, at least not yet. And Turnbull apparently had no back-up in the lobby.

There had to be plainclothes security in the lobby for the other unlucky VIP guests exiled so far away from the action, but none of them acted. The clerks at the front desk were a bit agitated – no doubt someone had just called about the shooting up top – but Crane saw that his way was clear. He got Barnes to the parking elevator bank and hit "P1-VALET."

The door opened as Turnbull burst out of an elevator car across the lobby.

Crane spun Barnes around and backed into the open elevator car, firing several rounds in Turnbull's general direction. It had the desired effect – chaos in the lobby.

Turnbull took aim, but he had no shot, and a second later the door closed. He sprinted full speed across the lobby, pushing terrified guests out of his way.

The elevator opened to the first floor of the underground parking lot. The valet station was there, and a short man in a vest with a red bow-tie was standing by a Silver E-Class Mercedes, keys in hand.

Crane shot him in the chest as the other people in the area ran away. He dragged the now screaming Barnes along with him, forcing her into the passenger seat and pausing to pick up the keys before slipping behind the wheel.

"You killed him!" she shouted.

"Yes," Crane said. "And?"

He hit the gas and the sedan accelerated toward the exit.

Turnbull burst out of the elevators, his Wilson seeking targets. There was a body on the concrete driveway at the valet station and he heard screeching tires.

He ran at a full sprint around the valet station and up the driveway to the exit. A silver sedan, probably a Mercedes, was turning right. He kept running, pumping his legs up the incline to the exit.

"Your friend Chris is back there," Crane said, looking at the figure emerging from the hotel driveway a few hundred yards back. She turned to look.

"Put down your window," Crane said.

Her fingers found the button and she pushed it. The window dropped and the cold wind filled the car.

"Why, do you want to freeze me?" she asked.

"No," Crane said. "I don't want to go deaf."

He shot her through the temple.

The sedan slowed and stopped ahead, its brake lights on. Turnbull started running. It was at least two hundred yards. The passenger door opened and something fell into the street.

Something orange.

Turnbull fired until the slide on his Wilson locked back, an arc of spent brass launching out of its port and clattering on the street. By the time he reloaded, the silver sedan had turned right and disappeared.

24.

The Gateway Arch National Park had been converted in a matter of days into an enormous outdoor amphitheater, with massive risers to hold the crowds who managed to get tickets to the most important signing ceremony since the Founders had affixed their names to the Declaration of Independence.

But what they were signing today would undo what those men achieved almost two and a half centuries before.

"I thought you would want to see it with your own eyes, Kelly," Deeds said. He was in a long winter coat with a hat covering his Roman senator haircut. Turnbull wore a heavy jacket that hid his pistol and magazines. Identification cards noting that Deeds and Turnbull were a key government official and a security officer of the United States of America – such as it was now – were affixed to the front of their clothing. The US flag was prominent. Jarringly, around them, some of the others in the audience were wearing ID from the new People's Republic of North America, its idiosyncratic rainbow flag similarly prominent.

Those two flags flanked the platform before them under the Arch, where the signatures would be put to paper to bring the Treaty of St. Louis into being.

"This is bullshit," Turnbull said, probably louder than necessary. An angry woman and her soft-looking husband turned and scowled.

"Don't eyeball me," Turnbull said unpleasantly.

"Please don't reignite the war this was designed to stop, Kelly," Deeds asked.

"Splitting up the country is not going to stop anything," Turnbull replied. "This is a mistake. I'm no historian, but didn't Lincoln say that a house divided will fall?"

"I think that was originally in the Bible," Deeds said.

"And half of North America is going to be a place where they hate both the Bible and Lincoln. How do you think that's going to work out?"

"Badly," Deeds conceded. "But that's why I'll need you more than ever."

"Didn't someone else say only the dead have seen the end of war? Remember how I'm dead?"

"Oh, Kelly, you aren't getting out of it that easily. You're still in the US Army, which I expect to get a bit bigger if the Roman Republic's legion model your pal General Scott admires so much gets enacted. Every citizen serves. He's quite the politician now, the prime opponent of the Split and now one of the key designers of our new country."

"He told me he had no political ambitions," Turnbull said. "So, basically, he's already started lying. A natural politician."

"Careful, he might be our president someday."

"I'll never vote for a general," Turnbull scoffed. "We are having voting, right?"

"The US Congress's first act will be to ratify the old Constitution. I hear the People's Republic is writing a new one."

"Because guys like Senator Harrington are smarter than James Madison?" asked Turnbull. "I should have shot him, amnesty or not."

"The argument is that a general amnesty is vital to reconciliation, Kelly."

"I'm not issuing any amnesty, Clay."

"Regardless, the new US of A is going to be different from the old one. I expect the red gets redder and the blue bluer."

"Isn't that called 'irreconcilable differences'? You know, there's a reason couples who split up don't live next door to each other."

Deeds offered a soft guffaw.

"We're going to be busy, here and overseas."

"Most of the world seems to be lining up with the PR already. Foreigners prefer their Americans blue and pliable," Turnbull said. "Which is one of many reasons I tend to hate foreigners."

"All enemies, foreign and domestic. That won't change," Deeds said. "Today is just the basic treaty. There are myriad details to work out in what is going to be the messiest divorce in human history. There will be lots for my Task Force Zulu Zombies to do."

Turnbull grunted.

"Crane has to be found," Deeds said.

Turnbull was silent for a moment before he responded.

"What about the amnesty?"

"He's an exception."

"Good. That mission I want in on."

Deeds looked over Turnbull, who was habitually scanning the area for threats. "I am sorry about your friend."

"Acquaintance," Turnbull said. "I don't have any friends."

"You'll get the first shot at Crane. I'll make sure of it when he comes up for air."

Turnbull stopped scanning and locked eyes with his boss.

"Oh, I insist," Turnbull said. "I do have to give Crane credit for one thing."

"What's that, Kelly?"

"He showed me that there really are no rules. Avery Barnes is dead because I didn't slot him when I had the chance. In Baghdad I would not have thought twice. But here at home, with other Americans, I did. He showed me that it is them or us. I won't make that mistake again."

Deeds paused. "I shudder to think of Kelly Turnbull liberated from restraint."

"Crane should shudder. I told him I would do him, and I pity anyone who gets in my way."

The cold wind whipped through the audience, and down below on the long platform the politicians from the two countries were streaming out to take their places. There would be speeches, and promises of eternal friendship and cooperation between the two nations that had once been together but had grown apart.

"They will try to make this positive," Turnbull said. "That we're moving forward to a brighter tomorrow. But I've been in the middle of the blue. There's no peace with them. We're just putting off the reckoning, Clay."

Deeds sighed, fearing that his operative was right.

"It's starting," Deeds said, looking at the preparations on the podium. "We're looking at history in the making, Kelly."

Turnbull looked down at the politicians preparing to divide up his country, and said, "Then I guess we better stop talking."

AUTHOR'S NOTE

As always, the technical stuff is invented. Even if I knew about that stuff, I would not write about it! I just hope it sounds plausible.

Crisis covers the beginning of the Kelly Turnbull saga and when I have something funny and interesting to say, I'll say it in Novel No. 6. The response to these novels has been remarkably gratifying. When I first put fingers to keyboard in 2016 to tell a story of what could be in the style of the airplane flight thrillers mixed with my own bizarre sense of humor, I thought some people might like them. Then they started charting at the top of the various Amazon bestsellers lists. People dug them – well, not the Never Trump Fredocons, but masculinity in the face of aggressive liberal fascism was never their thing.

I thought that I was being over the top, but time has demonstrated that I might not have been outrageous enough. When, in the face of a deadly epidemic, the left's biggest concern is people being "racist" by accurately identifying the virus by the name of its place of origin, we have gone beyond parody.

These books remain a warning, not a goal or objective. As I tell you in every one of these books, don't let this work of fiction become nonfiction.

KAS, November 2020

Kelly Turnbull will return in...

The Split

ABOUT THE AUTHOR

Kurt Schlichter is a senior columnist for *Townhall.com*. He is also a Los Angeles trial lawyer admitted in California, Texas, and Washington, DC, and a retired Army Infantry colonel.

A Twitter activist (@KurtSchlichter) with over 330,000 followers, Kurt was personally recruited by Andrew Breitbart. His writings on political and cultural issues have also been published in *IJ Review*, *The Federalist*, the *New York Post*, the *Washington Examiner*, the *Los Angeles Times*, the *Boston Globe*, the *Washington Times*, *Army Times*, the *San Francisco Examiner*, and elsewhere.

Kurt serves as a news source, an on-screen commentator, and a guest on nationally syndicated radio programs regarding political, military, and legal issues, at Fox News, Fox Business News, CNN, NewsMax, One America Network, The Blaze, and with hosts such as Hugh Hewitt, Larry O'Connor, Cam Edwards, Chris Stigall, Dennis Prager, Tony Katz, John Cardillo, Dana Loesch, and Derek Hunter, among others.

Kurt was a stand-up comic for several years, which led him to write three e-books that each reached number one on the Amazon Kindle "Political Humor" bestsellers list: *I Am a Conservative: Uncensored, Undiluted, and Absolutely Un-PC*, *I Am a Liberal: A Conservative's Guide to Dealing with Nature's Most Irritating Mistake*, and *Fetch My Latte: Sharing Feelings with Stupid People*.

In 2014, his book *Conservative Insurgency: The Struggle to Take America Back 2013-2041* was published by Post Hill Press.

His 2016 novel *People's Republic* and its 2017 prequel *Indian Country* reached No. 1 and No. 2 on the Amazon Kindle "Political Thriller" bestsellers list. *Wildfire*, the third book in the series, hit No. 1 on the Amazon "Thrillers – Espionage" bestsellers list and No. 122 in all Amazon Kindle books. *Collapse*, the fourth book, hit 121.

His non-fiction book *Militant Normals: How Regular Americans Are Rebelling Against the Elite to Reclaim Our Democracy* was published by Center Street Books in October 2018. It made the USA Today Bestsellers List.

His Regnery book *The 21 Biggest Lies About Donald Trump (and You)* was released in 2020 and hit Number #1 on an Amazon list.

Kurt is a successful trial lawyer and name partner in a Los Angeles law firm representing Fortune 500 companies and individuals in matters ranging from routine business cases to confidential Hollywood disputes and political controversies. A member of the Million Dollar Advocates Forum, which recognizes attorneys who have won trial verdicts in excess of $1 million, his litigation strategy and legal analysis articles have been published in legal publications such as the *Los Angeles Daily Journal* and *California Lawyer.*

He is frequently engaged by noted conservatives in need of legal representation, and he was counsel for political commentator and author Ben Shapiro in the widely publicized "Clock Boy" defamation lawsuit, which resulted in the case being dismissed and the victory being upheld on appeal.

Kurt is a 1994 graduate of Loyola Law School, where he was a law review editor. He majored in communications and political science as an undergraduate at the University of California, San Diego, co-editing the conservative student paper *California Review* while also writing a regular column in the student humor paper *The Koala.*

Kurt served as a US Army infantry officer on active duty and in the California Army National Guard, retiring at the rank of full colonel. He wears the silver "jump wings" of a paratrooper and commanded the 1st Squadron, 18th Cavalry Regiment (Reconnaissance-Surveillance-Target Acquisition). A veteran of both the Persian Gulf War and Operation Enduring Freedom (Kosovo), he is a graduate of the Army's Combined Arms and Services Staff School, the Command and General Staff College, and the United States Army War College, where he received a master's degree in strategic studies.

He lives with his wife Irina and their monstrous dogs Bitey and Barkey in the Los Angeles area, and he enjoys sarcasm and red meat.

His favorite caliber is .45.

The Kelly Turnbull Novels

People's Republic (2016)

Indian Country (2017)

Wildfire (2018)

Collapse (2019)

Crisis (2020)

Also By Kurt Schlichter

Conservative Insurgency: The Struggle to Take America Back 2013-2041 (Post Hill Press, 2014)

Militant Normals: How Regular Americans Are Rebelling Against the Elite to Reclaim Our Democracy (Center Street Books, 2018)

The 21 Biggest Lies About Donald Trump (and You) (Regnery, 2020)